Demons of Gadara

ISBN: 1483960099
ISBN 13: 9781483960098

Demons of Gadara

John A. Cassara

To those who endeavor to
make the world a
"better place for our children."

Author's Note

After writing my first non-fictions books, *Hide & Seek: Intelligence, Law Enforcement and the Stalled War on Terror Finance* (Potomac Books, 2006) and *On the Trail of Terror Finance: What Law Enforcement and Intelligence Officers Need to Know* (Red Cell IG, 2010), I continue to be concerned about the intertwined threats of what the US military calls "asymmetric warfare" and "threat finance." In searching for a new teaching medium, I decided to tell a story.

Demons of Gadara takes place in various locations in the Middle East, South Asia and Europe. I have traveled, lived, and worked in most of the locations described. Although the book is fiction, much of the material is based on personal knowledge and experience. The story and characters are not James Bond fantasy. The crimes do not get solved in 24 hours. The heroes, villains and cultures, including cultures of the bureaucracies involved, are all too real. *Demons of Gadara* is best categorized as narrative fiction based on fact.

During the story, I try to explain some of the history, complexities and interconnectivity of international events, diverse beliefs and terror finance. *Demons of Gadara* explores topics that have not yet broken into the mainstream. Yet we will assuredly be facing many of the issues surfaced in the not too distant future.

Certain facts have been slightly altered to fit the story. Some might feel the dangers identified are suggestive in nature. However, I intentionally left out elements in the threat equation. Hidden countermeasures remain hidden. The manuscript was subject to prepublication review by the Central Intelligence Agency to prevent the disclosure of classified information. The manuscript was also submitted to the United States Secret Service.

The dialog, narrative, and all statements of fact and analysis are mine and do not reflect the official positions or views of any US government agency or department.

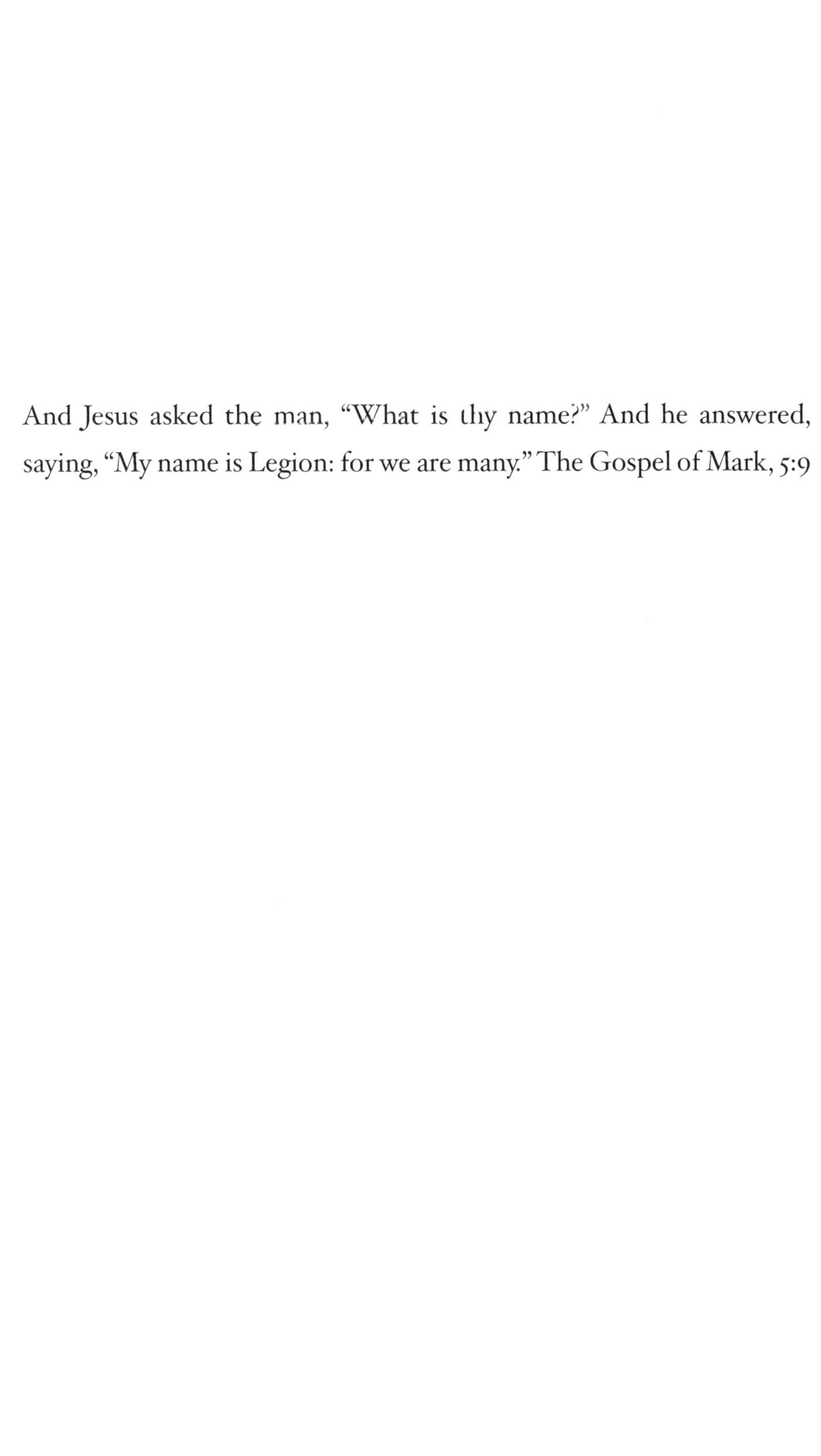

And Jesus asked the man, "What is thy name?" And he answered, saying, "My name is Legion: for we are many." The Gospel of Mark, 5:9

Prologue

At precisely 1500 hours on Friday, August 29th the first high explosive fragmentation shell fell from a cloudless blue sky. The explosive landed in a school courtyard in the village of Fardis. The school was closed for the weekend. Yet in a cruel twist of fate, five young boys had gathered in the courtyard to play soccer. Their game and shouts of play were instantly cut short with the falling projectile. The tremendous explosion precipitated five young souls into eternity.

Thirty seconds after the first shell landed, another struck. This time the explosive device fell through the steeple roof of the red tiled school house. The impact jarred the foundation of the old school. The roof was dislodged from its footings and it began to slide. Following the laws of physics, the first wave of falling timbers and tiles was trailed by a second. Finally, the entire side of the steeple that just a few minutes before had been facing the bright afternoon sun slid downward in an avalanche of dust and debris. It landed directly on top of the five young playmates. The children's already lifeless bodies were buried in ruble.

Billowing smoke and dust from the blasts began to waft towards heaven like incense burning on an altar. Prayers of the stunned villagers of Fardis were similarly directed towards God.

For long minutes nothing else happened. The resulting silence was more deafening then the two previous explosions. Even the buzz of the ever present August flies and the barks of the village dogs were silenced. Finally, a lonesome scream pierced the air. The anguished cry of a mother echoed throughout the village. Families started to cautiously appear on their doorsteps. Shopkeepers emerged from their stores. Their collective gaze was fixed on the empty space on the main street that used to be filled by a red tile steeple roof.

Slowly leaving the presumed safety of their front stoops, the stunned citizens of Fardis stepped into the dusty streets. It was almost as if they were at the seashore determining who had the courage to first put their feet into the cold surf. Finally, an anguished mother tore off her apron and left her home. She began to frantically run in the direction of where two of her children had gone to play. Pure terror filled her voice as she shouted their names, "Ilham!" "Ibrahim!" Her shouts jolted the other villagers more than the two explosions. Many joined the distraught mother in the race to the school yard. Others, trembling with shock, began to congregate with neighbors and family.

The delayed reaction seemingly triggered the next cruel game of chance. Once again shells began to fall from the sky. These munitions were different from the first. The thud of the blast and the feel of the percussion were not as dense. But the resulting sound - the crack of the shell breaking into smaller pieces - was far more terrifying.

Like a farmer haphazardly throwing seeds in a field, clusters of bomblets were scattered throughout Fardis. They fell in random patterns. Some tore into the sides of the stone and white-washed plaster buildings. Shards of shrapnel pockmarked walls of homes and shops. Other bomblets skipped and bounced and slammed into the stone fences that guarded the nearby fields. A few fell into the main street and bracketed those racing towards their loved ones. For those unfortunates, it was almost as if a tumbling marble had been thrown from above into a spinning roulette wheel that controlled their fate. The anti-personnel cluster bombs tore through flesh, bone, and sinew. The mothers, fathers, and citizens of Fardis racing to the school were shredded. Body parts and entrails spilled. Blood soaked the ground where new victims lay contorted in death.

A lone truck raced through the streets. Racing, weaving, careening, the truck somehow remained unscathed as it ran the gauntlet of the clustered explosions. Clearing the village, the truck finally came to a stop under the cover of olive trees in the fields outside the village. The driver jumped out of the cab of his truck and took cover behind a stone wall. As he lay trembling in the hardened late summer earth, the driver noticed some unexploded bomblets scattered in the nearby weeds.

Just as there was no forewarning of the anonymous attack, likewise there was no signal when it was finally over. The explosions simply stopped. So did time. Fardis was shattered along with the lives of the survivors.

Only much later when the stunned villagers talked quietly among themselves did they ask themselves, "Why?" A shepherd that had been with his sheep in nearby fields prior to the attack said he may have seen Hezbollah fighters on the hillside above the village. A bricklayer working on a new storefront said that he remembered before the attack hearing what he surmised was the buzz of a circling drone.

Yet the villagers told themselves, because nobody else seemed to care, none of this made sense. Why did innocents have to suffer? What did it all mean? Why on this particular August day did the finger of God point at them?

chapter 1

The landscape seemed biblical. Orchards of olive trees, vegetable gardens, and sun-washed stone fences were all planted in the same ancient earth that also sprouted the ruins of Umm Qais. The crumbling skeleton of the forgotten civilization was tucked away in a corner of Jordan far off the usual tourist track. The gravel and dirt road we traveled skirted the remains of brick, stone, and marble. We were driving on a promontory high above the Sea of Galilee and the Tiberius countryside where, two thousand years ago, Jesus began his ministry. The view of the Galilee where God walked on water was my reward for the three-hour drive from Amman.

"The Decapolis, which means 'ten cities' in Greek, was a ten-city Greco-Roman federation that occupied all of this territory of northeastern Palestine. Umm Qais was one of the ten."

My companion, driver, and impromptu tour guide was Colonel Faisal Abbadi of the Jordanian Dairat al-Mukhabarat al-Ammah, the General Intelligence Department, or GID.

Colonel Abbadi knew this land well. "If you cut me, I bleed this earth. My family has been living in this area since before the Corinthian columns on the Decumanus Maxium began to fall."

I smiled and nodded my head with his running commentary.

"What you see now are scattered ruins, but this road was once lined with shops and homes that stretched for nearly two kilometers."

Before Colonel Abbadi had picked me up earlier that morning from the Marriott Hotel in Amman, I had read in a tour book that the Decapolis had formed part of the Roman Empire's defense on its eastern frontier. In those times, Gadara was a thriving metropolis strategically located and linked by well-used trading routes connecting Syria and Palestine. Gadara no longer existed, but it still boasted the ruins of Umm Qais.

As a special agent for the US Department of Homeland Security Investigations HSI, sometimes known as Immigration and Customs Enforcement, or ICE, I had worked on a large number of investigations in Jordan and many other countries in the Middle East. Interspersed between conducting interviews, meeting with Jordanian counterparts, and coordinating my visits with the American Embassy in Amman, I had enjoyed previous opportunities to visit the ancient ruins of Petra and Jerash. However, this was my first visit to the northwest border area of Jordan.

I listened as Colonel Abbadi told me the story of how, during the years of Roman rule, the Nabataeans (with their capital in Petra), controlled the trade routes as far north as Damascus. Some of the modern asphalt and cement highways we had traveled earlier that morning were imprinted on the remnants of those earlier roads. Unhappy with the competition, Mark Anthony ordered King Herod the Great to weaken the Nabataeans. King Herod was the father of Herod Antipas, who was the ruler of Galilee during the time of John the Baptist and Jesus of Nazareth. In appreciation for his efforts in securing its eastern trade, Rome rewarded Herod with Gadara.

The city reached its peak of prosperity in the second century AD. New colonnaded streets, temples, theaters, and baths sprouted. Some contemporary observers compared ancient Gadara with Athens, a city and culture admired by the ancient Romans. Gadara was the regional center of Hellenism. The Greeks were here before the Romans. The ancient civilizations were long gone. But looking out the window of Abbadi's car, I saw the ruins and felt the ghosts.

Abbadi navigated his BMW down the rough road, keeping a watchful eye for potholes. This wasn't a GID car but Abbadi's own personal vehicle. Just like Americans and the Italians I knew so well back in Rome, Arabs had a love affair with their cars. A shining new BMW was a prized status symbol. Because of his high position in GID, Abbadi legally did not have to pay the exorbitant import taxes that made luxury cars unaffordable to the average Jordanian. It was an expected perk of the job and part of the culture of the GID bureaucracy. A prestigious vehicle also added to the mystique of the *mukhabarat* or secret police.

Driving past the hilltop castle of Aljoun, we passed an orchard of fig trees. Spraying gravel, Abbadi turned off the road and entered a dirt lane headed toward a small stone and white-plastered farmhouse. A side patio was trellised with grape vines. I spotted a middle-aged man in a worn and sun bleached New York Yankees baseball cap sitting on a cheap plastic patio chair. His smile transformed his face the moment he saw Abbadi's BMW approach in a cloud of dust.

"That's my cousin Ayman," said Colonel Abbadi. "I telephoned him this morning. I knew he would be waiting for us."

Getting out of the car, Abbadi and Ayman greeted each other with the traditional three kisses—cheek to cheek to cheek.

"Asalaam alykum,"—Peace be upon you, Ayman said to me as he took my hand.

"Wa `Alaykum as-salaam," —Peace upon you as well, I replied, returning a firm handshake.

"Mr. Joe, I know you understand a little Arabic, but we will speak English," said Abbadi. "Ayman drove a taxi in New York City for a few years." Laughing, he added, "In fact, he even has a bit of an accent."

"How are my Yankees doin'? I don't follow them much now anymore, but I still have my cap."

I smiled at the mixed Brooklyn-tainted Arab-accented English. "The Yankees are still in first place. They should just about have the playoffs locked up by now."

"I would like to go back to New York just to see the new stadium."

"Ayman, your English is excellent. I make no pretense of even trying to speak Arabic. I picked up a couple of expressions over the years, but it is a big regret of mine that I have never learned to speak the language. For most Americans, learning a language is very difficult."

"This is all very good because your visit gives me an opportunity to practice my English. As my cousin said, I lived in America many years ago." After a slight pause, he sheepishly added, "I had to leave because of visa issues." His unease didn't last long. "But Allah knows best. I am back where I belong." Under his Yankee cap, his expressive, weather-beaten face was punctuated by dark, joyful eyes. He tightly clasped my hand. "Come. Let's sit here on the patio under the shade."

Settling into our chairs, Ayman soon produced sweet tea, juice, and a platter of September-ripened brown figs.

"I would love to serve you a local Hashimiyya feast, but my cousin Faisal made me promise that we would just have tea. I know you will be visiting with Nanna later. She will feed you."

The appearance of a wide grin emerging from the white-flecked stubble of beard around his mouth was a telltale hint that Colonel Abbadi and I would enjoy the next nearby stop.

"You are near the village of Hashimiyya," Ayman continued. "As you saw on your drive here, Hashimiyya is small. In fact, this village used to be called *farah* or mouse in Arabic. We didn't even have a mosque here until 1949. But everything changed after the 1967 war." Ayman paused. "We had, how do you say in English, a *flood* of refugees—both Christians and Palestinians. I was a boy then, but I remember it well."

"The refugees brought development, businesses, schools, and mosques." Colonel Abbadi picked up the story. "When decent roads came in the 1970s, buses between Hashimiyya and Ajloun followed. A member of Jordan's royal family visited the town in the 1980s. He was so impressed that he no longer wanted it to be called 'mouse.' So the name was changed to Hashimiyya or Hashemite, the king's family name."

As I sipped the sweetened tea, I listened to the cousins' conversation and asked them many questions about the area and its history. As I had learned from traveling to the region for many years, one takes time with pleasantries. Courtesy and respect are all-important. American directness is not always appropriate. After a suitable period, Colonel Abbadi tilted back his chair and cleared his throat.

"Ayman, I will let Mr. Joe explain to you his work and his interests. As I told you on the phone, Mr. Joe visits me occasionally when he travels to Amman. We talk about things of interest to both of our countries. A few days ago he was in my office, and we were discussing the recent incidents in Lebanon and Syria over the Golan. I told him that you had just returned from some of the areas that had been shelled. Mr. Joe was very interested. Since he had never before seen this part of our country, I invited him to accompany me on a visit."

"He is most welcome."

There is that word 'welcome' again, I thought. I felt the constant use of the word was an endearing trait of Jordanians speaking English.

Taking the colonel's introduction as my cue, I began to tell Ayman about myself and my professional interests in Jordan. I explained that I was a senior special agent assigned to the office of the ICE attaché, attached to the American Embassy in Rome, Italy. Our office had regional responsibilities in the Middle East, including Jordan. As a special agent with ICE's Homeland Security Investigations, or HSI, I had investigative authority similar to the much better known FBI. The difference was that the FBI was part of the American Department of Justice and ICE was part of the Department of Homeland Security, which was created in the aftermath of September 11. Most of ICE's investigations and inquiries took place within the US, but since ICE dealt with violations of American law that had to do with people, goods, and money crossing the border, sometimes agents were sent overseas to further the investigative process. In those instances, ICE worked in cooperation with local police and customs forces. That is why I was meeting with the GID. I told Ayman that my particular area of interest was international money-laundering investigations. Yet I also had a lot of experience with other cross-border crimes, including the diversion and transshipment of prohibited American manufactured munitions and technology.

"Ayman, as I am sure you remember, back in 2006 there was a month-long war between Israel and Hezbollah. Many people were killed on both sides. However, the majority of the casualties were Lebanese civilians."

"Mr. Joe, I had just returned from New York. I remember the fighting well. It began after Hezbollah kidnapped two Israeli soldiers and the Israeli military responded." His smile disappeared. "I was here in Hashimiyya during the fighting. But I have many friends in the region, and some of them were involved. It was awful."

"Then you probably know that during the last few days of the conflict, Israel shelled areas in southern Lebanon with cluster bombs. Cluster bombs can be dropped from aircraft. They can also be fired from cannons. When they explode, they scatter hundreds of small bomblets. They have lots of uses but are most often used to kill people."

I paused to let Ayman digest what I was saying. I had learned over the years to speak slowly with my foreign counterparts. Even though many can speak English well, rapid-fire speech combined with slang and the American penchant for acronyms and jargon could be very confusing.

I continued. "As we have learned from other incidents in places like Kosovo, Iraq, and Gaza, not all the bomblets explode immediately. Over the course of time, many children and other civilians are seriously injured or killed."

This time it was Colonel Abbadi who nodded with my commentary. "It seems it is always the children who suffer the most."

My mouth suddenly became dry as I remembered my three children. I swallowed hard at the truism and then took a sip of tea. "Cluster bombs are crude and imprecise. Today, there is an international movement to ban their use, but neither Israel nor the United States have ratified the global treaty." My eyes were fixed on Ayman. "Unfortunately, some of the cluster bombs used by Israel in 2006 were manufactured in the United States. The use of those bombs violated agreements between my country and Israel. I assisted in the subsequent investigation."

Ayman's downcast eyes looked up towards mine. "Now I understand why you are here and why you wish to speak to me," he said hauntingly.

"Yes. Your cousin told me that you had just returned from the recent shelling and that you had seen the probable use of cluster bombs." Pausing for a few moments I added, "I am interested in finding out if American-manufactured weapons were used in possible violation of US law."

"But don't the Americans know everything?"

I chuckled. "Ayman, you lived in New York. You should know better!" With a smile on my face I added, "But that is a common misperception in this region. That and people believing in conspiracies!"

"You mean the CIA and the US Air Force were not behind September 11?" Ayman asked facetiously.

I returned to seriousness. "It is hard for us to get information from Lebanon, Syria, and even Israel. I know your cousin understands the use of information and intelligence."

Colonel Abbadi continued his nodding.

"I want to see if I can develop information in order to see if an investigation is warranted regarding any possible violations of US law. If so, I'll work with my colleagues in the States and we will present our findings to the US Department of Justice for possible prosecution of those involved. Certainly, our Department of State and our military services will also be interested."

I knew I had his attention. "Ayman, I would really appreciate it if you could tell me what you know and particularly what you saw."

Ayman looked at his cousin. The Colonel gave a slight nod of his head.

"Mr. Joe, I returned from Lebanon and Syria last week. What I saw concerned me so much that I telephoned Faisal as soon as I returned home. Somebody has to know what is going on. The situation is really getting dangerous."

"What do you mean?"

"Well, since the demonstrations over water shortages began in the West Bank and Gaza a few months ago, I saw from my travels through Lebanon that Hezbollah was once again trying to rally the people against Israel. The recent Israeli retaliation is exactly what Hezbollah wanted."

Colonel Abbadi jumped in. "Of course, when you say Hezbollah, you also mean that Shia Iran is trying to stir things up. I don't know whether it is the mullahs or the Revolutionary Guard calling the shots, but Iran is dangerous." As if to give added emphasis to his remarks, he held up a closed fist. "Although Hezbollah is a legitimate political party in Lebanon, everybody knows it still acts as a proxy for the Iranians."

With the mention of Iran, Ayman and Colonel Abbadi began an animated discussion in Arabic. Although I couldn't understand everything, I could tell they were discussing recent news reports. It was apparent that Hezbollah had seized on the water crisis in the West Bank and Gaza and had used it for their own propaganda purposes. AlManar (a Hezbollah-run TV channel) broadcast images of withering crops and thirsty children. However, the long running drought and resulting humanitarian crisis were not in a poor sub-Saharan Africa country but in a comparatively wealthy region where the country with the most powerful military also controlled the most important natural resource—water.

There was seemingly plenty of water for Israeli purposes. Yet decades of manipulation and diversion of scarce water by Israel had finally reached a crisis point. The situation was exacerbated by the two-year regional drought and the rapidly growing West Bank and Gaza populations.

Shia Hezbollah joined in a de facto tactical agreement with Sunni Hammas in the West Bank and Gaza to exploit the crisis to advance their respective political objectives. Widespread marches, riots, and demonstrations had broken out. The tactics seemed to be a repeat of the 2011 Arab Spring that occurred just a few short years ago. The surrounding countries of Egypt, Lebanon, and Jordan were also expressing their solidarity with their Arab brothers. The countries' governments were using the crisis to divert attention from their respective internal problems and continuing turmoil. Individual Gulf and North African states had made their views known, both privately and in public forums. The Arab League had released statements condemning the Israeli policies that used water supply as a weapon.

I knew from my previous trips to the region that the Jordanian population was also on edge because Jordan had its own water shortage. Moreover, the Jordanian population was increasingly Palestinian. Seemingly everyone in Jordan had direct family ties to the West Bank and knew the suffering all too well. The exodus of Syrians coming across the border exacerbated the situation. Decades of humiliation and feelings of powerlessness and resentment combined to make a dangerous mix.

All they needed was a spark to ignite the situation. Unfortunately, there was an incident. In early August, Israeli Defense Forces (IDF) using live ammunition fired on rock-throwing demonstrators near Ramallah. Three fifteen-year-old boys were killed. Their comrades carried their blood-soaked, Palestinian flag-draped bodies aloft and marched through the streets chanting for revenge. As had happened in previous Arab-Israeli conflicts, the scenes played out on television screens around the world. In response, Hezbollah launched rockets supplied by Iran toward Israel from positions in southern Lebanon. Innocent Israeli civilians were killed. Israel responded with a massive bombardment, firing from IDF positions in Israel. The Israeli Air Force (IAF) dropped anti-personnel cluster bombs from the air. Having learned the lessons of the short 2006 campaign, Hezbollah fired from civilian areas and then fled. The resulting Israeli retaliation caused massive civilian casualties. Both sides now seemed to be watching the other warily and trying to determine if this was the time for escalation.

"Mr. Joe, I'm sorry we were speaking Arabic," Colonel Abbadi said. "It is just that we feel very strongly about recent events. When we become emotional we speak our native language."

I nodded. Wanting to take control of the interview, I turned again to Ayman. "So, how did you happen to be in Lebanon?"

"I travel throughout the region," Ayman explained. "I drive a truck. I haul goods and produce to and from Turkey, Lebanon, Syria, Iraq, and Jordan. I see a lot."

"What do you mean?"

"It was the end of a trip, headed back here to Hashimiyya with my truck empty. It happened around Fardis in southern Lebanon. I took a short cut trying to skirt the Golan and cut across to Route 5 heading south into Jordan."

"What happened?"

"I was stupid. I had no idea Hezbollah would fire their rockets and the Jews would respond. I was caught in . . .I don't know the words in English. . . bombs were falling . . . I pulled off the road and into a field of olive trees. I was looking for a hiding place. It was only through Allah's mercy that I escaped."

As a "senior" special agent, I had lots of experience interviewing subjects. I found that the best technique was to use open-ended questions and let the subject talk while interjecting pointed questions that kept the subject on track. I used the same technique with Ayman. I also asked him if he was comfortable with me taking notes. He nodded his permission.

Ayman was animated as he told the story of the bombardment and the resulting devastation. Villagers congregated after the attacks, trying to find loved ones. He described how they desperately tried to put out fires and rescue those trapped in collapsed buildings. He used his truck to help transport some of the injured to a nearby medical clinic that was overflowing with casualties. Neither Hezbollah nor Lebanese security forces were anywhere to be seen. According to Ayman, he heard the Israeli air attacks had also strayed into neighboring Syria. As far as he knew, there were not any Syrian casualties.

Abbadi turned and looked at me intently. "I don't believe this is common knowledge. Syria has not yet publicly announced the attacks or responded militarily. Maybe Syria is not yet ready to be drawn into any more conflicts. Their military is discredited. The country is still so unsettled from the uprising against Assad."

Ayman's description of the cluster bomb and bomblets sounded to me like they could possibly be from the American-manufactured CBU-100, also known as the MK-20. I was familiar with the ordnance from my previous investigations. There was also a very strong possibility that the cluster bombs Ayman encountered were manufactured in Israel. If that was the case, there was no violation of US law. I needed specifics. I explained the issues to Ayman.

"Mr. Joe, I don't know whether those bombs were American manufactured or not. I also don't know whether the rockets that were also fired from Israel into other villages in southern Lebanon are Israeli or American." Ayman grinned as he added, "But I have something that might help you."

He brought out his cell phone and showed me photographs he had taken with the phone's camera. The destruction captured in the pictures was abhorrent, particularly a few haunting images of mangled and bloodied bodies. But some of the photos showed unexploded bomblets littered around a field, and others showed bomb fragments in the rubble.

"These pictures are very good. They could really help me with the investigation."

Looking at Colonel Abbadi, I asked Ayman if I could have copies of the photos. I also wanted the precise location of the attacks that he witnessed. The GID colonel nodded his approval.

"I also have something else you might be interested in."

Ayman reached for a plastic container that rested on a nearby wooden bench. Removing the lid, he presented metal fragments to me. These were not remnants of a nearby ancient civilization but rather pieces of shrapnel from twenty-first century warfare. Some of the larger pieces had markings in both English and Hebrew.

"These are pieces of the cluster bombs. I took them as souvenirs of my escape. You are welcome to them if they will help your investigation."

"Shukran,"—Thank you. I paused to examine them.

Ayman is too polite to point out that the United States—the country I represent—might be responsible for supplying Israel with the very weapons that almost killed him.

I didn't know what to say. Although there are many causes for anti-Americanism in the region, I had found throughout my travels that the long-running US support of Israel fuels the fires most. I put the fragments back in the box and closed the lid.

I looked directly into Ayman's eyes, which had changed during the course of our conversation from joy to sorrow. He must have known what I was thinking about and slowly pulled down the brim of his beloved New York Yankees cap.

I reached out to clasp him on the shoulder. "Ayman, I want to thank you again. These could be very helpful."

He replied softly, "Mr. Joe, you are most welcome."

chapter 2

MAJEED WAS A heavy-set man in his mid fifties with a halo of white hair. Black bushy eyebrows capped his wire-rimmed reading glasses, and a full salt-and-pepper beard hung from his face. But his soft, fleshy hands were his pride. They were hands that served him well. They were not the dirt-encrusted hands of laborers or the strong, scarred, tanned hands of his former comrades in the mujahideen. Rather, they were hands lined with the wisdom and knowledge gained through the keeping of books. Some older men have faces lined with age and experience. Majeed's hands better conveyed his insight, hard-won knowledge, and oversized ego. Perhaps that is why he chose to crown his hands with matching massive gold rings on his little fingers.

He sat behind a solid wooden desk. Like his well-scrubbed hands, Majeed's desk was immaculate. Everything was in order. His laptop computer, notepad, and pen and pencil set were precisely arranged. A calendar with pictorial scenes of the Swat Valley hung on the wall above his desk. Otherwise, there were no pictures or personal knick-knacks. His desk was his workplace. Yet the harmony and purposefulness of his desk stood in stark contrast to the open file cabinets, eviscerated cassette player, compact discs, pillows, metal folding chairs, and other items scattered haphazardly around the room. A small, single-weft Heriz carpet with long piles and a beautiful sheen lay on the floor away from the clutter. When Majeed did not have time to go to the mosque, he used it for prayer.

Majeed's office was located on a backstreet of a slum in west Karachi. The neighborhood of ramshackle homes, interspersed with businesses and trades of every sort, was built around the area's cliffs and marble quarry. The smell of raw sewage, diesel fumes, body odor, and spices in the market stalls and restaurants was an interesting mixture of sweet and rancid. During Karachi's most humid days, the smell in the slums could be overpowering. Majeed could certainly afford to work in a better environment. But for reasons of piety, security, and old habits, he opted for the slums.

The shortage of dwelling units in the teeming metropolis, a consequence of massive immigration, was largely responsible for the emergence of Karachi's *katchi abadis* or squatter settlements. The settlements began to crop up during the early fifties, shortly following the partition and migration of Muslims from India. An extensive, unorganized land invasion led to the establishment of *katchi abadis* on the then outskirts of the city as well as some open urban lands. Unfortunately, Karachi's traditional social order based on municipal government, clans, tribes, and religious edicts quickly fell apart under the invasion of people. It has never recovered.

After Pakistan's civil war in 1971, the housing situation grew even worse. Refugees from Bangladesh flooded into the city, followed by additional Muslim migrants from Burma to Uganda. Since 1979 and the Soviet invasion of Afghanistan, a steady stream of Afghan refugees also flooded the city. The Afghans were mostly Pashtuns. Karachi hosted one of the largest Pashtun populations in the world. There were also Tajiks, Hazaras, Uzbeks, Turkmen, and other ethnic groups from Iran and the surrounding "stan" countries.

Majeed did not flee Afghanistan after the Soviet invasion. Rather he joined the Mujahideen and fought the Godless communist invaders, just like his ancestors had fought successive foreign invaders since the time of Alexander the Great. In 1989, when the Soviets withdrew from Afghanistan in disgrace, Majeed was caught up in the resulting civil war. It was only a short time before the collapse of the Berlin Wall and the beginning of the end of the Soviet empire. Within Afghanistan, alliances between warlords, clans, and tribes shifted, and they engaged in pitched battles that devastated the land and the people. There was anarchy. Afghanistan was a failed state. It could no longer be called a country.

Most of Majeed's Mujahideen colleagues were illiterate. However, before running away to war, Majeed had attended a private school for a few years as a boy. His father also had given him practical experience in his Kandahar import-export business. His education marked him as especially useful. During the civil war, both Majeed and his commanders recognized his affinity and skill for logistics and finding creative funding sources.

In 1998, Majeed joined the newly ascendant Taliban. Originally, it was a group of "Talib" (student) militants trained by Pakistan's Inter-Services Intelligence (ISI). The group was formed in order to help put an end to the Afghan civil war. Yet the Taliban movement became more than that. The ISI was playing its equivalent of nineteenth century colonial Britain's "great game"; the Pakistan-Afghanistan link was designed to help protect western Pakistan in case of an Indian invasion. After the Pakistan-India split at the time of independence, India was perceived as Pakistan's chief threat. India's 1971 conquest of East Pakistan, a thousand miles east of West Pakistan, turned East Pakistan into Bangladesh. The antagonism was exacerbated because of the long-simmering dispute over Kashmir—a beautiful borderland claimed by both India and Pakistan.

The fundamentalist Pashtun, Sunni-Islamist Taliban welcomed the "bookkeeper" with open arms. Majeed soon proved his worth by helping senior Taliban leadership obtain funding from a wide variety of sources. He was just as adept at protecting financial assets and disbursing payments securely and efficiently. His success as a fund-raiser, accountant, and money-launderer was also due to his ability to cultivate relationships with people. Over the years, his financial network and contacts stretched from South Asia to the Arabian Gulf and beyond. Majeed was a man of his word; a man of trust. He did not question senior leadership. And although he was not personally corrupt, he knew how to corrupt others. It was one of his primary attributes. He was adept at finding vulnerabilities. In addition, his intelligence, allegiance, international networking, and bookkeeping skills made him very valuable to senior Taliban leadership.

One of the better-known Pashtunwali tenets was *melmastia*, or hospitality and asylum to all guests—even outsiders—seeking help.

During the years immediately prior to September 11, Osama bin Laden and his al Qaeda movement took advantage of Pashtunwali *melmastia*. Traditional Pashtun hospitality, sugared with plentiful funding, allowed al Qaeda to maintain its sanctuary in Afghanistan. Although there were some natural conflicts between the leadership of the Pashtun-dominated Taliban and the Arab Wahhabi-dominated al Qaeda, for the most part the two fundamentalist jihadist organizations had a mutually supportive relationship. Majeed became a trusted financial go-between.

In 1996, Osama bin Laden declared war on the United States from his mountain sanctuary in Afghanistan. Outside of a haphazard and futile response to the al Qaeda-sponsored attacks against the American Embassies in Kenya and Tanzania in 1998, for the most part he was ignored. However, everything changed after September 11. The United States Congress authorized the use of force against al Qaeda and those who harbored them. For the first time in its history, the North Atlantic Treaty Organization (NATO) invoked Article 5—the commitment that says an attack on one member nation is an attack on all. And the United Nations Security Council endorsed the use of all necessary steps to respond to the attacks.

Due in part to the Pashtun creed of hospitality to guests, the Taliban refused to turn over Osama bin Laden. As a result, US and coalition forces invaded Afghanistan. In December 2001, Osama bin Laden and the remnants of al Qaeda were bombarded and almost trapped in the mountains of Tora Bora. Majeed and small groups of Taliban used the hidden smuggling routes in southern Afghanistan they knew so well to cross into Pakistan. They were given refuge by the Pakistani fundamentalist Jumiat Ulema-e-Islam organization and protected by the Pakistani ISI. Eventually Majeed, together with other Taliban refugees, found his way to the *katchi abadis* of west Karachi. In a short time, the bookkeeper was once again in business.

While most of the Taliban were forced to leave Afghanistan, it was only a tactical withdrawal. A few years later, the Taliban returned in force. Their return was facilitated by the US invasion of Iraq. Despite setbacks resulting from the 2010 build-up of US and coalition forces, the Taliban were growing stronger. When US forces began their withdrawal, Majeed had no doubt that the Taliban would once again eventually take power. They were already at the doorstep of Kabul and had infiltrated all government organs. Just like the other invaders before them, the infidels would eventually exhaust themselves and leave Afghanistan for the Afghans.

Afghanistan was a very poor country, and the Taliban in Afghanistan was insular. Afghan Taliban leadership had no desire to actively spread worldwide Islamic fundamentalism.

In contrast, Majeed was convinced that the big prize for fundamentalist Islam was Pakistan itself, potentially a very powerful country. It even boasted the Islamic world's only nuclear weapons. And Karachi was the economic engine driving Pakistan.

Majeed had first-hand knowledge of the Taliban's ambitions in Pakistan. His financing schemes supported the Taliban in Pakistan's continuing attempts to destabilize a succession of weak and fragmented governments. The Taliban engaged in devastating attacks of terrorism against the Pakistani people, including the assassination of political figures such as Benazir Bhutto and horrific suicide bombings in mosques, marketplaces, and other public forums. The primary goal of the terror campaign was to help the Pakistani Taliban take power. But in contrast to their cousins in Afghanistan, another goal included international jihad to impose upon the rest of the world an Islamic caliphate. To this end, they joined with other radical Islamic groups. The relationships were sometimes tenuous and fraught with mistrust. But their overall common interests trumped their tactical wariness. And to further their common aims, lots of money was required. So was the bookkeeper's expertise.

Majeed had been reviewing his computerized Excel spreadsheet since the early-morning hours. It was habit. Every morning he was awakened just before dawn by the *adhān*, the Islamic call to prayer recited by the muezzin at the local mosque. The morning prayers, or *fajr*, were the first of the five daily mandatory prayers for Muslims. During the *fajr* prayers, the pious recited in unison, "*Al-salatu khayru min an-nawm*," or "prayer is better than sleep." While his right hand, crowned with a massive gold ring, deftly manipulated the computer's mouse, Majeed's left hand involuntarily rose and muffled an early morning yawn. The bookkeeper remembered the line in the prayer. His beard framed a smile of contentment. Majeed believed in jihadist Islam, the cause, his work. His life had purpose.

Staring blankly at the numbers on his computer screen while immersed in his thoughts, he was startled with the opening of the office door.

"Salām"

Majeed brightened. "Tariq? Come in, my son. I have some water ready for tea. Please, join me. What brings you here so early?

"My father, good morning," Tariq replied in Pashto. "I didn't sleep all night. It is the end of the month and I have been distributing our 'presents,' just as you taught me years ago."

Majeed smiled. He looked approvingly at Tariq. "Well done, my child. Were there any issues?"

"None at all," Tariq laughed as he poured his tea. "The fiscal police are as corrupt as ever. I'm surprised they don't ask for more. Maybe we are too generous."

"We have the means to be generous. And generosity ensures our continued success."

Tariq was not Majeed's son by blood. In fact, as far as Majeed knew, he had no offspring. However, Majeed thought of Tariq as a proud father thinks of his son.

Now in his early twenties, Tariq was a Pashtu-Afghan orphan and refugee whom Majeed first met in a Karachi *madrassa* or religious school. Since Pakistan had a poorly developed secular public education system, the madrassa network filled a social services void by providing a rudimentary education, food, and even clothes to the poor and destitute. The schools also provided religious indoctrination, which often included sitting cross-legged on the floor seven hours a day memorizing the Koran in Arabic and the basics of Islamic law as interpreted by barely literate teachers. Neither the teachers nor the students received any formal grounding in math, science, or history, and they were not exposed to critical ways of thinking. In addition to Pakistani students, madrassas also attracted thousands of Islamic young men from Thailand, Indonesia, Africa, and other locations who wished to pursue a fundamentalist education. The madrassa attended by Tariq was run by Jumiat Ulema-e-Islam and financed primarily by wealthy donors from Saudi Arabia who wanted to spread the fundamentalist Sunni-Wahhabi doctrine of Islam.

The madrassass also promoted the fundamentalist Islamic *Sharia* or "the way or path." For believers, *Sharia* governs everything from law, finance, and the social order. *Sharia* is the ultimate authority—not the government. The Taliban based their rule of law on *Sharia* and the ultimate goal for *Sharia* adherents is to engage in jihad, or holy war, to bring about the triumph of Islam under a global theocracy, one that will impose *Sharia* on Muslims and non-Muslims alike.

Handling the funding for the madrassa was something else that Majeed did for his circle of contacts and as a form of personal tithing for the poor. One day years ago, as Majeed hand-delivered funds to the madrassa headmaster, he mentioned that he had need of a few boys to help him with his work. Majeed said that he would personally see to their continued education. He asked for boys who were smart and pious. He also wanted the boys to show signs of imagination. In fact, Majeed wanted to take the boys under his wing before the well-known madrassa rigidity stifled all worldliness and creativity.

Months later, on a subsequent visit to the madrassa, the headmaster presented Majeed with Tariq and Rafi. They were both ten years old. Majeed brought them into his home and began preparing them to serve both radical Islam and himself. He was successful.

"When will you be making the collections?" asked Majeed.

Tariq finished a sip of tea. "Our clients have come to expect me at the beginning of the month." Tariq chuckled. "I don't want to disappoint them."

"This business has truly worked out well for us. The people want their cigarettes and the government will not cut taxes. And we are the ones who benefit!"

When Majeed first arrived in Karachi, he was asked by the Taliban leadership to find new sources of income. Having previous experience in smuggling, Majeed found the city's thriving black market particularly appealing. He felt that the Taliban in Pakistan could successfully break into the well-established underground network of buying and selling cigarettes.

Pakistan had some of the highest cigarette taxes in the world—accounting for almost ninety percent of the cost per pack. The onerous taxes drove the market, production, distribution, and sales of counterfeit cigarettes. By discounting the official tax, both smuggled and counterfeit "name brand" cigarettes were available at retail outlets and through street vendors at substantially lower prices than the government-dictated rate. Majeed had discovered it was a very lucrative business.

Most of the worldwide counterfeit market in cigarettes was supplied by China. In addition to the cigarettes themselves, China provided state-of-the art cigarette manufacturing machines, packaging, paper, boxes, holograms, and other necessary items. It was a relatively simple matter to set up shop using Chinese supply. He soon made the necessary contacts with Chinese intermediaries. As a result, Majeed and his colleagues moved into the production and distribution of counterfeit cigarettes for the Pakistani market. They started in Karachi and later expanded their production facilities in Mirpur, Chakwal, and Sargodha. Majeed directed the Karachi operation's finances. While they did not physically run the production and distribution facilities, they bought people who did. They also provided the Pakistani fiscal police and other government inspectors generous "presents" to ensure that they would look the other way.

While the production and distribution of counterfeit cigarettes was very lucrative, Majeed wanted to profit even further. At his direction, Taliban strongmen would visit the owners of both illegal and legal cigarette factories and demand payment of taxes. Sometimes the request for payments took the form of "*zakat*" or an Islamic "charitable contribution" to further the "struggle." The reality was that the Taliban borrowed a page from other organized criminal groups in Karachi and elsewhere. Victims were intimidated and payment extorted. In return, their "clients" were guaranteed "protection," safe passage, and distribution of their cigarettes. The money-spinning operation helped build the Taliban network in Karachi and elsewhere Pakistan. It helped fund their long term strategic plans and tactical operations

Majeed was pleased with the role Tariq played in the Karachi cigarette operation. He had developed a good sense of the street. Moreover, Tariq had received his promised education and Majeed was now tutoring him in international business and finance. His future was promising.

"My son, after the collections are complete, we are going to start using a new money exchange."

Startled, Tariq looked hard at his father. "That means we are no longer going to use Jafar?"

"No. Jafar is still our friend and we will still bring him occasional business. But considering the volume of our business, I think it only fair that we get a better rate. Jafar refused."

"He is shortsighted."

Majeed grinned. "That is precisely what I told him."

"Then who do we use?"

"Take your collections to Ahmad at Express Exchange. You will find him in the business district on Club Road. He will be expecting you."

"We are getting a better rate?"

"Yes. I've known Ahmad for years, and he is anxious to get a part of our business. They have money couriers every day traveling from Karachi to Dubai."

Tariq's dark brooding eyes suddenly widened. "With the volume of money we are generating, this will further increase both our profits."

"Yes, that is true. But I am thinking about the money exchanger and hawaladar that Ahmad works with in Dubai. Of course, we want our accounts to continue to be credited there. The hawaladar is Shia. But in business, sometimes we look the other way." Majeed grinned. "Besides, Rafi knows him."

"Father, I'll introduce myself to Ahmad later today."

"Wait until tomorrow. It will be impossible to get in or out of the business district. There is going to be a very large demonstration to show support of our Palestinian brothers and sisters. I listened to the news last night, and they expect tens of thousands of people."

News reports in Pakistan closely covered the growing West Bank and Gaza water crisis. Islamic groups, both Sunni and Shia, were stirring up the populace. They wanted to demonstrate solidarity with the Palestinians but were also posturing to advance their own internal political objectives.

"Western infidels want to eradicate Muslims. The modern crusaders invaded Iraq and Afghanistan. They support the corrupt puppet government here in Pakistan. Now the US government does nothing as Israel continues to harass the Palestinians." Tariq's words parroted the phrases found in radical Islamic sermons, madrassas, websites, chat rooms, blogs, message boards, and Pakistani media. Talk on the street was becoming increasingly strident.

Majeed nodded. "Many here in Karachi are poor; they have nothing. But at least we have water."

Tariq put down his tea and paced a few steps. He stepped over a cardboard box that had tipped on its side revealing its contents of old accounting ledgers. He turned back to look at his father. "Isn't there something we can do?"

"I understand that there are discussions taking place now." Majeed paused and took off his glasses. He absentmindedly wiped them on the sleeve of his *kameez.* His eyes met Tariq's and held his gaze. Finally he said, "My son, patience is difficult for young men. If our leadership wants our assistance, they will let us know in due course. In the meantime, worship Allah and be content to know that your work is important."

chapter 3

Colonel Abbadi and I left Ayman with more thanks and well wishes. We followed some back country roads that curved around rocky hillsides. When the roads cleared to the west, we once again had panoramic views of the Sea of Galilee. As we drove, Colonel Abbadi pointed out landmarks, homes, and farms of friends and family members.

"This is the area in which I grew up. When I was eighteen, I went away to school and later joined the army and then GID. Most of my career has been in Amman, but I am still rooted to this land."

"Do you get back often?"

"It is hard now. On the weekends I sometimes come here with my wife and children. But there are so many things to do in Amman that it is hard to break away. The children have their friends and my wife has her family and obligations. That is why bringing you here is also a good excuse for me to come back to my real home. This is also a much more civilized pace of life."

I understood what Colonel Abbadi meant about not having enough time. Living in Rome with my wife and three children, we were hard-pressed to take advantage of all that Rome and Italy offered. If I was home on the weekends during intervals from my many trips, there were always errands for my wife and I to run. The children also had their friends, sport teams, and school-sponsored events. Life was hectic.

"Yet it is different coming back here now," Colonel Abbadi continued with a wistful look in his eyes. "Both my parents and grandfather passed away over the last few years. I have many memories."

As he said this, he brightened and added, "But Nanna, my grandmother, is still here. I'm sure she is waiting for us."

"Colonel, I thought seniors are called by their eldest son's first name; for example 'Um Ali' which would mean mother of Ali."

"Joe, your understanding of Arabic is improving," he said with a wry grin. "But in my family we use a diminutive or Nanna. You'll soon understand."

As soon as the colonel said this, he pulled up to a gated drive. He got out of the car and took a key from his pocket. The colonel opened an old wrought-iron gate that still had some specks of flaked green paint. Following the long pebbled drive, we soon arrived at a beautiful home built of stone that in many ways reminded me of some villas I had seen in the Tuscan countryside.

Nanna could have easily been an Italian "Nonna," or grandmother. The white-haired lady dressed in black was a bit stooped as she came down the stairs of the house, but there was a bounce in her step and energy in her eyes. She welcomed her grandson with a big hug.

"*Asalaam alykum*,"—Peace be upon you. "*Keef haluk?*"—How are you?

"*Ana bikhayr, shukran,*"—I am fine, thank you. "But let's speak English for our guest, Mr. Joe."

"Mr. Joe, it is so nice to meet you. Welcome to our home."

"I am very happy to meet you. I am also impressed with your English. Aptitude for languages must run in the family."

Nanna beamed. "Actually, my late husband insisted that the family learn English. Many years ago, he worked with the British in what was then the Transjordan. He learned the language. After World War II, he realized that English is the language of international commerce and he insisted that all of our family members learn the language—including me!"

Nanna's eyes moistened. "My husband was a man ahead of his time." She paused as if momentarily lost in her memories. "In any event, speaking English helps keep my mind sharp. Please, come in."

Ushering us into her beautiful home, Nanna then escorted us out the back and sat us around a table under a veranda covered by trellised grape vines. Ripening quickly in the pleasant Jordanian sunshine, clusters of grapes hung low over our heads. The view from the terracotta tiled patio was breathtaking. Stony hillsides were the back-drop for the glistening Sea of Galilee. White rocks like lumps of feta cheese lay strewn amongst the cypress groves and farms. It was a familiar Mediterranean picture; the carefully tended olive orchards that lined the hillside slopes formed a similar background to paintings of Tuscan or Grecian landscapes.

All the while busying herself with our comfort, Nanna kept up a steady banter of regional news and family gossip interspersed with simultaneous inquiries about her grandchildren's well-being back in Amman. After a few minutes, a matronly woman emerged from the kitchen door carrying platters of food. Nanna introduced us to Amal, her "helper, best friend, and part of the family."

The late lunch began with a round of *mezze,* including the ever-present hummus and baba ghanoush. Amal also brought freshly baked bread, halloumi cheese, olives, and tabbouleh. Chilled lemonade churned with mint leaves quenched our thirst.

Nanna was a gracious hostess. Having traveled to most countries in the Middle East, I knew that the words "Arab" and "hospitality" were synonymous. Arab hospitality, the art of welcoming a traveler into the home, was said to be the same now as it was a millennium ago when lonely travelers crossed deserts and remote wastelands. The travelers were dependent on others to provide water and sustenance. Hospitality was an intrinsic part of the Arab culture. Normally it was the male who played the role of host. In this case, Nanna, the matron of the Abbadi family, provided a welcoming environment to the visiting American guest.

"I moved into this house sixty-eight years ago, the day I married my late husband. Of course, the house did not look like it does now. We worked hard over the years to develop our business and properties. But my children were all born here, my husband died here, and *Inshallah,* God willing, I will die here as well."

I listened to Nanna's stories of family as I helped myself to the overflowing plates of *mezze*. The conversation drifted to recent events. Nonna said that everybody in the area was talking about the demonstrations and water shortages in the West Bank and the exchanges of rocket attacks between Israel and Hezbollah in southern Lebanon.

"This is just one more legacy of the 1967 Six-Day War."

"What do you mean?" I asked Nanna.

"Mr. Joe, the Arab-Israeli dispute is a conflict about land. But just as crucial is the water that flows through that land. The Six-Day War that changed the map of the area arguably had its origins in a water dispute."

I gave her a quizzical look. "Water was an issue in 1967?"

"Israel has wanted to control the regional water supply since its creation. The issues have not gone away and are getting worse."

I knew the Six-Day War was a spectacular victory for Israel, and a humiliating defeat for three Arab countries. Egypt lost Gaza and the entire Sinai Peninsula. Jordan lost East Jerusalem and the West Bank. Syria lost the Golan and has not yet recovered the strategic heights. Although the Sinai was returned after the 1973 Yom Kippur War, and Gaza is now controlled by the Palestinians, the loss of East Jerusalem and the West Bank was a tremendous blow not only to the Jordanians but to pan-Arab nationalism, pride, and the psyche of the Arab "man in the street."

Reportedly, Jordan's King Hussein was tricked into the war with a phone call from Egypt's Nasser telling him that a look at his radar would show scores of Egyptian planes on their way to attack Israel. However, the radar blips were actually Israeli aircraft returning to base in Israel after they had effectively destroyed Nasser's entire air force of 350 Soviet-supplied planes. The subsequent Jordanian attack was overwhelmingly repulsed, and Israel's army entered East Jerusalem on a wave of fury and once again claimed the remnants, the supporting retaining wall, or "Wailing Wall," of their holy temple.

Israel lost no time in constructing new settlements in the captured territory. During my trips to Israel with HSI, I had seen dozens and dozens of settlements raised near Jerusalem. There were hundreds more throughout the West Bank. They were home to hundreds of thousands of Israeli settlers. The settlements changed both the topography of wide swaths of the Holy Land and the political dynamics.

As Amal began to clear the *mezze* from the table, Nanna continued her commentary. "I am an old woman. I have seen a lot. As a result of the 1967 War, Israel gained control of the waters of the West Bank and the Sea of Galilee. Those resources—the West Bank's mountain aquifer and the Sea of Galilee—give Israel about sixty percent of its fresh water."

Looking at Colonel Abbadi, I said that I was aware that the wall running through the West Bank that Israel created in the mid 1990s had also exacerbated the whole water situation.

He nodded his head in agreement. "Due primarily to the intifadas and attacks against Israeli civilians, Israel erected a solid thousand-kilometer-long wall that is in some sections ten meters high. It physically separates the Jews and the Palestinians. However, it juts into Palestinian territory for eighty-five percent of its length."

"You can hardly blame successive Israeli governments for wanting to protect their people." I said. "Something had to be done to stop the suicide attacks."

Abbadi paused. It appeared he was carefully considering his words. "The wall has served many purposes. It has secured Israeli enclaves in Palestinian territory. It also doubles as a defensive line. Most Israeli settlements are sheltered behind the barrier. Conveniently, they also sit astride the water aquifer that runs north-south."

"I didn't realize."

"Joe, the wall put ninety percent of the territory's aquifer west of the demarcation under Israeli control."

What was left unsaid by Colonel Abbadi was that the US had given tacit political and financial support to Israel in constructing the wall. In order to survive, the Palestinians were forced to buy water from their hated occupiers at inflated prices. But lately Israel had curtailed Palestinian access to water even further. The result was demonstrations, riots, and an exchange of rockets.

Amal came from the kitchen and put a massive platter heaped with the signature Jordanian dish on the table in front of me.

Mansaf is a tender lamb cooked in *jameed*, sheep's milk yogurt. The lamb is served on a bed of rice garnished with toasted pine nuts and almonds. The lamb's head was on top, which signifies respect for the guest. As I extolled the dish, Colonel Abbadi took a pinch of flat bread and expertly used his fingers to scoop up a mouth-watering ball of *mansaf* rice and lamb. Since I was the guest, he personally fed me the delicious morsel.

Amal joined us at the table.

"Mr. Joe, I heard you talking about the West Bank. I'm from Aboud, a small village northwest of Jerusalem and only a few kilometers from the Green Line, Israel's pre-1967 border."

"If I may ask, why are you now here?"

"I'm Christian. I believe I am here through the grace of God and the hospitality of Nanna and her family."

Nanna smiled warmly. "Amal came here in the early 1980s. She was a refugee and alone. Her family did not survive the move from Aboud. My husband had business in a refugee camp further south in Jordan. He met Amal and brought her here. She is the daughter I never had."

"Mr. Joe, Aboud was a wonderful place to grow up. It was a very peaceful village. We only had a few thousand residents. At the time I left, the village had about the same number of Christians and Muslims. For centuries, we lived together peacefully."

"I know there has been an exodus of Christians from the Holy Land. It is such a shame."

Nanna added, "That is probably another casualty of the 1967 War. Christians fleeing Israel and having their lands confiscated. It is a continuation of when Israel was founded in 1948."

"Look to the Sea of Galilee below you," said Colonel Abbadi. "The region around Galilee was only one-quarter Jewish. But when the Israeli army moved in, they forced many Muslims and Christians out of their ancestral homes without compensation. Many of the refugees came to this area. That is the primary reason why Hashimiyya and the surrounding area have grown so rapidly."

I knew that Palestinian refugee camps were found throughout the West Bank, Gaza, Lebanon, and Jordan. Most were squalid. They bred both resentment and terrorists. The refugees had no choice but to struggle to survive in horrible conditions and hope against hope for a settlement that would allow them to reclaim their land.

"Any comprehensive peace settlement will have to address the refugees' right of return."

"That will never happen," said Colonel Abbadi. "Israel will never allow it. The Palestinians know that and it adds to their feelings of helplessness."

Amal spoke up again. "Mr. Joe, we were here for thousands of years. In the case of Aboud, our history dates from when Jesus and the Holy Family passed through Aboud en route from the Galilee to Jerusalem. We also believe that Jesus preached in Aboud."

I nodded. Unlike the United States, people in the Middle East—Muslims, Jews, and Christians—readily spoke of their religion. It was the central part of their lives. The entire area was holy to all three religions. One could not understand the region without understanding the overriding importance of religion.

Amal continued. "My life changed in 1982. Israel established a settlement near our property. We were concerned but believed we could all live together. Then they converted the settlement into a military base, and then they confiscated all of our land."

She looked down and her voice trembled. "We never received a shekel in payment. When we were forced to leave, my mother and father just gave up. It was too much for them to leave our home and ancestral land."

"I'm so sorry."

"This is my home now. I am blessed. But sometimes I hear from friends back in Aboud. They are really suffering now through the further loss of water."

"Are they also rioting?"

"I don't know. But since the '67 War, Israel has severely restricted Aboud's use of the aquifer and prevented the drilling of wells to access fresh water beneath the village. The people are forced to purchase their water from Israel's national water company. The people are also upset about the loss of their olive trees."

"Olive trees?"

"The creation of the wall, military base, and settlements has destroyed much of Aboud's olive groves. We've lost more than ten thousand trees. Some of them were over a thousand years old. Those trees were in the village's families for centuries."

Nanna's face was solemn. "The loss of olive trees is happening throughout Palestine. The olive tree is a symbol of life. Generations of families have been provided for from the fruit of the olive tree. Our way of life is disappearing."

"Mr. Joe, it is good that you hear of these things. In order to understand the current conflict, you must understand the history behind the events. You must understand that people feel helpless," said Colonel Abbadi.

Our lengthy discussion over the platter of *mansaf* continued with dessert. Amal had prepared *kunafeh,* a dessert of creamy cheese topped with sweetened tangerine-colored semolina, speckled with green pistachios, and drizzled with saffron-infused sugar syrup. And Nonna served sweetened black tea flavored with sage "to help the digestion."

We slowly sipped our tea. Colonel Abbadi lit a cigarette.

Nanna began to speak. "In Islam we believe that your Jesus was a very great prophet." She swept up her hand and pointed. "Look. You can see the hillsides sloping to the Sea of Galilee."

The view from the patio was incredible. The sky was turning hues of gold and red as the sun began its descent over the deep blue lake.

"Jesus was here two thousand years ago. Today, this area is safe. This area is prosperous. We do not have a water problem. The radicals have not come to this area."

"And we will not allow it," interjected the colonel.

"Mr. Joe, do you know the gospel of Matthew that tells the story of the land of Gadara—the land where we are now? I have known this story since I was a little girl. When I came here to live with the Abbadi family I was so happy to see the area where my savior Jesus performed miracles and preached."

I nodded. Amal continued. She wanted to tell the story.

"I know the passage well. Jesus came here after he spent the night on the Sea of Galilee in a boat with his disciples. As Jesus lay sleeping, a great storm came and the boat was swamped by the waves. His disciples awakened him and Jesus rose and settled the winds and the sea and there was calm. In the morning they came to the other side of the sea. When Jesus stepped on land, demons approached. They asked Him, 'Have you come here to torment us before the time?' There was a herd of swine feeding nearby. The demons begged Jesus, 'If you cast us out, send us into the swine.' Jesus said to them, 'Go,' and they went into the swine; and the whole herd rushed down the steep bank and perished in the waters."

Amal finished the story and looked at me. She then turned her gaze toward the steep hills rushing down to the sea. Almost to herself she murmured, "Of course, nobody knows exactly where that happened. But I feel it was nearby."

Colonel Abbadi blew out a puff of smoke and snuffed out his cigarette in an overflowing ashtray. "I don't know your bible. But there are passages from Greek and Latin classic literature in which petitioners beg their gods to transfer an evil from one place to another, or from one person to another. It's almost as if the amount of evil in the world is constant and evil cannot be destroyed but can only change location."

I nodded and waited for him to continue. *He is trying to tell me something.*

"Mr. Joe, the GID is very good. I see a lot of intelligence reports from Jordan and from other areas. I am very worried. There are many different kinds of demons today. And they are changing locations."

chapter 4

WALKING OUT OF the parking complex near the American Embassy Rome's Boncompagni gate, I turned on Via Lucallo and headed toward the law enforcement annex. The embassy and its nearby annex were part of the Palazzo Margarita complex, which faced the Via Veneto, one of the most famous and fashionable avenues in the world. During the 1950s, the Veneto was synonymous with the *dolce vita*, with its elegant cafes and shops. The cafes and posh hotels were still there, as was the monumental Aurelian Wall found at the upper end of the avenue. In fact, the wall and its Porta Pinciana, which formed the entrance to the Veneto, had surrounded Rome for almost eighteen centuries. When the wall was originally constructed, the decline of the Roman Empire was already underway. Emperor Aurelio launched the massive construction of towering walls and fortifications in an unsuccessful attempt to hold off the inevitable sack of Rome by the demons of a previous age—the barbarians. Modern Rome still boasted impressive ruins of the empire that once ruled the world, including the far away Roman outposts in Gadara.

Walking briskly down Via Lucallo, I spotted Special Agent Pete Gonzalez of the United States Secret Service. Pete stood erect by the front door of the annex. His arms were folded and he had his sunglasses on. He was obviously waiting for someone.

"Hey Pete, are you practicing standing post?"

He smiled. "Yeah, being overseas I miss it so much I thought I would just stand out here by the door for the next few hours," he said facetiously. "I have to stay in post-standing shape."

"Well, you certainly cut a *bella figura*," I replied, using the Italian expression that roughly translated to beautiful image or style, a trait very important to Italians.

"Actually, I'm waiting out here for the rest of the guys. We are going to start our day with a cappuccino at the Mozart coffee bar. Would you like to join us?"

"No thanks. I just got back from a trip to Jordan, and I've got a lot of paperwork to do."

"I was there on a counterfeit currency investigation a couple of months ago." Pete said. "Jordan's great."

I nodded my agreement.

"Hey Joe, speaking of standing next to doors, I know you have had a lot of experience yourself. POTUS is coming out here in November. Would you like to help us out and be a post-stander again? We always need bodies."

I smiled. "Sure, why not? It would be like old times. Just let me know the exact dates and I'll block them out on my calendar."

The good-natured bantering and camaraderie among Secret Service agents was something that I missed. However, I did not miss "standing post" or guard. I began my law enforcement career as a special agent with the Secret Service. I only lasted three years.

The current Secret Service was part of the Department of Homeland Security. But when I joined, it was part of the Department of the Treasury. The Secret Service, or "Service" as it was often called among the rank-and-file, boasted a long and distinguished history. The mission of the Secret Serviced evolved over the years, but its core mandates of combating various types of financial crimes and protection of the president and other "protectees" designated by Congress remained. Investigation and protection were actually complimentary. The Service had found that their criminal investigations helped prepare their agents for protective responsibilities. During investigations, the agent learned to read people, size up situations, and if necessary react quickly and decisively. These were all essential attributes for protection.

I started my Secret Service career assigned to the Washington, DC, field office. Although I cut my teeth on investigations in the greater Washington, DC, area following counterfeit currency and forged US checks, because of the office's location I was heavily involved in protection—the Secret Service's priority mission. I was constantly used as a guard or post-stander at various functions in Washington where the president, vice president, and other dignitaries protected by the Secret Service were in attendance.

During a typical event, I would be assigned a door, entryway, or a position near a stage to stand watch or "post." In order to secure the environment where the "protectee" would pass, the agents would typically stand post hours in advance of the arrival. In addition, my colleagues and I were pulled to assist the Service during presidential campaigns and sometimes foreign travel. Although the work looked very glamorous from the outside, it could be deadly tedious. I had the utmost respect for the people, the organization, and its mission, but I soon realized that I did not want to make the Secret Service my career. The travel and shift work wreaked havoc on my family life. I also wanted to pursue investigative work. When a transfer to the Presidential Protective Detail or PPD looked imminent, I knew I had to make a decision. I decided to leave the Secret Service but continue my career as a Treasury agent. I joined the US Customs Service.

Leaving Pete and his newly arrived colleagues at the front door of the annex with a promise that I would try to join them the following morning for that cappuccino, I took the stairs up a few flights to the office of the ICE attaché.

Walking in the front door, I almost bumped into the new attaché, Susan Martinelli, as she was walking out.

"Hi, Joe, welcome back! How was your trip?"

"It went well," I replied. "Let me know when you have some time and I'll give you a brief. I developed some pretty good leads and got some solid information back from the Jordanians on a couple of cases. I'll be writing up some ROI's." Reports of Investigation were an important means of communicating information to colleagues.

"I look forward to that brief. Actually, I saw some cable traffic from Embassy Amman."

"Yeah, when I got the information about the cluster bombs, I knew I had to report it to the Embassy Amman regional security officer and the Agency."

"The cables got some attention, but we'll talk about that later. Right now, I've got some appointments. A presto!" she said in a bubbly voice. "See you soon!"

I watched Susan head toward the annex's elevator until the door closed behind her. Susan was in her early fifties. A single career woman, she was trim, fit, and wore her frosted-blonde hair short. She had arrived in Rome only a few weeks before—about the time I departed for Jordan. I smiled because Susan had not yet adopted the Italian style of dress. Having been in Rome for five years, I had seen a steady stream of both American men and women change their typically frumpy, loose-fitting, and sometimes sloppy attire to adapt to the more stylish and professional Italian fashion. Clothes are a part of making the Italian *bella figura.*

It was common knowledge that Susan was on her "retirement tour." In her meteoric career, she had been promoted far too rapidly and for many of the wrong reasons. She became one more example of the Peter Principle, whereby an employee tends to rise to his or her level of incompetence. By all accounts, during her previous assignment as the special agent in charge of the HSI office in Houston, she had been a disaster. Amid allegations of office improprieties, a spike in Equal Employment Opportunity grievances filed, Internal Affairs investigations, and a severe drop-off in successful investigations, the HSI director of investigations in Washington, DC, prevailed upon his colleague, the director of international affairs, to take Susan off of his hands. Eventually, a personnel quid pro quo would repay the favor between directors. But the short-term solution to the problem in Houston was to transfer the problem overseas; out of sight and out of mind. Since Susan was well connected politically within the HSI hierarchy, face had to be saved. Management protected management and presented the transfer to Rome to both Susan and the troops as a reward for her years of service and as a way of fulfilling her Italian heritage. Everybody knew better.

I saw the office manager, Terri Donato, standing in the foyer. Simultaneously, she gave me a smile and arched an eyebrow. Terri was the real boss of the office. Her job description was handling administrative and budgeting matters. But Terri was much more than that. An Italian-American, she had been living in Rome for thirty years and had been working at the embassy for twenty. She spoke the language fluently, had a wide circle of contacts, and knew the inner workings of the embassy better than most. Attachés, agents, and analysts had come and gone. Terri was the constant in the office. She made the place work.

"Welcome back, Joe."

"Well, I *think* it is good to be back." There wasn't anybody else around, but still I leaned over and whispered, "How is Susan getting along?"

Likewise lowering her voice, she responded, "It's too early to tell. Outside of going to a few country-team meetings at the embassy and courtesy calls with some Italian counterparts, she hasn't really done anything yet. She has been preoccupied with furnishing her office and apartment."

"What? Here we go again," I said. "It seems like one manager after the other is more concerned with the perks of the position than doing actual work."

Terry lowered her voice another few decibels. "I have been directed to find thousands of dollars in the budget to have new drapes put up in the attaché's office. Those are the 'appointments' she is going to now. She is picking out fabric."

"You've got to be kidding. What's wrong with the old drapes?"

"Absolutely nothing. If the taxpayers only knew . . ."

She continued, "Joe, I know you have a lot of paperwork waiting for you. I'll let you go, but how are Ana and the kids?"

"They're fine. Thanks for asking. I had quite a welcome home. The kids are still in the, 'Daddy, what did you bring me?' stage. It's fun."

"They are cute kids. You are lucky."

"In many ways. Ana is used to holding down the fort while I'm away. As you know, she has adapted very well to Rome. Many spouses do not."

My office was down the hallway. I sat down behind my desk and flipped on the computer. Looking in my paper inbox, I let out an audible groan. Every time I came back from a trip, it took days and sometimes weeks to catch up with the paperwork and miscellaneous bureaucratic tasks. For example, I knew I would spend most of that morning just on the accounting for the trip. Despite what the media portrayed, agents spent the majority of their time handling seemingly never-ending administrative matters, writing reports, pleading for operational funding, and playing political and bureaucratic games trying to ensure that their next transfer took them someplace they wanted to go. My foreign trips and investigations were only a temporary respite from the all-encompassing bureaucracy.

Looking past the computer screen, I saw an old US Customs ensign hanging on the wall in front of me. Despite the fatigue, occasional aggravations, increasing paperwork, and bureaucratic changes over the years, the old Customs flag made me smile. I still loved my job.

Unfortunately, the ensign was one more legacy of the old Customs Service that no longer existed. Like the Secret Service, US Customs was once part of the Department of Treasury. In fact, it had an even longer history within Treasury and its accomplishments were just as impressive. When most Americans thought of Customs, they undoubtedly thought of the uniformed customs officers' duties of inspection and control at airports and land border crossings. Although this was important work, it didn't sound glamorous. However, Customs also had an investigatory side staffed by special agents. The investigators never received a lot of public recognition, but within law enforcement circles they were well-respected.

Customs investigated things that had to do with crossing the border of the United States. Its mission involving transnational crime appealed to me. So when I decided that I did not want to spend an entire career with the Secret Service, Customs was a logical alternative. Since both the Secret Service and Customs were sister Treasury enforcement agencies, the transfer was not complicated. I finished work with the Secret Service on a Friday and started with Customs on a Monday.

Customs' Office of Enforcement boasted about three thousand special agents and other support personnel. Enforcement was responsible for various investigative programs, tactical interdiction, and intelligence support. Customs' Office of Enforcement was charged with enforcing over four hundred laws, more than the FBI handled. Although the primary focus at the time was the "War on Narcotics," just about anything that had nexus to the border came under the Customs domain. Long before September 11, the US Customs Service was part of the United States' first line of defense.

However, everything changed after September 11. In the rush to react to the terrorist attacks, politicians of both political parties hurriedly created the new Department of Homeland Security, or DHS. The new department combined about 170,000 federal workers from twenty-two separate agencies, including Customs and the Secret Service—the two proud former Treasury agencies. The Department of Treasury also lost the Bureau of Alcohol Tobacco and Firearms, which was incorporated into the Department of Justice. Outside of Treasury's Internal Revenue Service, which concentrated primarily on tax issues, Treasury's legacy and proud history of law enforcement were jettisoned primarily for reasons of political expediency.

It never made sense to me why the two US agencies most responsible for the events surrounding September 11, the CIA and the FBI, were rewarded with additional staff, resources, and mandates. Yet bureaucratically, the Department of Treasury's enforcement arm suffered the most. It had never recovered.

Customs' inclusion into the new DHS bureaucracy was further complicated by the forced merger with the former Immigration and Naturalization Service, or INS, an extremely weak and frankly incompetent agency. The criminal investigators in both Customs and INS were combined into the new Immigration and Customs Enforcement, or ICE.

The forced merger, which took place during a time of war, created horrendous logistical, administrative, financial, and personnel issues. Some issues took years to sort out and others had never been resolved. For some in "legacy Customs," it was hard to adapt. Morale suffered. Many left. I found refuge in the office of the Customs attaché in Rome.

Homeland Security Investigations had twenty-six principal field offices throughout the United States. Yet ICE's Office of International Affairs had more than fifty international offices in more than forty countries around the world, including the office of the ICE attaché in Rome. Other US law enforcement agencies, such as the FBI, DEA, and Secret Service, also had law enforcement attaché offices overseas. There were many reasons for this. For example, if the FBI was working an investigation in the United States and an "investigative lead" went overseas, the FBI would task the appropriate "Legatt" (legal attaché) office or offices to continue to follow the investigative trail. Generally, the requested overseas information was obtained in conjunction with "host government" counterpart agencies, like police and customs services. Depending on the country involved and operational agreements with counterpart agencies, US law enforcement might also be allowed to conduct limited investigations or interviews, such as the one I conducted in Jordan with Colonel Abbadi. Obviously, US law enforcement had no jurisdiction overseas. There were also reciprocal agreements with our foreign law enforcement counterparts where we tried to respond to their requests for information in kind.

It was a common misperception, particularly among those who believe pulp novels and James Bond-type thrillers, that INTERPOL conducted international investigations. Simply put, that was erroneous. There was no such thing as an international police agency that actually investigated across borders, let alone had the power to arrest. INTERPOL did facilitate an international law enforcement information exchange by issuing electronic alerts and requests for information through its "in-country" representatives. It was currently building and improving databases and the technical means to share information. But INTERPOL would always be hampered by sovereignty concerns and the fact that member countries had diverse legal standards and systems. Conversely, attaché offices had a history of being able to build effective bilateral relationships: the single most important attribute in conducting international criminal investigations. It was exactly the kind of work I enjoyed and I was thankful that Customs—and now HSI—had given me the opportunity.

Staring at the old Customs ensign and immersed in my thoughts, I was startled to hear the assistant attaché, Dennis LaFarge, enter my office.

"Hey Joe, I thought I heard you come in. How was your trip?"

"Hi, Dennis. Jordan is always a pleasure. I really enjoy the people. And I think I got some good information."

"I saw the cables."

"I almost bumped into Susan as I was walking in. I offered to brief her when she comes back. Why don't you sit in?"

"I'd like that," Dennis said as he settled uninvited into the visitor's chair opposite my desk.

Dennis was a tall man. His height helped proportion his large belly, which was noticeably protruding from his sport coat. The weight, receding hairline, and double chin made him look much older than his 42 years. Although at times I found him professionally annoying, I thought he was very nice on a personal level. I enjoyed having the occasional beer with him. Our wives and children were friends. However, as much as I enjoyed Dennis's company in a social situation, I thought he never should have been sent overseas. To put it politely, he had trouble "adapting."

Dennis was Susan's deputy. He was legacy INS. He was fine with immigration matters but knew very little about customs issues such as money-laundering, fraud, and the transshipments of weapons and high technology. It was also his first supervisory position, and it sometimes showed. He too was posted overseas via the "old boy's network"—not the normal competitive bidding process. Dennis benefited from an unwritten quota system of trying to even the overseas representation of legacy Customs and legacy INS personnel.

Dennis had been in the Rome office about a year. During that time, I never saw him work a case, write a report, or develop an informant. I did hear him practice his Italian every morning with the Italian custodial staff, but to the best of my knowledge he had not once visited an Italian law enforcement agency on his own. When he arrived overseas, he didn't know how to drive a manual transmission car and soon ground down the gears in his government-issued "G-ride." Finding it hard to adjust to the swirling Roman traffic, he had already been in three fender-benders. As Terri said, Dennis was both "budget and labor intensive." Outside of over-editing the reports of the three agents in the office, giving unsolicited advice on customs matters he knew little about, and attending the occasional administrative meeting at the embassy, I honestly didn't know what he did to justify the approximately one million dollars per year it took in salary and allowances to keep him and his family overseas in Rome.

"Joe, I'm not sure when we will have this brief with Susan, but things are moving fast and I want to give you a heads-up."

"What's that?"

"Well, you know the situation in the Middle East is getting volatile."

"I saw the news reports last night. There are massive demonstrations up and down the Gulf. CNN is also reporting some ugly incidents in Beirut, Cairo, and Karachi."

"Obviously, Washington is concerned. The cables from Amman got a lot more attention in the community than you probably intended."

"Dennis, I didn't *intend* anything. I just reported the facts as they were reported to me. That's my job."

"Joe, you are not an intelligence officer. You are a criminal investigator."

"And there might be criminal violations," I responded, perhaps a little too forcefully and with a little too much sarcasm.

Dennis didn't show any reaction to the tone of my rejoinder. He was either being diplomatic or just didn't grasp the issues. "In any event," he continued, "headquarters wants a quick follow-up. I got a phone call from the director of international affairs this morning. Since you are the one who reported the information and also have a background in cluster bombs, there is talk about sending you to Israel."

"I'm O.K. with that."

"It could be quickly. That's why I wanted to give you a heads-up."

"How quickly?"

"Well," he paused, "Today is Monday. The Israeli weekend is Friday and Saturday. We would like you there and working by Sunday."

I smiled the smile of someone with jet lag, an overflowing inbox, and a family anxious to spend some time with him. "There is a lot to do to get ready."

"Do what you have to do. Give the regional security officer in Tel Aviv a call. Sound him out. Tel Aviv has been copied on all the cable traffic. Have him start setting up appointments. You'll have to get a country clearance cable out ASAP. Terri will make all the travel arrangements for you."

"Do we even know if the Israelis will talk to us?

"We have to at least be able to document the fact that we tried."

"O.K."

"One more thing. A report came in from the SAC/New York regarding an investigation into Iranian sanctions-busting linked to a hawala network. The investigation is also getting some notice in headquarters. The powers that be are getting snippy because Congress is starting to ask questions about the effectiveness of sanctions. It's getting political." I nodded my understanding. "Anyway," Dennis continued, "one of the hawaladars that reportedly is involved is located in Dubai."

"That's not a surprise."

"In doing record checks, the case agent found that you have met the guy."

"Farid? He's not a documented source. He obviously has good access to information. But it is hard to get him to talk specifics. I would like to try to develop him."

"Anyway, the New York report has undeveloped leads for our office. There are some other cases involving Dubai that also need attention, and we have your training initiatives to pin down. I printed out the reports and put them all in your inbox."

"I saw the stack of paper when I came in."

"Susan and I were talking. This is the end of the fiscal year. Travel money is tight right now. We have to consolidate our work."

This can't be good, I thought.

"We thought that since you have to go to Israel, you might as well keep going to Dubai. They are both in the Middle East and it might provide some travel savings."

I didn't say a thing as I unsuccessfully tried to keep the grimace off my face. As Dennis got up to leave, he also didn't say anything. He either didn't care or just didn't comprehend the logistics and administrative and investigative issues involved. Either way, the end result was that I was going to be on the road again.

chapter 5

SHAMROZ SLAMMED HIS fist down on the desk. He shook his head and cursed. Rubbing eyes that ached from strain and reddened from lack of sleep, he looked again at the flickering screen above the keyboard. The encrypted email was short and direct. It stood in polar opposite to the flowering language of diplomacy and propaganda that was his norm.

He took a moment to re-read the cryptic text and cursed again. His mind raced with the implications of the message. Why couldn't his comrades in Zahedan have been more forceful? Couldn't they have headed off this summons? What was so important that he had to return once again to that cursed Iranian cesspool of a city? Couldn't they have included some insight in their cryptic message?

The Shura councilman was worn and tired. Shamroz closed his eyes. Although only 58, he felt much older. The last few years as the Taliban's de facto chief diplomat had been grueling. He longed for the simplicity of his youth and the sense of purposefulness of the battlefield. Where did the years go?

Willing himself a momentary escape, he thought again of the momentous days of 1989. It was the year he received his nom de guerre while fighting with the Mujahedeen. He had severed the head of a captured Soviet colonel and had been photographed holding the grizzly trophy. The picture had been widely circulated. The caption labeled him "Shamroz" or "Master of the Sword." The grizzled warrior smirked at the memory. This was the incident where he first learned the value of propaganda.

Shamroz unconsciously touched his breast. He simultaneously gave thanks and praise in silent prayer. He rejoiced that he had experienced a time when all of Afghanistan seemed united in their successful efforts to expel the Soviet invaders. That sense of unity and shared purpose lasted until the last Soviet tank rumbled home in disgrace across the Termez Bridge.

Strife and civil war followed. Shamroz was well acquainted with the tribalism that divided his countrymen. The ancient discords and rivalries were exacerbated by modernism and western influences. Yet he believed the major fault line was just below the surface; it was the disunion within Islam itself.

The two major denominations of Islam, Sunni and Shia, were originally divided by a dispute that began when the Islamic prophet Muhammad died in the year 632 AD. An argument over succession developed between his followers. The young religion split. Differences in the Islamic denominations evolved and included religious practice, belief, traditions, and customs. Over the centuries, the relationship between Sunni and Shia was marked by periods of both cooperation and conflict. In recent years, conflict dominated.

In the modern era, approximately eighty-five percent of the world's Muslims were Sunni, including the majority Muslim population in the Arabian Peninsula, South Asia, and Africa. Almost eighty percent of Pakistan's population was Sunni, but a strong Shia presence remained. Shia was the majority in Iran, Iraq, and Bahrain. There was also a very large Shia presence in Lebanon, including Hezbollah.

Although Sunni-Shia strife in Iraq, Bahrain, Syria and Lebanon received the most international attention, the same type of discord existed in both Pakistan and Afghanistan. The issues were ancient, complex, and intertwined. Riots, sectarian killings, and assassinations were common results. Thousands of people had died in both countries. In recent years, the violence had often been the result of direct involvement of both the Taliban and al Qaeda and associated splinter groups, such as the Lashkar-e Taiba, responsible for the 2008 attacks on Mumbai.

Shamroz again rubbed his eyes. Only last night there had been another horrendous attack a few kilometers from his Quetta office. Gunmen rode motorcycles into a queue of football fans in front of Shaheed Nauoroz Stadium – the largest stadium in the city. They had sprayed the crowd with fire from automatic weapons. Dozens were killed and injured. He had stayed up all night trying to determine what happened.

Shamroz hoped the incident was generated by Baluch separatists that were fighting a low-level insurgency. They had been trying for years to gain political autonomy and a greater share of the profits from the region's natural resources. But Shamroz knew the incident could just as well be the result of a pro-Taliban faction. His frustration mounting, he pounded his fist yet again. He was a member of the Shura and he didn't have a clue about the latest outrage. Maybe the summons from Zahedan was a blessing in disguise, he thought. A quick departure would avoid the official Pakistani inquiries. Shamroz had learned that evasion is sometimes the best form of diplomacy.

The Taliban recognized Shamroz's talents. The Shura councilmen first used his bona-fides, intellect, grasp of issues, and biting wit to produce videos and later on-line Taliban propaganda. Later, his polished demeanor, longevity and interpersonal skills were found useful for sensitive negotiations. In the summer of 2012, the Shura selected Shamroz to open the first Taliban mission in Iran.

Iran's theocratic Shia regime had been an enemy of the Sunni Taliban when the latter ruled most of Afghanistan. For example, when Taliban forces captured the city of Mazar-i-Sharif in 1998, they murdered nine Iranian diplomats. Yet despite the ancient Shia/Sunni split, over the years there had been a gradual rapprochement. The Afghan/Pakistan Taliban and the hardline Iranian mullahs realized they faced common threats and had shared interests; "An enemy of my enemy is my friend."

Both sides desperately wanted to force the Western infidels from the region. The Taliban were battling a physical invasion. Iran felt encircled. Although there were no foreign armies on its soil, there was a strong American influence on its Iraq, Turkish, Afghan and Gulf borders. The ruling mullahs also felt they were combatting stealth attacks that threatened the very survival of the Islamic Republic of Iran. Sanctions, designations, international diplomatic countermeasures, hyper-inflation and a simmering rebellion by a large segment of a disillusioned populace had taken their toll. The hard-liners were increasingly concerned about terrorist attacks, cyber-warfare, covert operations within the country and assassinations of some of their top nuclear scientists. Despite tremendous costs and international censure, the mullahs told themselves that nuclear arms were the key to safeguard their power and their Islamic revolution.

By 2005, a tentative dialog gained momentum. Shipments of Iranian arms, rockets, and explosives were smuggled to the Taliban fighting forces. The Taliban made payment via smuggled shipments of opium, gems, and timber; a percentage of the proceeds of the illicit trade often routed to the ruling cadre and facilitators within the Iranian Revolutionary Guards.

The Taliban's official presence in Zahedan was the next step. As chief of mission, Shamroz was instrumental in solidifying the burgeoning relationship. First he secured specialized operational training for Taliban guerilla fighters by the Quds Force of Iran's Revolutionary Guard Corps. Playing on Iranian fears of American aggression, Shamroz next convinced Tehran to furnish the latest generation of specially designed IEDs that were so effective against US forces in Iraq. Yet before he could get Iranian concurrence for his third major request – shoulder fired and laser guided surface-to-air missiles that could threaten American and coalition air dominance over the skies of Afghanistan - the Shura recalled Shamroz to Quetta.

The arrival of CIA supplied stinger missiles on the Afghan battlefields had been the turning point in the mujahideen war against the Soviet invaders. The Shura had long believed history could repeat itself. The latest generation Iranian supplied surface-to-air missiles could expedite the withdrawal of the remaining air-dependent US and coalition forces. They would sow panic in the thinning ranks of Afghan pilots. Although the Taliban had been able to secure a trickle of the coveted weapons, Shamroz wanted a steady flow. The request had been left quietly on the negotiating table.

Shamroz knew the Iranians were getting increasingly desperate. Factions within Iran were battling. As Iran fell ever deeper into isolation and economic distress, some wanted to strike. Is this what the summons to Zahedan is about? What do they want from us? The uncertainty caused the "Master of the Sword" to pound his fist once again.

chapter 6

MAJEED STROLLED DOWN the west wharf at the international container terminal in the port of Karachi. It was a beautiful evening. He enjoyed the fresh air and sea breeze, so different from his native landlocked Afghanistan. He was dressed in the traditional *shalwar kameez*, a long, loose-fitting tunic with very baggy trousers. The legs were wide at the top and narrowed at the bottom, and the side seams of the tunic were left open at the waistline for greater freedom of movement. Conforming to his status and self-image as the gentleman "bookkeeper" and despite the Karachi heat, Majeed's white collared shirt was buttoned high. He wore a light-weight grey waistcoat over the *kameez*. Fashionable leather sandals were on his feet. To onlookers, Majeed unconsciously exuded striking dignity. His spectacles and precisely trimmed beard gave him a scholarly air. Prayer beads hung from a vest pocket. Sometimes on his walks, Majeed used the beads to count phrases of worship called *thikr*.

Due to its strategic geographical location, during British colonial rule the Karachi harbor was known as the "gateway to Asia." Although much had changed over the centuries, the port was still located in close proximity to major modern-era shipping routes including the Strait of Hormuz. The natural harbor lay in a sheltered bay to the southwest of the city, protected from storms by the Sandspit Beach, the Manora Island, and the Oyster Rocks. The port was located between the towns of Kiamari and Sadder, close to the heart of old Karachi and the main business district. The west wharf where Majeed was strolling extended southwest from Saddar town and the east wharf northeast from Kiamari Island.

Majeed was headed toward Berth 29, where the container ship *Ocean Star* had arrived early that day from Dubai. He looked forward to seeing his son, Rafi. Along the quay, there was a commotion of activity, including pedestrian workers dodging a variety of motor vehicles, such as forklifts and the ubiquitous light trucks. Majeed had to stay alert. Technically, he was not supposed to be in this area. But the authorities along the terminal appreciated Majeed's ready presents and largesse. He was never questioned.

When Majeed approached the berth, he smiled at the sight of his son. He was a very handsome and impressive looking young man. Even from a distance, Rafi exuded an aura of confidence. Although of medium height, he had a powerful build. Majeed knew that Rafi spent a lot of time working out in a favorite upscale Karachi gym. Instead of the traditional *shalwar qameez,* Rafi wore a tailored dark blue suit with an athletic cut over a white open-collared shirt. Tan-colored Italian shoes were on his feet. His medium-length hair was coal black and combed back in the latest Karachi style. In contrast to the Taliban cadre, Rafi was clean shaven. Majeed saw that Rafi was deep in conversation. He noted that Rafi's powerful arms punctuated his remarks with stabbing motions in the air. Majeed observed his son's bearing, mannerisms, and polished sophistication; he was much different from his brother Tariq. It was only natural.

After Tariq and Rafi came to him from the *madrassa* many years ago, Majeed raised the boys together. He educated, mentored, and counseled them. He ensured their continuing *Sharia*-based Islamic education. As time went by, he discerned their strengths, weaknesses, and personality traits. He determined that Tariq had the characteristics of a man of the streets. As a result, Majeed steered him in the direction of the Karachi black market. In contrast, Rafi was more urbane. He had a sharp intellect and excelled in his studies. He developed a facility for both foreign languages and math. Although Rafi exuded confidence and power, Majeed knew he had a sensitive side. He was also very introspective. These traits manifested themselves in different ways. One of the most obvious was that Rafi had a soft spot in his heart for Western music and stylish things. These traits were anathema to Islamic fundamentalists.

However, Majeed felt these qualities could be used to the Taliban in Pakistan's long-term advantage. With tacit approval from the Taliban leadership, Rafi was allowed to socialize in Karachi's best clubs and fraternize with Western businessmen and tourists. Majeed wanted Rafi to understand Western mannerisms, outlooks, and ways of doing business.

With his facility for languages, Rafi developed passable Arabic, French, and Italian that complemented his already fluent English, Pashtu, Dari, and Urdu. It wasn't long before Majeed could send Rafi as his representative on business trips of increasing complexity and responsibility. With little guidance, Rafi now operated the trading business Majeed had started. He traveled regularly throughout Pakistan and to the Gulf, primarily Dubai. Following in his father's footsteps, he became adept at building a network of business contacts.

Traditionally, most Afghan Pashtuns only used a first name. For practical reasons, Afghans who had any contact with the Western world almost always adopted a surname. Having surnames was also considered a status symbol. Those from prosperous or influential families used surnames for added recognition. Pashtuns frequently adopted the names of their tribes as their last names. Since Rafi was being groomed for international business, Majeed insisted that he use a last name. As a sign of respect, he adopted the tribal name of his adoptive father, "Durrani."

Rafi's education, dress, mannerisms, and exposure to worldly things were good for business. But for Majeed, Rafi, the Pakistani Taliban, and al Qaeda, business was the means to an end; the promulgation of a worldwide Islamic caliphate based on *Sharia*. Where violent jihad was impractical or counterproductive, *Sharia* directed faithful Muslims to use other means in order to accomplish the same goal. As a result, at times Islamic fundamentalists adopted the concept of *taqiyah*—sometimes called Islamic subterfuge—whereby deceiving non-believers by concealment, disguise, and deception was an important and fundamental part of the art of war. Although unspoken, Rafi's image, development in international business, and association with worldly things was a conscious form of subterfuge.

As his discussion ended, Rafi abruptly dismissed his interlocutor. Out of the corner of his eye, he noticed his father approach. As Rafi turned toward him, Majeed could clearly see his son's handsome features. Rafi's brown eyes gleamed with the joy of seeing his adoptive father. He walked briskly toward Majeed and embraced him.

"*Asalaam alykum.*"

"And peace be with you, my son," Majeed replied. "Who were you talking to?"

"The customs broker for the shipment to be off-loaded. I generally meet him in his office, but there were some issues at the ship that needed to be resolved."

"My son, this is a beautiful evening. Thank you for meeting me here. Do you have time for a walk?"

"Father, it is I who will always thank you. Of course I have time. Let's head toward the end of the wharf and watch the ships, just like we did when Tariq and I were boys."

Majeed smiled at the memory of evenings spent on this same wharf years ago, the three of them watching ships from around the world sail in and out of the Port of Karachi. Sometimes the boys' focus and imagination would also turn toward small islands in the harbor called Oyster Rocks. Their name and strange shapes captivated the impressionable young boys. Majeed told them stories of long-ago pirates and hidden treasure. The pleasant memory of those evenings on the wharf was the reason Majeed named his Karachi-based import-export company Oyster Rocks Trading.

"Are you down here for the shipment of cars?"

"Yes, Father. Two dozen used cars bought mainly in Japan and shipped in duty-free from Dubai."

"Are these destined on paper for Afghanistan?"

"Of course," Rafi laughed. "I'm working with Ahmer in Spin Boldak. Our operation is very profitable."

"Rafi, remember, I am your father but I am also 'the bookkeeper.' I know very well the profit this trade is generating," Majeed replied with a chuckle.

"You were very shrewd to establish this trade."

"If the governments of Afghanistan and Pakistan will allow us to import duty-free, it is our obligation to take advantage of their generosity."

Rafi responded in a serious manner. "The governments are really both very corrupt and very stupid. The profits that we are making out of the Afghan Transit Trade they promote are being used for their very downfall."

"Nobody ever accused those two governments of being honest or astute," Majeed said. "But I am old enough to remember how and why this trade started."

Afghanistan was a land-locked country. Under a 1965 bilateral treaty signed by Afghanistan and Pakistan called the Afghan Transit Trade Agreement, or ATTA, trade goods for import or export into Afghanistan that transited through the Pakistani port of Karachi were exempt from Pakistani duties or customs tariffs. In 1974, the ATTA was expanded to include other neighbors of Afghanistan, including an agreement with Iran that allowed free transit through the Iranian port city of Bandar Abbas and in 2003 for transit through Chabahar. Access to the Pakistani or Iranian port cities by rail or vehicle provided Afghanistan direct access to the Arabian Sea and the opportunity to transport goods internationally by ship.

The majority of commodities, such as electronics, construction supplies, foodstuffs, and automobiles that were traded and smuggled in the region originated or transited in Dubai. One of the seven emirates of the United Arab Emirates, Dubai acted as a sort of regional supermarket. Trading goods and commodities of all sorts were available for purchase from Dubai's souks and free-trade zones. Majeed had set up Oyster Rocks Trading primarily to handle the shipments of trade goods from Dubai to be off-loaded in Karachi. Taking advantage of the ATTA, Majeed's business avoided Pakistan's stringent taxes and customs duties and the goods were then transported to Afghanistan via rail or truck. Since the various brokers and middlemen involved in the trade operated on very small margins, the avoidance of taxes was a common measure to ensure profit. Once in Karachi, the goods were sent into Afghanistan for sale, barter, or payment. Often, payment was made via counter-valuation and invoice manipulation in hawala transactions. Sometimes the goods did a U-turn and were smuggled right back into Pakistan for sale on the Pakistani black market.

Just as the avoidance of taxation was central to Tariq's cigarette trade, it was also the catalyst for Majeed's business plan for Rafi, who now directed the Afghan transit trade operation.

"I don't really care about why and how the transit trade was established," Rafi said to Majeed. "All I know is that there is a huge demand for cars here in Pakistan, but they are too expensive. We give our customers a good product at a good price. Our colleague Ahmer is the one who helped set this up."

Majeed smiled. He approved of the way Rafi was working with his old friend Ahmer, back in Afghanistan.

Rafi continued. "The cars that just arrived on the *Ocean Star*, we will handle just like previous shipments. They will be sent overland from Karachi in sealed containers for Afghanistan. The containers are unpacked in Spin Boldak, and the cars sent right back across the border, with forged papers and *baksheesh* given to various officials along the way."

"And the serial numbers on the vehicles?

"Ahmer takes care of that too. He has a network of *tamper-wallahs* in both Afghanistan and Pakistan that specialize in changing a car's serial and chassis numbers."

"I like that." As he strolled with his son, Majeed absentmindedly fingered his prayer beads. "And your plans for our junk business?"

Rafi laughed. "Father, you are so old-fashioned. The West doesn't call it 'junk.' The merchandise is called 'used' or 'previously owned.' In any event, we import a lot of inexpensive things that originate in Europe and North America. We get container loads of the stuff via Dubai."

"Still used clothes? As you remember, that is how I started Oyster Rocks Trading," Majeed said with a wistful look. Blinking back his emotions, he continued. "Since I gave that part of the business to you, I don't look at those books anymore."

"Yes, but also used microwave ovens, electric appliances, DVD players, bicycles, camcorders, propane stoves, generators, children's toys, TV sets: just about everything the West wants to discard. But the car business is most profitable."

"What about exports?"

"There isn't as much, but we also export Pakistani textiles, animal hides, and furniture. Sometimes we use these exports for counter-valuation and to build up our export credits."

"Is the junk cargo you import still going all the way to Afghanistan?"

"It depends on the market. We import the goods duty-free via the transit trade agreement. But many times the only part of the shipments that actually leave Pakistan for Afghanistan is the paperwork. The goods never actually cross the border."

Majeed laughed. "Let me know if you ever have any trouble with our friends in customs or the border police. I have good contacts."

"So do I," said a smiling Rafi. As they were strolling, he playfully squeezed his adoptive father's shoulders. "I learned from the best."

His face turned serious. "Father, we could do more with the Afghan transit trade. There is the narcotics business. But I know how you feel about it."

Majeed stopped walking. He turned and looked directly at Rafi. "You remember what I taught you. Yes, we always need to diversify. But we are doing very well with Tariq's cigarette business and your transit trade operation. We also continue to get substantial contributions from our Arab brothers in Saudi Arabia and elsewhere."

"Ahmer and others tell me how much the Taliban in Afghanistan are making from the drug trade. Often they exchange narcotics for things that are imported from the transit trade. The drug trade is now financing most of their operations."

"I understand. But the narcotics business is something I will not do. We will leave that to others." Majeed paused and continued, "I have seen personally what heroin addiction does. It is one thing to poison the infidels, but we are also poisoning ourselves. It is against Islam."

Like other senior Taliban, Majeed's religious beliefs were combined with a heavy dose of native Pashtunwali, a pre-Islamic tribal honor code that over the centuries had somewhat fused with Sunni

Islamic tradition. The resulting mix of creeds regulated nearly all aspects of Pashtun life, ranging from tribal affairs to individual *nang* (honor) and behavior. The use of mind altering drugs was contrary to both Majeed's religious and cultural beliefs.

Yet a few years after September 11, after coalition forces occupied much of Afghanistan, Afghanistan was producing about ninety percent of the world's supply of opium. The drug was one of the few products Afghanistan produced that outsiders valued. It was conservatively estimated that over one-third of Afghanistan's (licit plus illicit) gross domestic product was derived directly from narcotics activities. Afghan opium was refined into morphine and heroin by production labs, more of which were being established inside Afghanistan's borders all the time. The narcotics were often broken into small shipments and smuggled across porous borders via truck or mule caravan for resale abroad. The ancient smuggling routes followed mountainous trails out of Afghanistan into Pakistan, Iran, Turkmenistan, Uzbekistan, and neighboring countries. Many of these very same trails were used by al Qaeda and Taliban forces, including Majeed, when they fled coalition forces in the fall and winter of 2001 and 2002.

In Afghanistan, opium gum itself was often used as a currency, especially by rural farmers. Opium stockpiles were a store of value in prime production areas. As a result, a type of barter trade had developed whereby narcotics were sometimes exchanged for commodities or services. A few grams of opium could be traded in rural areas for a meter of fabric or even a visit to a barber shop. In some areas in the region, the going rate for a kilo of heroin was a color television set. The same kilo of heroin smuggled to markets in Europe could be worth tens of thousands of dollars wholesale. The European, Russian, and Iranian market for Afghan heroin was large, but comparatively little was sent to the United States.

Deep in conversation, Majeed and Rafi reached the end of the wharf.

"I have always enjoyed this view," Majeed said.

Looking into the harbor, they could see all sorts of water craft, including giant container ships, fishing boats, and even modern multi-night ferries that offered service to Dubai, Mumbai, and Mombassa. The harbor sea was starting to still. The blue of the water contrasted with the pastel-colored clouds. The sun was going to set within the hour. Squawking seagulls flew overhead, chasing a nearby fishing boat coming in with the day's catch. Looking out toward the Baba Channel and the sea and the faraway lands beyond, they knew better than most the interconnectivity of the modern world. In their devout Islamic faith and humility, living in one of the largest cities on earth, they knew they were like no more than the small pebbles on nearby Manora Beach. But in their jihadist ambitions, they felt they could impact the world.

Rafi finally broke the spell. "I leave for Dubai tomorrow morning."

"When will you return?"

"Thursday."

"My son, this is why I wanted to talk to you. I know you have heard about the situation in Palestine. It is getting progressively worse. Our leadership has been monitoring developments closely."

"How does that concern us?" Rafi replied.

"I do not know the details yet. I received a message this morning from a courier. He brings news from Quetta."

The provincial capital of the province of Baluchistan, Quetta bordered both Iran and Afghanistan. The rugged and remote area had swirled in controversy since the establishment of the Durand Line in 1893, which divided the Pashtun and Baluch tribes living in Afghanistan from those living in what later became Pakistan. The Durand Line was named after Henry Mortimer Durand, the foreign secretary of British India at the time. His agreement with Amier Abdur Rahman Khan set the frontier between Afghanistan and what was then colonial British India—now Pakistan. Afghanistan vigorously protested the inclusion of Pashtun and Baluch areas within Pakistan without providing the inhabitants with an opportunity for self-determination. Although shown on most maps as the western border of Pakistan, the Durand line was unrecognized by Afghanistan and remains a source of much friction between the two countries. The largely lawless and semi-autonomous area had been infiltrated by both the Taliban and al Qaeda, including much of its senior leadership.

Rafi had, for the most part, stayed away from the machinations of the jihadists. He knew his father—the bookkeeper—handled some of their Karachi-based financing and occasionally received their directives. He also knew from his father that the jihadist leadership monitored and approved his Western-oriented activities. Rafi was torn. His youth, ambition, and faith urged him to do more for the cause. At the same time, he enjoyed his interactions with the West and Western things. Perhaps because of that, his direct contact with the loose-knit Taliban in Karachi was rare. Rarer still was any form of communication from senior leadership scattered in remote tribal areas in Pakistan's frontier areas. When communication was required, the use of phones, faxes, and even the open Internet was forbidden. Those methods were prone to interception. When messages of import needed to be passed, trusted couriers were often used. It was the same primitive communications system that had been used in warfare for thousands of years and was impervious to modern warfare's technical countermeasures. Although it was an open secret that Osama bin Laden was located and killed by Americans focusing on the comings and goings of a long-time trusted courier, the use of messengers for mid-level leadership was still judged to be safe and effective.

"Does the message actually mention me?" Rafi asked.

"The message was very brief, but yes, it did." Majeed turned from the view of the harbor and looked directly at Rafi. "They asked that both of us be available for further communication next week."

"I will be back from Dubai by then." Rafi paused before asking, "Do you know what any of this means?"

"I don't know. There has been quiet talk of a sensitive operation. I only know about it because periodically I was asked to put aside large amounts of money. But I don't know the details, and I don't know if this might involve you."

"Well, Father, I am not going to worry about it. It is as Allah wills."

Majeed smiled. The father and son turned away from the setting sun and started walking back the other way down the wharf. The setting sun cast heavy shadows to darken their path.

"By the way, when you go to Dubai, please do me a favor."

"Of course," answered Rafi.

"You know the big Shia hawaladar in Dubai, Farid?"

Rafi paused before responding. He knew Farid well but wasn't sure which way Majeed was going with the questioning. "He has tentacles all over the world. I sometimes work with him. He has brokered some transit trade business. But I haven't had any problems."

"Tariq and I will be sending quite a bit of new business to him through an agreement with Ahmad Exchange."

"I know Ahmad as well."

"Ahmad I trust completely. I only know Farid by reputation. I have some doubts. Please, assess him further. Ask around about him."

chapter 7

"JOE, IT IS always good to see you, but I'm afraid you are going to have an unproductive trip," said Steve Glennon, the regional security officer of the American Embassy in Tel Aviv.

"I was afraid of that," I replied.

The previous evening, I had arrived at Ben Gurion International Airport, flying Alitalia from Rome. An embassy facilitator met me at the airport and drove me to my Tel Aviv hotel near the Mediterranean waterfront. In the morning, I walked the few blocks down Hayarkon Street from my hotel to the American Embassy. My appointment with Glennon was at 0900 hours.

Steve was part of the State Department's Diplomatic Security Service, or DSS. His primary responsibility was the physical security of the American Embassy and its staff. He also worked with DSS colleagues in Jerusalem to likewise secure the American consulate and those assigned to work there. As a secondary function, the regional security officer assisted with miscellaneous law enforcement matters, including the coordination of requests for investigative assistance from those US law enforcement agencies that did not have a direct in-country attaché presence, including my office. The HSI office in Rome covered Israel.

"I'm just sorry everything was so rushed," I continued. "Thank you for granting country clearance."

"Well, particularly with the current water crisis, we normally would not grant clearance without specific meetings lined up, but I understand this case is a bit different."

"As I explained over the phone, there has been some pressure from Washington to get to the bottom of these allegations about the possibility of Israel using US-manufactured cluster munitions."

Steve arched an eyebrow. "I can only imagine. However, the bottom line is that the embassy, and that includes all of its representatives, has no knowledge of the recent use of these munitions in Israel, Lebanon, Syria, or elsewhere." He put stress on the words "all of its representatives."

"Do you think the allegations are plausible?"

Steve stretched back in his chair. "Well, as you know, in the past Israel has periodically violated military-to-military agreements governing the use of such munitions. The problem is that we cannot get anybody on the Israeli side to talk to us."

I opened my notebook and took some notes for my case report. "Unfortunately," I replied, "this is not a normal law enforcement or customs matter. My regular Israeli contacts will not work."

"We also had the Deputy Chief of Mission contact the Israeli Ministry of Foreign Affairs. According to the DCM, the Ministry understood our concerns, but they would not or could not get us an interview."

I knew from my past investigations how difficult it sometimes was to get straightforward information out of Israel. For example, the Israeli Police would generally grant my requests for simple criminal records checks, a common professional courtesy between international law enforcement agencies. However, if the subject was an Israeli citizen, the requests were routinely denied.

"What about our Defense attaché? Could he get anywhere?"

"I'll let Colonel Pence tell you himself. Hold on, I'll ring his office. He should be joining us shortly."

While Steve was on the phone, I looked around his office. It was apparent he had been in diplomatic security for at least twenty years, and most of his foreign assignments had been in the Middle East. Plaques presented to him by the State Department and a host of US and foreign law enforcement agencies covered one wall. A giant map of the Middle East covered another. A window with an outside blast screen took up a third. Assorted Middle Eastern trinkets and souvenirs were scattered over his overflowing credenza and filing cabinet. An antique copper Bedouin coffee pot stood on a low coffee table directly in front of me. The bottom of the coffee pot still had scorch marks; undoubtedly from long-ago campfires in the Arabian deserts. In earlier times, the offering of coffee was an important part of the wandering Bedouin and their ritual of hospitality. When I folded my long legs, my left foot almost kicked over some half-filled Styrofoam cups of coffee and tea haphazardly placed next to the antique. It was an interesting contrast.

A few moments later, the door to Steve's office opened and Colonel William Pence of the United States Marine Corps, the Embassy Tel Aviv Defense attaché, walked in. I stood up and was greeted with a firm handshake. Steve made the introductions.

"Joe, welcome to Tel Aviv. When did you get in?"

"It's a pleasure to meet you." I replied. "I got in last night. I'm sure you have been briefed on the reason for my visit."

"Yes, and I will get right to the point. We are being stiffed." The colonel paused to let his words sink in and then continued. "I first reviewed all of the cable traffic and talked to our intel folks about the allegations. In preparation for your visit, I made all the appropriate contacts in the IDF and IAF. However, nobody on the Israeli side will talk to us about the allegations. I'm afraid you wasted a trip."

"Well, I appreciate your efforts," I said, slowly giving myself time to digest the news. "However, the trip is not wasted. From a law enforcement perspective, I still have to document the fact that we made official inquiries and that they were rejected. From a bureaucratic perspective, I had to come."

"What about investigating it domestically?" Steve asked.

"We will make some inquiries with the manufacturer," I replied. "We have some photographs and pieces of shrapnel that could prove helpful. But once the munitions leave the US, tracking them further is difficult. If this is a repeat of what happened in 2006, we will need Israeli cooperation."

"It is just so frustrating," said the colonel. "Do you know that the United States gives Israel billions of dollars every year in military aid, loans, indirect loans, and preferential contracts?"

"Probably hundreds of billions since Israel was founded in 1949," added Steve.

"You would think for that much money we at least would get the courtesy of an official response."

The colonel settled into an adjoining chair facing Steve's desk. "Joe, I've had two tours in Iraq and one in Afghanistan. I spent two years at US Central Command in Tampa and another two at the Pentagon. The more I learn, the more I realize I haven't even begun to scratch the surface of the complexity of this region." He turned and looked directly at me. "There has always been mistrust on both sides, but this situation seems different." The colonel continued, "I have never been so pessimistic. The water issue is the catalyst for a coming crisis. I can feel it. Yet nobody knows how it will play out."

Pausing, he looked away from me and toward the wall map of the Middle East. "It must have been easier in the Cold War," he said almost wistfully. "Things were comparatively straightforward."

"Well, for one thing, the political process in Israel today is dysfunctional," Steve said. "For example, there are about one hundred settlements not authorized by the Israeli government in the West Bank. But nothing is done about them. The religious extremists backing the settlements have inordinate influence over the policy makers."

"In a way it's somewhat similar to the Islamic fundamentalists having undue political influence in some of the Islamic countries," I added.

"Yes, that's true," said Steve. "But just about everybody in the Arab world hates Israel. The extremists also think that we are the villains, that we sustain Israel. They believe the US and what we represent are the cause of all their problems."

I nodded. "There is blame on all sides."

"Unfortunately, particularly in Palestine, when you take away hope, when you treat people like they are undeserving of respect, when you humiliate your adversaries, you can't be surprised when one day they rise up and rebel," Steve added.

"Things just aren't clear," said the colonel, going back to his previous line of thinking. "This is the Middle East. The issues are historical and intertwined. Here, ancient history is just yesterday."

"What bothers me is how the American media and our politicians try to simplify everything," Steve said. I could tell he was warming to the topic. "We always want to conveniently label sides the 'good guys' and the 'bad guys.' The media facilitates the politicians' dividing complex issues into black and white. Sometimes there are shades of gray." He sat upright in his chair. "I'm just disgusted. The American people get sound bites. News is now entertainment."

"Speaking of which . . . I was watching CNN before I left my hotel room this morning. The water issue is huge. More solidarity demonstrations are breaking out in European cities. There have been rallies in the United States. From a PR perspective, Israel is really taking a beating."

"The religious right and the settlers here in Israel are putting enormous political pressure on the current government not to give in to the demonstrations," said Steve. "The government can't be seen as weak or it will topple."

"So what?" I asked. "Let it fall."

"The problem is that it is no longer possible to cobble together a moderate coalition. Politically, water rights now seem synonymous with Israel's right to exist," the colonel said, trying to frame the issue. "They can't control the high Palestinian birthrate, which is the real long-term threat to Israel's survival. Demograhics is destiny. But Israel *can* control the water." He continued, "It is no longer possible to have rational conversations. Emotions are taking over—not only in Israel but elsewhere."

"Well, a new twist is developing," said Steve. "There has been a lot of US Embassy message traffic that Hamas, Hezbollah, and other radical groups are finally going to play smart; they are going to follow the playbook of Gandhi and Dr. Martin Luther King."

"Do you mean Shia-Sunni unity? The Gulf states' acceptance of Iranian ambitions? Palestinian unity? Fatah and Hamas coming together? You're kidding!"

"No, I'm not. I doubt they can pull it off. And if they do it will be for short term tactical advantage only. There are too many angry young men and too many factions and political agendas. But I think they finally realize this pacifist tactic is far more dangerous to Israel in the long run than a rock-throwing intifada, suicide bombers, or missiles fired from Lebanon and Gaza."

"They are trying to recapture the early days of the 2011 Arab Spring," Colonel Pence said. "This time instead of venting their frustrations over oppression and misery at home and overthrowing despots like Hosni Mubarak, Zine el Abidine Ben-Ali, Moammar Gadahafi, and the others, they are going to focus their attention on Israel. They sense that this water issue can be used to manipulate public opinion. Using social media and instant communications, they will mobilize global opposition against Israeli policies that oppress the Palestinians."

"What could be dangerous about that?" I asked. "Publicly, this is something Israel has always demanded. No violence and no terrorism."

"That's right," Colonel Pence continued. "The talk is that the various groups are going to publicly renounce violence and orchestrate massive pacifist worldwide anti-Israel demonstrations and peaceful strikes. As Steve said, they are playing for international sympathy and moral superiority."

"I can see it now. There is an incident. Israel uses overpowering force and responds. But instead of violence, people in the crowds hold hands and sing the equivalent of 'We Shall Overcome.' The scenes are broadcast around the world."

"Complex issues presented in sound bites. News as entertainment. Here we go again," added Steve.

Colonel Pence stood up and walked over to the window. Staring outside, his back was turned to both Steve and I. He slowly turned around and said in a low voice, "I was wondering when they were going to get smart."

"Smart like a fox; apparently they are prepared to renounce violence, but they haven't said anything about recognizing Israel's right to exist." Steve paused and considered his words. "Arabs can be very shrewd. Like the colonel said, I always wondered when they would put their rivalries aside and use their cleverness to further their political aims."

I nodded. Steve continued speaking very slowly, as if he was developing his thoughts in process. "If this nonviolent movement goes forward, they will back Israel into a corner where it will either have to back down, offer true concessions, and be internationally humiliated, or lash out. Either of those outcomes is a loss for Israel and a win for Arabs."

The colonel walked away from the window. His gaze went back to the map of the Middle East. "I'm not so certain it will play out that way," he said quietly. "This is about more than water shortages and embarrassing Israel. There is a lot of evil out there. People and groups will feel threatened. They will not let it happen."

chapter 8

SHORTLY BEFORE MIDNIGHT, Rafi exited an old, un-mufflered Morris taxi. He walked down Nishtar Road in the heart of the Karachi business district. Even at the late hour there were flashing lights, neon signs, and plenty of traffic—both vehicular and pedestrian. Yet the light show and movement swirling around him was nothing compared to his racing mind. *What was this summons all about?*

The courier had arrived earlier that same evening. Rafi had never seen the man before. The verbal message was short; he was directed to go to a public Internet café and log on that very midnight. The courier next gave him a small piece of paper which contained a URL, the name of the virtual world he was to enter, and the password to an encrypted chat room. There were also brief directions telling him that upon entering the chat room, he was to select an avatar of a falcon. That was to be his online identity. The use of real names and descriptions of location were forbidden in the chat messaging. No further information was given.

This was the first time Rafi had received a message via courier. Although he didn't know for certain, he assumed it was from the Taliban in Pakistan leadership. He didn't personally know them or their whereabouts. They could be scattered in remote regions or ensconced in a major city. He knew many were in Karachi itself. In the past, his few interactions with them had been facilitated by Majeed acting as an intermediary. Like Majeed, he did not question. He was raised that way. Rafi remembered the conversation on the wharf with his adoptive father shortly before he departed for Dubai, when he was told to expect something like this. However, this was all happening much too quickly. He had only returned from Dubai yesterday. His mind was still engaged in his business endeavors. His thoughts were racing.

Rafi knew the business district had a number of Internet cafes. He remembered one nearby that had a prominent sign stating that it was open twenty-four hours a day—something unusual in this area of Karachi. Walking briskly toward the location, he unconsciously looked over his shoulder before entering the door.

The room was softly lit by the glow of about two dozen computer screens. The person behind the counter gave him a blank nod and directed him to terminal #11, located toward the back of the room. A glance around the rather austere surroundings mitigated Rafi's concerns about privacy. There was only one other customer in the shop. He was located near the entrance and was engrossed in some type of computer game. Rafi walked toward #11. Reaching into the front pocket of his jeans, he pulled out the waded paper containing the URL and instructions given to him by the courier. Sitting down, he logged on.

Although Rafi had only occasionally participated in cyber games, he knew well from both his business and social contacts that virtual reality universe games were becoming increasingly popular around the world. Some cyberspace games were not just a source of entertainment but a venue for both social and secure communication and for real commercial activity. Both al Qaeda and Taliban leadership had learned over the years that communicating was one of their weak links; insecure communications had led directly to missile attacks fired from unmanned Predator and Rapier airborne drones directed by the hated American infidels. Intercepted communications by Pakistani security forces had also led to the capture or killing of some of the Taliban's most important leaders. As a result, senior Taliban leadership increasingly used secure email or chat room facilities to lessen security concerns.

After logging onto his assigned computer, Rafi was initially taken aback at the welcome screen banner of the website. The software was engineered to provide 3-D browsing. The graphics and interface were first rate. A new user began as a "tourist" and was invited to explore dozens of unique virtual reality cyberworlds. Participants could build their own virtual home, castle, or community in cyberspace and interact with invited guests. Rafi surmised that the group he was dealing with was piggybacking on the site. Participants in the welcoming cyberworld could customize their avatars' physical appearance, characteristics, and dress. The avatars could also walk, run, fly, and interact in multiple ways. Rafi bypassed the invitation to become a "tourist" and explore all the website had to offer. Rather, as per his instructions, from a drop-down menu he selected his assigned cyberworld. He was next prompted for a password and then asked to select an avatar. He used the mouse to designate a peregrine falcon and watched as the character opened its black-tipped wings and flew into a new 3-D cyberworld.

"*Bismillah ir-Rahman ir-Rahim,*"—In the name of Allah Almighty, the merciful and compassionate. "*As-Salaam Alaaikum,*"—Peace be upon you.

The text emanated from an avatar in the form of an unsheathed sword with rivulets of blood dripping from the blade. The sword moved next to an AK-47 assault rifle. Both avatars were set against a backdrop of a post-action battle scene in the high desert. The realistic 3-D terrain was complete with burned-out fighting vehicles, billowing smoke, and uniformed soldiers sprawled lifeless on the ground.

Rafi watched as the AK-47 spelled out the following message: "This is a secure environment. We can speak freely. However, we will not use names or locations."

Rafi found the text prompt for the Falcon. "I understand," he wrote. "It is an honor to be with you."

"We have followed your progress for many years," wrote the sword. "We thank you and your family for your continued assistance."

They have been following my progress, thought Rafi. It was a few moments before he replied. "My contributions have been small in comparison to our brothers on the battlefield."

The sword moved to hover over a burned-out fighting vehicle. "The battles continue. The threat is great. You have seen how the Crusader armies are sweeping over the Islamic world."

"And now our Palestinian brothers are rebelling again against the Zionist entity," wrote the unknown AK-47. "Rallies and demonstrations in their support are occurring around the world."

"The demonstrations are also about justice and Muslim dignity and pride," wrote Rafi almost automatically. His immediate response somewhat startled him. He smiled to himself; the phrases from the years in the madrassa and the incessant sermons in the mosques had become reflexive.

In the cyberworld of Rafi's computer, he saw the AK-47 swoop to the top of his screen, overlooking the battle scene. The assault rifle messaged, "We should continue jihad to liberate Palestinian land and establish an Islamic state. Believers should wage jihad against Jews and all those who support them, whether they are Americans or other Westerners."

"This new movement toward nonviolence is a threat. A plot. It is misguided and a ruse. It is something that we cannot tolerate," added the sword.

Rafi started to type a response but saw the sword was continuing. "Rather than peaceful protests, in these times in which wickedness is spreading and Islam is threatened, we must pursue and strengthen jihad."

The sword on Rafi's screen flew next to his hovering falcon avatar. "My son, we ask you to consider something of great import."

"With the grace of Allah, I am ready," replied Rafi.

"There is to be a large meeting of leaders of infidel nations. Allah willing, we will destroy them," typed the sword. The words on the screen continued. "Our movement has access to a special weapon. As we defeated the crusader nation in New York and Washington, this time we will terrorize them all."

In the virtual battlefield, the AK-47 fired a clip of tracer rounds directly at a burned-out personnel carrier. Afterward, as if for emphasis, the avatar typed a well-known Islamic verse, 'The curse of Allah is on disbelievers.'

"This meeting of Westerners is just part of the Crusader and Zionist campaign to enslave and humiliate us, and to occupy our land and steal our wealth," added the sword.

With a flick of his keyboard mouse, Rafi maneuvered his avatar to the top of the screen.

"How can I help?"

"We believe you have the background and skills necessary to carry out this operation," wrote the AK-47.

Me? But what can I do? Rafi thought. *What do they want with me?* Slowly he typed, "I know very little about weapons and warfare."

"The weapon to be used is simple. It is non-conventional. We will give you the training you need," texted the sword.

The AK-47 fired another burst of tracer rounds. "In this operation, if it pleases Allah, you may become a martyr. We do not know what you will encounter. But if sacrifice is necessary in the cause of jihad, you will surely gain access to paradise."

Martyrdom? For long moments Rafi thought. He did not respond. His mind was now racing between the virtual reality cyberworld and the true reality of himself. This was something he had never considered. From his early introduction to Islam as a young boy, later reinforced by teachings in the madrassa, sermons in the mosques, and even in conversations with his adoptive father, the concept of martyrdom in Islamic jihad had always been extolled. But he never entertained the thought that one day he might be called.

Martyrdom was inextricably linked with the entire religion of Islam. As had been explained to Rafi since he was a child, the term 'Islam' was based on the Arabic root *salama*, which meant 'surrender' and 'peace'. As such, Islam was a complete and peaceful submission to the will of Allah. As countless sermons preached in countless mosques over countless years had declared, being prepared to die to further the cause of Islam was a natural part of the submission to Allah.

Martyrdom, like all other Islamic concepts, could not be understood in isolation but only appreciated in the light of the Islamic doctrine of *tawhid*, or the absolute unity of Allah and full submission to His will and command. Rafi was taught the concept in the madrassa. It was reinforced with countless orations preaching that it was the duty of all Muslims to obey His will and that His will included the destruction of unbelievers. The ultimate goal was to create a worldwide Islamic caliphate based on *Sharia* law that would honor Allah.

Thoughts swirled through his mind. "Please do not misinterpret my delay in responding," Rafi finally typed. "Although I work to support jihad, I have never before thought about martyrdom."

"There is neither jihad nor martyrdom outside the realm of truth. Martyrdom applies only when it is preceded by jihad and jihad is a constant struggle for the cause of the truth—the cause of Allah," responded the sword.

"Jihad and the glory of Islam are linked," added the AK-47.

"But I still do not understand why you selected me," typed Rafi.

"This operation will take place in a foreign country. We need somebody who is sophisticated, comfortable in dealing with the infidels and who can speak multiple languages," answered the sword.

"Prior to this conversation, we spoke with your father. He was effusive in his praise for your abilities."

Rafi's mind began to swirl again. *They have spoken to Majeed? I owe him everything. I want to honor him. I know I was being prepared for something . . . but rescuing me from the madrassa . . . my training, was it all deceit . . . subterfuge? Was this the ultimate objective?*

On impulse, Rafi wrote, "I owe my life to both Allah and my father."

On Rafi's computer screen, the sword slowly circled the falcon. "I believe that is your answer."

"Martyrs and their families are rewarded by Allah. By your martyrdom, you will repay your debts," added the AK-47.

Rafi waited a few moments before typing, "When does all of this happen?"

The AK-47 responded, "Soon. Over the next few days you will be contacted again. A trusted brother will give you instructions and training. Everything will be done with complete security and secrecy. Do not talk to others about this. Even your father. He only knows what he needs to know."

"We will arrange for a clean passport, visa, credit cards, cash, and all necessary documents and travel arrangements," wrote the sword. "We will also arrange for the transport of the weapon."

"When you arrive at your destination, you will link up with another brother who is aware of the local environment. He also has lots of battlefield experience with explosive devices. Depending on what you find, it will be up to the two of you to determine the final tactical strategy to detonate the special weapon. Contact instructions will be provided," added the AK-47.

Rafi's swirling thoughts were now focused. Pride and religious fervor consumed him. The great honor of being selected for this assignment appealed to his young man's sense of duty and adventure. He used his mouse and manipulated the falcon avatar to soar around the 3-D battle scene. "I have no other questions. With the grace of Allah, we will have success," he typed.

The sword and the AK-47 responded.

"May Allah bless and protect you in jihad."

"May Allah's mercy be upon us all."

chapter 9

DUBAI WAS ONE of the seven emirates of the United Arab Emirates. Not many years ago, it was a backwater pearling village on the shores of the Arabian Gulf. But today it is an ultra-modern cosmopolitan city-state that was also a world-class transportation, communication, commercial, and financial hub. In ancient times, it was said that "all roads lead to Rome." I had learned in my time as a criminal investigator coming from Rome that many of the transnational criminal roads I followed eventually led to Dubai.

Over the years, each return trip to Dubai had inspired amazement and a head-scratching incredulity. Both visitors and residents marveled at the rapid growth. The ever-changing skyline was a source of wonder; new structures sprouted from the desert sands or the Gulf water itself - from Jumeirah International's Burj Al Arab sail-shaped hotel to the Dubai Palm artificial islands to a man-made ski slope inside one of the countless air-conditioned shopping malls to the Burj Khalifa, the tallest structure ever erected by mankind. Equally impressive was how, at least on the surface, peoples of diverse cultures and backgrounds had worked together to create the ultra-modern city-state.

Yet during my occasional visits I also heard about growing pains and resentments. Approximately ninety percent of Dubai's population was non-native. Most were from South Asia, but there were also many from the Philippines, Africa, and other countries in the Middle East. Most migrants resided on the other side of Dubai Creek in the old quarter called Deira. Other laborers lived in squalid conditions far removed from the modern city they built. A manual worker's pay was minimal, and many were no more than indentured servants. The migrant laborers resented the ostentatious wealth on display, even though that wealth was built primarily by their strong backs and the sweat of their brow. There was also a scattering of European, Asian, and American technocrats, engineers, and advisors. The well-to-do expatriates seemed to congregate in the smart districts of Satwa and Jumeirah. The influx of so many people in such a short amount of time had resulted in both opportunities and problems. Emiratis had seen their numbers diluted in a sea of migrants. Increasingly, the foreign workforce and a dissipation of local culture scared the natives.

Most of the new immigrants came to make money in an honest manner. Unfortunately, a few took advantage of Dubai's openness, location, and first-class infrastructure and turned Dubai into a global hub of regional ethnic and white-collar crime. Non-native organized criminal groups and those that support terrorists increasingly lurked just below the surface of the modern "City of Gold."

After the attacks of September 11, UAE officials became very nervous. Investigation by the FBI discovered that much of the funding for the terrorist attacks either originated or transited through Dubai. Moreover, two of the nineteen hijackers were Emirati citizens. The terrorists took advantage of many of the same factors that made Dubai such a hub for international business: finance, transportation, trade, and communication. Heading off US and international criticism, the government of the UAE cooperated. In addition to opening their financial books and assisting in the investigations, the UAE government was receptive to various training initiatives, primarily by the United States and the United Kingdom, but also by the UAE itself.

One of the most successful initiatives was a series of annual conferences hosted by the Central Bank of the UAE that focused on *hawala*, or the regional underground financial network. In the timeframe immediately following September 11, the West grappled to understand the remittance system used primarily by immigrant workers to send a portion of their salaries back to their home countries in order to help support loved ones. Unfortunately, the "parallel" or "alternative remittance system" was also abused by both criminals and terrorists. During the hawala conferences, the UAE Central Bank invited individuals from industry, law enforcement, academia, and banking, as well as traders and hawaladars themselves, to come together and discuss the issues involved and try to agree on steps that could be taken to provide transparency and accountability in the remittance industry.

As an ICE representative at one of the later conferences, I was invited to give a presentation on US investigations into hawaladars and their abuse by criminal and terrorist groups. After my remarks, I was approached by one of the largest hawaladars in Dubai. Our conversation was pleasant and professional. I was very impressed with his apparent openness and business acumen. As a matter of course, I indexed Farid Harandi's name and known identifiers in HSI's information database. Thus I should not have been surprised when years later, the New York office associated his name with an investigation into the laundering of narcotics proceeds via hawala networks. The referral from New York brought me once again to one of the most fascinating cities in the world.

October evenings in the Gulf were pleasant. The warm weather, setting sun, long shadows, and bustling streets gave a boost to the senses. Enjoying the stroll from my nearby hotel, I spent nearly thirty minutes wandering in the back streets of Old Dubai near the spice souk, trying to locate Farid's shop. The sights, sounds, and smells were intoxicating. There were few addresses in the old souk or market area of Dubai. People just learned where things were. I finally found the shop tucked away on one of the many backstreets. It wasn't the small neon sign that spelled out "remittances" that called my attention but rather the line of customers that stretched out the door.

The customers were a mixed group but most probably all "guest workers." Most of them appeared to be from South and Central Asia. Finding my way inside the shop, I asked a harried worker behind the busy counter for Farid. Disappearing for a moment, the staff assistant returned with a polite smile and a wave of his hand. I was ushered upstairs and into a back office. Farid looked up from his desk. His most prominent feature was a long narrow nose that made its owner look rather aristocratic. His dark eyes were framed with creases yet they seemed to dance when he smiled.

"Mr. Joe, welcome! It is good to see you again." Farid Harandi got up and gave me a warm handshake. "Please sit down." Without pausing, he said, "Of course, you will have some chai." He picked up one of the many cell phones on his desk and quickly sent a text.

"Farid, thank you for seeing me. I know you are a busy man."

"It is my pleasure. When did you arrive?"

"Actually, I arrived in Abu Dhabi a couple of days ago. I had some meetings with the embassy and the Emirati Financial Intelligence Unit within the Central Bank."

Farid grinned. "I occasionally have to deal with them as well. Those hawala conferences resulted in a Central Bank edict that all hawaladars have to register and file financial suspicious activity reports."

I good naturedly slapped his shoulder and asked with a laugh, "Well do they?"

He chuckled in return, "Not really."

The pleasantries were interrupted by a *chai walah* or tea runner who rushed a little too quickly into Farid's office. He was not more than twelve years old. His shalwar was drenched in sweat. For the chai courier, the faster he could run through the congested city, the more chai he could sell. The boy's dark brown eyes and wide smile accentuated his fluid motions as he silently and expertly poured chai into Persian teacups on a tray atop Farid's desk. Many *chai walahs* prepared their chai in small batches on a per-order basis. However, in a large city like Dubai, the chai business was often divided. A central chai maker would prepare enormous batches of chai and then send teams of runners to deliver the chai to local shops. The *chai walahs* sometimes even offered the drink to shoppers and pedestrians strolling through the streets. Some *chai walahs* put a little something special in the tea; it could be a pinch of ginger or a strand of saffron to make their product unique and keep their customers coming back for more. The distinct aroma of cardamom disclosed this *chai walah's* favored ingredient.

With a nod of thanks, I took the scented tea from the offered tray and resumed the pleasantries. After a respectful interval, I began to seek an opening to discuss the reason for my visit.

"After my appointments in Abu Dhabi, I came down to visit with some staff at the consulate in Dubai. We are trying to arrange some training initiatives with the Dubai police, customs, and possibly the Ministry of Economy and Commerce."

Farid leaned back in his chair, "Mr. Joc, if you keep coming to Dubai, you may become a resident yourself!"

I grinned. "I really like it here. Every time I come back, I'm amazed. If I may ask, how long have you been here?"

"I came with my family in 1979. I was just a teenager. We fled Ayatollah Khomenini's Islamic Revolution."

Farid put down his tea and picked up a *midwakh*, a little pipe of Arabian origin. He took some *dacha* out of a small enameled container on his desk and tamped it into the bowl of the pipe. *Dacha* is Iranian tobacco that is mixed with foliage and herbs. The *midwakh* appeared to be carved out of bone, and the opening of the bowl resembled the mouth of a camel. Manipulating the *midwakh,* Farid's countenance visibly changed. With a quiver in his hands, he lit the pipe and deeply inhaled. Blowing out the acrid smoke, he finally continued.

"Those were hard times. The revolution made Islamic fundamentalism a growing force from Iran to Indonesia; many suffered and continue to suffer."

"Did many other Iranians also come to Dubai because of the revolution?"

"Oh yes." Farid held up the palms of his hands as if to emphasize the point. "Today there are more than 400,000 Iranians in Dubai out of a total population of four million. There are more Iranians than Emiratis. The ten thousand Iranian companies in Dubai are involved in every type of trade, finance, and business."

I smiled. "Including hawala?"

"Including hawala. As you can see from the line of people outside, I perform a service. But in addition to remitting funds from

Iranians working here to their families back in Iran, Iranian capital flows here too."

"I know there is capital flight."

"There is. Dubai has become a satellite state for Iranian capital. Iranians are some of the city's largest merchants and developers and some of the top buyers of homes. With all the difficulties in Iran today, wealthy Iranians invest here. I help facilitate the movement of funds and trade in both directions."

I nodded while Farid continued.

"After Tehran, Dubai is the most important city on earth to the Islamic Republic of Iran. Mr. Joe, have you ever been to Tehran?"

"Unfortunately, travel to Iran is difficult for Americans on official government business. However, one day I would very much like to visit."

"If you ever go, you will see the incredible number of ads for apartments, travel, and investment in Dubai. Billions of dollars flow out of Iran every year into Dubai. For wealthy Iranians in particular, Dubai is a haven for capital."

"If I may ask, how did you get involved in the hawala business?"

Farid's eyes narrowed even further. "Mr. Joe, in Farsi hawala is pronounced *hawah-leh.* It is spelled the same as Arabic, but the pronunciation of a common character is different.

I nodded again. "Thank you. Actually that is one of the reasons I'm here. I would very much appreciate it if you could teach me more about *hawala* or *havah-leh.* It is such a foreign concept for Americans to understand."

In my travels and interviews, I had found that people were happy to talk about their professions if approached with courtesy and a sincere desire to learn. Hawala is a very efficient money service that Farid and other practitioners could be proud of. Moreover, I had learned from countless interviews that people liked to talk about themselves. And in talking, they sometimes dropped their guard.

Farid put down his teacup and smiled. "Well. . .getting back to your original question, soon after our arrival, my father established an import-export business not far from here along Dubai Creek. It was only a few years after Dubai and the other emirates received their independence from the UK. But my father very perceptively recognized that this was a good place for business. There is a kind of a laissez-faire attitude."

"Is your father still in the business?"

"No. He passed away a few years after we arrived."

"I'm sorry."

"I think he died of a broken heart. Except for his immediate family he lost just about everything in the Iranian Revolution." Farid took another long puff from the *midwakh.* As if talking to himself, he added, "My father died far too young." He diverted his gaze toward the floor.

I waited for Farid to continue.

"Anyway, Mr. Joe, as you know, trade is directly linked to hawala. Our trading company was used to help settle debts between hawaladars, both here and in Iran. The goods we traded were often used in counter-valuation."

"You mean over-or-under-invoiced?"

"There are lots of different ways, but generally that is correct."

"Could you give me an example?"

"Mr. Joe, you know how hawala works."

"Farid, I think I do understand, but from your experience here in Dubai, give me a typical example of a hawala transation."

Farid was astute; he knew I was asking him a leading question designed to get him to talk and explain. I watched as he drained the last of his chai. Tilting his head back toward the ceiling, he inhaled once again from his *midwakh.* Farid got up from his chair and walked over to a window. He looked out and his gaze must have hit the line of people winding out from the door of his hawala shop. It was a Thursday evening - the last work day of the week. Many laborers had just been paid and wanted to send a portion of their paycheck back to their home countries to help support their families. Turning around, he put his hands behind his back He started to pace the few steps between the window and his desk.

"O.K. I will give you an example of my work here in Dubai."

Farid began to tell the story of a typical customer - Ali, an Afghan laborer and guest worker in Dubai. During the later half of the 1990s during the long Taliban occupation of his country, Ali immigrated to Dubai in order to help support his family back home in Afghanistan. He continued to work as a skilled laborer on construction projects in Dubai and every month sent a portion of his salary (about 700 UAE dirhams - the local currency - or about $200 American) back to his elderly father, Jafar, who lived in a village outside of Herat in western Afghanistan near the Iranian border. He used the hawala remittance system.

Farid explained that if Ali went to a bank in Dubai to send money home to his father, he would have to open an account. Ali didn't want to do that because he didn't trust banks. It was simply a matter of culture and societal development. He was afraid of possible government scrutiny of his financial transactions. And, like eighty percent of Afghans, Ali was illiterate and could not fill out the necessary bank forms. Farid explained that many of his customers, particularly those from rural areas of some South Asian countries, were intimidated by twenty-first century banking practices. In addition, banks charged their customers assorted transfer fees and offered unfavorable exchange rates. For example, in Dubai, Ali was paid in dirhams, but his family in Afghanistan needed either the local currency (the afghani) or US dollars. A bank would charge a hefty commission to convert dirhams to other currencies. Bank fees and exchange rate valuations could have meant that fifteen percent or more of the money remitted would not reach the recipient.

The delivery of the money to Jafar posed another problem. Farid said that even though the number of banks in Afghanistan was increasing, most of the country was still non-banked. And even if banks were available, like Ali, Jafar and other family members were illiterate and sometimes were intimidated by financial institutions. In addition, the security situation in many parts of Afghanistan was not good. Farid said that as a result of these issues, Ali opted to use a hawaladar, both because it made good business sense and also because he felt more comfortable.

"Farid," I interrupted, "I thought that hawaladars were generally of the same tribe, family, or clan. In the example you are using, why would Ali—an Afghani—use your services if you are Iranian?

"Mr. Joe, that's a good question. In my case, it is because my business is well established and trustworthy. Remember, *hawala* means 'trust' in both Urdu and Arabic. Hawala is called *hundi* in Pashtu in Pakistan. It is the same system."

I chuckled. "Farid, that was said like a true businessman. But we are talking about separate countries. And what about the Shia-Sunni issue?"

Still slowly pacing the room, Farid paused and inhaled deeply from the mouth of his midwakh. Resuming his professorial bearing, he began to explain.

Resuming his professorial bearing, he began to explain.

"Mr. Joe, sometimes borders are just lines drawn on a map." Farid chuckled. "In fact, that is what the British colonial masters did in many parts of South Asia and Africa. That is one of the main reasons we have so many problems today." He walked a few steps back and forth before continuing. "Borders have divided tribes, clans, and religious groups."

I nodded my head in agreement.

"As you know, Iran is primarily Shia. Many of the major ethnic groups in Afghanistan are Sunni. But not all. For example, Pashtuns in Afghanistan are found along a large crescent-shaped belt stretching along the Pakistani border on the east, southward from Nuristan, across the south, and northward along the Iranian border almost to Herat. Pushtuns are generally Hanafi Sunni Muslims, but some are Ithna Asharia Shia. So Ali could be a Shia Pashtun. He could also be a Shia Hazara or other Afghan Shia ethnic group. But of course, there are other reasons I have many clients like Ali."

"For example?"

"Cost. Depending on many variables, the commission I charge is much lower—perhaps one to three percent of the amount transferred. That is very competitive with other hawaladars and certainly far less than commercial banks or formal money remitters charge."

I nodded.

"In addition, I offer a much better currency exchange rate than some of my competitors."

"When Ali gives you the money he wants transferred to Afghanistan, do you give him a receipt?

"If he asks for one, of course. But we know our regular customers." Farid smiled. "This isn't a Western-style remittance system. Remember, hawala is based on trust."

"So that's it? There aren't any forms to fill out?"

"Well . . . if Ali is a new customer, we may give him a transfer code that generally takes the form of numerical digits. Ali, in turn, forwards the code to Jafar. His father will present the code to the courier, who delivers the money right to his door. If it is a recurring delivery, say every month, there is no need for a transfer code because undoubtedly the courier and Jafar know each other. In fact, Jafar's entire village probably knows he is receiving regular remittances from his son Ali in Dubai."

"And how long does it take for Jafar to receive the money in his village outside Herat from the time Ali gives you the funds here in Dubai?"

Farid smiled. "Probably twenty-four hours. Depending on where the money goes, we either send an email or a fax to the local hawaladar. Sometimes we might go through a colleague in a major hawala center. We have people we deal with throughout Iran, Afghanistan, Pakistan, and many other countries. They, in turn, have networks of regional representatives and couriers."

"Do you keep records of your transactions?

"Yes, we do. We have to keep track of the clients, the date of the transaction, amounts involved, the destination, exchange rate, and that type of thing."

"So in theory the authorities here in Dubai could come in and ask to see your books?"

"Mr. Joe, that doesn't happen. Banks here in Dubai and in most countries around the world are obligated to keep records of transactions. But hawala is not regulated banking. Most hawaladars only keep records until they periodically settle accounts."

I knew from first-hand experience that Farid was right. The financial transactions involving hawaladars were not monitored by authorities in the UAE or Afghanistan or even the United States. And hawala was perfectly legal in those countries—as long as the hawaladar registered his business with the authorities. In the United

States, for example, a hawala operation was classified as a "money service business." In addition to registering with the Department of Treasury, a hawaladar also generally had to be licensed in the state in which it did business. Reforms put in place after September 11 required that hawaladars, like other money service businesses, were supposed to file suspicious activity reports with the Department of Treasury. Since hawala was built on trust and engaged in underground finance, the required forms were generally not filed.

Although Farid's example occurred in Dubai and Afghanistan, I knew it could just as easily have taken place in New York City, Minneapolis, London, Frankfurt, Karachi, Mumbai, Johannesburg, and many other locations around the world. Money or value was transferred without physical money actually moving. And it was almost completely under the radar screens of government officials. While authorities generally had no wish to interfere with guest workers sending money back home to help support their loved ones, unfortunately law enforcement and intelligence agencies were very aware that criminals and terrorists abused the very same hawala networks.

"Farid, you mentioned both 'settling accounts' and 'countervaluation.' How does that happen with your business?"

Farid moved away from the window and sat down again behind his desk. He momentarily closed his eyes and inhaled powerfully from the *midwakh*. "It is important to understand that money transfers between hawaladars are not settled on a one-to-one basis but are generally bundled over a period of time after a series of transactions. Payments go in both directions. Remittances and value flow from Dubai into South Asia via hawala, but money and value also go out of South Asia into Dubai. The same is true for hawala operations in the United States, Europe, and Africa. It is multi-directional."

Farid continued his explanation by pointing out that currency restrictions in South Asian countries often limited the amount of currency that could be sent out of the country. To get around the restrictions, hawaladars were able to provide "hard currencies," such as dollars or euros, in exchange for local currencies, such as rupees, dinars, the Iranian rial, or afghanis. These hawaladars also operated as currency exchangers and charged a small commission. Some hawaladars profited from currency speculation or black market currency dealing. Currency speculation was one of the principal reasons, in addition to low overhead, why hawaladars could beat the official exchange rates banks offered.

Eventually accounts had to be balanced between hawaladars. Hawaladars would be running deficits or surpluses with their partners. Kinship, family, and tribal ties often facilitated the settlement process. In Afghanistan, for example, intermarriages between the families of hawaladars were commonplace because they helped cement trust between the parties. It was very common for brothers or other relations to operate in the same hawala enterprise. Yet although there were often familial relationships, Farid and other hawaladars that I spoke with always emphasized that hawala is a business concerned with profit.

A variety of methods were used to settle accounts. Sometimes direct bank-to-bank wire transfers or cash couriers were involved. Payments could also be made via Internet payment providers. But most often, historically and culturally, trade was the method employed to provide "counter-valuation" or a way of balancing the books.

Farid explained that if a Dubai-based hawaladar owed money to a hawaladar in Kabul, he could settle the account by under-invoicing a shipment of trade goods. For example, most large hawaladars like Farid either operated a trading company or worked closely with "import-export" groups. A shipment of telecommunications equipment could easily be under-invoiced to reflect the amount owed and settle the debt. To move money the other way, in this case from Kabul to Dubai, over-invoicing could be used. For example, if a shipment of electronics was worth $50,000 but was over-invoiced for $100,000, the subsequent payment of $100,000 would pay for both the legitimate cost of the merchandise ($50,000) and also allow an extra $50,000 to be remitted abroad. Invoice manipulation "counter-valued" the debt and provided a way to balance the books between traders and hawaladars. The cover of the business transaction and the documentation involved washed the money clean. Moreover, the transfer of money for business purposes also generally negated the governments' currency controls.

Farid's explanation was helpful, but it was time to shift the conversation. "Farid, thank you again for taking the time to see me. I really appreciate your explanation. It has been very helpful.

"You are welcome."

"I know that your business is involved in helping people support their families back home. In fact, a Somali banker once told me that hawala is the poor man's banking system."

Farid laughed. "That is a good way of putting it. But believe me, many wealthy people use hawala as well."

"Unfortunately, criminals and terrorists also use hawala. For example, in 1998 the bombings of the US Embassies in Kenya and Tanzania were financed in part by hawala. In 2010 the unsuccessful Times Square bombing was also financed by hawala transfers from Pakistan."

Farid's eyes narrowed. "It is unfortunate."

"As I indicated to you over the phone, your name surfaced in an investigation by our New York office."

"Can you give me some details?"

"Well, Homeland Security Investigations has many offices around the United States. Our New York City office was conducting an investigation into a company based in Manhattan that was involved with sending prohibited computer software to Iran. The transaction is a violation of our Iranian sanctions. Pursuant to a search warrant, when the investigators examined the firm's records, they found documents that indicate that your company was the financial intermediary for the transaction."

"Mr. Joe, I don't know anything about the specifics of what you are talking about, but those are your sanctions, not mine."

I smiled. Of course he was right. It was exactly the answer I expected. "Do you know the name of the New York company—S Solutions Ltd.?"

"As you can see, our volume of business is very high." Farid looked puzzled. "Isn't the English expression, *the name doesn't ring a bell*?"

I laughed. "Your point is well made and your English is excellent."

"Do you have the name of other companies involved?"

"The documents show that S Solutions was dealing with a trading company based in Sharjah named Unlimited Imports and Exports."

Farid continued to sit behind his desk. His face was expressionless. "I don't know that company either. Why don't you talk to the authorities in Sharjah and have them help you?"

"We're doing that." In fact, a formal inquiry was being coordinated via the American Embassy in Abu Dhabi.

"By chance, do you have any records of doing business with S Solutions or Unlimited Imports and Exports?"

"I just explained that hawaladars don't generally keep records. And even if I did, I'm under no obligation to turn the records over to you or the UAE authorities."

He was right. I didn't respond.

"Mr. Joe, if I may, these sanctions against Iran are another example of American arrogance. They also don't work."

"Farid, I just enforce our laws. I don't make them."

"I think you should explain to your bosses back in Washington that Iran and Dubai have ties that go back hundreds of years through marriage, traditions, religion, and even shared cuisine. You probably don't realize it, but even the Arabic spoken in Dubai is different. It has a Farsi inflection. Neighborhoods and sports teams here in Dubai are named after counterparts in Iran. It is impossible to break these bonds through sanctions."

"Farid, my bosses in Washington don't listen to me. They also have to enforce the laws that are made by our politicians. And our politicians feel they have to be seen doing something, even if most everybody understands that sanctions are for the most part ineffectual."

"I remember when America started to tighten its embargo against Iran back in 2003 and 2004. At that time there were less than three thousand Iranian-run businesses in Dubai. Today we have over three times that many." He laughed. "Do you think that was just a coincidence? If you put a barrier in front of somebody and they are determined enough, they will find a way around it."

"It isn't just American sanctions. The UN began applying sanctions in 2006 after Ahmadinejad announced Iran's nuclear enrichment program. In fact, the UAE has somewhat cooperated with the UN's mild sanctions, as it must under its treaty obligations."

"Mr. Joe, when you leave here, take a walk down by Dubai Creek. It is still sometimes called 'Smugglers' Creek.' Look at the *dhows*. Those wooden sailing vessels have been going back and forth across the Gulf for hundreds of years. Nobody can stop the trade between Dubai and Iran."

"I know from a customs and law enforcement perspective that there is very little inspection of the *dhows* and for that matter the thousands of forty-foot shipping containers in the Jebel Ali Free Trade Zone."

Farid grinned. "Today subsidized Iranian gasoline gets exchanged for all different kinds of things blocked by the US embargo. It is an open secret that narcotics from Afghanistan cross the Gulf. Whiskey, building materials, microchips, computers, and undoubtedly even prohibited software are sent from Dubai into Iran."

He got up from behind his desk and extended his hand. "I know you are just doing your job, but you can't control this kind of trade. These issues are very complex."

I knew Farid's getting up from his desk was his signal that the interview was over. "Because these issues are so complex, that is exactly why I appreciate your insight."

Farid extended his hand and walked me to the door.

"Thank you again for your time," I said. "I'm staying at the Sheraton Hotel on Dubai Creek and flying back to Rome Saturday night. Let me know if you would like to talk some more."

chapter 10

HAKIM FAGHOUL EXITED his tiny third-story apartment in the Via Zeno district of Brescia in northern Italy. The apartment complex was one of many in an urban low-income development project checker boarded with sterile and uniform cement block buildings. Hakim momentarily closed his eyes against the bright Italian sun and then headed for his nearby dark blue Fiat Punto. The car was conveniently parked on the sidewalk in front of the apartment building. His makeshift parking place was marked by Arabic graffiti sprayed on the cement wall above the Punto.

Driving down the Via Costalunga on a quiet Sunday morning, Hakim was soon in the *centro storico* or historical center of Brescia. The Via Zeno district stood in marked contrast to the wealthy and cultured side of Brescia. The *centro* boasted airy piazzas and picturesque streets, manicured parks and fountains, aristocratic residences, and a multitude of art treasures found in Renaissance-era churches and modern-day museums. This Brescia—the Brescia for the locals and the tourists—was clean, inviting, and beautiful. The stark difference between the two sides of the Italian city in which Hakim resided fueled his resentment. As Hakim shifted his Punto out of a corner turn and into third gear, he accelerated rapidly.

Hakim Faghoul was a native Algerian. In Italy, he was called a *clandestino*—an illegal immigrant. Hakim called himself a *ghurba*-somebody lost and adrift in a land of strangers. Yet he tried to make the best of the situation. The province of Brescia was home to one of Italy's largest immigrant populations, and the Via Zeno district had one of the highest concentrations of *clandestini*; most of them

Pakistani, Senegalese, or, like Hakim, North African. Many of the *clandestini* had survived perilous sea crossings or were smuggled in the back of trucks on dangerous cross-border land journeys. Once the immigrants arrived in Europe, organized criminal groups involved with human trafficking would sometimes charge a premium for those seeking employment and a new life in northern Italy.

Brescia was located off the A-4 *autostrada* or freeway, about equal distance between Milano and Venezia. The city's residents historically had been known for their work ethic. Primarily because of its inhabitants' fondness for work, Brescia was sometimes called the "the lioness of Italy." During Italy's industrialization and manufacturing boom years of the 1980s and early 1990s, modern Brescia specialized in engineering and automotive industries. It became the model for the rest of northern Italy.

The *clandestini* joined their fellow Bresciani in hard work; however, most of the jobs given to the *extracommunitari*—immigrants from outside 'the European community'—were what the Italians call *lavoro nero* or underground labor. Italy had a thriving underground economy and undocumented workers were always needed for light manufacturing and service jobs. The native Italian owners profited greatly, as they could pay low wages and avoid payroll taxes. The profits drove the development of the region. The new wealth also resulted in a large and growing class of flamboyant and materialistic Italians.

Hakim and most of the other *clandestini* despised *la nuova Italia*. Many of the new rich did not handle their conspicuous wealth well. Instead of the Italian ideal of *bella figura,* signifying good manners and culture, many with new money personified the opposite image of *bruta figura,* or ugly image. *La nouva Italia* often became a charade of social pretense. Many tried to pass themselves off as aristocracy. The worst were sometimes labeled *caffone*, someone with absolutely no class. *La nuova Italia* was the source of much conversation amongst the Bresciani, both Italians and *clandestini.*

Like much about the man, the name Hakim Faghoul was a lie. At one time he was Basem. His new identity was one more contradiction in a life of contradictions and deception. Hakim was proud of his ability to compartmentalize. He knew well that his mental discipline was the key to both his emotional and physical survival.

Although his father had passed away when Basem was a young boy, he enjoyed a poor but relatively happy childhood far from Brescia in both time and distance. Basem lived with his mother and siblings in the village of Oued Bouaicha, about 240 kilometers south of Algiers. In 1998, when he was fourteen years old, his life suddenly changed forever. As part of the long-running and barbaric Algerian civil war between the government and various Islamist rebel groups, fifty-two people were killed in Oured Bouaicha by a group of militants carrying axes and knives. Whether the murderers and thugs acted for a rebel group or the government, it didn't matter. What mattered to Basem was that when he returned to Oued Bouaicha that fateful day after a visit to a neighboring village, he found the town's butchered casualties included his mother, brother, and two younger sisters. Basem was alone.

After the massacre, Basem found his way to Algiers and soon adopted a life in the streets. In order to survive, he became adept at petty crime. His new life of crime was also a means for him to strike back. Using his quick hands, feet, and mind, he excelled in the Algerian underworld of crime. He was impetuous and a risk-taker. He also had a temper. By the time he turned sixteen, he had killed his first man. Hakim felt he had been insulted by a fellow thief. He reacted by plunging a knife into the man's back. Hakim surprised himself. He felt nothing. There was no emotion, no fear, and no regret.

The 2003 US invasion of Iraq was the catalyst for Hakim's adoption of radical Islam. The fiery sermons given in many mosques were spread further on cassettes, videos, and Islamic websites accessed in Internet cafes. They exhorted the faithful to jihad. The cries for the defense of Islam, coupled with a young man's quest for adventure, resonated within Basem.

He joined a small group of Algerian jihadists and traveled to Syria. They were smuggled across the border and joined al Qaeda in Iraq. After cursory training and indoctrination, Basem was selected to specialize in explosives. He became adept at roadside bombs triggered by improvised explosive devices. He was presented with many opportunities to practice jihad, kill infidels, and help defeat the foreign crusaders. His burgeoning bloodlust found additional outlets when he participated in atrocities against Shia Iraqis.

Within al Qaeda of Iraq, Basem was well regarded by his superiors for both his courage and his killing instincts. At one time, he fought with Abu Musab al-Zarqawi, the former Jordanian criminal who became the al-Qaeda leader in Iraq. Both in Iraq and in Jordan, Al-Zarqawi became notorious for waging a bloody campaign of suicide bombings and beheadings. Al-Zarqawi became Basem's hero and role model. He was also a bit of a father-figure. The relationship was shattered when, in 2006, al-Zarqawi was killed. US warplanes dropped two five-hundred-pound bombs on a house in which Zarqawi was meeting with other terrorists.

It was one of many narrow escapes for Basem. His profile was high. He was also exhausted. After three additional years of violence, he was told by his al Qaeda in Iraq superiors that his personal jihad must take another form. It was time to leave Iraq. While waiting for instructions that might never materialize, he was directed to integrate into the West, find a means to support himself, and maintain a low profile. Although fearless in battle, his new mission of *taqiyya*—Islamic subterfuge—frightened him. The West, the land of infidels, was for him repugnant. It was beyond his comprehension. His new life would only exacerbate his contradictions, deceptions, and resentments. However, he obeyed his superiors and longed for the day when he could continue jihad.

Basem arrived in northern Italy. His long journey was facilitated by a type of international jihadist underground railroad. From stop to stop—through Syria, Turkey, and into Germany—he was shepherded by a loose-knit network of radical Islamists and jihadist sympathizers. By the time he arrived in Italy, he was a *clandestino*, but not undocumented. Through a series of contacts and the payment of a considerable sum of money, his identity was changed and immigration and identity documents provided. He became Hakim.

Hakim was a rather small man with a slight, sinewy build. He was clean-shaven and wore his hair short. Forgoing popular Italian trends and fashion, he sometimes shopped for clothes on Saturday mornings at Brescia outdoor markets. They were one of the few venues where the immigrant and native Bresciani openly mingled. The markets were also a way for him to begin to assimilate the Italian language.

Yet, for the most part, Hakim followed his instructions and maintained a low profile. Even with his documents, he wanted to stay under the radar of Italian authorities. He disappeared into the anonymity of immigrant life in the Via Zeno district. During his waking hours, he successfully compartmentalized his previous life.

Hakim first found employment working with other *clandestini* in a small Brescia factory involved with reclaiming small amounts of gold from computer waste. Under the guise of "recycling," personal computers were collected and their contents dissembled and sorted. Hakim worked with the microprocessors and, using a mixture of hydrochloric and nitric acid, separated the gold from ceramic. The gold scrap particles were collected, smelted, and later turned into small gold bars that helped feed the Italian jewelry industry's ravenous appetite for the precious metal. The manufacture of fine gold was one of Italy's largest industries.

The large community of immigrants in Brescia, both legal and illegal, generally sent a portion of their earnings back to their homelands in order to support families. Although they felt the wages they earned were not just or commensurate with their Italian counterparts, they considered themselves fortunate. In comparison to the families they had left behind, the euro they earned was strong and the wages plentiful. They all felt it was their natural obligation to assist their families in need. As a result, money was sent to places like Afghanistan, Pakistan, Somalia, Sri Lanka, Bangladesh, the Philippines, Senegal, Nigeria, Algeria, and Tunisia. Particularly for remittances sent to South Asia countries and Somalia, Dubai was the regional hub or clearinghouse.

Hakim did not have a family to support. Yet he had a cause. Following the exhortations of the imams in the local mosque and the radical Islamic websites he frequented, Hakim sent money overseas in order to support his jihadist brothers. Hakim firmly believed in the teachings of *Sharia,* that those Muslims who cannot engage in physical jihad using force of arms must support jihad financially. As one of the chief spokespersons for jihad once explained, “God has ordered us to fight enemies with our lives and with our money.”

Thus Hakim felt it was a blessing when, through a series of friendships with other *clandestini,* he was able to assist the hawala operation in Brescia. Because so many remittances were leaving Brescia and other areas of northern Italy via hawala, there was a need for the regional hawala operation to balance accounts. Although virtually any commodity could be used in value transfer, gold was often preferred. There were many reasons: gold was both a commodity and a de-facto bearer instrument; depending on the need, gold could easily change form; more value could be transferred via gold than almost any other commodity; its relative constant value gave predictability to those involved in value transfer; and there was a tremendous demand for the precious metal. Particularly in neighboring Vicenza, there was a thriving gold manufacturing industry.

Hakim’s astute mind realized that there was literally a golden business opportunity in providing the local hawaladars with a means to an end. He found that “gold scrap” was not precisely defined by customs authorities and was readily susceptible to invoice fraud. By importing “gold scrap” from, for example, Dubai, at prices that were over-invoiced, payment was sent in return. Moreover, in Italy gold that was imported, “worked,” and then re-exported as “fine gold” was exempt from most customs duties.

After a few years in Brescia learning the gold recycling business, Hakim established his own small company that imported “gold scrap” and scrap metal. The scrap included used computers, machine filings, scrap jewelry, electronics, and even dental fillings. Some of the importations were genuine and some just occurred on paper. But more important than the physical importations, Hakim provided his hawaladar partners the invoices required to send payments abroad. The payments, of course, were part of the settling accounts between international hawaladars.

Hakim called his small import-export business *Riciclaggio di Oro* or RDO. Riciclaggio in Italian means washing, recycling, or laundering. He enjoyed the subtle joke. His business had nothing to do with the environmental movement sweeping the country. Rather, his recycling had everything to do with the disguising, transfer, and laundering of money and value.

The gold-scrap import business provided Hakim with a moderate income. It was the means for him to pay his rent, buy a car, and occasionally indulge in sending funds abroad to help support his jihadist brothers. Yet in Hakim's logic, he felt the most important fruit of his labors was that he provided a service to his fellow *clandestini.* Thanks to the gold imports, many of the northern Italian hawaladars were able to expand their services. And since hawala was a form of underground finance, he also felt he was obeying his guidance to maintain a low profile.

However, this morning was different. Hakim was headed to Milano to join tens of thousands of other "guest workers" and *extra-communitari* to protest substandard working conditions, lack of benefits, and a general lack of respect. The situation was made even worse by the current Italian economic downturn and belt-tightening. The pent up frustrations and real and perceived slights from *la nuova Italia* were finally finding an outlet. The authorities believed the rally and march from the Duomo would attract thousands of disaffected workers. Previously, Hakim had only worked with the *clandestini* in the shadows. He understood direct participation in the demonstration was not smart. He knew of the need to stay off the authorities' radar screens. But sometimes Hakim could not help himself. The feelings of repression played on his hidden impetuousness.

Before entering the *autostrada* for the short ride to Milano, Hakim stopped off at a coffee bar that doubled as an Internet café. After a restless night punctuated with horrid dreams, he desperately needed his morning espresso. Hakim also wanted to check if he had received any messages. It had been almost two weeks since he had last had the opportunity to check his encrypted email.

Back in his Fiat Punto, Hakim again gunned the engine while driving up the ramp to the autostrada. His mind was racing as fast as his engine. It wasn't because of the caffeine in the espresso. After all the years of waiting, he had finally received his first operation.

Unfortunately, the message was short on specifics. Interspersed among the promise of eternal glory and the promise that further details would be provided, there was a request to confirm his availability to strike the infidels. True to his sometimes impulsive nature, Hakim quickly replied "yes."

chapter 11

THE PHONE RANG in my hotel room. "Mr. Joe? It's Farid. I'm down in the lobby. Can you come down and talk?"

"Farid? This is a pleasant surprise. I'm just starting to pack my things. I've got to be at the airport by ten p.m. for a midnight flight. But I have a little time. Give me ten minutes and I'll be right down."

I hung up the phone and shrugged. *Why is he calling now?* Looking around the room, I saw my suitcase open on the bed. Some neatly folded clothes were stacked nearby, ready to be packed. Others were thrown crumpled over a nearby chair. A wet towel from my shower hung from the closet door. I had just finished typing up the draft of my trip report and shut down my laptop. My travel briefcase was open on the desk. Repeating stories from CNN International hummed from the television. The low-volume news reports cycled like elevator music and provided the accompaniment for my travels: another country, another hotel, another room, another day on the road. I wanted to go home.

Taking off my jeans, I put on a more presentable pair of slacks. *Why does Farid want to see me? Could this be some kind of a set-up?* I wasn't really worried. If he reported our recent conversation to the local authorities, I didn't care. If they wanted to know anything about my activities, I would be more than happy to tell them. I had no secrets. Most of my work helped the host countries. I hadn't done anything to upset the embassy in Abu Dhabi or consulate in Dubai. I always received country clearance from the embassy prior to my arrival. My activities were cleared with appropriate embassy staff. Over the years, I had learned the necessity of staying on good terms with the embassy. I understood all too well that the American ambassador was in charge of all official US functions and the boss of all official Americans present—whether permanently stationed or just on temporary duty status. The ambassador's authority covered representatives from all US agencies and departments in the country on official business. Logically, the embassy had to know who was traveling to the country and for what purpose. In addition to security concerns, the embassy also wanted to ensure that business was conducted both efficiently and expeditiously. As in this trip to Dubai, the embassy staff helped both to provide local points of contact and broker the right introductions. And I always delivered an "out-brief" to the appropriate embassy staffer at the end of my visit, summarizing my activities. Again, I had no secrets. *Well . . . maybe just a few.*

Making sure I had a pen in my shirt pocket, I next put the hotel key card into my wallet. Closing the hotel room door, I turned to walk down the corridor to the elevator. *Left? Right? I've already been here a few days and I'm still confused. Too many hotels.*

When the elevator door opened, I stepped into Dubai diversity. It was one of the things that I found so attractive about the city-state. In my travels, I often played a game of guessing people's country of origin. Sometimes I could spot telltale signs in their manner of dress or the shoes they were wearing. In other cases, it was just their overall look or the way they carried themselves. Of course, hearing them speak was often the giveaway. The game was a bit of private and harmless entertainment. I also told myself the game helped me develop my assessment skills and stay alert about who was around me.

In the back of the elevator was a middle-aged Arab man dressed in a loose, long-sleeved, ankle-length white *thobe,* perfectly suited for the hot climate of the Gulf. On his head was the ever present *ghutra*, a square scarf folded in a triangle and typically worn over a white knitted skull cap called a *tagiyah.* The *ghutra* was patterned in white and red checks. There is no particular significance to the colors; sometimes the ghutra is all white and sometimes it is checked in black and white. However, the red and white check pattern is very popular in the Kingdom of Saudi Arabia and gave me a possible indication of his nationality. The black cord—the *agal*—was wrapped around the *ghutra* to hold it in place on his head. According to the Quran, a man should be judged by his deeds, not his appearance, so the plain white *thobe* also expresses equality. However, the man in the *thobe* still managed to express his individuality and probable status with a gold pen in his breast pocket and gold watch on his wrist.

The Arab in the white thobe was accompanied by what appeared to be two wives; they stood quietly on each side. They were dressed from head to toe in tent-like black *abayas.* When young Saudi women reached the approximate age of thirteen, the garment became obligatory. In the more cosmopolitan city of Jeddah, many young women increasingly wore colored head scarves around their shoulders and left their *abayas* open to reveal pants and colorful T-shirts. However, these ladies in the elevator were dressed completely in black, which was a possible tip-off that if they were from Saudi Arabia, they very likely were from a more conservative area, such as Riyadh. Again, each woman revealed a hint of individuality with multiple gold bands and bracelets that peeked just out of their long black sleeves. I knew that the buying and selling of gold jewelry was very popular with Saudi women and was both a pastime and a kind of informal investment and savings account. Gold was an extremely important part of Saudi culture. Except for their eyes, the women's faces were completely covered by a black mask-like garment called the *niqab*. Many women wore the *niqab* to protect their modesty. But being confronted by a black scarf where a face should be could be startling for a Westerner. Not wanting to give offense, I tried not to stare. I did notice their eyes turn toward the floor as soon as I entered the elevator.

An elderly gentleman with a weathered face and a stubble of white beard also stood at the rear of the large elevator. He wore a simple, ankle-length, collarless gown with long sleeves similar to a *thobe* that some call a *dishdasha*. The garment was lilac in color, which indicated to me that he was probably from Oman. Although white was the most popular clothing color in Oman, the Gulf country was famous for its men wearing *dishdashas* in baby blue, orange, soft brown, and lavender. On his head was a *muzzar,* or a square of finely woven woolen or cotton fabric, wrapped and folded into a turban. The turban was another indicator he was probably Omani. He wore leather sandals on his feet.

Others joining us for the short ride down to the hotel lobby included a forty-something couple that appeared to be from Germany. Dubai was increasingly popular for European tourists. Dressed inappropriately in shorts, ratty T-shirts, and Ecco sandals, they could very well have been headed for a stroll along Dubai Creek or to a local Western hangout for a cold beer on a warm evening.

The elevator doors opened. I was the last to exit. Walking past the busy reception desk, I spotted Farid on the other side of the lobby, seated in an overstuffed chair. The area surrounding him was deserted of people and I did not sense anything amiss.

"Farid, it is very nice to see you again."

"Mr. Joe, I know you have to leave shortly for the airport. Pardon me for not giving you more notice. I will not keep you long."

"It is a pleasure to see you. Is this a good place to talk, or would you prefer to go somewhere else?"

"This is fine." With an almost imperceptible nod of his head, he motioned me toward an adjoining chair.

I waited a few moments as Farid stared momentarily at the armrest of his chair and seemed to collect his thoughts. He then turned his dark eyes directly toward mine.

"Mr. Joe, are you aware of the demonstration yesterday protesting the situation in Palestine?"

"Of course. I watched some coverage of the demonstration on my hotel TV. Normally the authorities here do not allow demonstrations. They made an exception. There was even a short segment on CNN. I made it a point to stay away from the downtown area of Burg Dubai."

"They have allowed demonstrations in Dubai before that show support for the Palestinians." Farid's eyes darted around the room before he continued. "But this one was the largest yet."

"These marches are materializing around the world," I said. "They are happening in the developing and developed countries alike. But thank God they have always been peaceful. I think that is why they may prove effective in finally getting Israel to change its policies regarding water and the West Bank. I understand that Israel is in convulsions right now. They don't know how to respond to this."

Farid slowly shook his head. "Mr. Joe, do you know the term *takfiri*?

"Aren't *takfiris* those who believe in a strict interpretation of Islam? They reject any change from the religion as it was originally conceived in the time of the prophet?"

"Very good. But sometimes it goes even further than that. The most radical of *takfiris* believe that Muslims who practice a more liberal form of faith or obey anything other than Islam, including modernity, are apostates from Islam."

I nodded. "Of course, *takfiris* also despise infidels."

"Unfortunately, these beliefs allow them to justify the use of violence against those who do not believe what they believe. That was one of the main reasons behind the sectarian violence in the Iraq insurgency."

"That kind of hate and sectarian warfare is so hard to understand."

"*Takfiri*s believe that political authority that does not follow their interpretation of Islam is illegitimate. The long-running sectarian strife in Iraq is just one example of the problem. The same thing is happening in many other areas of the world, such as Syria, Afghanistan and Pakistan. And, of course, we have our problems of extreme fundamentalists in Iran."

I knew he was trying to tell me something, but he seemed reluctant to get to the point. I thought I would try a direct approach. "But Farid, what does this have to do with the demonstrations?"

Farid waited a few moments before replying. "Mr. Joe, do you have children?"

"I have been blessed with three."

Farid's eyes sparkled as he smiled momentarily. "I too have three children." He paused and his eyes shifted from mine and began to again scan the hotel lobby. His fingers started to tap the armrest of his chair.

I knew he needed a nudge. "Farid, one of the reasons I do what I do is to try to make the world a better place—a safer place—for our children." I waited a bit before continuing. "I know the United States has done much to cause suspicion and mistrust in this part of the world. But my country is also a force for good. We still have the strength and sometimes the courage to do what others cannot."

His head turned back toward mine and his eyes looked intently at me. I shifted slightly in my chair and leaned toward him.

"As I told you in your office, one of the reasons I visited with you is to ask for your help. These issues are very complex. The culture and way of doing business in this part of the world are so difficult for outsiders to understand. I depend—and my colleagues depend—on information that people like you provide. And most of the time people cooperate with me and the government I represent because they are afraid for their children. They are afraid of the various evils they sense coming."

There was another long pause before Farid began to speak quietly. "The case you spoke to me about in New York is nothing. It is not worth your time."

The nod of my head was meant as an encouragement for him to continue.

"In my business, I see and hear much. I know many people. There are things happening right now. I cannot give you specific information because I do not have it yet. However, I do have my suspicions."

"Is there anything that you can share with me?"

"Now is not the time or the place. I need to see if I can—how do you say—connect the dots?"

"I understand."

"Maybe my fears are nothing at all. But I have some interesting business connections. Some of them could be called *takfiris*."

This time I was the one who looked away. There was some commotion by the entrance to the hotel. A large group of tourists and their luggage had just arrived. A tour guide hovered about like a mother hen. She held a closed red umbrella that acted as a beacon. I didn't have to guess their nationality; they were Chinese. The hotel staff began to scurry. A din of voices and activity filled the lobby. I turned my gaze back to the man who was seated next to me. *Something is troubling him. It took a lot of courage for him to come here.*

"Farid, I trust you. And I give you my word that you can trust me. I appreciate you coming here tonight."

"Mr. Joe, you are going back to Rome. What if I want to reach you?"

"You already have my business card." I took another card from my wallet and began to write. Handing it to him, I said, "Here is another. It has my personal phone number and email address. Let me know if I can help."

chapter 12

THE SEA SURROUNDING Karachi Harbor shimmered in the late afternoon sun. Rafi savored the feeling of walking along the beach on the wet sand. The rushing surf and tide splashed seawater up his rolled pant legs. His stroll along the beach was for him like walking back through time. This was the first occasion Rafi had been here since he was a boy.

Shortly after he and Tariq were adopted by Majeed, they all came to spend a week together at this very beach. Leaving behind the rigidity and hopelessness of the madrassa, they began the bonding process at the seashore. The wonderful memories were the catalyst for the salty tears he began to feel well in his eyes. He could not help himself. For him, French Beach was a special place—a perfect place for families. It was one of the few beaches in Karachi left unspoiled. Until this day, French Beach had also remained uncorrupted in his memory.

The locals knew the area as *Haji Ismill Goth*. It was sandwiched between Hawkes Bay and Paradise Point, not far from downtown Karachi. A private beach popular with Pakistani elites and Karachi's expatriate community, the area was surrounded by a wall that restricted unauthorized entries. The local villagers had constructed a number of beach huts for rent during high season. French Beach was neat and orderly. In contrast, most of Karachi's other beaches stretching along the outskirts of the city were polluted and had a dearth of facilities. Petty crime along the beaches was rampant. Karachi beaches were also notorious as death traps for innocent visitors due to the strong currents that swept swimmers away.

Over the last two weeks, Rafi had begun to think that his cyberworld invitation to jihad and martyrdom was an illusion. He had heard nothing more. After the days of silence, Rafi found refuge in his business. He redoubled his efforts to make deals. His efforts reached from Karachi to Dubai and beyond. When his mind did wander back to the strange evening in the Internet café, he began to think that his virtual-world encounter with unknown avatars was nothing more than just some sort of loyalty test. His confusion was compounded because he was directed not to discuss the matter with anybody.

This was the time he truly needed his adoptive father. But he could not get himself to approach him. To Rafi, his entire relationship with Majeed was now open to question. Although Rafi told himself he was willing to sacrifice his life in jihad if that was the will of Allah, he did not like the gnawing feeling that he was little more than a pawn to be used by others and then discarded. When the messenger finally came to him with word of the meeting on the beach, it was almost a relief. He swallowed hard at the irony that the meeting place was this very same spot that held such significance for him.

Rafi had arrived a half hour earlier. Per his instructions, he entered a gate off nearby Mauripur Road. He noted that this particular entrance to French Beach did not have a gatekeeper. His subsequent stroll along the beach led him to an outcrop of jumbled rocks that formed a small natural jetty jutting out into the sea. He remembered it from his youth. He looked at his watch. It was almost the designated 1600 hours. On this delightful October day, the beach was nearly deserted. He was startled to hear the greeting, "*Asalaam alykum*."

A man in his mid forties suddenly appeared from around the other side of a large rock. Dressed in a traditional white *shalwar qameez*, he smiled as he walked toward Rafi with an extended hand. Rafi acknowledged his greeting with a nod of his head and politely clasped the outstretched hand.

Before he could say a word, the stranger continued. "Rafi, I saw you coming. It is an honor to meet you. I have heard many good things about you. My name is Abdul Ghafoor. If you do not mind, it is best that we speak English."

Rafi closely studied the man. His eyes were dark and framed with rimless glasses. His mid-length black beard was sprinkled with grey. A gold tooth added a touch of sparkling color to his smile. Though of medium height and build, the man's bearing, manner, and coloring did not suggest fitness. On the contrary; his hand felt soft. Rafi intuitively knew that the use of English and the common name of Abdul Ghafoor were to protect his identity.

Rafi, fearing that tears might still be in his eyes, forced himself to smile. "It is a pleasure to meet you." Making a conscious effort to compose himself, he added, "I have not been to this beach for many years. I have good memories."

Abdul smiled and then replied, "Then, Allah willing, let us make some more."

There was something in the words that triggered Rafi's emotions anew. With bitterness that he was having a hard time controlling, Rafi said, "I'm assuming you are you here to tell me about my mission? I do not believe there will be time for many more memories."

For long moments nobody spoke. "I can give you some insight but not all," Abdul finally replied curtly.

Rafi lowered his head and looked at his sand-covered feet. For a moment, he felt again like the boy at the beach. He slowly raised his eyes. "It is a pleasure to meet you. I am sorry for having spoken like that. I am honored to fight jihad. It is just not what I expected. Not now." His voice trailed and ended in a hard swallow.

"The inevitable laughs at man's schemes," Abdul said, this time in Pashtu. The expression was a well-known proverb. "It is as Allah wills."

"Yes. As Allah wills," Rafi replied.

Abdul circled back behind the rock from which he had mysteriously emerged just minutes before. He quickly came back with a small rolled carpet, thermos, and tea cups.

"Let us begin again," said Abdul.

Sitting cross-legged on the carpet, Rafi accepted the offered tea with gratitude. Watching each other and the nearby surf, they began to talk of everything and nothing. The conversation was harmonious. Both consciously avoided the reason for the meeting. The thermos was emptied. Finally, Abdul Ghafoor abruptly stood up and motioned for Rafi to do the same. "Let us leave these things here," he said, "and stroll down the beach together."

The sun was beginning to lower in the western sky. The seagulls shrieked as they darted from the sky to sand to surf, frantically searching for their evening meal. Leaving footprints in the sand, only to have them erased by the charging surf, Rabi and Abdul began to walk.

"Rafi, you are aware of the situation in Palestine and the worldwide reaction?" It wasn't so much a question as a statement of fact, and Abdul's effort to shift the conversation to the reason for the meeting.

"Of course. There seems to be a sense that this time it is different. The injustices will no longer be tolerated. The peaceful marches, strikes, and boycotts are gathering momentum." Before Abdul could respond, Rafi added, "Apparently, these incidents are going to be the catalyst for our action?"

"Rafi, I am but a technician. I do not understand the politics of these things. But it appears that you are right." Abdul abruptly stopped walking and reached down and picked up a rock. He threw it into the sea. "Our leadership has decided that this is the opportune time. Abdul continued. "There are too many grievances, and they have accumulated for many years. The Jews and the crusaders will misinterpret peaceful actions. We have to fight back."

"You are Afghan. You understand the expression, "a tree only moves in the wind."

Rafi nodded.

"Now is our time. We have the means to strike. We are not going to just create wind but a hurricane."

Turning directly toward Abdul, Rafi asked, "And what, specifically, is my role?"

Abdul walked a half a dozen steps before responding. "We have accumulated sufficient radioactive material to construct a 'dirty bomb.' Your mission will be to assist in the delivery and activation of this weapon in a western city. The time and the place for the operation have been chosen to exert maximum terror."

The statement floated away in the sea breeze. Rafi did not say anything.

Finally Abdul added, "You should be honored to be selected for such a mission."

Rafi waited again. "I am. I just have many questions."

"That is what I am here for. I will explain the operation and answer what I can." Abdul turned and held Rafi's hand—a Pakistani sign of friendship. They began to walk again down the beach.

After a dozen steps together, Rafi finally said, "I am impressed. Of course, Pakistan is a nuclear power, but how did we obtain these materials?"

Abdul's golden tooth sparkled anew as a wide smile formed underneath his beard. "It was the fruit of a lot of hard work and money going to the right places. Regarding the financing, the money came from multiple sources. We owe a lot to Majeed. Regarding the technical aspects of this operation, I sometimes felt like I was playing the part of A.Q. Khan."

Rafi, like all Pakistanis, was well aware of the revered nuclear engineer regarded as the "father" of the Pakistani nuclear program. However, it was the 1947 calamitous partition of primarily Hindu India from what is now known as Muslim Pakistan that caused the perceived need for the "bomb."

The breakup of the British Empire in the years after World War II had far-reaching consequences. Israel and Pakistan were both founded as religious homelands. In both cases, the handiwork of an exhausted and guilt-ridden colonial power resulted in a series of wars and never-ending threats of war against a continual backdrop of terrorism.

For years Pakistan was more of an idea than a country. The name was originally coined by a Muslim nationalist attending Cambridge. "P" is for Punjab, "A" is for the Afghan region, "K" is for Kashmir, S" is for Sindh, and "tan" is for the area of Balochistan. In the Urdu language, *pak* means pure and *stan* means land, giving the new country the favored name of Pure Land. However, it was the

K in the acronym that had been the root of most of the subsequent problems. To many in Pakistan, Kashmir became a symbol of all the indignities Muslims suffered as British India unraveled. Kashmir, a beautiful border area claimed by both Pakistan and India, had seen two bloody wars.

As a result of the wars and the constant tension, India publically announced efforts to develop a nuclear bomb. Pakistan was comparatively poor and weak. Yet the situation for Pakistan's nationalists was not hopeless. Despite the humiliating defeats and Pakistan's inferiority complex, Zulfikar Ali Bhutto, a rising young Pakistani politician, responded that Pakistan "will eat grass or leaves—even go hungry—but we will get one of our own."

The nuclear race was exacerbated in 1974 when India tested a nuclear device in an underground cavern only a short distance from the Pakistan border. Passions on all sides flared. At the time, Abdul Qadeer Khan was earning a doctorate in metallurgical engineering in Belgium. He later landed a position in a European nuclear power plant. Using his training, talent, and charm—plus surreptitiously copying diagrams and blueprints—Khan soon developed a scheme that put Pakistan on the road to developing the coveted bomb. He received full backing from President Bhutto.

What Pakistan could not develop on its own, it procured in the international market through a labyrinth of front companies centered in Dubai. Driven by greed, European companies in particular were only too happy to sell "dual-use" products. Dubai also played a prominent role in Khan's plans to disguise the financing of the nuclear program through the misuse of the international gold trade and the regional hawala operations. The original stealth efforts paid off, and Pakistan's quest for the bomb began to emerge from the shadows. In fact, Khan himself boasted in a statement to a newspaper that, "Nobody can undo Pakistan or take us for granted. We are here to stay, and let it be clear that we shall use the bomb if our existence is threatened."

In 1998, Pakistan tested five nuclear weapons inside shafts bored into the side of a mountain. For the first time, an Islamic country had developed a nuclear bomb. It was the source of jubilation and tremendous national pride. A.Q. Khan was a Pakistani hero.

The legacy of colonialism and modern perceptions of backwardness and political rot were wiped away. The bomb was seen by many as a symbol of unity and national respect. Pakistan, and the Islamic world, had joined the nuclear age.

Khan's reputation was later tarnished by revelations that he was involved in the proliferation of nuclear knowledge to countries that the US Department of State labeled "state sponsors of terrorism," including Iran, Libya, and North Korea. Whether his motive was profit or misguided ideology, it is improbable that official Pakistan was not aware of Khan's efforts to spread nuclear technology. Khan crisscrossed the globe in his proliferation efforts; most of his travels were on official Pakistan government aircraft. He was often accompanied by senior members of the Pakistan nuclear establishment. Khan had also developed close ties to Pakistan's generals—the perennial powerbrokers in the country—and to senior officials in Pakistan's Inter-Services Intelligence, or ISI.

However, in the eyes of many in Pakistan, Americans and the other members of the "nuclear club" were the hypocrites. They worked to deny nuclear security for others, yet they maintained huge arsenals of their own. Many felt this was just another vestige of humiliating colonialism. It was a particular affront to Muslims. They had not recovered from the time centuries before during the "Golden Age" of Islam when they had been the intellectual and military masters of the world. They desperately wanted to emerge from the nuclear boot heal of the West.

Radical Islamists who worked to deny modernity, progress, and innovation in so many facets of life wholeheartedly endorsed the quest for nuclear arms. Osama bin Laden said it was a "religious duty" for Muslims to acquire nuclear weapons in defense against the West. In fact, the same year Pakistan became a nuclear power, bin Laden issued a statement labeled "The Nuclear Bomb of Islam," sponsored by the "International Islamic Front for Fighting the Jews and the Crusaders." He argued that "it is the duty of the Muslims to prepare as much force as possible to terrorize the enemies of God."

Reviewing the history of Pakistan's nuclear quest with Rafi, Abdul explained some of the enormous technical, financial, and logistical challenges involved.

"So how did we develop a weapon?"

"Although some of those in charge of Pakistan's nuclear arsenal are our supporters, the safeguards imposed on the weaponry are too tight," Abdul answered. "It is also an open secret that over the years we have tried and failed to acquire nuclear materials and weaponry, both directly and through middlemen."

"I know my father has some familiarity with the underworld of technology and arms."

"Yes, but nothing we tried worked. There was nothing we could do. We couldn't steal the devices and we couldn't buy them." Abdul paused before continuing. "It was finally decided that we would adopt a new strategy—the procurement of enough radioactive material to construct a radioactive dispersal device. It is sometimes called a 'dirty' bomb."

"I think I know in general terms but what exactly do you mean by a dirty bomb?"

Before answering, Abdul took off his glasses and looked out to sea. He wiped the lenses on the sleeve of his *shalwar qameez*. "The term means the bomb will be a conventional explosive device laced with radioactive material. It is not like the nuclear bomb that destroyed Hiroshima. There will not be a mushroom cloud. It will be more like the radiation from Japan's Fukushima nuclear reactor. The only destructive power will be as a result of the explosive. However, it is nuclear contamination—both real and imagined—that will cause panic and terror. And the target city could be deemed uninhabitable for years."

Rafi stopped walking and turned to look directly at the sea. The sun was beginning to set. The scene was peaceful. Serene. A gift from God. In a short while, it would be time to pray the *salutu-al-maghrib*, which began immediately after sunset and would extend till the red glow in the western horizon disappeared. "Please continue," he said softly.

"The basic idea of this device is that the explosion will blast the radioactive material into the air. The material will be further dispersed by the wind. The explosion itself will only cover a small area, but the radioactive cloud—most importantly even the *perception* of such a cloud—should easily cause panic throughout the entire city."

Abdul was warming to his topic. "Although the technical details are not important for you to understand, the destructive force of the bomb will be the ionizing radiation. The energized particles disrupt the orbital electron of an atom, throwing off the balance between the positively charged protons and negatively charged electrons. The atom then becomes an ion. Atoms collide and more ions are created."

"I haven't had much training in science," Rafi replied quietly.

"I have," Abdul chuckled. "What is going to happen—we believe—is that these ions will cause a lot of problems in the human bodies that are exposed. For example, DNA chains can be broken. If a lot DNA is mutated and cells die, the body will probably develop radiation poisoning and sickness—similar to what happened in the area around Chernobyl. However, as I said, this will be a comparatively minor explosion. And blowing a dirty bomb up into the air minimizes the effects." Abdul paused while he shook some wet sand from his pant legs. "I believe our device will still be effective because we have succeeded in obtaining a fairly high-level radiation emitter. We don't know with certainty what will happen to those who are exposed. I believe for most people, if they get rid of their contaminated clothes, take a shower, and evacuate the area they will probably be O.K." As if reminding himself, Abdul added, "However, that is not important. The point of our efforts is to terrorize the infidels by causing panic so that we will achieve our political goals."

Rafi weighed Abdul's words carefully. "And what about casualties? Innocents will suffer."

Abdul stopped walking. He turned slowly to face Rafi. "I too have thought of this. But innocents are suffering now. What about the Palestinians? What about the Muslim victims who have died at the hands of the crusaders through the centuries?"

Rafi nodded.

Abdul continued. "I am a technician. Rafi, you are a businessman. But we are both believers. Remember the holy book . . . 'once the sacred months are past and they refuse to make peace, you may kill the idol worshipers when you encounter them, punish them, and resist every move they make.'"

Rafi knew the phrase well. It was often quoted by those who sought to justify jihad. "And we are not worried about a response?"

"I understand our leadership will make clear that we have additional radioactive material. Force will be met by force. We believe the infidels do not have an appetite for this kind of conflict."

"Wasn't this hard to build?"

"Not really. The challenge for us was to obtain sufficient radioactive material. We tried a lot of different sources."

"I cannot help myself. I'm curious," Rafi said.

"Brother, don't concern yourself with these things. All you need to know is that there are a number of sources of radioactive material, both in Pakistan and around the world. For example, some hospitals use cesium in nuclear medicine, and universities use materials in nuclear research. Cobalt-60 is sometimes used to kill harmful food bacteria. Cobalt-60 is also used in fabrication work, especially for welding steel. A few years ago, a significant quantity was found in a New Delhi scrapyard. There are also a number of thermoelectric generators that contain strontium-90 in countries that were members of the former Soviet Union. There are other sources. We have friends."

Abdul and Rafi turned and started to walk back along the beach toward the outcropping of rocks where they had started.

Abdul continued. "Money is persuasive. Although we could not buy a ready-made bomb, enough people who have access to fissile materials are sympathetic to our appeals. They don't care where the materials are going. They would sell their own mothers if the price was right. Our long-term efforts in finance—of which your family is well aware—have paid dividends."

Rafi knew the truth of Abdul's words. He had been taught by Majeed to recognize and take advantage of human failings to advance radical jihad. And one of the primary weaknesses in most men was greed. It was a fact that Majeed exploited over the years. He intertwined his network of underground finance by exploiting human avarice.

"Through our networks, sufficient material was gathered and stored safely. My technical challenge was to mix what I call a radioactive cocktail. I'm quite confident I succeeded." Rafi noted Abdul's hint of smile and countenance of self-satisfaction.

"Everything is already packed and ready to go," he continued. The radioactive device is actually not that large. To minimize radiation and the possibility of detection, the dirty bomb is wrapped in lead sheathing and form-fitted into the drum of an old washing machine. The actual explosive device is stored in a used commercial freezer. Both are already loaded on a forty-foot shipping container filled with similar used kitchen appliances, machine parts, and Pakistani scrap metal that is destined to be recycled."

Rafi was momentarily staggered. He finally stammered, "I have experience with international trade. I can tell a lot of thought went into the shipment."

Abdul smiled. "There are multiple layers of protection for you and the operation. First of all, customs services know that radiation is a naturally occurring event and is present in many materials—particularly scrap metal. The metal could easily be from old lab equipment, x-ray machines, and other sources." He paused a moment before continuing. "Scrap metal emits a lot of nuisance alerts on radiation portal monitors that custom services sometimes use in examining shipping containers."

Rafi nodded his understanding.

Abdul continued, "As a result, if they do detect radiation from the container, they will probably discount it as a false positive."

"I don't know whether they use those devices in Pakistan or not," Rafi said.

Abdul winked at Rafi through his thick glasses. "They are used, but don't concern yourself. It is taken care of."

"What about at the destination country?"

"That's a good question. First of all, the device is shielded in lead, which has minimized the radioactive emissions. I will not go into the technical details, but lead is used for shielding in x-ray machines, research labs, military equipment, certain businesses, and other places radiation is encountered."

"But won't their radiation detection devices still detect the emissions from the container?"

"We don't think so. As I said, we encased the device in lead, minimizing the emissions. Using our equipment, the readings of the container here in Karachi are not alarming. Particularly factoring in false positives, we don't think it will cause undue suspicion."

"I know customs services are overwhelmed in the ports. The sheer numbers alone work in our favor," Rafi said. "However, something concerns me."

"What's that?"

"The container is coming from Pakistan. Everybody knows what the West thinks of us. We are labeled as a threat. That by itself should cause alarm."

"Yes, unfortunately, that is true. But put yourself in a customs inspector's place. Would you open up every single container of scrap metal coming in from Pakistan? Do you understand how labor-intensive it would be to conduct such examinations?

Rafi smiled at the logic. "They can't do it. If they opened up and inspected every container from a threat country, commerce would be paralyzed. Businessmen would complain."

"Exactly. And if, by chance, they do open the container, the device is located toward the back. After an initial examination, they may well grow discouraged."

"Forgive me, but what about my own exposure to radiation?"

"Do not be concerned. I will explain momentarily, but you will not have to handle the device. Besides, you will have personal shielding equipment available that is designed to protect against radiation."

"What are they?"

"A variety of things, such as aprons, gloves, and goggles. I used them and I'm fine."

"You mentioned other precautions?"

"All of the paperwork is in order. I do not know the details, but the shipper and consignee have done business before. And let me add that your father has some excellent contacts both in Karachi and in the destination port."

Abdul glanced at Rafi through his thick glasses and smiled. "To sum up, we are quite sure that the container will avoid scrutiny."

"So what do I have to do?" asked Rafi.

"Your assignment is to be at the receiving end. You know the business of clearing cargo and handling the freight forwarders and brokers. I also understand you can speak multiple languages. We do not anticipate any problems, but if there are complications you will be there to facilitate the safe entry of the cargo."

"I can do that."

"Rafi, the leadership has also told me they want you there because you make considered decisions. In an operation of this nature, things can go wrong. We want somebody who can make the right choices under pressure."

Rafi acknowledged the statement with his silence.

Abdul added, "You will also assist in scouting the location where the device will be placed and detonated."

"Can you tell me the location—the city where this is to happen?"

"Not yet, brother. You will know shortly."

"And what about the detonation?" Rafi lowered his voice. "My martyrdom?"

"Rafi, I'm not actually sure whether martyrdom will be necessary," Abdul said slowly. "One of the two devices—the old freezer—is packed with explosives. It is common TNT. We have sufficient supply. There is also an arming device. When the TNT is detonated, the radioactive material will disperse. But what I am saying is that there are a number of ways to arrange detonation. You may not have to be in close proximity."

"What do you mean?"

"Well," replied Abdul, "There are dozens of different ways to detonate the bomb. We could use a variety of timing devices, infrared beams, microwave beams, motion detectors, tremble or mercury switches, pressure plates, and many more. Because of the security countermeasures that are sure to be in place for the event we have in mind, we have to be prepared for various contingencies."

"That makes sense." Rafi's mind began to race once again.

"We know you are not an explosives expert. That is why you will be conducting this operation with somebody who is. He has had a lot of experience on the battlefield. He has fought against the infidels. Regarding the manner of detonation, both of you will have to make the correct decision at the time given the circumstances that you find."

"Will I be meeting the explosives expert here and travel with him?

"No. You will link up with him in the destination country. We do not want him traveling to Pakistan. We do not want his travel documents to receive scrutiny."

"I understand." Rafi said.

"The specific date, time, and place for the meeting will be given to both of you later."

The sun was starting to set. Rafi noted that Abdul was now leading him away from the beach and back toward Mauripur Road. There was no vehicle or pedestrian traffic. The area was deserted. Abdul abruptly stopped at a battered delivery van that was parked on the side of the road. He reached into a pocket, pulled out keys, and unlocked the back door of the truck. Rafi could immediately see an old washing machine and freezer sitting in the back of the van. His heart skipped a beat.

"Brother, these are not the real devices. They are empty. However, these machines are very similar to the originals containing the devices. They are exactly as you will see them delivered in the target country. Do you see that they both have red duct tape on the tops?

"Yes."

"There will be parts of other washers and freezers in the shipment. In case you get confused, just remember that the ones you are looking for will be very close to each other. They are placed about two-thirds of the way in from the container door and marked with red tape."

"I understand."

"You and your colleague will not have to open or adjust the washer containing the radioactive material. I assure you there is no need to touch anything."

Rafi nodded his head. He could not take his eyes off of the worn machines.

Abdul continued. "The explosives expert will affix the proper triggering apparatus on the real freezer that contains the TNT. He is also receiving his instructions."

"What about the delivery device?" Rafi asked. "Should we use a similar truck or a van?"

"I think so, but that will also be a part of your scouting mission. We gave it much thought, but we decided against hauling the forty-foot shipping container itself to the point of detonation. With the security precautions that are sure to be in place, they would never let such a large truck get close to the event we have in mind. Besides, most of the big trucks require special licenses and permits."

Rafi nodded as Abdul continued. "Both you and your partner will have sufficient funds to purchase a suitable van or delivery truck. There is no need to steal one. The back of the delivery vehicle will probably look very similar to what you see in front of you. Park the van as close to the event as you can without triggering our adversaries' security countermeasures. The rest is as Allah wills."

As if on cue, a muezzin from a nearby mosque began his call to evening prayer. The ancient cry, tinged with advocacy of faith and duty, sounded to Rafi as if it was a call to action.

chapter 13

It started routinely enough. At noon a group of villagers from Dura al-Qari marched quietly toward the Israeli settlement of Beit El. There had been similar marches in the Holy Land every day for the last week in the pleasant fall sunshine. The organizers of the march were using the same tactics deployed in much of the occupied territories: peaceful marches, work stoppages, and demonstrations designed to keep pressure on the Israeli government over its confiscatory water policies. The marches also served as an outlet for the frustrations of the Palestinians. Surprisingly to many, the organizers' discipline of nonviolence had been maintained. The nonviolence strategy turned out to be a catalyst for both worldwide moral encouragement and financial assistance. The mass popular movement was spurred in large part by social networking on the Internet and the ubiquitous cell phone. Following the lead inaugurated by the "Arab Spring," a new age of global mass protests and organization of the "street" had begun.

Nerves were particularly raw for the Dura al-Qari villagers and in the adjoining towns of Beitein, Ein Yabroud, and al-Beireh. In addition to the lack of water, the villagers had been the victims of recent land-grabs and the bulldozing of their treasured ancient olive groves. Their sense of helplessness and despair was overwhelming. Beit El cast long shadows over the land.

In Biblical times, the area of Beit El was the location where Jacob slept and dreamed of angels going up and down a ladder from heaven to earth. The description of Jacob's Ladder appears in the Book of Genesis.

Thousands of years after Jacob's dream and ten years after the Six-Day War, Beit El was founded when several Jewish families moved onto the Israel Defense Force base. Additional settlers occupied nearby hilltops. The settlement grew rapidly and became part of the Religious Zionist Movement. The settlers were strident in their belief that they had an innate, God-given right to the land. Successive Israeli governments tacitly, actively, and covertly backed the establishment of the settlements, or, in the words of the former Prime Minister Menachem Begin, "the establishment of facts."

The daily Palestinian protest began a few kilometers from the Israeli settlement. Picking up support along the way, the demonstrators would lock arms and march in the style made famous by Dr. Martin Luther King and his supporters in the segregationist South. The Palestinians and their enthusiasts around the world were copying King's tactics, which, themselves, had been modeled on Gandhi's nonviolence strategy. They made no apologies. Sometimes they chanted or held aloft placards demanding water, a release of prisoners, and a return of land. But more often, the demonstrators marched in silence right up to the fence surrounding Beit El. They stopped at the security checkpoint and presented a petition asking for the release of water. During the previous seven days, when the demonstration reached the security gate of Beit El, a copy of the petition would be given to an IDF soldier. After a short period of time, the demonstrators would march back to the villages from which they had come. The symbolism was manifest and the political point was delivered peacefully. As the daily demonstration became more and more routine, the number of the participants started to decline.

On this particular day, a film crew from Sky News International was trying to make its way from Jerusalem to the Palestinian town of Hebron. Since the direct route had been closed due to a security incident, the news team tried an alternate route that took them to the Beit El checkpoint. In a coincidence of fate, the film crew was stopped by Israeli security at approximately the same time the demonstrators arrived.

Nerves were also tight on the Israeli side. For one week, the settlers watched the demonstrators approach and withdraw. They were indignant that the world now seemed united in supporting the rights of the Palestinians. "But what about us?" they asked themselves because nobody else was listening. Israel had won this very land in a war of aggression perpetrated by the Arabs, who had as their stated objective driving Israel into the sea. The settlers had claimed land that was for the most part barren and unproductive. Within a generation, they had transformed it into a veritable garden containing modern homes, schools, synagogues, and amenities. The water came with the land. And the land belonged to their ancestors—the chosen ones. It was land given to them by God. In unison, the settlers felt they had been called to Beit El.

Amongst themselves, the settlers told each other that the Palestinians and their patriarchal society couldn't stand being bested by the Jews. Attempts at friendship had been rebuffed. Israel believed it had tried repeatedly to negotiate a fair and lasting peace. The Arabs would not agree. There would always be a substantial segment of the Palestinian people and the surrounding region that would not be satisfied until Israel ceased to exist. That would mean another Holocaust—something that all Jews agreed would never happen again.

Feelings of resentment and rage swelled within a few of the settlers. There was a growing sense of isolation. There was likewise a strengthening of belief that international criticism was mostly hyperbole linked to centuries of anti-Jewish persecution—and was something that could be readily discounted. As the politicians in the fractured political parties bickered in the Knesset about how to respond to the mounting international condemnation, a faction among the most radical settlers in Beit El decided enough was enough.

Earlier that morning, armed with nothing but clubs, a group of settlers hid themselves under the tarp of an old and battered Leyland flatbed truck that was parked near the main entrance to the settlement. They waited silently and unobserved. At the exact moment the petition was presented, the Leyland raced around the security checkpoint. IDF security faced out toward the perceived threat and did not anticipate danger from its rear. Roaring through the gate, the Leyland headed straight for the crowd of protestors. Without taking his foot off the gas, the driver slammed into the crowd. Bodies crumpled under the tires. Demonstrators were thrown through the air. The tarp was removed and clubs rained down on those who were still standing. The truck never stopped. Not a shot was fired by the IDF forces manning the security barriers.

Mangled and crushed bodies were strewn along the road. Horrible piercing, wailing screams filled the air. Those who were left unhurt rushed to attend the wounded. And still, the Palestinians committed no violence. In the final analysis, it didn't matter whether the docility was caused by shock, exhaustion, discipline, or the fact that only a few were left standing. What did matter was that the Sky News crew captured the carnage and the stoic reaction.

Two scenes in particular were played over and over again on the international twenty-four-hour news cycle and Internet video-link postings. The first was of a screaming three-year-old clutching the bloodied and lifeless body of her mother. The second was the blood-soaked Palestinian petition for water rights lying in the dirt.

The angels on Jacob's Ladder had been replaced by demons.

chapter 14

THE BEDROOM WAS dark. Only the small glow of a nightlight allowed me to see my daughter's head peaking out from the covers. Her face was turned to me. The bedtime story was over. As I watched Marie drift into sleep, I noticed that there was the faint contour of a smile on her lips. I gently brushed away some hair that fell over her forehead. Leaning down, I gave her a light kiss on the cheek. For a few moments, I sat still on the side of the bed savoring her innocence.

Murmuring a soft prayer for the countless blessings and graces I had received, I could not help but reflect on those less fortunate. During my work and travels, I was constantly exposed to the courser side of human nature. Whether it was the avarice of white collar businessmen I interviewed, the violence and intolerance I found in some of the countries I visited, or the dire warnings in the law enforcement and intelligence reports that crossed my desk, sometimes it was all simply too much. Particularly in the developing world, I was affected by the cycle of poverty and, in particular, the suffering of blameless children. Some of the scenes I had witnessed broke my heart. Innocent children were suffering for the sins of others, often caught in humanity's vice grip of selfishness and cruelty.

Although it had been many weeks since I had interviewed Ayman in the Jordanian village of Hashimiyya, I could not get his story or the pictures of terror out of my mind. It was like a recycled song one hears over and over again. The catalyst undoubtedly was the non-stop news broadcasts of the latest clashes in the Middle East and the growing international protests. Tensions were rising around the world. I had this anxious sense that this time something was different and I was on edge. Sitting in peaceful silence, I could only compare and contrast horrible images with the angelic vision of my slumbering daughter.

Interrupting my thoughts, Ana slowly opened the bedroom door. She whispered to me that my cell phone was ringing. After giving Marie another kiss, I walked into the kitchen. Ana handed me the still-ringing phone. We both looked at each other and grimaced. *This can't be good.* We had both learned to dread unexpected phone calls in the evening.

"*Pronto*? Hello?" I said in my normal Italian/English greeting.

"Mr. Joe, is that you? This is Farid."

"Farid? I could not mask the surprise in my voice. "It's a pleasure to hear from you. How are you? How is your family?"

"We are fine, thanks be to God."

"I really enjoyed our discussions last week in Dubai."

"I did as well," Farid replied. "That is why I am calling."

"What can I do for you?

"Mr. Joe, I need to see you."

After a pause to collect my thoughts I decided a direct and honest response would be best. "Farid, I can't go back to Dubai so soon. I'm sorry, but I work in a bureaucracy. The trip wouldn't be approved. Is it something we can discuss over the phone?"

"I need to talk to you in person. I understand about not being able to travel to Dubai. But how about meeting me this Sunday at Frankfurt International Airport? I'll pay for your trip if need be."

"Frankfurt? This Sunday? I'll try. But getting approval to travel will still be hard." I thought a few moments before continuing. "I appreciate your offer to reimburse me for my travel, but I can't accept that. I hate to ask you this, but since you are traveling so far, can you come to Rome?"

"No. I have my reasons, which I will explain to you in Frankfurt. As it is, I'm using a safe phone."

"O.K."

"Mr. Joe, you told me in the hotel lobby to reach out to you for help. Something is going on that you need to know about."

"Is it something you would be willing to discuss with somebody from the American Embassy in Abu Dhabi or the consulate in Dubai?"

I could almost hear Farid thinking over the telephone. "No, I will not meet somebody else. Mr. Joe, I know you and trust you. There are some complicated issues involved."

This is something I have to do. "O.K., Farid. This is not going to be easy, but I'll be there."

"Thank you. I'll send you an email with my flight information. The flight arrives early in the morning. I have a long layover."

"I'm familiar with Frankfurt Airport. I'm not sure at what terminal you will be arriving, but there is a Sheraton Hotel near Terminal One, close to the train station. Take the shuttle train and just follow the signs. I have to check flights, but I'll try to get up there early. Let's tentatively plan on meeting Sunday at 1000 hours in the lobby of the Sheraton. I'll confirm in my return email."

"I know the hotel. That will work perfectly."

"Good. I look forward to seeing you again."

"Thank you. Safe travels."

Clicking off my phone, I turned to Ana. She knew the look on my face.

Before I could say a thing she said, "I heard something about Frankfurt this Sunday?"

"I'm sorry, but it looks that way. I have to meet a source. He says it is very important."

Ana's dark brown eyes highlighted her bemused look. "Joe, you probably forgot, but we had plans to have lunch after church this Sunday with the LaFarge family. We were going to go to the Quatro Venti restaurant up in the hills. You know how much the children love to play there."

"I didn't forget, but I have to do this. Everybody else can still go."

"That isn't the issue and you know it. You just came back from two long trips to the Middle East and now you will miss another weekend?"

"Not the whole weekend. I'll be here Saturday, and we can do something with the kids. I think I can fly to Frankfurt Sunday morning and get back by evening. I'm really sorry. This is unexpected for me too."

"But why you? Why Frankfurt? Why can't somebody else meet with this source?"

"Ana, you are always so supportive. Please try to continue to understand. This is something I just have to do."

"Is it really?" she replied. "Or do you want to go to Frankfurt?"

I looked hard at my wife. We had been married for twelve years. She had given me three wonderful children. Standing in front of me in the kitchen, Ana had just finished the dinner dishes while simultaneously helping our two eldest children with their homework. I thought she was just as beautiful now as when we were dating. Ana gave up her promising career to raise children and follow me half way around the world. She had been my steadfast partner and a source of much needed support. I didn't want to disappoint her. I was torn but I knew I had to go.

"I'm sorry. Perhaps you know me better than I know myself," I finally said. "I just feel like something is going on. I sense it. Something in my work is starting to haunt me. I just can't put it into words."

Ana smiled and squeezed my hand.

"Then go," she said.

The next morning I found Dennis LaFarge seated behind his desk.

"Dennis, do you have a few minutes?"

"Sure, Joe, come on in."

I didn't take the open seat in front of his desk, but rather walked over to the window. Looking out, I could see the traffic snarled. Roman traffic was almost always bad. However, I had been in the *citta eterna* long enough to know that the time frame of fall leading to Christmas and New Year's was the worst. It was like a Verdi opera building toward a crescendo finish. To me, the cacophony of noise from the street four stories below was just as unpleasant. The window had a ledge seat on which were stacked some books and memorabilia. Leaning against the ledge, I turned toward Dennis.

"I received a phone call last night from Farid—the hawaladar in Dubai. He wants to talk to me."

"That's good. Maybe now you can document him as a source."

"Perhaps. He still hasn't really provided any operational intelligence, but without a doubt he has great access to information. As you know, he is one of the principal hawaladars in the region. He is very knowledgeable." I looked directly at Dennis so as to try to impress upon him the importance of what I was about to say. "Potentially, this could be a first-rate source. We don't have anybody like him. It could open the doors to underground finance in the Middle East and beyond. The fact that he called me means that I established more credibility and rapport with him in Dubai. I'm encouraged."

Dennis directed his gaze from me to his computer screen. From where I was standing by the window I could see that there was a game of solitaire on his computer. With a tone suggesting he would prefer to contemplate his next computerized flip of cards, he asked, "Any idea what he wants to talk to you about?"

"Not really. But he insists it is important. Apparently, he is going on a trip and will be transiting Frankfurt this Sunday. He wants to meet me there."

Dennis looked up. "Frankfurt? This Sunday? That is highly unusual. What about him coming to Rome?"

"That's exactly what I asked him. But he will not do it. He said he has his reasons. Farid wants to meet me in Frankfurt, and he said he will only deal with me."

Dennis absentmindedly scratched the top of his balding head and then pushed back the chair from his desk. Swiveling to face me, he crossed his legs and folded his hands over his rather large belly. "Joe, it is Susan's call, but I don't think a visit to Frankfurt is going to happen. There are lots of issues involved. The first is funding. We don't have the money. A directive came in from headquarters this morning telling us to stand down on all non-emergency travel until Congress and the administration finally agree on a budget. And you are well aware that Frankfurt is not our territory. HSI has an attaché office in Frankfurt. Let him meet one of our Frankfurt agents."

"Dennis, I can't have him meet another agent. First of all, he is not recruited and not documented. He is a developmental, and I am building a personal relationship with him. Farid said he had important information and so I asked him if he would meet somebody from our embassy or consulate in the UAE. He refused. He said he would only meet with me. Regarding money, a trip to Frankfurt will not cost much. In fact, I can go up and back the same day."

"Outside of Susan's trip to Washington, there is no travel."

"Susan's going to Washington?"

Dennis smiled. "Yeah. They have some end-of-fiscal-year money left, which they have to spend or they'll lose it. Months ago they put together a diversity forum in DC. Susan is one of HSI's diversity directors. Since the money was obligated before October 1, apparently they can spend it. She is leaving next week."

"Unbelievable. What you are telling me is that there is money to send the attaché to a conference in Washington, DC, but there isn't any money to send me on a one-day trip to Frankfurt to meet with a source that perhaps will provide us with important information."

"Joe, you know as well as I do that this is how the government works."

I stood there shaking my head. It was this kind of frustration that often made me consider quitting the government.

"Is it worth my while asking Susan about Frankfurt?"

"Go ahead if you want, but I am quite certain she will tell you what I did. Outside of her trip, there is a freeze on non-essential travel. And source development is considered non-essential."

I moved away from the window. Walking back toward Dennis' desk, I stopped and looked down at him. His face was turned back to his solitaire game. His hand hovering over the mouse, he appeared to be calculating which card to flip. I took those same moments to weigh my options. It didn't take long.

"Dennis, I'm sorry that I am going to miss our get-together Sunday. But Ana and the kids will still be going."

"Huh? Oh, yeah. We're looking forward to it. But where will you be?"

"Frankfurt. It's a weekend. I don't have to take leave. I'm going on a one-day vacation. I'll pay out of my pocket to fly up there."

"You can't do that."

"Why not?"

"It is Frankfurt's territory. We have to clear it with them first."

As I walked out of his office I said, "I'm vacationing in the transit area of the airport. They don't have jurisdiction over that."

chapter 15

MAJEED EXITED HIS shop and walked to a nearby road. He clutched a package under his right arm. The traffic was heavy. Within minutes he caught a bus headed away from the *katchi abadis* slums of west Karachi and toward Port Qasim. He always enjoyed bus rides. Majeed hoped the ride would distract his mind from his thoughts of Rafi's departure.

For Majeed, and most inhabitants of Karachi, a bus ride was an adventure. The buses were hot, crowded, unsafe, adventurous, fast, noisy, and offered a cornucopia of smells. In short, the rides were a microcosm of Karachi. Many of the buses were art galleries on wheels. They boasted ornaments of all sorts, including heavy cable chains and oddly shaped outgrowths of tin in the style of punk rockers' piercings. The metal that covered the buses clanged incessantly, exacerbating the roar of the surrounding traffic. Some buses were painted with floral images or boasted a design of the splashing waters of a fountain or the graceful white wing of a swan flying over the bright blue of a mountain lake. The scenes represented the homeland districts of the bus drivers; they were like rolling tourism advertisements for places like Swat, Chitral, and Mardan.

Like the exterior, the interior of the bus in which Majeed was riding was wildly decorated. On the walls were photos of beloved Bollywood stars, twinkling lights, silver ornaments. A large bouquet of faded orange and pink plastic flowers was fastened to the dashboard. Near the flowers was a set of buttons for different sounds of horns. The driver on Majeed's bus honked the various horns, repeatedly warning pedestrians and other vehicles to get out of his way. Like a musical conductor, the driver chose the sounds to fit the occasion and his mood. However, on this bus the buttons were broken. The bus driver played the horns by holding the exposed wires together.

Most Karachi bus drivers left their home districts and came to the teeming city to make money. Yet with their decorated buses, they were proudly able to bring a bit of home with them. And the more colors and more ornaments a bus had, the more respect the bus driver commanded. A Karachi bus driver, or pilot, as he was sometimes called, was the lord of the bus. The pilot's prestige was enhanced by the measures of speed and cunning he displayed while navigating through Karachi traffic. Arrogance was also on display, as no self-respecting bus driver would stop anywhere but the middle of the road. Any place that potentially had a large number of passengers became a bus stop, regardless of the countless crashes and the car pileups that the bus's sudden stop might cause.

Majeed considered himself fortunate to find an open seat by a window. The wind blowing in his face was an added bonus. Since the air conditioning unit had long since been removed and undoubtedly sold at Chor Bazaar, the only vent for the passengers' sweat (and other assorted bodily odors) was either the exit with no door, or the various windows with no glass. However, Majeed was constantly on his guard because of the occasional fountain of *paan*—or juice from the betel leaf filled with areca nut and seasonings that many Pakistanis chewed—spraying out of the driver's window and marking both the Karachi streets and the sides of the bus.

Majeed also amused himself by watching his fellow male passengers. In a scene that would have been familiar in the American segregationist South of many years ago, the bus was divided. However, in the case of modern Pakistan, it was the sexes that were separated. Since Majeed's seat was directly in front of the women's section, he had an unobstructed view of many of the men's not-so-subtle leering. The women dressed in Egyptian-style *hijabs* and seated in the back of the bus could not help but feel uncomfortable—because of both the stifling heat inside the bus and the penetrating x-ray stares directed their way.

Despite the myriad distractions along the twenty-kilometer ride to Port Qasim, Majeed still could not help but reflect on his actions in support of the Pakistani Taliban and his relationship with his adopted sons. He had never considered himself a *terrorist.* His work kept him far removed from the Taliban's bombings of mosques, marketplaces, government buildings, and religious shrines. Although immensely profitable for the Pakistani Taliban, he never supported the wave of cruel kidnappings in the country. Religious extremists had escalated their attacks over the years, from the inner security cordon of a Benazir Bhutto rally to the army's general headquarters in Rawalpindi. Increasingly, the attacks were sectarian—more violent and more brutal. The historical distrust between Sunni and Shia, between Sunni sects, and between tribes was playing itself out on the streets of Karachi. Rival Muslim groups called each other heretics and increasingly used the tenet of *takfirism* to condemn and eliminate their rivals. In his few moments of reflection, Majeed knew that his financing and money-laundering facilitated many of those attacks. As much as he told himself he regretted the lost lives, he continued to believe in the *takfiri* notion that the end justifies the means. Majeed sincerely believed that his life's work and overall cause was noble—the eventual implementation of a worldwide Sunni Islamic caliphate based on *Sharia* law. To this end, Majeed simply thought of himself as humble servant of Allah: an enabler, a businessman, a financier, and a bookkeeper.

The bouncing, jarring, malodorous bus ride did not distract Majeed from his troubled thoughts. He was certain that his life was about to radically change. The Pakistani Taliban was embarking on an irreversible path. The countdown had begun. He knew the shipment containing the dirty bomb had already left port. He realized full well the enormity of Rafi's mission. And he could not escape thoughts of his adopted son's impending martyrdom.

Despite the Pakistani Taliban's leadership insistence on strict secrecy, they finally acquiesced to his repeated appeals to see Rafi before his departure. And since Majeed's financing and organizational skills had facilitated much of the operation, he knew just where to find his son. For the last few days, Rafi had been staying in a Taliban safehouse in Port Qasim, Pakistan's second busiest port. It was established during the 1970s to relieve the congestion of the Port of Karachi and also to facilitate massive imports of raw materials for steel production by the nearby steel mill. The port was constructed in an old channel of the Indus River. The safehouse was located in an industrial zone.

Despite the almost indecipherable routing and numerous interim stops, the bus in which he was riding headed toward Port Qasim. As it approached his destination, Majeed kept looking out the window, trying to orient himself to his surroundings and determine when he should exit. The decision was made for him when he heard a *thump-thump* on the roof of the bus. It was a signal from one of the passengers seated or sprawled on the roof that he wanted the bus to stop. As the bus came to a standstill, the passenger climbed down using Majeed's window as a toehold. A quick exchange with his fellow passenger revealed that Majeed should likewise exit. Once out of the bus, he again found good fortune. Hailing a passing taxi, he was soon at the entrance of the nondescript safehouse marked only by a rusted sign that read "Metal Works."

Without waiting for a response to his knock on the corrugated tin door, Majeed entered. He immediately spotted Rafi on the other side of the almost barren warehouse. He was stripped to his T-shirt and running pants and doing bench presses. Majeed waited until Rafi lowered the dumbbells.

"Rafi, my son, a*salaam alykum.*"

Rafi immediately sat up on the bench and rubbed the sweat from his eyes. Realizing the greeting was from Majeed, the initial puzzled look vanished from his face and was immediately replaced by a broad smile. Rafi stood and slightly bowed. He placed his right hand over his heart in a sign of affection and respect. Both men hurried toward the other and embraced.

"And peace be with you, Father. Thank you for coming," Rafi said warmly. "I was not sure if I would see you again."

"Are you alone?" Majeed whispered.

"Yes," Rafi replied in a normal tone of voice. "I assume you know what is happening. There have been a few visitors from the

Shura over the last two days. I understand they will return this evening and again tomorrow."

"I am aware of the logistics." Majeed swallowed hard. "I'm sorry my visit was delayed. I was told not to see you. They finally relented."

Rafi stepped away from his father and wiped the perspiration from his face with an old towel that was haphazardly draped over the bench.

"I'm sorry I cannot offer you anything. I only have water. I walk to the local tea shop for tea and snacks."

Majeed smiled. He presented Rafi with a package wrapped in paper and secured in twine that he had carried with him on the bus from the *katchi abadis.* "I brought you some *dal* and rice and *sohan halwa.* I remember it has been your favorite meal since you were a boy."

This time it was Rafi's turn to smile. "You remember? Thank you. I will particularly enjoy the sweet. It is still my favorite."

Rafi took his father by the arm and led him to a carpet in a far corner of the warehouse. The rest of the warehouse floor was bare cement stained with grease or colored with flecked paint in places. Seated on the carpet and reclining against pillows propped up by a wall of peeling plaster, they began to speak of things in a way they had in the old days. For a long while, no mention was made of the impending mission. Finally, Rafi could not hold the questions burning inside him any longer.

"Father, forgive me but I must ask you, how long have you known of this? Was this planned from the beginning? Was our eventual martyrdom the reason why you adopted Tariq and I?"

For a moment, Majeed felt much older than his years. Rafi could easily read the pain and hurt in his eyes. He had not previously seen this emotion in his father.

"My son, I did not know this was going to happen. I was as surprised as you must have been when I was told of your selection. Of course, I am very proud of you. It is an honor to be chosen to conduct an operation of this magnitude. You have the qualifications they were looking for." Majeed paused to collect his thoughts and looked out across the vacant warehouse. His eyes then returned to Rafi. "As you know, I had big plans for both you and Tariq. However, my personal plans are not important now. If you become a martyr, you will be in paradise. *Inshallah*, I will follow." Lowering both his voice and his eyes he added, "But selfishly, I wish they would have picked someone else."

Rafi grasped his father's hands in his. Simultaneous emotions of relief and affection seemed to flood back into him. With a voice choked with feeling, he finally managed to say, "Father, thank you. That is what I needed to hear."

For long minutes nothing more was said. Majeed was glad that his thick glasses covered his eyes. He was surprised by the depth of his feelings. Looking down at his outstretched hands framed with large gold rings, he murmured a prayer to Allah and then resumed the role of bookkeeper. "Do you have everything you need?"

"Yes. I've been given a clean passport with a visa. I also have credit cards and plenty of euros and dollars. A technician has explained the dirty bomb, and I will be meeting with an explosives expert here who will brief me on the options for detonation."

"When do you leave?"

"In two days. They gave me round-trip tickets." Rafi smiled at the irony.

"That is to lessen scrutiny of your travels," Majeed said knowingly. "But only Allah knows. Maybe you will be coming back."

"Only if it is the will of Allah. Yet if the operation is successful and I survive, I will not soon return to Pakistan. It is far too risky." As an afterthought he added, "Do you think they will respond?"

"What can they do? The crusaders already invaded Afghanistan and Iraq." Majeed chuckled. "They are not going to do that again." And in a more serious tone he added, "They will never invade Pakistan. They are not that stupid."

"What about the shipment? Are you confident it will not be detected?'

"It already left the Port of Karachi. It will arrive in Naples on the twentieth of November."

"I'll be there on the fifteenth," Rafi interjected. "That will give us plenty of time to prepare."

"I'm very confident that the container will be easily cleared. I used my Chinese contacts—the same ones that facilitate our cigarette trade here in Pakistan."

"But how will that help us in Naples?"

"Chinese gangs control much of the port operations, particularly the black market. Of course, they don't know what is in the shipment, but by the amount of money that we paid them they realize its importance. They guaranteed the container will not be inspected."

Rafi shook his head and looked at his adoptive father with even more admiration. "I continue to be amazed with your contacts."

"World trade is becoming increasingly intertwined. So is the international black market."

"I still have much to learn."

"I'm sure they already provided copies of the shipping documents, including the bill of lading, insurance, and invoices."

"Yes. I have everything. All the documents are in order."

Majeed looked tenderly at his son. He wanted to continue to give guidance. "I insisted that the shipment be made by an importer-exporter who regularly conducts business with Italy. It will lessen scrutiny."

"Yes, thank you. I was told that those involved have helped us in the past. I don't know any further details."

"That is as it should be. I do not know the specifics of this operation, but from a financial and logistics perspective, I am confident of success."

"Of course, it is as Allah wills, but if you are confident then so am I." Rafi slowly got up from the carpet. He walked in a small circle in part to stretch his legs and also to focus his mind. Majeed quietly let him think.

"Father, what of our business? Who will look after our dealings? What about our contacts in Dubai and elsewhere?"

"Rafi, you are young. That is a blessing and a curse. Let me give you one final lesson," Majeed said softly, "Nobody is irreplaceable." As he spoke with downcast eyes, he noticed his hands with the matching gold rings trembling.

Rafi nodded. "Tariq. Use him." He paused before continuing. "Does he know any of this?"

"No. Only a very few are aware of this operation. I'll tell Tariq you are on a long business trip. When and if the truth comes out, I'll explain everything to him. He will be proud. He will understand."

"Please tell him that I truly feel he is my brother."

Majeed silently nodded. He looked with affection at one of his two adopted sons. He saw only peace, calm, and resignation. Majeed wondered if perhaps he had trained him too well.

chapter 16

I SPOTTED FARID as soon as I entered the lobby of the hotel. Wearing dress slacks and a sweater, his appearance was much different from what it was when I had last seen him in the spicy warmth of Dubai. Yet despite the long overnight flight, his dark eyes somehow maintained the same sparkle. I grasped his outstretched hand.

"Mr. Joe, it is wonderful to see you again. Thank you so much for meeting me in Frankfurt."

"It is my pleasure. I look forward to our conversation. When did you get in?"

"A few hours ago. My flight doesn't leave until 1500 hours, so we have plenty of time. How was your trip from Rome?"

"Uneventful, on time, and quick—just the way I like to fly," I replied with a grin.

Farid turned and pointed toward the far end of the hotel. "I saw a café in the lobby underneath that large glass dome. I'm sure you would enjoy some coffee and a pastry after your flight. It looks like a good place to talk."

Within a few minutes, we were seated comfortably around a small table toward the back of the café. Perhaps because it was a Sunday morning, there were not many other customers. Shortly after the exchange of additional pleasantries and obligatory inquiries about families, the waitress returned to our table with our order of cappuccinos and apple strudel. Farid slowly stirred sugar into the frothy coffee.

"Thank you again for meeting me. I know this was a bit of an inconvenience."

"Bureaucracies are sometimes an inconvenience. You're not," I replied and then waited for him to continue.

Putting down the spoon, Farid said "Do you remember, when we last spoke in your hotel in Dubai, how you said that we need to try to keep the world safe for our children?"

"Yes, I do. I sincerely believe that."

"Our children . . . well, that is why I called you." Farid shifted in his chair. "A few weeks ago I didn't have enough information. I still don't have the complete picture. But the pieces I have been able to put together and the conversations I hear are increasingly troubling."

"Please, continue."

Farid looked closely at me. "Mr. Joe, I am not trying to be dramatic, but I must be assured that the information I provide will not be publicly released and associated with me. The safety of my family, my business, and my own life could be in jeopardy." He looked at me hard. "This is very real."

I folded my hands on the top of the table and fixed my eyes on his. "Farid, I do not know what you will tell me. However, I promise to safeguard any information you give. The information will not be publicly released. And within government reporting circles, your name will be protected." I paused a moment to give him time to think. "I have an idea. Why don't you tell me what you can and then we will discuss how to go forward?"

There was a long pause. "As you said, 'what I can.'" Farid swallowed hard. "Mr. Joe, you know that my business is doing well. In order for that to happen in Dubai, and for that matter almost anywhere in the Middle East, one must be well connected. I admit I have benefitted from *wasta.*"

"As I understand the expression *wasta* basically means influence through high-level connections."

"Exactly. In my case, my Father was sponsored by a member of Dubai's ruling family. I've worked hard to maintain that sponsorship and nurture a mutually beneficial relationship."

"I understand."

"Because of the nature of my business, I also maintain close ties with the Iranian expatriate community in Dubai. I also deal with many from South Asia and other locations that are involved with . . . what is the term that you use, underground finance?"

"In bureaucratic jargon, sometimes we say underground finance, other times parallel banking, underground banking, or informal value-transfer systems. Sometimes my colleagues who don't know better lump everything together and say *hawala*."

Farid laughed. "I know. Hawala is an easy label, and it gets blamed for everything."

"So you are concerned about a specific hawala transaction?"

"Before I answer that, I remember when we spoke in my office I gave you an illustration of how hawala works, using the example of a guest worker in Dubai wanting to support a family member in Afghanistan."

"Yes, I remember. It was a good example of how hawala can be the poor man's banking system."

"Exactly. But say, for example, somebody wants to launder or legalize black money in Pakistan or finance an illegal activity."

"Go on."

"Often times they use fictitious exports or invoice manipulation."

"That is something that customs services around the world observe. We talked about that a little bit."

"It is very common in Pakistan for unscrupulous businessmen, criminals, and even terrorist financiers to show fake export transactions to the government in order to claim duty drawbacks. But they don't really trade anything. For example, if a person has a lot of black money in Pakistan and he wants to legalize it, the first step is to establish a fake company in Dubai or any other international location, to show that foreign buyers are interested in purchasing Pakistani products."

"I understand."

"I know you are aware of false invoicing. An item worth fifty dollars could be easily shown as being worth one hundred dollars or more on the same invoice. So a fifty-dollar-per-unit price is sent to the foreign buyer through hawala/hundi, and export proceeds that reflect a one-hundred-dollar-per-unit price are received through normal banking channels."

Listening to Farid, I kept wondering where he was going with his explanation. But I knew from many conversations in the Middle East that direct explanations are often not forthcoming.

"In the next phase of the transaction," Farid continued, "documents are prepared stating that exports have been made to the foreign buyer. The owner of the foreign buyer company bogusly established in Dubai, Frankfurt, Rome, New York, or any foreign location is actually working with the exporter in Pakistan. The actual exported goods might be inexpensive or of low quality, having little value. On the other hand, the declared exports on the accompanying documentation reflect high quality and price. The goods are over-invoiced. By showing exports in the fraudulently prepared documents, the business transactions and foreign exchange earned from such exports become legal. So their billions of rupees in black money are now legal."

"Farid, I appreciate the explanation, but what are you trying to tell me? You didn't ask me to meet you in Frankfurt to discuss fraudulent trading."

"Only when that trading masks threats to our children."

"What specifically do you mean?"

"Mr. Joe, I cannot give you the specifics I know you want. I cannot, as you say, connect all the dots."

"Then, as I said earlier, tell me what you can."

Farid paused to sip his coffee and again swallowed hard. "A few weeks ago, I was visited by a young Pashtu businessman from Karachi. His name is Rafi Durrani. I've done business with him for a few years. I've also recently started some additional business with his father Majeed and his brother Tariq. They have a Karachi import-export trading company they call Oyster Rocks. It is common knowledge in my circles that Majeed and his sons are involved with financing and money-laundering for the Pakistani Taliban."

"Do you mind if I take notes?"

"No, in fact I wrote out the names for you." Farid smiled and reached into his shirt pocket. He handed me a piece of paper with the names typed. "I know how hard foreign names can be for Americans."

I smiled appreciatively. "Thank you. I can tell you are an excellent businessman."

Farid ignored the compliment. "As I said, I've known Rafi for a few years. He is a very impressive individual—very smart and energetic. We come from different worlds but have become friends. In part because of that it is hard to betray confidences."

"I understand, but please tell me what you can."

"Well, on the last few visits and communications I can only describe his actions as peculiar."

"What do you mean?"

"Instead of his normal upbeat self he was very depressed. Normally, Rafi is apolitical. He is just concerned about business. Now he talks incessantly about the Palestinian demonstrations, the West' oppression of the Middle East and South Asia, and how it is time to strike back."

"Strike? Anything else?"

"He said not to be surprised if I hear something in the news about a weapon of mass destruction."

"What?"

"That's right. That is why I am talking to you. I'm worried about what might happen. The world is a tinderbox right now. If something should happen, I don't want this on my conscience."

I looked directly at Farid. "This is very important," I said slowly. "Did this Rafi contact of yours give any additional information or details about this weapon of mass destruction? Do you know what kind—chemical, biological, nuclear?

"No, he didn't. I wish I had more specifics for you."

"What makes you think he wasn't just expressing frustration? Many people say things they don't really mean."

"I know that. But I am very troubled by his demeanor. He acted very differently from the man I have come to know. I cannot stop thinking about that conversation and about his subsequent demeanor. It haunts me. I'm certain something is going to happen."

I put down my pen and folded my hands on the top of the table. "In America we have the expression that something like that is a *gut feeling*."

"Gut feeling? Like stomach? Oh, I understand. Exactly. What makes things worse for me is that I am also hearing worrying things from some of my other contacts."

"For example?"

"The West seems to think that the leaders of the Taliban are just sitting in mountainous caves up along the Afghan-Pakistan border. Undoubtedly some of them are. But some of them live quite opulently. Some of them are in Karachi, Dubai, and other cities in the region."

"Please give me specifics."

"Mr. Joe, I'm sorry, but I told you that I would tell you only what I can. I have to be very careful. That is why I insisted on meeting you here in Frankfurt."

"Isn't there anything else you can tell me? In order to take action, I need something tangible. Something more than a gut feeling."

Farid's right hand reached for his breast pocket and then abruptly stopped in mid-air. He chuckled. "I desperately need a smoke, but it is not allowed here." Taking another sip of his coffee he continued, "As I said, a businessman involved in transferring money and value in the Middle East and South Asia hears many things."

"Go on."

"Well, I can tell you a bit more about my conversation with Rafi."

"Please."

"He mentioned that he was going to travel to Italy shortly on a business trip."

"Italy?"

"Exactly. That's one of the reasons why we are talking. Of course, you also know that the G-20 will be meeting in Rome in about ten days."

There was a long pause. My mind raced as the magnitude of what my source had just said hit me. Things started to fall into place.

My eyes locked onto Farid. "Oh, my God," I finally gasped. "The leaders of the most important economic countries of the world will be there . . . including the President of the United States."

Farid lowered his eyes and, half in prayer, whispered, "May Allah have mercy on us all." He looked up and then used the napkin that was folded in his lap to wipe the perspiration from his forehead. The natural light in the atrium café reflected off his face. His worry visible, I knew his concern was genuine. Farid continued, "For the last two weeks I kept telling myself that my suspicions might be nothing. I hope I am wrong but I fear not. I am doing very well in business in large part because I have a number of important contacts and I'm a good judge of people. If something happens, I don't want this hanging over my head. I had to tell somebody."

Half to myself and half to Farid, I said, "My family is in Rome."

"I know."

My thoughts still swirling, sorting out the professional and personal implications, I noticed I continued to speak very softly. "I'm going to be assisting the Secret Service with protection when the president visits Rome. I was asked to help the Presidential Protective Detail. With a visit of this magnitude, they are going to need additional people."

"Mr. Joe, I'm sorry."

"I've got to alert some people. Both strategically and tactically this makes sense. We always believed our adversaries would strike with weapons of mass destruction if they had an opportunity—if they could somehow get their hands on them." Thinking of current events I added, "But assuming they actually have such weapons, why now? The worldwide demonstrations are peaceful in nature. There is a sense that maybe this time peace will finally come to Israel and Palestine."

"Mr. Joe, don't you understand? That is precisely why this might happen. The crazy people, the militants, the *takfiris* don't want peace. Real peace is a threat to their political objectives, as well as their power-grabs and money-making operations. They perceive Gandhi-like nonviolence as a danger that must be stopped."

I nodded. Farid continued, "Al Qaeda's and the Taliban's Islamic radicalism isn't a result of the Soviet-Afghan war. It isn't a byproduct of the Israeli-Palestinian confrontation. It isn't about avenging the crusades. It's organized crime. Radicalism is also the most recent violent reaction to the modernization of the Muslim Middle East and South Asia. Many do not want that to happen."

"I believe what you are telling me."

"There is another reason I am speaking to you. You understand that the core tenants of Islam are justice, tolerance, and charity. The great majority of Muslims are not terrorists, but good and simple people."

"I personally know many Muslims and have traveled frequently to Islamic lands. I truly believe that."

Farid nodded. "Many of our countries are stricken with poverty and backwardness because of the lack of education and because of corruption among our ruling elites. This exacerbates the radicalism."

I knew I had to refocus the conversation. "Farid, I agree with what you say. But we have an immediate issue that we must confront. I will be very candid with you. Bureaucratically speaking, if I am going to sound the alarm, I have to have something more concrete to work with. I'm going to also have to answer a lot of pointed questions that I don't have answers to."

"Like what?"

"Well, a number of questions come immediately to mind. For one thing, people will ask me why we should believe somebody who facilitates funding for the Taliban."

"Mr. Joe, that is also one of the reasons why I am talking to you. You understand hawala." Farid paused. "Don't you have an American legal expression, *willful blindness*?"

"Yes."

"I can understand how outsiders accuse my colleagues and I in Dubai and elsewhere of willingly closing our eyes to suspicious transactions. But I don't really know or care if we provide trade goods such as cement, cigarettes, or cars that are sent into Afghanistan and Pakistan as part of counter-valuing hawala transactions. That is what we do. That is our business. Value transfer is part of what you yourself once said is the "poor man's banking system."

"Farid, I've gotten a lot of information over the years from a lot of different people. Not infrequently businessmen try to give me information to discredit their business rivals. I don't believe that is happening here, but I can see how others might believe that."

Farid's face reddened. "Mr. Joe, I'm not telling you these things to punish a business rival. By coming forward and talking to an American official, I have more to lose than anybody. Besides, who am I punishing? Rafi Durrani and his family's business are located in Karachi. He isn't a rival. I'm making money from working with him. And I have not given you the names and positions of other contacts because . . . you just have to trust me. I can't."

"I know this is hard, but these questions are going to pale in comparison to the hard questions I am going to get." I paused. I knew I had to get the hardest question of all on the table. "Would you be willing to meet with another American official to discuss these allegations? There might be a desire to administer a polygraph."

"A lie-detector test?" Farid replied indignantly. "Do you think I am making this up?"

I slowly shook my head. "I don't. I trust you, but I also know how the system works. The bureaucracies are filled with people who sit behind their desks and second-guess others. Somebody could say, for example, that you are fabricating information for your own personal reasons—that you want money."

"I don't want money," he almost shouted. "Do you think I would risk everything for a few dollars? That is ridiculous."

Through the corner of my eye I saw customers at a nearby table looking in our direction. I smiled and motioned with my hands for Farid to keep his voice low. "I know it is ridiculous, but accusations and misunderstandings are likely to happen. HSI doesn't normally use polygraphs, but this is extremely important. Other agencies will be involved. It would really help if I reported that you would agree to meet with another official and, if necessary, take a polygraph." I knew I was pushing him. But I also knew I had to ask.

For long moments Farid was silent. I could tell he was both seething inside and calculating.

"Mr. Joe, the answer is no. I will not meet with anybody else. I reported this information at great risk to myself, my family, and my business. I reported it to you because I trust you and because I know you understand many of the issues involved." He paused and then continued, "I have not told you where I am going and how long I will be away from Dubai. I know you can find out. But I promise you if I am approached by an American official during my travels or upon my return by local officials, I will deny this conversation ever took place."

The obligatory question had caused the expected damage. Now I knew I had to start to repair the relationship. "Farid, I understand your feelings. I respect you and admire the courage it took to come forward with this information. I am personally grateful for the information you provided and so is my country. But you have to understand; I work in a bureaucracy and I have to ask bureaucratic questions." I smiled and added, "I laugh when I see James Bond movies or TV shows that solve complex international crimes within twenty-four hours. The real world is not like that." I could see Farid begin to relax a little bit. "Bureaucracies are a fact of life," I continued. "And in my government the information that you are reporting to me overlaps many different agencies and departments. This is going to be complicated."

"I understand, but I will not meet with other officials," he firmly replied.

"O.K. But from an investigative point of view, I need more. The names you provided are a start. Is there anything else you can tell me regarding Rafi and his business? Where can we begin to focus our inquiries?"

The cappuccino and strudel had long since disappeared. Farid shifted in his chair. His dark brown eyes began to squint. I could not tell whether he was lost in thought or if he was squinting from the morning sunlight filling the atrium café. He finally clasped his hands on his placemat and looked at me intently. "I wrote what I know about Rafi and his business on that piece of paper. For example, his approximate age."

"That's helpful, but isn't there something else you can add?"

Farid paused before he said, "Take a look at Italy's trade of scrap metal and scrap gold from Pakistan."

"What do you mean?"

"Remember, any commodity can be used in counter-valuation. An examination of trade can be the back door to underground finance such as hawala."

"Yes," I said and once again began taking notes.

"In money-laundering I know you use the expression *follow the money.*"

"Actually that saying was first coined by an informant during our Watergate scandal back in the 1970s. By following the money trail, investigative journalists brought down the presidency of Richard Nixon."

Farid stared straight into my eyes. "Mr. Joe, this time follow the value trail."

chapter 17

"Joe, where is the US Customs violation? Where is the US Immigration violation? What is the actual nexus to the US border here?"

Dennis practically shouted his rapid-fire questions at me. He clutched the report of my meeting with Farid in his right hand. His left hand was leaning on my desk and his reddened face was far too close to mine. "Do I have to remind you that you work for DHS/ICE? You are not an intelligence officer, and you are not working for the Secret Service. As much as you might disagree, we do not do this kind of thing."

Trying to maintain a calm exterior, I replied, "Dennis, I do not disagree with you. However, you have to understand that I did not actively seek this information. In the course of my HSI duties, I happened upon it. The source contacted me when I was here in Rome. I had no idea what he might report. But it was exactly because of my HSI duties I felt I had to go up to Frankfurt and talk with him."

Dennis was still furious. Despite his cutting words, I didn't believe he was as upset with me for collecting information that was not part of HSI's mandate as for the fact that I had gone around him and Susan by going on my own time and dime to meet with Farid.

"In any event, how can we trust this guy? He has more than likely facilitated the transfer of technology from the US to Iran in violation of our sanctions. Even worse than that, according to your own report he has apparently been working with financiers for the

Taliban. He paused for emphasis and then continued in a scathing tone of voice, "Joe, in case you forgot, the Taliban is killing US and coalition forces."

That was too much. I got up from my desk and faced him directly. "Dennis, back off. What are you insinuating?"

Returning my glare he said, "We really do not know who this guy is . . . or his true motivation for giving you this information."

"Again, I don't disagree. But we can't ignore the information either."

"I'm not so sure about that."

"What?" I asked incredulously.

"I exchanged some emails with Susan this morning."

"Dennis," I interrupted. "I hope you used a secure message system. That information is highly sensitive."

Ignoring my admonition, he continued. "In fact, Susan is more upset than I am. She is insistent that you focus on ICE work. ICE pays your salary. She does not want you going around playing James Bond."

"Dennis, I've worked for the government for a long time. I didn't expect a pat on the back upon my return, but I thought management would at least recognize the potential importance of this information."

That seemed to quiet him. "I recognize this information has to be reported."

That was the opening I was waiting for. "Of course, I'll do what you and Susan wish, but this is what I believe we should do. First of all, I think we should keep the reporting of this interview completely out of HSI channels. For now, I'm not going to write an electronic report of the interview with Farid. The memorandum you have documents the interview. Next, I would like to brief the Secret Service attaché. With the president coming to Rome, this is their jurisdiction. I think we should let them decide what to do."

"I'm O.K. with that," he replied, "but what about the Bureau?"

Dennis and I both knew that the Federal Bureau of Investigation was the eight-hundred-pound gorilla that hovered over any bureaucratic discussion over the jurisdiction of terror finance.

Because of the nature of US Customs Service's, and now ICE's, work, on numerous occasions investigators uncovered criminal networks that had ties to the possible funding of terror. Over the years, the issue had proven divisive. Bureaucratic squabbling reached its peak after September 11. Both the FBI and the newly created ICE established competing terror finance task forces. The task forces ended up bickering over dominance of investigative leads, financial intelligence, informants, personnel, and cases. The turf wars were finally settled via the National Security Council when in May, 2003, a memorandum of agreement was signed between the Department of Justice and the new Department of Homeland Security giving the FBI primacy of investigations and operations relating to terror finance. From that point on, if an ICE agent happened upon a possible investigative lead into terror finance, he or she was bound to turn it over to the Bureau. Needless to say, the edict proved unpopular with both ICE management and the troops. Why should ICE spend time, resources, and personnel on an investigation that might have ties to terrorism finance if the case could be turned over to the Bureau? The end result was that possible investigations into terror finance were stopped—negating possible trails to terrorist acts and organizations.

"Of course I'll do what you want, but Farid's information is thus far unsubstantiated. In my opinion, turning over this raw information to the Bureau is premature. I think we should defer to the Secret Service regarding the further dissemination of the information."

"I'll check with Susan, but I agree. By the way, aren't you going to be working with the Secret Service when the president comes to Rome?"

It was the first time during the conversation with Dennis that I smiled. "I worked presidential foreign visits years ago when I was in the Secret Service. They are manpower-intensive. They are going to need all the post-standers they can find—particularly now. If they still want me, I would like to help out."

"That's fine with Susan and me," Dennis said with a wave of his hand. "But one more thing. Are you going to document Farid as a source of information?"

"That's a good question . . . he isn't really a formally recruited source. But if I don't document him and other agencies get wind of what is going on, they could move in . . . not that documenting him as a HSI source would stop them."

We both chuckled. There was a fierce competition among the various law enforcement and intelligence agencies over good human reporting sources. It was not uncommon for one agency to pinch off an informant from another. Moreover, certain CIA chiefs of station felt that if ICE, DEA, FBI, or even the US military met an informant in "their country," they wanted to know about it. There had been various proposals over the years to form a central source registry for the intelligence, law enforcement, and military communities. In theory, the idea of stopping duplication of effort and preventing recruitment efforts against the same target was valid. It would also stop potential sources shopping information from one agency to the other looking for the best "deal." However, everybody knew that much of the posturing over sources of information or human informants was simply another manifestation of bureaucratic turf battles. Despite various post-September 11 reforms, bureaucratic posturing and games were still being played.

"One other thing," I continued, "the information in this report will probably end up going interagency. I've got to protect Farid by issuing him a source number."

"Perhaps you're right," replied Dennis in a tone that indicated he was thinking out loud, "but we might never see or hear from Farid again."

"That's very true."

"Besides, having him as a documented HSI source may or may not work in our best interests. As this thing develops, I think we should wait and see which way the wind blows." Dennis almost looked embarrassed as we both heard what came out of his mouth.

The conversation paused. I decided to ignore his indiscretion. Finally I said, "Let me get a source number for Farid. I'll create a developmental file. I'll include the report I wrote from Dubai and the memorandum about our meeting in Frankfurt. If we develop additional information, I'll also add it to the file. I'll put everything in the safe with the other source folders." I paused and looked at my memorandum of the interview that Dennis was still holding in his hand. My eyes returned to Dennis. "I gave him my word that I would protect his identify and the information he provided."

Dennis nodded.

"Is that O.K.?" I wanted him to audibly acknowledge what I had proposed.

"Yes, that's fine. Issue him a source number. Depending on what happens, we can always say he isn't a real source but just a developmental." He turned and left my office.

As I watched him go out the door, I started to shake my head. Immediately I sat down and began to type a "memorandum to file." I had spent many years in government bureaucracies. I knew all too well the importance of covering myself by putting everything in writing, just in case something controversial developed. And in this case I believed management's response to Farid's information could later receive close scrutiny. I was still seething inside. Writing the memorandum helped me vent. I could not believe management had told me in effect not to waste my time reporting information about a possible weapon of mass destruction because there was no nexus to the United States. The premise was absurd. Even the President of the United States might be a target. Dennis's nonchalant attitude about operational security infuriated me. Lost in my thoughts, I didn't hear Terri enter the room.

"Joe, are you O.K.?" she asked.

I looked up from my keyboard. "I'm fine. Did you hear what happened?"

"I couldn't help but hear. Dennis closed the door, but your voices went right through the wall into my office."

"I can't believe Dennis and Susan are not able to get past their narrow interests. I have no idea if the information the source gave me is true or not, but it deserves attention."

"I don't know the details—and I'm not sure I want to know," responded Terri. She seemed a bit shaken.

"You shouldn't know. But actually I am glad that you overheard us. I'm writing a memorandum to the file right now documenting the conversation I just had with Dennis. I'm going to print it out, sign, and date it. It will not be on the office hard drive. If this thing blows up, I want there to be a contemporaneous record. You are my witness that I am writing this memorandum immediately after the conversation."

Terri nodded.

"When is Susan getting back from DC?"

"She'll be back by the end of next week. She has that diversity conference and then she is taking some personal leave. However, I spoke to her this morning and she said she definitely will be back here by the time of the G-20 meeting and the presidential visit. The scuttlebutt going around the embassy is that the president will pay a courtesy visit and meet embassy country team staff. Susan wants to be here for that."

"But of course," I said with a roll of my eyes. "I'm not sure if her being away is good or bad. In any event, I'm going to finish this memo and then go downstairs and talk to the Secret Service attaché."

The Secret Service was one floor below the office of the ICE attaché. With the exception of the FBI's legal attaché or Legatt, representatives of American law enforcement agencies were located in the same annex building of the American embassy. The Legatt was located in the main embassy building. The close proximity aided both camaraderie and the coordination of cases. After ringing the buzzer to the office, the office secretary ushered me into a small reception area decorated with framed photos and memorabilia highlighting the service's twin missions of investigations and protection. The displays brought back fond memories. Within a few minutes, I was in the office of the Secret Service Attaché Frank Fortuna. Frank and I knew each other from the days when we were both hump post-standers assigned to the Washington, DC field office. He greeted me with a warm handshake and a big grin.

"Joe, I thought you might be paying me a visit. Are you down here politicking for a good post standing assignment for the POTUS visit?"

"Maybe you can assign me a kitchen post," I said smiling. "Remember that time in the Washington Hilton when we both had the kitchen?"

"Oh I remember," he said. "Great food! They let us eat our fill when the event was over." Frank's face turned serious. "Dennis was just down here about an hour ago. He gave me a copy of your interview of the Iranian hawaladar in Frankfurt."

I slowly shook my head. "I thought he wanted me to tell you. I shouldn't be surprised he came down here first. But it doesn't matter. I'm glad you already had a chance to see it. I was bringing you a copy myself." I placed a plain folder on his desk.

"Thanks Joe."

"I know you need Farid's identifiers. But please if you have to disseminate the report in your channels refer to him by using the source number that was just issued. The report in the folder incorporates the use of the number."

"Of course. Before we go any further, Roy Williams of the Intelligence Division is here. He is part of the PPD advance team. Do you know him?"

"Maybe I'll recognize his face but I don't recall the name."

"Roy's very good. He's in Pete Gonzalez's office right now reading your report. Let me call him in."

Prior to a presidential visit overseas, a small group of agents and technicians arrive in the host country about ten days in advance of the visit. They work with the embassy, host country officials – including their security counterparts, and study all aspects of security, logistics, communications, and transportation. The advance team conducts specific site surveys of locations the president and other protectees are going to visit. Manpower, communication, and equipment needs are assessed. Hospitals and evacuation routes for emergencies are also identified. Most of the advance team consists of individuals from the Presidential Protective Division or PPD but it is very common for specialists outside the division to accompany the advance team as well – particularly to a nice location such as Rome. The advance team always has at least a few people that work to coordinate intelligence at the host location. They also help bring together the interagency threat assessment for the visit.

The door opened and a very big man walked in. He had the look, bearing, and firm handshake of a football linebacker. "Hi Joe. I'm Roy. Good to meet you. I've heard great things about you."

"You've heard great things even though I left the service?" I responded with a laugh.

"By all accounts you're doing well in HSI. I'm happy for you."

"I enjoyed the SS. But I knew I couldn't make a career out of it. Anyway, Customs and now HSI have been good to me. And this latest assignment in Rome has been a lot of fun. I have really enjoyed the work and most of the travels."

"You mean you aren't spending all of your time sipping espresso on the Via Veneto?"

"Not quite."

"I know Roy has a meeting in a few minutes with the rest of the advance team," Frank interjected. "I suggest we find time to socialize later on over a beer. Roy, did you read Joe's report? Do you have any questions for him?"

"Joe, the report was comprehensive. Thank you. But between us, momentarily forget what is written in your report and I'll also forget what Dennis told me. This guy, Farid, what do you think of him?"

I could feel my face starting to burn when I heard the mention of Dennis. Gathering myself I said, "I don't know what Dennis told you but I'm playing it straight with you. In my professional opinion, I think we have to take what Farid says very seriously. I'm not sure of his true motivation but I think I can read people pretty well. Do I think he is holding back additional information? Yes. Do I think he is telling the truth? Also, yes." Roy nodded his head. I continued. "That might seem like a contradiction but as you know many sources hold back."

"In your report, you mentioned a number of reasons why we could also be skeptical of his reporting," Roy said. "You also did a good job of refuting the possible allegations. However, there is one point that you missed."

"What's that?"

"We don't really know who this Farid is. We are going to try to find out. However, we do know he is Iranian. Could this possibly be misinformation from the Iranian intelligence services? I've seen a lot of troubling reports of Iran using just this kind of subterfuge."

I paused before answering. "Roy, that's a good point. I admit I hadn't thought of it. But it isn't just the Iranians that do that kind of thing. We've been known to do a bit of it ourselves." Everybody shared a quiet laugh. "Deception and scheming are very common in Islam, Sunni and Shia alike. I believe the term is *al makr.*"

Roy nodded. "I can't even hypothesize why the Iranians might want to plant this type of information."

"Well not many people realize that Iran - a majority Shiite country - and the Sunni Taliban almost went to war with one another in the late 1990s. So there is no love lost between the groups. At the same time, there are reports that the Iranians are providing arms to the Taliban. In that part of the world, the history is long and the culture is strong. Besides, there are a lot of independent actors. Groups often do their own thing without knowledge or backing from their governments." I paused a few moments before continuing. "In dealing with South Asia and the Middle East, our normal western linear analysis is very difficult. There is so much dissimilation and deception. But even if some group wanted to plant mis-information, why would they use me? I'm very low level. There are many other ways."

"Joe, I hear what you say. Iranians have a persecution complex. They are very suspicious. Their actions also can reflect hidden meanings. Maybe there is an Iranian tie and maybe there isn't. This whole scenario is a puzzle." Roy paused and first looked at the Attaché and then back at me. "In any event, let us work with the information we have and see what we can come up with."

"Perfect. That is what I suggested to Dennis. This is your jurisdiction not ours."

Roy grinned. "Spoken like a former Secret Service agent. This will definitely get some attention both here and in D.C. Leave it to me. I'll coordinate with the Agency and the FBI. We'll also see if NSA can pull something up. We'll get full traces. Maybe we already have something in our databases on these characters."

"Don't forget the Durrani family company - Oyster Rocks," Frank added.

"What about our Italian counterparts?" I asked.

"I'm already meeting with both AISE and AISI. I'll coordinate with them," Roy said. "By the way, I get them confused. Which one is internal and which is external?"

Frank and I simultaneously looked at each other. He beat me to the answer. "AISE is the Agenzia Informazioni e Securezza Esterna. It is the external information and security agency. And AISI is the Agenzia Informazioni e Sicurezza Interna or internal security service."

"If Rafi Durrani is, in fact, traveling to Italy, let's see if the Italians can pull his visa application," I added. "Even if he is traveling in alias, you may also want to think about what agency would be best to approach the appropriate Pakistani service to see if we can get Rafi Durrani's identifiers and photo. We know he has traveled before under that name. They don't have to know why a request is being made."

"Excellent ideas." "I hate to give up this investigation," I said. "Is there anything I can do?"

"Yes there is," Roy said. "See what you can find in your databases. Most importantly, as Farid said, follow the value trail. We can't do that. HSI can."

"I'll try. The problem is that both the money and value trails probably don't have any nexus to the United States. That means there likely will be nothing in our databases."

"Isn't there anything else you can do?" Frank asked.

I grinned. "I've got a few ideas. Is it O.K. with you if I talk to the Italian Guardia di Finanza – the fiscal police – and through them the Italian customs service – the *dogana*?"

"Joe, I'm not going to tell you how to do your business. Do what you think needs to be done."

"That's what I wanted to hear. *Grazie.* I'm sure we will all be using that word a lot over the next few weeks."

chapter 18

Salvatore Gargiulo returned to his desk after his mid-morning coffee break. Sal was a creature of habit—particularly now that he was reaching the end of his career. His wife called his morning espresso, accompanied by one or two Marlboro cigarettes, a vice. She was worried about his high blood pressure. But for Sal it was one of life's pleasures. Unconsciously smacking his lips, he could still taste the last sip of coffee. He also appreciated the rush of caffeine and nicotine that worked to give him a burst of morning energy. Adding to his upbeat mood, over his coffee he had good-naturedly engaged in yet another debate with his close friend and patron over the fortunes of the Italian Series A football team. Sal was convinced that team Napoli—a perennial loser—was on the rebound. Marco, on the other hand, was equally dogmatic that until Napoli's inept management opened its purse strings to sign better players, nothing would change. In the *napolitano* way, both argued animatedly and passionately.

Before sitting down in front of his desktop computer, Sal looked out his office window. The seventh floor office offered a panoramic view. Scanning the harbor was also part of his routine. Although he had worked on the docks of Naples for over thirty-five years, his view overlooking the Flavio Gioia pier continued to amaze him. The pier had an overall length of over six hundred linear meters and boasted two fifteen-ton cranes. The pier, and its terminals, was one of the busiest in the region. Devoted exclusively to container traffic, it played a vital role both in Napoli's and Italy's robust commerce. As a customs officer in the Italian *dogana*, Sal had intimate knowledge of the huge and thriving port. His current assignment was to help keep track of container traffic on the pier in front of him. The task was daunting. Approximately ninety percent of international cargo was shipped via container, and some days Sal felt the containers all came to his pier.

The incredible views stretching out before him made Sal reflect. At age fifteen, he began his working life on the Naples docks. Those days were long gone, but the memories were not dissipated by time. Sal could still feel the strain of loading and unloading cargo. The work was hard but steady. Work on the docks not only built his body but exposed him very quickly to some of life's hard lessons. He grew up fast. Sal learned a lot about the good of international shipping and human nature. He also witnessed the sometimes sordid business of smuggling, theft, influence, fraud, extortion, and retribution. Naples was one of the largest centers of economic and political corruption in Italy. Although the name Camorra was not openly used, everybody knew the organized crime families had both direct and indirect influence along the piers and terminals. Sal occasionally augmented his meager wages by doing small favors for friends that facilitated the routing of trade goods from the waterfront to the local black market. A crate "falling off the truck" was one of his specialties.

Sal could easily have remained a dock worker. However, his obligatory military duty changed his life. In addition to the mandatory military training, Sal completed a special program that allowed him to obtain his *diploma di maturita.* By the time his service was over, he had the qualifications to apply to the Italian customs service—the *dogana.*

He first met Marco in his customs basic training course. Everyone knew that Marco was destined to rise quickly up the ranks. In addition to being polished, intelligent, and well-spoken, Marco had the most important attribute of all—connections. He had married the daughter of a ranking Guardia general. As his career rapidly advanced, Marco also took care of some special friends. After serving fifteen years inspecting cargo along the pier, Sal's knees had started to give out. He was also beginning to suffer from high blood pressure. Thanks to Marco's influence, Sal was moved to his current position of reviewing electronic manifests and clearing shipments. His promotion roughly coincided with the exponential growth in worldwide containerization, the flood of Chinese imports into Italy, the tremendous expansion of the Naples Port Authority, and the growing regional influence of organized crime.

Sal and his customs colleagues knew all too well that time is money. On a daily basis they were under incredible pressure to simultaneously balance security against commerce—to collect revenue and to facilitate trade. The resulting stress contributed to Sal's high blood pressure.

In order to try to more efficiently accomplish the contradicting missions of security and commerce, the *dogana*—like most modern customs services—had begun to electronically examine shipping manifests long before the ship actually made it to port. In fact, sometimes the electronic analysis began before the shipments actually left the port of embarkation. Using a vast database and modern analytics, today's customs inspector examined trade patterns and possible trade anomalies. Factors such as content, pricing, weight, port of departure, threat levels, past history of the exporter or importer, previous customs alerts, and other variables entered into the electronic equation. Possible targets of concern were developed based on specific criteria and adjustable thresholds. The computer then coded and prioritized questionable shipments.

Due primarily to the sheer numbers involved by the time the ship arrived in port, most containers were electronically "precleared." The results were forwarded to waiting customs brokers and others involved in expediting discharge procedures. Increasingly, the customs information systems were able to interface with port and interport management information systems. Depending on the customer's specific wishes, the customs broker then took possession of the cleared shipments, which were generally transferred by truck for immediate delivery. Only a very small percentage of shipments were actually "red-flagged" and marked for additional examination, including manual inspection.

Much had changed since the old days. From his customs perspective, Sal had witnessed how containerization also improved cargo security. Since freight in a container was not visible to the casual viewer, goods were less likely to be stolen. Moreover, containers in transit had locked doors. They were increasingly protected by tamper-resistant customs seals. As a result, the "falling off the truck" syndrome of Sal's youth had just about become a thing of the past. But Sal knew all too well that the new safeguards were not infallible. Organized crime used other methods to divert, steal, and pilfer. And he was quite aware that the serious theft occurred far away from the docks via white-collar trade fraud and trade-based money-laundering—particularly through the over- and under-invoicing of goods.

Although it was not the same as being on the docks, the older Sal got the more agreeable his desk job had become. He came to terms with his growing physical limitations. Sal became quite adept at using twenty-first century technology to remotely clear cargo. But he still made a concerted effort to maintain his old friendships. He enjoyed the good-natured bantering with his colleagues—even if increasingly he only had face-to-face contact with them during breaks away from the computer. Sal was particularly gratified that even after so many years, Marco remained his friend and patron. Despite Marco's rank, he occasionally would stop by Sal's desk and inquire about his family. Sal was honored. On some of his visits, his patron asked for a special favor or gave him a recommendation on how to expedite a task. And from time to time, Marco would show his appreciation by giving Sal premium tickets to his beloved Napoli team or perhaps some extra cash for the holidays.

When Sal finally left the window and settled behind his desk, he looked in his jacket pocket and pulled out the *busta* or envelope that Marco had given him during the coffee break. The wad of five hundred euro notes surprised him. He had never received so much money before. He smiled at his good fortune. The money was wrapped in a typewritten paper with a request to pre-clear a shipment of scrap metal arriving from Karachi. The note included the container's identifying information.

Sal logged back on to his computer. With a few clicks of his keyboard, Sal soon found the ship and scrolled down the electronic manifest. Locating the shipment and container number, he noticed that the consignment had not yet been flagged by the computer. Sal didn't understand Marco's concern for this particular shipment or the electronic algorithms of his computer. He didn't care. He moved the cursor of his mouse to highlight the entry on his screen showing the container from Karachi. With a quick click of the mouse, the container was pre-cleared. Sal smiled. He was already looking forward to his lunch break.

chapter 19

RAFI SOFTLY CLUTCHED the leather steering wheel of his rented Alfa Romeo 159 sedan. The finely engineered Alfa was a joy to drive. Although he was careful to accelerate no more than the posted speed limit of 120 kilometers an hour, Rafi delighted in the automobile's immediate response. In his previous travels he had never had the opportunity to drive such a superb machine matched to an equally magnificent highway. Headed south toward Naples on the A-1 autostrada, Rafi was enchanted by the beautiful valley of the Sacco River surrounded by the rugged Ernici and Lepini mountain ranges. The ancient city of Frosinone was on his left, perched on a hill overlooking the A-1. Lost in the mesmerizing ride that boasted such spectacular views, for a few blissful minutes Rafi forgot the reason he was in Italy. Reality rudely intruded when he saw the road sign listing the distance to Monte Cassino. Turning down the volume of the Alfa's stereo, Rafi went over his mental checklist one more time.

He had arrived at Rome's Fiumicino Airport three days earlier via an Emirates Air flight from Karachi to Rome via Dubai. Passing through Italian immigration and customs, he was heartened that his Pakistani passport and Italian visa did not draw any suspicion. The passport was genuine. It was purchased from a corrupt official in the Directorate General of Immigration and Passports in the Ministry of Interior. The visa and entries were created by a skilled Taliban forger. In Pakistan a small industry in identity papers and forgery had developed during the anti-Soviet war to serve the mujahideen. Like so many other legacies of the anti-Soviet War – calls to jihad, training camp, smuggling routes, the

ISI's duplicitious behavior - the forged document industry continued unabated. Rafi was pleased and honored with his alias—Shuja Kaker. In the Pashto language, Shuja means brave and Kaker is the name of one of the largest tribes. His Pakistani Taliban facilitators also gave Rafi credit and debit cards in his new alias, issued by a Dubai-based bank. He was also given miscellaneous wallet identifiers and calling cards. Rafi was assured the identifiers were backstopped with storefront addresses. Thus far the documents had worked perfectly. Rafi had no problems renting the car, registering in a hotel his first two nights in Rome, renting a cell phone, and buying Italian business suits, shoes, and casual clothes. He did not want anybody to give him a second look because of the way he was dressed. So far, everything was going according to the plan formulated in Karachi.

Rafi had memorized his meeting instructions and knew he was quickly approaching the exit, or *uscita*, for Monte Casino. Located about 125 kilometers south of Rome just off of the *autostrada*, the historical monastery could not be missed. The massive building dominated a nearby hilltop. It served as a landmark easily visible in the surrounding Ciociaria region. Rafi surmised that it was exactly for this reason—plus the direct route from Rome and the proximity to Naples—that his handlers in Karachi had chosen it for the initial meeting with his still-unnamed explosives technician partner.

Exiting the autostrada, Rafi paid the toll and followed the numerous signs pointing the way to the Monte Cassino monastery. It felt good to work the gears of the Alfa again as he quickly traversed the adjoining town and began his winding ascent to the top of the outsized hill. It was late afternoon. The rocks and junipers jutting from the hillside cast long shadows. Yet another glance at his watch reassured him that he was right on time. His was the only car on the switchback road. Climbing rapidly, he rounded the last bend before the monastery. Following the signs, he spotted the large parking lot he was looking for. It was obviously designed to have ample space for both cars and tour buses. It was apparent that not many religious people or tourists made their pilgrimage to the ancient abbey during a mid-November afternoon. Downshifting into second gear, he entered the lot. Per his instructions, Rafi had his eyes peeled for one car in particular. He immediately spotted it in the almost vacant lot—a dark blue Fiat Punto.

Pulling up a few spaces behind the parked car, Rafi saw the driver immediately open his door. He had a slight, sinewy build. Rafi's first impression was that the man was North African. With quick steps, he walked the short distance to the Alfa. Rafi opened his car door and the man extended his hand in greeting.

"*Asalaam alykum,*" he said with a smile.

Rafi responded with the directed Pashto proverb of recognition, "One cannot clap with one hand alone."

In rapid succession, the stranger kissed Rafi on both cheeks and touched his heart with his right hand—the agreed sign of recognition.

Both men then rotated attempts to communicate—first in Pashtu, then, in rapid succession, Arabic, French, and even Italian. Although one or the other knew a little or a lot of each language, amid increasing laughter they quickly determined that their lingua franca was primarily English.

"Brother, my name is Hakim Faghoul."

"It is an honor to meet you. Please call me Rafi."

"The honor is mine. I have looked forward to this day."

"As have I," Rafi answered. "Do you know this place?"

"I have been here for a while. The grounds and the cemeteries are beautiful. Come, let us walk together. We have much to discuss."

Ignoring the monastery and the museum, the two began walking. Although it was late fall, the garden paths were still striking. The grounds were a picture of tranquility. Noting the many signs advising visitors to be respectful and keep their voices down, Hakim and Rafi spoke softly. They discussed their respective backgrounds, their journeys that brought them together in Italy, and their shared instructions. Strolling quietly, immersed in intense conversation, and occasionally reading the posted signs that featured multi-language explanations of the grounds and the rich history of the surrounding area, the two appeared as pilgrims at a holy sight.

Before their arrival, both Rafi and Hakim had been ignorant of both the religious and historical significance of Monte Cassino. The area was founded by Saint Benedict in 529. Born to a noble family, he did not intend to become a leader of a great monastic order. Hearing the call of God, he initially became a hermit. He lived a life of prayer and contemplation in a small cave near Subiaco, located about seventy-five kilometers from Rome along Aniene River. However, Benedict's quest for solitude was interrupted by disciples attracted to his virtuous character and lifestyle, teachings, and ability to work miracles. As a result, Benedict and his followers retreated to the Monte Cassino hilltop. There he wrote guidelines for laymen wishing to live a life pleasing to God. The *Rule of Saint Benedict* soon became the model for monastic orders in medieval Europe. Benedict died in 543. By the eleventh century, Monte Cassino was the wealthiest monastery in Europe.

During World War II, the area surrounding Monte Cassino became part of the German defensive line guarding against the Allies' southern approach to Rome. The monastery was turned into a fortress. As a result, it became the target of both air bombardment and land assault. The hill was finally captured after the loss of 54,000 Allied lives. The monastery was destroyed. It was later rebuilt based on the original plans. The relics of St. Benedict survived.

Still deep in conversation, Rafi and Hakim turned away from the Polish cemetery that contained the remains of over one thousand Polish soldiers—many of whom died in the final assault on the monastery ruins. Evening was coming and they started to walk back toward the central buildings. Despite their pleasant stroll and wide-ranging conversation, something was bothering Rafi. His partner appeared devout, sincere, motivated, and exceedingly polite. Yet something seemed off. He could not pinpoint the cause of his concern.

"I checked online but also confirmed with the Naples broker," Rafi said. "The ship arrived yesterday as scheduled. The container is here."

Hakim smiled. "That is very good news."

"Yes. Ocean freight shipments are almost always on time. The issue we have to be concerned about is whether or not the container will be electronically cleared by Italian customs or whether it will be targeted and pulled for inspection." Rafi looked up at the beautiful sweeping view of the valley below. He continued. "The real danger is the possibility that some type of radiation detector might issue an alert."

"I was told that there shouldn't be any problems," Hakim said. "In addition to taking steps to minimize the radiation, I understand we have a Chinese connection."

Rafi hesitated before replying. He didn't realize Hakim had been told that much detail about their plans for clearance. "I understand a significant amount of money was paid to a Chinese expediter to ensure smooth delivery. But I wasn't given any details. As you know, this is my first time in Italy. Frankly, I'm amazed that the Chinese apparently have such power in Naples."

"Not Chinese," Hakim laughed. "The Chinese Mafia."

"What?"

"That's right. When most people think of Italian organized crime, they think of the Mafia based in Sicily. But today the most threatening organized crime group is the Camorra, based in Naples. Increasingly, they are forming a partnership with Chinese organized crime."

"How do you know these things? You're an Algerian living in Brescia."

"That's right. But everybody in Italy knows the Chinese have penetrated the underworld of Italy—northern Italy as well."

"What do they do?"

"They primarily specialize in flooding both the commercial and underground markets with cheap knock-offs and counterfeit trade goods—everything from designer bags, pirated DVDs, and electronic gadgets to Rolex watches and counterfeit cigarettes."

"We have that in Pakistan as well," Rafi said with a knowing smile. "The trade is very profitable. We use it for our purposes."

"The Chinese counterfeit trade is everywhere," Hakim replied. "But if we are talking about Italy and the rest of Europe, Naples is the primary entryway."

"What about the Italian authorities? Why do they allow it?"

"The Chinese and their enablers in the Camorra are smart. They flood the port of Naples with so many entries that they overwhelm the Italian customs and police services. There is so much trade fraud, they can't keep up with it all. Besides, payoffs are common," Hakim said. Warming to the topic, he added, "I detest Italians for many reasons. That's one explanation of why I only speak Italian when absolutely necessary. But what I particularly dislike about Italians is their greed." He waited a moment before continuing, "Do you know what Italy's national pastime is?"

Taken aback by the non sequitur, Rafi said, "I assume it is football or soccer—*calcio* in Italian."

"No. It's tax evasion," Hakim laughed at his own joke. "Everybody cheats. Greed and corruption facilitate everything here. That's true in most places I have been, but here the hypocrisy is particularly staggering. But the rich and powerful look the other way. They do not want to crack down too hard because they benefit from the status quo."

"Pakistan is like that as well. I just didn't think it would be like that in Italy."

Hakim laughed again. "It is particularly common in Naples."

"Well, that's what we are counting on." Rafi said. His eyes twinkled with an inner smile. He thought of Majeed's lessons in business and human nature. "We'll use their weakness to our advantage."

The sun began to set as the two partners followed the trail back to the monastery. They entered a partially covered walk that was part of the cloisters. Dark green ivy vines straining for sunlight hung from the walls of the passageway. In a voice lowered even further, Rafi continued the conversation. "We still have a few more issues that need to be discussed."

"What are they?" Hakim asked.

Hakim and Rafi continued to stroll for a few moments side by side along a bricked walkway that marked the perimeter of the courtyard. "I had no idea before I met you that the consignee is also our explosive expert," Rafi finally said. "I'm worried."

Hakim shrugged. "Things are as Allah wills. I have been facilitating the import of gold scrap and scrap metal for a couple of years.

The business has not only provided cover for my presence in Brescia but has also assisted many brothers in their efforts to remit funds home. But don't worry. My record is clean here in Italy. The authorities don't know about me."

Rafi nodded his head. "O.K." He was still uncomfortable with the arrangement and furious that he had not been told in advance. However, there was nothing he could do. "I was told in Karachi that you have a great deal of operational experience." He paused a moment before continuing. "Did you arrange for the warehouse? What about the van?"

"I've been working on both for the last few weeks. Everything is taken care of."

"Excellent."

"We have an abandoned warehouse outside of a town called Caivano. It isn't too far from Naples. It should work perfectly."

"How did you find it?"

"Campania—the province of Naples—is beautiful. But it is also known within Italy for its trash dumps and illegal landfills. And since the shipment is scrap metal, I thought being near a landfill would add to our cover. It wasn't hard to find an empty warehouse in the area and an owner eager for some unexpected money."

"Perfect. Give me the address and we will arrange with the Naples freight forwarder for delivery. What about the van?"

"After giving the operation a lot of thought, I became convinced that it will be necessary to put the devices in a van or delivery truck."

"That's what they also suggested in Karachi," Rafi said.

"A couple of days ago I purchased a used delivery truck – a Scudo - for cash. It is large enough to do the job and should blend in with Roman traffic very well. There are a lot of them on the road."

"Where is it?"

"At the warehouse. I also have all the tools we need there. I'll show you everything tomorrow."

"Did you purchase the Scudo in your real name?

Hakim chuckled. "Brother, it doesn't really matter. I'm going to rig this van so they cannot identify the pieces. But to be on the safe side, I already eliminated the vehicle's identification numbers.

And even if they somehow piece things together, we will either be dead or long out of Italy," he said with finality.

Rafi did not speak. He was deep in thought. Finally, spotting an exit sign directing them toward the parking lot, they turned and headed away from the monastery.

"It's sunset," Hakim said. "Let's say our evening prayers by the cars and give thanks to God."

"O.K."

"I always felt that the *adhan* at sunset is one of the prettiest sounds on earth. 'There is no god but God, and Muhammad is the prophet of God.' It will be good when this is over and we will be amongst the believers again—either on earth or in paradise." Almost as an afterthought, Hakim added, "Afterward, we can get something to eat and rooms for tonight in the town of Cassino. I noticed some places on the drive up."

Rafi turned to mutter his approval to his partner's proposal. When he saw Hakim's face in the dimming glow of the setting sun, he was momentarily stunned. He finally realized what had been bothering him. Hakim's eyes appeared haunted; as if they were windows to a soul already consigned to hell. At that very moment, the heavenly refrains of vespers began to sound from Saint Benedict's monastery.

chapter 20

I HAD BEEN at it since very early in the morning. My eyes began the all-too-familiar glaze. A low-grade headache was intensifying. The numbness in my right arm was getting progressively worse. I knew what these symptoms meant: I had spent far too much time in front of my office computer.

Although working the street was still essential, the modern criminal investigator increasingly relied on data-mining, analytics, and Internet-surfing to facilitate investigations. I found that my international sleuthing was taking place more and more often in front of a computer screen. As suspected, the information and names provided by Farid had no identifiable nexus to the United States. Despite my repeated attempts to find something—anything that could possibly be associated with the subject names—there were no "hits" in the financial, trade, criminal, travel, immigration, and other databases I was desperately searching.

I was not surprised. Despite public pronouncements over the years by various administrations and the US Department of Treasury about our "success" in fighting terrorist finance, in reality there had been precious few victories. For example, approximately eighteen million pieces of financial intelligence were filed every year with the Department of Treasury's Financial Crimes Enforcement Network (FinCEN)—the US Financial Intelligence Unit (FIU). Financial intelligence covered things like high-cash deposits and withdrawals with financial institutions, cross-border currency declarations, large cash purchases, and suspicious transaction reports filed by banks and, increasingly, money service businesses.

Financial transparency reporting requirements were originally imposed with the passage of the Bank Secrecy Act of 1970. During the so-called "War on Drugs," the idea was to give criminal investigators the ability to follow the money trails. Now, countless millions of additional pieces of financial intelligence were filed internationally with the more than one hundred individual financial intelligence units located worldwide. However, out of all that information, at the time of September 11 not one piece of financial intelligence was filed on any of the nineteen hijackers. The same lack of financial data has held true for subsequent terrorist attacks from Bali to Baghdad.

I knew far too well that the dearth of information was not an accident. Our adversaries were smart. Osama bin Laden, in one of his few public pronouncements about finance, stated that ". . . al Qaeda and other jihadist groups . . . are aware of the cracks in the Western financial systems." Terrorist financiers had simply maneuvered around US and international financial transparency reporting requirements and other anti-money-laundering and counter-terrorist finance countermeasures. I was quite certain that if the allegations by Farid were correct, once again there would be precious little to find in the databases.

It was easy to confirm that there were no importations of Pakistani scrap metal into the United States linked to any of the names that Farid had given me. However, I put electronic alerts into the system that could possibly flag any future shipments. I also created a special electronic notice for US Customs Border and Protection (CBP) personnel assigned to the Container Security Initiative (CSI) at various Italian ports. The CSI initiative involved US officers working together with host foreign government counterparts. Cargo destined for the United States is pre-screened and targeted if judged to be at risk. Various screening criteria, non-intrusive inspection, and radiation technology to screen high-risk containers are used before cargo is actually shipped to US ports. Although I was quite certain CSI personnel would share tactical intelligence with their Italian counterparts, they had no mandate or authority to take action regarding shipments not destined for the United States. It seemed that wherever I turned there were roadblocks.

Before my headache got even worse, I knew I had to get up from behind the computer. I picked up the phone on my desk and called Pete Gonzalez of the Secret Service.

"Pete, do you have a couple of free hours? I would really appreciate it if you could go with me to the Italian Guardia di Finanza. I have an appointment with Colonnello Dario Rossi, and I know I would have a better chance of impressing him with the gravity of the situation if I had a representative of the Secret Service with me."

"Is this about the information you gave the attaché and Roy Williams?"

"Yes, it is."

"I know it's important, but I'm not really involved."

"I understand. But I would really appreciate the favor. I can brief you on the walk over. Rossi works at the IV Reparto of the Guardia. It is only a few blocks from the annex."

"When do you want to leave?"

"Uh . . . how about right now?"

"Thanks for the notice," he said glibly, "but I have to be back within two hours. I'm scheduled to participate in the advance team's walk-through at Ciampino Airport late this afternoon. We have POTUS's wheels-down at Ciampino the day after tomorrow." Pausing a bit for emphasis, he added, "The lead-up to the G-20 Summit has made Roman traffic even worse than usual. In addition to the usual circus, with all of these heads-of-state in attendance, demonstrators are pouring into the city." I could sense his growing frustration over the phone. "I can only imagine what the traffic will be like during the actual visit," he said.

"*Grazie infinite*," I said sincerely. "I owe you a cappuccino. I'll be down in a few minutes and we can head right out."

Walking northeast on Via XX Settembre toward the Porta Pia gate, Pete and I were engrossed in conversation. He gave me the latest updates relating to the presidential visit and, in turn, I shared with him what Farid had told me about a possible attack on Rome with a weapon of mass destruction. Pete confided that although the allegation was taken seriously by the Secret Service, Farid's information was just one of many threatening reports received on a daily basis relating to the G-20 Summit. The almost global demonstrations on behalf of the Palestinians over water rights—exacerbated by the massacre at Beit Eil—were causing an incredible amount of "noise" in the intelligence and law enforcement communities. Even working with foreign counterparts, there were far too many threats to assess, digest, and investigate in the short time remaining before the conference.

Despite the mid-morning hour, traffic on one of the main arteries of Rome was almost at a standstill. Pete and I were happy to be walking. However, we still had to dodge the many cars illegally parked on the sidewalk as well as the numerous *motorini*—or motorcycles—that swarmed both the road and the sidewalk like annoying, buzzing bees. The ever-present tour buses were also a major problem. In addition, groups of demonstrators in large buses were pouring into Rome to make their demands known at the summit. They were also flooding into the *citta eterna* on trains, cars, and airplanes. They were joined by a small army of journalists coming to cover the event. It was almost impossible to find a hotel room. The city was just about at its bursting point.

Approaching Porta Pia we found complete traffic gridlock. The chaos was accompanied by an Italian symphony of car horns and shouts. The few *vigili* present—traffic police—were mere observers. There was little they could do to control the situation. Porta Pia had become a bottleneck for traffic trying to surge into the historical center of Rome.

Porta Pia was originally an ancient gate in the Aurelian walls. Surprisingly, the Renaissance-era entryway was designed by none other than Michelangelo. It is Michelangelo's legacy as an artist rather than as a traffic engineer that survives today. He never could have anticipated the traffic situation in Rome half a millennium into the future. The beautiful but unworkable Porta Pia exacerbates modern-day traffic that attempts entry to the current Via XX Settembre. From Porta Pia there is direct line of sight and transportation to the Quirinale—a palace built by Pope Gregory XIII in 1574 as a summer residence. Today the palace serves as the residence of Italy's president. Leaving both the beauty and the chaos, which in many respects characterizes Rome, Pete and I cut through some backstreets until we finally reached the nondescript walls of the Guardia di Finanza's IV Reparto. After stopping at the reception desk, a smartly uniformed *maresciallo* escorted us to Colonnello Rossi's office.

"*Colonnello, vorrei presentarle il mio collega del Secret Service, Pete Gonzalez*," I said as I was introducing Pete."

"It is a pleasure to meet you," replied Rossi. "Do you mind if we speak English? I need the practice."

"Actually you would do me a big favor," said Pete. "I haven't been in Italy as long as Joe. I'm still struggling with the language."

"How do you find Rome?"

"I love it," Pete replied enthusiastically. "There is so much to do and see. The history and culture of Italy are amazing. The food and wine are fantastic. And the women are beautiful."

Rossi's eyes twinkled in response. "That just about sums it up," I said. "Gentlemen, I propose we get right down to business. Special Agent Gonzalez doesn't have a lot of time. He has an appointment this afternoon in preparation for the president's visit to Rome."

"I understand," said Rossi. "Things are hectic here too. The Guardia di Finanza is very much involved in the entire G-20 Summit. The security will be very tight."

The Guardia di Finanza, also sometimes known as simply the "Guardia" or the "GdF," was best described as Italy's fiscal police. It enforced the country's revenue laws, including anti-money-laundering and customs fraud. It had approximately 100,000 employees, including a large police force, investigators, and a small air force and navy. The GdF fell under the authority of the Italian Ministry of Economy and Finance. I knew that an event the magnitude of the G-20 Summit, would require Italy to deploy the considerable resources of the GdF to augment the Carabinieri—the national gendarmerie of Italy—as well as the Polizia di Stato.

"Colonnello, you may have heard from the AISE or the AISI, but HSI in collaboration with the Secret Service has developed some information regarding a possible attack here in Italy involving a weapon of mass destruction."

Momentarily stunned, the major finally said, "I have not heard anything about it."

I continued. "The information is closely held. It originated from an informant of mine based in the Middle East. I don't want to cause undue alarm. We have no way to judge the credibility of the informant, but, of course, we are taking the report very seriously."

"What kind of weapon of mass destruction? Are there any other details?" asked Rossi.

"I'm sorry, but we don't have any details. We are trying desperately to develop additional information." I briefly recounted what I knew and the steps taken thus far.

"What can we do to help?"

"Well, do you remember the trade-transparency unit initiative I spoke to you about a couple of months ago?"

"Yes, I do," replied Rossi. "We are examining the issues involved. I believe it has a lot of potential for Italy."

"Trade-transparency unit?" Pete asked. "Could you explain what it is?"

"Sure. Actually, I know the guy who invented the concept. He is a former US Customs agent. Right after September 11, he was very concerned about underground finance—particularly hawala."

"Hawala also exists in Italy and most countries in western Europe," volunteered Rossi.

"Hawala is also found in the US. In fact, in 2010 the Times Square bombing attack was financed by hawala," I said. "Anyway, the former customs agent was talking to a source of his from South Asia. If I remember the story correctly, the source told the agent that the drug lords and terrorists were laughing at us. They said they were moving money and value right under our noses, but we didn't see it. The agent knew it was true and it pissed him off."

"I can understand that," said Pete.

"Anyway, this agent understood from first-hand experience that in the Middle East and South Asia, trade is often used to provide counter-valuation in hawala transactions. He thought that by examining suspicious trade, we might be able to identify underground finance."

"Counter-valuation?" Pete asked. "That sounds like a customs term."

"Sort of," I replied. "Hawaladars periodically have to settle their accounts. Although they use a variety of methods, trade is favored."

"It's customs fraud. That is quite common here in Italy, and the Guardia di Finanza investigates it," said Rossi.

"That is one of the reasons why we're here," I said. "We know you do excellent investigative work."

Rossi smiled and nodded his head. He was obviously pleased with the compliment.

"You were explaining trade-transparency units," said Pete.

"Yes, I'm sorry. The short version is that every country has a customs service. Countries keep track of what comes in and what goes out for revenue purposes, if nothing else. For many countries, customs duties are the chief source of revenue. And by comparing one country's record of exports with the corresponding record of imports in the trading country, anomalies can be readily identified. With the exception of some recognized variables, what goes out should match with what comes in. For example, if there are large discrepancies in the declared import and export unit prices, it could be an indication of customs fraud at the least but perhaps trade-based money-laundering or even an indicator of underground finance, such as hawala."

"It is a very good investigative technique," added Colonnello Rossi.

"The idea is to create a worldwide network of trade-transparency units or TTUs. The network would be somewhat analogous to the Egmont Group—the international network of financial intelligence units that examines financial intelligence," I continued. "ICE has taken the lead on the initiative. We have already worked with interested partners and established about a dozen TTUs, primarily in South and Central America. But the concept should be expanded. I proposed to Colonnello Rossi that Italy would be an excellent candidate country."

Pete glanced down at his watch. I took the hint.

"Colonnello, the source gave me the names of some individuals and the name of a trading company based in Karachi that might be involved." Taking the envelope from my jacket pocket, I handed it to Rossi. "I wrote down the information that we have."

"*Grazie*. This will be very helpful."

"In this case, you probably will not have the corresponding country's export data. However, you can certainly check Italy's import data."

"We can do that. We get the records directly from Italian customs."

"The source told me he didn't have any details. I don't know if he is telling the truth or not, but he did give me one lead he said was very important."

"What is that?" asked Rossi.

"He said to examine Italy's importation of scrap metal and scrap gold from Pakistan."

Colonnello Rossi had a look of concern. "Is it possible that the goods are being transshipped through a third or even fourth country?"

"The source didn't say, but it is quite possible."

"Do you think the importation of scrap metal could also hide this weapon of mass destruction?" asked Pete.

"Hide it or pay for it," I said. "I don't know. The source specifically advised us to follow the value trail."

Rossi looked hard at Pete and then turned his direct gaze at me. "I assume the competent American law enforcement and intelligence agencies are also examining this?"

"Absolutely," said Pete. "This is being fully coordinated. As we said, this information has also been turned over to the Italian intelligence services. I understand it has also been given to the Carabinieri unit in charge of protection for the G-20 Summit." Pete paused momentarily before continuing. "Obviously the information is very sensitive and should continue to be protected. The services involved are also investigating many other threats. We are swamped with too much information. That's probably why you and the Guardia have not previously heard of it."

"Colonnello, I examined all of our relevant databases. I couldn't find anything. There is no identifiable nexus to the United States. However, in addition to the trade data, perhaps you could also check Italy's financial, immigration, and criminal databases."

"I'll take care of it personally," replied Colonnello Rossi.

chapter 21

THE CAMPANIA REGION was celebrated throughout Italy for its superb climate, fertile soil, and spectacular views. The land consisted primarily of gentle hills, interspersed with the Matese mountains and the rugged area around Irpinia. The still-active Vesuvius volcano, located on the Gulf of Naples, was part of the splendor of Campania as well as an important element of its history. Vesuvius exploded in 79 AD, destroying the thriving Roman cites of Pompeii and Herculaneum. Modern-day tourists delighted in walking the ancient cities' excavated and well-preserved streets. The gulfs of Naples and Salerno, separated by the Sorrento peninsula, boasted steep cliffs that drop to the sea, hiding sandy bays and hidden green grottoes. The Amalfi coast, with its magnificent vistas and villages, seemed to be backdropped in pastels of lemon and orange. The fragrance of citrus and pine floated in the sea breeze. And Campania's beautiful offshore islands of Ischia, Procida, and Capri sat like precious jewels against the coastal azure sea. It was no wonder that in antiquity Campania was called the "felix ager" or happy land.

Approximately fourteen kilometers northeast of Naples, the trash dumps of Caivano lay in stark contrast to the storied Campania of picture postcards. Included among shopping centers, industrial parks, unfinished buildings, and apricot and peach orchards were impromptu dumps and landfills. They spewed forth a putrefying stench of every matter of filth, decay, and garbage. Urban rubbish, including household waste, tires, old refrigerators and TV sets, and all manner of plastic trash, was trucked to Caivano. No trash was refused: metallurgical dross, sludge from tanneries, rotting animal carcasses, and medical wastes were all included in the recipe for the contaminated stew. In some of the dumps, the rubbish was supposed to be sorted at waste-treatment centers. The centers sorted the material into solid and liquid waste, compacted it into "eco-balls," and then burned the refuse. However, often times the balls of garbage could not be burned because they were not properly sorted. Burning the filth would emit even more toxic fumes. And leaving the filth to decompose produced toxic waste that seeped into the ground and contaminated the water table. The reports of cancers and other diseases from the surrounding populace were alarmingly high.

Trash disposal was a lucrative business. Camorra organized crime families paid truckers to haul urban and industrial waste from northern Italy and other parts of Europe to Campania's trash processing and disposal sites for fees that undercut those of the legal trade. On the same majestic A-1 autostrada that had brought Rafi to Naples, there was a never-ending stream of trucks transporting waste to the south. The railroads brought more. The waste was funneled to illegal dumps in Campania like the ones around Caivano. Other destinations were Campania's unlicensed landfills, often made by blasting holes in the sides of hills. The dumps and landfills pockmarked the land. The trash business had gradually driven away farmers. The Camorra bought agricultural land that had been held in families for generations so that they could dump even more waste.

The Camorra had made international alliances. For example, the very same shipping containers that arrived in Naples from China containing cheap household goods and counterfeit clothing and electronics were filled with excess waste and garbage for their return trip to China. It was the classic case of supply meeting demand. It was not efficient to transport empty carriers back to China, and Campania's mountains of trash had become a thriving Italian export.

Despite the establishment of various law enforcement task forces to combat the entrenched problem, the establishment of "trash czars," the spending of billions of euros given by the Italian government and the European Union, the crisis of Campania's trash was not going away. The business of trash had become too lucrative for both organized crime and the politicians at the local and national levels who provided Camorra's cover.

Rafi and Hakim stood in an old abandoned industrial warehouse at the outskirts of Caivano—a nondescript town in the heart of Campania and one of the focal points of the garbage industry. Nearby was their prized forty-foot shipping container, recently arrived from Karachi. The warehouse's front doors were wide open. Directly across the street was a new trash dump located just off the Via Neicropoli that headed toward Pascarola. Rafi thought it ironic that their "dirty" bomb would be unloaded, packed, and readied for detonation in a place surrounded with so much filth and pollution.

Just thirty minutes earlier, the container had been delivered. Everything went according to plan. Rafi played the role of the visiting businessman and did all of the talking with the driver while Hakim signed for the consignment. He checked and double-checked to make sure that the seal on the door of the rust-red-colored container was not broken and the number shown on the bill of lading and other documents in his possession exactly matched the number on the container's seal. After the paperwork was completed, the driver simply unhitched the container and left it sitting on wheels in the middle of the warehouse. After watching the truck cab exit the warehouse and depart the grounds in a spray of gravel and a cloud of dust, Rafi and Hakim turned around together and simply stood and stared at the container. It was hard to believe.

After long moments of disbelief, they finally laughed and embraced each other. "Did everything go O.K.?" Hakim asked Rafi. "I couldn't understand everything that you and the driver were saying."

"I had a hard time with his Neopolitan dialect," Rafi said. "But everything is fine. The delivery driver wasn't involved with any of the customs or clearance issues. As it turned out, it appears the container was electronically pre-cleared before it even entered the port of Naples. As you can see, the customs seal is still intact on the container door. It was not physically inspected." Although Rafi did not voice his thoughts, he realized full well that Majeed had worked his magic yet again.

"That's a relief," Hakim said abruptly. He turned and walked to the back end of the container and looked closely at the sealed door. "But now I'm anxious to get to work. Although everything is going according to our schedule, we don't have any time to waste. I'll be right back."

Moments later, Hakim returned driving an old windowless van. Rafi watched as Hakim backed it next to the side of the container. After securing the parking brake, he exited the driver's door with a big smile on his face. Walking to the rear of the vehicle, he opened the back doors. He then walked to the front of the warehouse and closed the doors to prying eyes.

Rafi turned and looked admiringly at the large van. "This Scudo is going to work well. Actually, it is very similar to the van the technician showed me outside of Karachi that contained the mockup of the device." He paused and then added, "It was very smart of you to park it behind the warehouse. There is no need to let the delivery driver see it."

Hakim smiled at the compliments. "There is plenty of space inside for the dirty bomb plus a lot of scrap metal. We will pack it tight," he said. "The tighter it is, the more effective the blast. However, at the same time we have to be careful with the weight so as not to overload it." Hakim's amusement and satisfaction were bubbling to the surface. "I haven't done this since Iraq. I can't tell you how much I have missed blowing up infidels."

Ignoring Hakim's attempt at humor, Rafi said, "I see you have lots of tools with you."

"I brought some with me from Brescia and I bought some additional ones that might prove necessary. I've also got a trolley and a portable lift." Hakim turned and pointed. "The blue plastic container in the back holds a variety of timing devices. I have been working on them ever since I was initially briefed." With the twisted smile that Rafi was beginning to find more and more irritating, he added, "I'm confident they are going to work fine." Hakim popped the lid on the container and Rafi saw a jumble of cell phones, wires, electronics and tape. "I'm not going to select or set a timer until we get to Rome. We will have to see where we can park the van and the conditions in which we will operate. Then we can choose the right timing device."

Rafi nodded. "We also have to decide when to detonate it. A lot is going to depend on the announced agenda of the G-20 meeting."

"Exactly." Hakim looked at his watch once again. "We might as well get started."

While Rafi changed into some work clothes, Hakim retrieved his tool boxes from the van and placed them on the ground between the container and the Scudo. He gave Raffi a pair of leather gloves. "I also have some protective gear for the radioactivity. But I was told it's not necessary, so I'm not going to use it. The work will be hot enough as it is. You do what you want."

Picking up a heavy-duty cable cutter, Hakim walked again toward the doors located on the rear of the container. Each door had two lock rods. Generally, since the left door closed first, the customs seal was placed on the right door that had to be opened first. The container they were working on had the seals on both of the lock rods. Seals were placed on the container to maintain the integrity of the contents. Although there were ways for thieves, smugglers, and those who committed customs fraud to get around the seals, the procedures were generally adequate to thwart blatant tampering. Hakim made short work of the seals. He lifted the rods and opened the container doors. It was stuffed floor to ceiling and wall to wall with scrap metal. Some of the material started cascading out of the back.

Rafi and Hakim jumped away at the falling material. Then they started patting each other on the back again. Seeing the actual scrap was a further sign that all was going well. Their task now was to dig and sort through the metal junk in order to find the devices hidden inside. For a moment, Rafi thought of Oyster Rocks and his father's stories many years ago about pirates digging for buried treasure.

Hakim showed Rafi how to unload the scrap. They started with the junk that was near the opened doors—various parts of air compressors, automobiles, bicycles, construction and industrial equipment, and metal shards and shavings.

"I've talked to our people in Karachi about the right weight and ratio of high explosives or TNT and the scrap metal," Hakim explained. "I've already worked out the calculations. I just have to select the right metal pieces. We have lots to work with here. For example, grenades use hundreds of tiny metal pieces about the size of one quarter of a pencil eraser. For a grenade the explosive weight is roughly two hundred grams and a typical grenade weighs about half a kilogram."

Rafi kept working. He was pleased to see Hakim concentrating on the task at hand.

"When I was in Iraq," Hakim continued, "I made a lot of improvised bombs out of American 81 mm mortars shells. The steel in those shells is up to 3.2 centimeters thick. For aerial bombs and anti-tank bombs that we sometimes were able to use, the fragmentation is high density. About one-third of the total weight is explosives." Hakim paused as he lifted a heavy metal bumper out of the way. "It just depends on the device, he continued. "But the more high-explosive used, the bigger and thicker the fragmentation needs to be or the small pieces of metal will be vaporized due to the high heat and the immense pressure created at the time of explosion."

Hakim jumped down off the elevated container and started to create two separate piles of metal. The overwhelming majority of scrap metal being unloaded was rejected and piled together on the far side of the container. The rejected scrap would be left behind. He started to carefully select pieces that in his judgment would be the right size and density to create deadly shrapnel. The scrap metal he selected was placed near the Scudo van. Hakim and Rafi would later put the selected metal pieces into cardboard boxes, which would be stacked in the back of the van.

Rafi knew nothing about explosive devices, but with the professional eyes of a trader, he noted that whoever had packed the container was skilled at his craft. "Packing it tight to ride right" is a common expression in the international shipping business. He quickly estimated that this forty-foot container had a cargo capacity of about 55,000 pounds and a cubic capacity of a little over two thousand cubic feet. As they removed more and more junk and scrap, he could tell how the weight was expertly spread evenly over its entire length and width. There was a lot of scrap metal to unload.

Rafi was in excellent shape, but after just thirty minutes of work he began to sweat profusely. He had long since discarded his protective lead apron. His jeans were already ripped in a few places. He had never before unloaded a container. Now he understood why customs services around the world were so reluctant to physically inspect containers, preferring instead to simply examine the paperwork or, if possible, run containers through giant x-ray machines. With millions of containers in worldwide circulation, he knew the smugglers had a distinct advantage over customs and law enforcement. Depending on the port, the percentages of containers that were actually physically inspected by customs officers were in the lower single digits. The vulnerability was yet another "crack" in Western safeguards that Majeed had taught him to exploit.

As they slowly and methodically unloaded the container, Hakim kept up a running commentary. He was in high spirits. The realization of what they were doing magnified his hatred and contempt. After many years in Italy filled with pent-up frustrations, haunted thoughts, and a longing to strike again, the work was a release. Turning from the container he pointed to a window and animatedly exclaimed, "Look at that trash!" Even from inside the warehouse, the view of the neighboring junkyards and landfills offered an incredible panorama. "This is what the West produces—garbage and filth. And they export it to the rest of the world." He was warming to his topic. "I'm not just talking about this garbage in front of us. It's a great metaphor for the West's moral perversions—their films, music, fashion, and vices. It is destroying our culture."

Rafi had heard all of this before. It was a popular theme of clerics and imams.

"This filth also represents the West's obsession with money. Did you see the filth that surrounds us in the landfills of Campania? Just as their corruption and greed poisons the land and air, it poisons our values," Hakim continued.

"Brother, where I come from in Pakistan there is also greed, corruption, and filth." Rafi grunted as he lifted a car bumper out of the container. "That is part of the human character. It is universal."

"Yes, but in Pakistan, Palestine, Algeria, and Iraq the people are poor. They have nothing. Here everybody is rich. They are selfish," Hakim replied. "Instead of giving they accumulate." Hakim's dark eyes glistened. "We are believers. Our cause is just. They believe in possessions; a short work week; a six week vacation in the summer." He continued, "Islam allows an individual to earn as much as he can. But some of the wealth he must give to the less fortunate as charity and zakat."

Rafi responded in Arabic with a well-known verse from the Quran, "No virtue of yours will be rewarded unless you perform charity—infaq—and give in the way of Allah things which you consider valuable to you . . ."

"Yes, Brother. God willing, now is the time for the infidels to be punished. The leaders of the G-20 will witness His message. They will be the victims of His wrath. His justice." Hakim threw down a rusty pipe and tore off his gloves. Looking down at his hands, his voice quivered with emotion and his eyes sparkled. The inner rage within Hakim was again bubbling to the surface. "Let our hands be the instruments of His will."

Rafi was silent. He did not respond to Hakim's outburst. The crazed look in Hakim's eyes and his twisted grin were more and more evident. Rafi kept on unloading the container. Yet inwardly, he was increasingly concerned. He was beginning to have doubts. At first he was troubled with his impending martyrdom—a death he accepted as a tenet of his faith, which called for sacrifices to fight jihad. Yet emotionally and intellectually, he was vacillating. Now that he was in Italy and the operation was a reality, he began to understand more and more that innocents were going to suffer. This was no longer a theoretical discussion among jihadists. He had not previously thought too much of the morality of the attack. He had stayed away from those thoughts. Now Rafi knew he was working on a dirty bomb that, if successfully detonated, would change the world. Finally, he was concerned about the mental stability of his partner.

The signs of Hakim's inner torments were becoming more and more apparent. Rafi knew he would have to watch his partner closely.

After working more than three hours with the occasional break for water and midday prayer, they felt they were making progress. Rafi judged they were halfway through the container. The pile of scrap outside the container was growing, along with the much smaller mound next to the van containing Hakim's choice pieces of metal to be used as shrapnel. He was collecting small projectiles: nuts, bolts, ball bearings, and large metal coils and shards. In Iraq, Hakim had seen the kind of bloody damage this form of anti-personnel bomb could inflict. His enthusiasm intensified. Both Rafi and Hakim were getting excited because they knew they should be approaching the washing machine and freezer containing the dirty bomb and the TNT.

Finally, after lifting away the bumper of an old bus, the partial top of a washing machine came into view. Removing a car wheel, both workers simultaneously saw red duct tape on the top and sides of the washer.

"That should be one of them," Hakim exclaimed. He worked to control his emotions. "Let's be even more careful now. Although they are inert we do not want to have any accidents. I saw too much complacency handling explosives in Iraq, and many of my colleagues were killed as a result."

Rafi did not need any reminding. Working gingerly, more and more pieces of scrap were removed until finally the two jihadists were staring down at an old freezer similarly marked with red duct tape. It stood beside the washing machine. They appeared just like the ones Abdul had shown to Rafi at French Beach. For a few moments, both Rafi and Hakim quietly stared. The enormity of what was happening momentarily staggered them.

Not knowing what to do or say, Rafi finally broke the silence. "The freezer with the red tape has the TNT."

Hakim nodded. "I know. That follows my instructions as well." In a short devout prayer of praise, he added "Allah Akbar."

Taking off their gloves they both turned and jumped down from the container. They grabbed their water bottles and headed outside into the Campania sunshine. Although it was not warm, they were both drenched in sweat. Taking long pulls from the plastic bottles, they headed toward an old apricot tree that stood alone by the side of the warehouse. Both the fruit and the leaves had long since fallen from the tree. The partners sat down under bare branches that stood in stark contrast against the blue autumn sky. After Hakim finished his water, his gaze turned to the landfills and trash dumps directly across the street from the warehouse. Trembling with renewed contempt, he quietly recited a short verse. "Soon shall we cast terror into the hearts of the unbelievers. Their place will be the fire, and evil is the home of the wrongdoers."

chapter 22

THE CHILDREN WALKED down the aisle of the school auditorium two abreast. Their sparkling eyes matched their beaming smiles. Dressed smartly, they held their country flags high. Seated on an aisle seat with my digital camcorder, I spotted our eldest son entering the procession.

"Jack is coming in now," I whispered to Ana. "What flag is he carrying?"

She reassuringly patted my shoulder. "It's the Peruvian flag." My astonished look caused an amused smile to envelope her face. Her brown eyes glimmered. In a soft voice she continued, "There are students from dozens of countries attending the school. Most are from Italy and the United States. Everybody wanted to carry those flags."

I whispered, "So how did he end up representing Peru?"

"They asked for volunteers to carry the flags of countries not represented by students. Jack wrote a paper about Machu Picchu in Peru so he asked to carry the flag."

I chuckled. "That makes sense," I said. I returned my focus to the viewfinder and began recording like a proud father.

The annual "International Day" at the American School in Rome was always a big hit with both the students and their families. Many of the students were the sons and daughters of the diplomatic representatives or businessmen stationed in Rome. Jack, our eldest, had attended ASR since our arrival in Rome. Paul was in first grade and too young to participate in the flag carrying ceremony. Nevertheless, he and his classmates were seated in the school assembly towards the front of the auditorium a number of rows away. Every so often, he would slyly peak over his shoulder and smile at his mother and I and wave to his little sister. Marie, our youngest, stood upright in Ana's lap. She was captivated by the procession and colorful flags.

I knew from past years that soon the headmaster would give welcoming remarks. His presentation would be followed by children's performances of singing and skits representing countries and cultures from around the world. My favorite part of the day followed. Tables laden with international fare waited for us outside along the courtyard in the middle of the manicured school grounds. Parents of the international students – some in native dress - delighted in sharing their countries and their cultures via food and drink. The courtyard became a microcosm of the international community.

The few hours at ASR with my family were a welcome break from work. Yet watching the children's parade of flags caused my thoughts to return once again to the pending terrorist threat. My mind flashed to a comment made by Colonel Abbadi in Jordan only a few short months ago. "It is always the children who suffer the most." Since that conversation near the ruins of ancient Gadara, it seemed like I had been living a nightmare. It was reinforced just a few days before when Farid talked to me about protecting our children.

The reality of the threat of a dirty bomb being detonated in Rome overlapped the innocence before my eyes. Yet I understood the uncertainties involved precluded the authorities from making the threat known to the public. Seated in the middle of the school auditorium with responsibilities as a husband, a father, US civil servant and a member of the community, I was caught in the middle of a dilemma with no good choices.

As I listened to the headmaster drone on and on about our "international village," once again I began to weigh my options.

chapter 23

Colonel Malik Khan of Pakistan's Directorate for Inter-Services Intelligence, more commonly known by its initials ISI, seldom left his Karachi office. During the middle of the week, he was rarely out of his immaculately clean and crisply starched uniform. In the sometimes sweltering heat and humidity of teeming Karachi, Khan worked to maintain his military bearing and appearance. His ramrod straight posture, taught physique, and flawless grooming contributed to his carefully cultivated self-image. Yet today Khan had shed the trappings of his rank and profession and wore a simple white *shalwar kameez*. He did not want to draw attention to himself. He knew his uniform's insignias would have been out of place on the bus rides to the *katchi abadis* of west Karachi. Khan had only been in this neighborhood once before. Leaving the latest in a series of jostling bus rides, Khan knew he had to negotiate another few blocks in the oppressive squatter settlement before reaching his destination.

Far in time and distance from his first deployment as a second lieutenant along the Kashmiri border and his subsequent assignment as a fast-rising captain in Waziristan, Khan nevertheless surveyed the urban slum with a soldier's trained eye and a love of discipline. In return he saw disorder and dismay. The surrounding area was repugnant to his military sense of organization as well as his senses of sight and smell. As a military intelligence officer, he understood why his contact desired to live and operate in such a place. But Khan was thankful that he didn't have to live here. On the contrary, he was able to provide his family with a comfortable suburban Karachi home. Khan permitted himself a small smile at the knowledge that his upper-crust lifestyle was not due to family wealth, political connections, and certainly not his government wages. Rather, Khan benefitted from the largesse of benefactors who appreciated the special favors and services he could provide. Picking his way along the open sewer and clogged walkway of the *katchi abadis,* Khan was hopeful that this afternoon's meeting would prove particularly lucrative.

Even though his career had been temporarily derailed, Khan believed that when the government changed again he would benefit. Politicians and generals fluctuated. Yet throughout the years he had remained loyal to the ISI. He was proud to be part of the institution that did so much to protect the fatherland. He knew its history and mission well.

The Pakistani intelligence service was established in 1948 in the aftermath of the first Indo-Pakistani War. The conflict exposed horrid intelligence weaknesses and lack of coordination between the various branches of the Pakistani armed forces. In 1950, the ISI was officially tasked to safeguard Pakistan's domestic and international interests—including its power base in the greater South Asian region. Over the years, the mission of the ISI further expanded to include the gathering, analysis, and dissemination of domestic and foreign intelligence, as well as also coordinating the intelligence of the military services. The mission soon evolved to include counterintelligence. During the Soviet occupation of Afghanistan, the ISI actively equipped and trained the Afghan mujahedeen. They sent the guerilla fighters across the mountains to attack the Soviet "evil empire." However, Pakistan paid a price for its activities. Afghan and Soviet forces also conducted raids against mujahedeen bases inside Pakistan.

After the terrorist attacks of September 11, Pakistan officially ended its support of the Taliban. Pakistan's military leader, General Pervez Musharraf, attempted to curb the ISI and purged Islamic fundamentalists from leadership positions. Additional reforms were made, including the disbanding of many of the ISI's Kashmir and Afghan units. Many involved had promoted Islamic militancy throughout South Asia. Some officials were forced to retire and others were transferred back to the military. There was a further purge after the US humiliated both the military and the ISI by locating and killing Osama bin Laden in the country's heartland.

Khan had been transferred to Karachi. He was given a bureaucratic wasteland position in foreign liaison. Although his ego suffered, he convinced himself and his family that the assignment was a career stepping stone. He also determined he could sometimes benefit from the information that came across his desk.

Rounding a corner, Khan's internal compass recognized that he had finally reached the correct street. There were no signs. Sensing that he had to turn left, he walked a few more steps and found the office he was looking for. Without pausing, he knocked brusquely and opened the door.

Majeed was seated behind his immaculate desk. Hearing the rap on the door, he looked up from the ledger he was examining. "Good afternoon, Colonel Khan. I was expecting you. Thank you for coming all the way here to my humble place of work."

"*Asalaam alykum*," Khan replied as he entered Majeed's spartan office.

"Please, sit down. I have some hot water ready for tea."

"Thank you," Khan replied. "The ride here was rather exhausting."

"I very much appreciate your coming here. At my age, it is getting more and more difficult to navigate around this city."

"It is my pleasure," Khan replied graciously.

Majeed stood up and busied himself with preparing the tea. The two men exchanged pleasantries and updates since their last meeting. After they had settled into their chairs and sipped their first taste of tea, Majeed said, "Colonel, I was a bit surprised with your request for a meeting. It was unexpected."

"Yes. I imagine. I too was surprised." Khan took another sip of tea and then said, "I will get right to the point." Khan shifted in his chair but maintained his ramrod straight posture. "Do you have any idea why a foreign government sent a request asking about you, your business, and your sons?"

"What do you mean?"

"As you know, my current position is with foreign liaison. A few days ago, I received a request from our headquarters in Islamabad for name checks. This is routine. Our service receives these kinds of requests from countries around the world." Majeed listened impassively. Khan continued, "Your names were included in a rather long list of names forwarded by a foreign embassy."

Majeed took off his glasses. He looked directly at the colonel sitting across from him. "This is very interesting. Which embassy?"

"Right now that is not important."

"Was there any explanation provided?"

"An explanation is why I am here. I was hoping you might be able to provide me with some information."

Majeed sat quietly. He was genuinely surprised. In moments, he analyzed the reason for Khan's visit. Due to operational security, he had not heard from Rafi since his departure. However, he understood from the leadership that things were proceeding according to plan. Had something happened? Majeed doubted it. A request like this could be weeks or months in the works. If the mission had been discovered, there would be more forceful inquiries than the one put forward by the greedy and self-important colonel. The name checks also included Tariq. Majeed knew his other son had nothing to do with the Italian operation. The bookkeeper had no idea how the names had surfaced, but he doubted the name checks had any link to Rafi's mission. Nevertheless, he was still uncomfortable.

"I don't know why they are asking about us," Majeed finally replied. "Our companies are active internationally. Maybe some of our business generated an inquiry."

"Perhaps," replied Khan. "But I think there must be more."

"Colonel Khan, if you would permit me to ask, in a typical response to such inquiries what do you do?"

"Well, it depends on what is in our files. Sometimes there is nothing. Sometimes we provide full identification, including, for example, if the subject has any criminal records."

"Colonel, if I may, I think that should be our answer."

"And what specifically is that?"

"Again, I don't know why our names were included in the request. Obviously, my sons and I have successful businesses with many international connections. Somehow, the foreign country concerned must have learned something and put in a routine request for additional information."

"Go on," said Khan.

"Well, it should be a simple matter for you to craft a reply that states that you have no information on me, my sons, or our businesses."

"I could do that," Khan replied slowly and pensively.

Majeed smiled. "In that case, it is agreed. Please give me a moment." Replacing his wire-rimmed glasses, he pushed back the chair from his desk and opened a drawer. The matching gold rings on his two pinkie fingers glistened as he quickly counted out an additional ten 500-euro notes and stuffed them into the already prepared envelope waiting for Colonel Khan. Under the rapt gaze of Khan, Majeed next took the latest issue of *Dawn* magazine that was placed on the upper left-hand corner of his desk. Flipping through the magazine, he quickly inserted the envelope. Handing the magazine to Khan, Majeed again smiled broadly. "Colonel, there is an excellent article in this magazine about the latest situation in Kashmir. I marked it for you."

chapter 24

"ALL RIGHT, EVERYBODY. Listen up," shouted one of the many men and women dressed in dark blue suits, white shirts, and brilliantly shined black shoes.

Instantly the small crowd of agents, officers, and assorted White House and US Embassy staffers quieted down and gathered around him.

"For those of you who do not know me, my name is Special Agent Steve Rucker of the Presidential Protective Detail, or PPD, of the United States Secret Service. I'm the lead advance agent for the Secret Service. The advance team and I have been here in Rome over the last two weeks getting ready for this visit."

Walking to the front of the impromptu briefing room at Rome's Ciampino Airport, Rucker unconsciously straightened his large frame a little further and assumed a command position.

"Wheels-down is on schedule. That's 1600 hours." Rucker looked down at his watch. "We've got about three hours. I was asked to get this briefing underway because Angie Coleman of the White House staff, the lead advance for this event, has been delayed in traffic." Just about everybody in the room smiled knowingly. "We expect her shortly." Rucker continued, "Before I begin the brief, I would like to thank the US Embassy and our Italian counterparts for their hospitality, support, and assistance."

Rucker's eyes scanned the group in front of him. "We've already had some long days and nights of hard work in preparation for this visit. But for those of you who have never been involved with an overseas presidential visit before—let alone an international summit of this magnitude—I want to be the first to tell you that our hard work thus far has just been the beginning." Rucker paused before continuing. "Ladies and gentlemen, Rome is called the eternal city. But I doubt it has ever seen anything like this before. Get ready. An unbelievably large circus is coming to town. There are approximately two thousand White House staffers, aides, military and security personnel, and media in the US delegation alone." Rucker's tone turned very serious. "For the next three days and nights, we will all be working together to make this a safe and very successful visit."

I stood in the back of the room next to Agent Pete Gonzalez. We had walked in just minutes before Rucker called the gathering to attention. Leaving the embassy two hours earlier in Pete's government-issued vehicle, or "G-ride," we should have had plenty of time to spare. However, a ride that would normally take thirty minutes was slowed to a crawl. In the days leading up to the summit, the Roman traffic was seemingly getting worse by the hour. Despite the best attempts by the Italian authorities to get vehicles off the roads, it was readily apparent that traffic gridlock would break out when the world leaders all arrived, and key streets and expressways were shut down to facilitate motorcade movement.

"Ladies and gentlemen," Rucker continued. "As you are aware, we are all here because POTUS will be attending the three-day G-20 Summit. This will be the largest G-20 meeting in history. It was going to be large when it was originally scheduled a year ago, but with the continuing economic downturn, the Palestinian crisis, and the worldwide reaction, it has taken on even more importance." Rucker paused and turned to the back corner of the room where a few embassy staffers who played an active role in the visit had been invited to the airport arrival. "I see Rome embassy economics officer Valerie Johnson standing in the back. Valerie, please come up here and give us a brief overview of the G-20."

A very petite and stylish forty-ish woman with fine facial features and striking cropped, carrot-colored hair slowly made her way through the packed meeting room. Clasping a thick black leather notebook in her folded arms, she joined Special Agent Rucker at the front of the room.

"Hello, everybody," she said. "I would like to begin by welcoming the newcomers to Rome." Smiling she continued. "For those of you who do not know, the G-20 refers to the group of twenty finance ministers and central bank governors from nineteen countries plus the European Union. For this Rome summit, they will be joined by their heads of government or heads of state. Collectively, the G-20 economies comprise well over eighty percent of world trade and the large majority of the world's population."

As she spoke, Valerie seemed to warm to the topic. "The G-20 was originally proposed to gather countries together to discuss matters relating to the international financial system. Cooperation and consultation is stressed and policy recommendations sometimes result. The G-20 often tackles issues that are beyond the scope of any single organization like the World Bank and the IMF." She paused a moment and ran a hand through her hair. "Many of you are more familiar with the G-8. But over the last few years, the G-20 has, in effect, replaced the smaller group. It is much more inclusive and representative."

Opening her notebook, she quickly scanned a page. "I'm not going to go over the entire list of participants, but in addition to host country Italy, some of the countries that will be in attendance are Argentina, Brazil, Canada, China, France, Germany, India, Japan, Russia, Saudi Arabia, the Republic of Korea, and the United Kingdom." Looking up, she continued. "When this summit was originally put together, Italy as the host country suggested the primary topics of discussion. They are clean energy and sustained growth in the developing world. Those topics will still be discussed. However, it appears this G-20 summit will also be drawn into the Palestinian water crisis and the brewing international reaction. Turning to Rucker, she said, "That is a little bit out of my area of expertise."

"Thank you, Valerie," replied Rucker. "I'll take it from here. Regarding the situation in the Middle East, I don't think much need be said. As everybody here knows, the water crisis in the West Bank has precipitated worldwide nonviolent demonstrations and sometimes work stoppages. International summits normally attract numerous groups that rally in support of various causes. They attempt visibility in front of the global media. This will be particularly true here. For the next three days, the world's attention will be focused on Rome."

His eyes again swept the group. "Demonstrators and political activists have been pouring into the city—most of them are focusing on the Palestinian issue. Although most of the groups are not linked, we expect the demonstrators to be fairly well coordinated via social networking sites. So far everything has remained peaceful. However, we are closely monitoring reports that others are attempting to exploit the situation for their own ends. Regarding possible threats, Secret Service personnel will be briefed shortly by Special Agent Roy Williams of the Intelligence Division."

A few more latecomers trickled into the back of the room as Rucker continued his briefing. "Most of the international delegations have already arrived. However, more will be arriving in Rome later this afternoon and evening. Some are using Ciampino and others Fiumicino airport. Because of the size of our delegation and the prominence of POTUS, we've been given a three-hour time slot here at Ciampino. It commences at 1400 hours. Immediately after the arrival and the official greeting, POTUS will be escorted to the waiting motorcade and driven directly to the ambassador's residence near Villa Borghese."

Rucker paused and pulled a vibrating cell phone out of his front pants pocket. He frowned, scanned it for a few moments, and then continued. "POTUS will have a few hours to rest up from the trip and be briefed by our ambassador. At 2000 hours this evening, the Italian president will be hosting a dinner for delegation principals at the Quirinale. At the conclusion of the event, POTUS will be driven back to the ambassador's residence and will remain overnight. President Rindler will spend all three nights of the summit at the residence. The working summit begins in earnest at 0900 tomorrow morning."

Rucker stopped momentarily and looked out the window. The Brazilian delegation had recently arrived. There was some commotion outside as the welcome ceremony ended and the delegation was escorted through the terminal to their waiting cars. "As most of you know, our command post is in the Excelsior Hotel—just a few blocks from the American Embassy," he continued. "Most of the accompanying White House staff and other members of the delegation are also staying at the Excelsior. During the length of the visit, hospitality and communications suites will be in operation at the Excelsior 24-7."

There was additional noise and a few shouts from outside. The door to the room flew open and a young woman walked in. She wore a scowl on her flushed face. Peering around the room, she saw Special Agent Rucker addressing the group. She immediately walked toward him and whispered animatedly into his ear.

Rucker nodded his head and then turned again toward the group, "Ladies and gentleman, Angie Coleman of the White House staff has just arrived. I've been working with her the last few weeks. As I said, she was unavoidably detained in traffic. Angie, I have just about finished the general brief, but perhaps you would like to say a few words."

Coleman appeared not to be any older than twenty-five. She was very thin, with mousy brown hair that fell to her shoulders. Although her outward appearance and dress were professional, her demeanor seemed stressed and agitated. Coleman must have realized it and took a few moments to compose herself before addressing the group.

"Thank you, Special Agent Rucker. Sorry I'm late. We ran into other motorcades coming into the city as we were going out. The traffic was simply horrible. I have never experienced anything like it."

The White House staffer turned to Rucker and said in a voice low but audible to all, "People will hear about this."

Turning back to the group in front of her she continued, "I have no wish to delay things any further by reiterating Agent Rucker's brief. I know we are running a bit behind schedule. Thank you for your assistance." She again turned back to Rucker and started whispering animatedly in his ear.

Pete Gonzales nudged my shoulder and said in a low tone of voice, "Coleman is a piece of work. I've done a few domestic trips with her, and I can't figure out why the White House keeps using her."

"She's so young," I replied. "It looks like she just graduated from college."

"I believe she graduated Wellesley a few years ago and through family influence received a very visible position in President Rindler's election campaign," Pete said.

"Nothing has changed," I said, shaking my head.

"You're right," Pete said. "It has only gotten worse. Daddy gives the Republican or Democratic Party a lot of money, and in return a son or daughter gets a plush appointment on the White House staff."

"That's just how the game is played," I said, keeping my voice low.

"The sad thing is," Pete said, "the position goes to these young staffers' heads. They have the power of the White House behind them."

"I've seen it before. These kids on the White House staff come into an embassy and order people around and sometimes make foolish decisions. Yet very senior people kowtow to them because they don't want to make waves with the White House."

"You got it, Joe. You should have seen Coleman's behavior at some of the meetings this last week."

Our tête-à-tête was interrupted. "O.K., everybody," Rucker shouted again. "The general brief is over. All Secret Service personnel stay behind for our intelligence brief and post-standing assignments. The rest of you can go to the hospitality room right outside the door. The Italians are wonderful hosts. They have quite a spread for you." Looking at his watch again, Rucker said in a loud voice, "The Secret Service brief will start in five minutes."

"I gotta get up there," Pete said above the din as the meeting broke up. "This is my site and I have to assist in the brief."

"Sure, go ahead."

"Come up with me. We have a few minutes before we get started. Let me introduce you to Rucker. He's a good guy."

Moving forward against a group of staffers and strap-hangers who were slowly exiting the room, Pete led me to where Rucker was standing. He was joined by Special Agent Roy Williams.

"Steve, you got a minute?" asked Pete. "I want to introduce you to DHS Investigations Special Agent and former Secret Service Agent Joe Costa."

Rucker turned and gave me his hand and a big smile. "Joe, it is a pleasure to finally meet you. I've talked to both the attaché and Roy Williams about you and your report. Thank you for assisting us."

"The pleasure is mine. It's great to work with the Secret Service again—at least temporarily."

Roy Williams from the Intelligence Division spoke up. "Joe, Pete briefed me on your meeting with the Guardia di Finanza. Have we heard anything back yet?"

"Not yet. It might take some time. And, unfortunately, we don't have any."

"Wheels-down is less than three hours from now," reiterated Rucker.

"Have you been able to pick anything up through your channels?" I asked.

"This isn't the time or place to discuss everything. We can confirm that the entities in your report exist, but that's about it. No derogatory data has been developed. However, we cannot locate the individuals' whereabouts. We are awaiting additional information from some of our foreign counterparts."

"Are you going to mention any of this in your briefings over the next few days?

"We've given this a lot of thought," Rucker said. "At this time, the answer is no. When Roy gives his brief in a couple of minutes, he will discuss the usual subjects and groups. As you will hear, many are coming out of the woodwork for this visit."

I saw Roy nodding his head.

"However, until such time as we get more specifics about your report—and hopefully some photographs of the alleged subjects involved—we don't have much to work with. In my discussions with the station and the Deputy Chief of Mission, they agree that the bottom line at this time is unsubstantiated information and conjecture." I saw Agent Williams slowly nodding his head. Rucker continued. "No sense in causing undue alarm. The Italians believe we should take precautions so that reports of this nature are not leaked to the press. It could cause panic."

"The Italians are notorious leakers. I'm surprised the information hasn't been released as yet," I said.

"Obviously, Secret Service technical security people and their Italian counterparts have been briefed," Rucker said. "The reality is that in today's world we regularly incorporate this kind of threat scenario into our countermeasures."

I knew what Rucker was saying made sense but I still felt frustrated. *Didn't they understand the gravity of the situation or was I overreacting?* "If there is anything I can do, please let me know."

"Joe, we've got you down for a few post-standing and liaison assignments. However, we don't want to overdo it because we want you to keep working on developing information on the threat you reported," Rucker said.

Turning to Pete he added, "Give Joe a heads-up about what we have in store for him over the next three days." Extending his hand, Rucker said, "Thanks again for your help. If you would excuse us, I've got to confer with Roy for a few minutes before we get the intelligence brief underway."

"Of course." I turned to Pete and said, "Well, what do you have me down for?"

"Joe, we only have a few Italian speakers. So what we would like for you to do this afternoon is to be by the motorcade for the departure. I'll introduce you to Special Agent Jim Jenson. Jim's got the motorcade. He'll give you the specific post. Jim has run the routes many times, and even with the traffic we are confident we will be fine with our Italian escort." I nodded. "Prior to departure there will be a lot of Italian cops around the motorcade, and if there are communication issues it will be nice for you to be there."

"Sure, that's fine. Can you tell me what else I'll be doing?"

Pete opened his notebook and pulled out a sheet of paper. I saw my name at the top.

"Tomorrow afternoon, after the first G-20 working session, POTUS is going to the American Embassy for a courtesy visit. We'd like for you to be there."

"It will be fun to see the president at the embassy and the reaction of the staff. I understand families have been invited as well. Do you have the reporting instructions?"

"Everything you need is on this piece of paper." He handed it to me. "Of course you know that is a close hold."

I nodded. "What else do you have me down for?"

Pete grinned and said, "Well, for old time's sake, we have you working a midnight shift at the ambassador's residence—Villa Taverna."

I laughed. "What's the Secret Service without midnights? Seriously, no problem."

"Well, it might be," replied Pete, "Because on the third day, we have you down again for a post-standing assignment at the Coliseum."

"I'll be fine."

"Joe, we wanted to use you for additional assignments, but the situation has changed."

"I'm just glad I can play a small part," I said with the seriousness that I felt. "I want to do everything I can. Besides the threat to international security and the safety of Rome itself, my family and friends are here. I have a very personal connection to what is going on."

chapter 25

"I NEED A coffee."

It was the first thing Hakim had said all morning that Rafi had agreed with. Since sunrise, the two of them had been scouting Rome. It was the first day of the G-20 conference. The cordoned-off streets, police checks, barricades, and re-routing of traffic patterns had tried their patience and put their nerves on edge. Disagreements were now out in the open. Rafi spotted a coffee bar across the piazza. Gesturing to Hakim to follow, he turned his motor bike around and navigated swiftly through other *motorini* and groups of pedestrians. Finding a convenient spot to park, he turned off the ignition. Straddling the bike, Rafi pulled off his helmet. Hakim pulled up right beside him. The two spotted an open table. As an added bonus, the table boasted a beautiful view of the piazza. It was swarming with people.

"Let's grab that table before somebody else does," Rafi said. "We need a break. We also need to make some decisions."

Within minutes, the two were seated and silently stirred small packets of sugar into their espressos. Looking up, Rafi was struck by the glimmering pastel hues of the surrounding buildings. The eternal city looked extraordinarily glamorous in the November sunshine. Late afternoon shadows highlighted the ancient Egyptian obelisk that stood like a sentry in the center of the Piazza del Popolo, or people's square. The Egyptian obelisk was brought to Rome in 10 BC by the order of Cesar Augustus. Despite the deadly intent of their excursion around Rome, Rafi could not help but admire the beauty, history, and culture of the city.

The Piazza del Popolo was located by the northern gate in the Aurelian Wall that once surrounded ancient Rome. In ancient times, it was said that "all roads lead to Rome." The beginning of the Via Flaminia marked the northern entry and one of the primary gateways into the capital of the Roman Empire. In the Middle Ages, the Piazza del Popolo was the first view of Rome that greeted travelers and pilgrims coming from the north. Over more recent centuries, the Piazza had been used as a market, gathering place, and center for demonstrations and political rallies.

Three major streets branched out from the Piazza. The Via del Corso was in the center and flanked on both sides by the Via del Babuino and the Via Ripetta. The Via del Corso—or racetrack—followed the course of the ancient Via Flaminia and led to the Piazza Venezia and the Roman Forum and Coliseum—the center of imperial Rome. The Via di Ripetta led past the mausoleum of Cesar Augustus to the Tiber River that bisected the city. The Via del Babuino linked the Piazza di Spagna and its famous Spanish Steps, or *Scalinata*, leading to the Piazza Trinita dei Monti and the church of Trinita dei Monti.

During their long day, Rafi and Hakim had either covered—or attempted to cover—all of those areas and more. The day before, they had left the Scudo van in a secured parking garage just off the *Grande Raccordo Anulare*—the *autostrada* expressway that circled the city. They rented motorbikes because they quickly realized that the bikes were the best way of navigating through the heavy Roman traffic. But as the sun came up and the city awakened to the G-20 Summit and its hundreds of thousands of participants and demonstrators, they quickly found that even transit by motorbike was difficult. They were often forced to leave their bikes and proceed on foot to scout potential sites. The two terrorists became increasingly frustrated, worrying that they would not be able to find a suitable place to detonate the dirty bomb. In one sense, all of this had been expected. Their handlers had known in advance that the security precautions for the G-20 Summit would be stringent. As a result, Rafi and Hakim were allowed flexibility to assess the situation as it developed and do their best to find an opportune location for detonation. Nevertheless, the overwhelming police presence and suffocating traffic still surprised them.

"The circumstances are not what we expected," Rafi finally said.

"I've lived in Italy for many years now," replied Hakim, "and I have never seen anything like this."

Rafi sipped his espresso. The sweetened hot and bitter coffee was an elixir. Within moments he could feel the calming of his nerves. He looked around and made certain that people seated at the adjoining tables could not overhear their conversation.

"If things continue this way over the next few days, we are not going to be able to get close to any of the G-20 events." Rafi took another sip of his espresso. "You are the expert here. What do you think we should do?"

"The best we can," Hakim replied curtly.

Rafi studied Hakim through his sunglasses. His partner was becoming increasingly irritating. Since their departure from Campania two days before, Hakim had been making sarcastic and biting comments. If wasn't always what he said that bothered Rafi so much, as the tone of his voice and the look in his eyes. Rafi could understand Hakim's antipathy toward the West. However, he had started to make personal comments and insinuations about him. Rafi knew the worst thing to do would be to get into an open argument with the moody and seemingly haunted Algerian. The success of the operation depended on them working as a team. It required clear thinking by both of them and the ability to get along. Rafi knew that this was one of the reasons he had been chosen to participate. He also realized that the operation was dependent on Hakim's skills. He had to keep trying.

"Let's go over this logically," Rafi said. "The newspapers have listed the events and their times. If we can't get close, what do you think is our best option?"

"As we have seen today, parking by the major announced events is impossible," Hakim replied. "We've covered them all. They are locked down. We're going to have to select a secondary site." He sipped his coffee before continuing. "In Iraq, when the infidels' security was too tight, we often had to do the same thing."

"Have you seen anything that you think might work?"

Before replying, Hakim looked over his shoulder to again determine nobody was within hearing distance. "We really have two options. If you want to be a martyr, you can drive the truck into a crowd of people. I'll rig the van for detonation." Hakim's twisted smile returned. "I'm not sure you would detonate it yourself. Besides, there are so many police around, you undoubtedly would be shot before you got too far."

Rafi let the slight or the misguided attempt at humor pass by. "So you don't think I can get close to an event?"

"Not really. But it doesn't really matter if the object is just to detonate the device. The radioactive cloud will achieve our goals."

"I agree, but for political reasons we should still try to get as close as possible. It isn't going to have the same effect if the bomb goes off in a Roman suburb far away from the G-20. What's the other option?"

"We'll park the truck as close as we can in *centro storico.* I'll use a remote device and detonate the bomb at a time of our choosing."

"Yes, but where? The streets near the events are either closed or closely monitored. We can't risk having the truck towed."

"When we were riding by the Circus Maximus, I saw a street that should work," Hakim said quietly.

Rafi took a map of Rome out of the inside pocket of his leather jacket. "Show me," he said.

Hakim momentarily examined the map and then pointed. "Right here. Via dei Cerchi. It fronts Circus Maximus and backs into the Palentine Hill."

"I remember," Rafi murmured. "It might work."

"On the other side of the hill, the police have got everything else controlled around the Piazza Venezia, the Forum, and Colliseum. It looks like they are going to use the Circus Maximus as a staging area for tour buses and demonstrators." Rafi nodded. He was appreciative that Hakim had lowered his stridency and was acting reasonably. Hakim continued. "If we go to Via dei Cerchi very early in the morning, we should find parking that will work."

"What about detonation?"

"Cell phones are our best option. Once we decide on the optimum time to detonate the bomb, I'll simply make a phone call. The call received at the cell attached to the triggering device will close the circuit and the whole thing will detonate."

"So there is no need for us to be there?"

"I know that disappoints you, but there is no need to be a martyr. Not now." Rafi saw Hakim's twisted grin returning. He let the comment go.

"You're confident the phone detonator will work?"

"Yes. However, I'm assuming the authorities will still not be using any jamming devices." Hakim paused to think. "I think that is a fair assumption, because if they do, people will not be able to communicate within the city. The authorities know that people will not stand for it. Italians are wedded to their *telefonini*." Pensively, Hakim slowly stroked his chin. "Actually, planting the bomb on the other side of the Palentine Hill could help counteract any tactical jamming devices in close proximity to the G-20 officials."

"But we don't know that for certain." Rafi said as he finished his coffee.

"I'm quite certain the cell phone detonator will work. I'm going to keep everything very simple. I never had a failure with my system in Iraq. And I'll engineer something else, just in case. A back-up system. I'll rig everything after we park the van."

"Then where do you make the call from, and how do we get out of the city?" Rafi lowered his voice even further. "With the explosion, there will be chaos."

"A hotel room or a *pensione* would be ideal; someplace within a kilometer or two of the parked van. We can monitor the G-20 event on television and choose the opportune time. I'll make the call from the room." Hakim grinned again. "Since we will be a kilometer or so away from the explosion, we will not get trapped in the initial panic and confusion."

"The room should also be a place where we can make a quick exit from the city." Rafi looked up at the piazza. He then turned his eyes back toward the map. "Actually, this area around Piazza del Popolo will work." Hakim slowly nodded. "If we can get a room nearby, there is easy access to both Ponte Milvio and the Flaminia.

"We'll have our bikes ready to go. When the bomb is detonated, we will get out of the city," Hakim said.

"On our motorbikes, we can easily ride up the Flaminia to our car before security has time to react and traffic is at a standstill. The garage is right by the *racordo* and quick access to the *autostrada,"* Rafi added, warming to the plan.

"From there we can head to Bari on the Adriatic Coast. I know a network of *clandestini* smugglers. We can go to Algiers," Hakim said grinning again.

Rafi slowly nodded his concurrence. It was a plan. It was logical. As if reading his mind, Hakim added, "It will work. Trust me. But we have to find a room. There are so many people in Rome now that finding one is going to be very hard."

Rafi smiled as he thought of his adoptive father. "Leave that to me. I've only been in Italy a short while. But I know people. Greed is universal."

chapter 26

I HAD ONLY been standing post for three hours, but my feet were killing me. My discomfort was tempered by the irony of it all. It was just like old times: the nice suit, shined shoes, sunglasses, earpiece, microphone attached to the end of my suit sleeve, the issued lapel pin, a mobile phone, secure digital Motorola radio on my belt, two extra clips of ammunition, and my FN 5.7 pistol holstered on my hip. The only difference was that my detail to the Secret Service would be over in just a few days. In prior years when I was a Secret Service agent, there was no end in sight to the protection details. This time when the president left town, I wouldn't accompany the protection detail home. Rather I would go back to my regular work as a HSI special agent. That made the post-standing more than bearable and actually encouraged a lot of good memories. Without thinking, I squared my shoulders a bit more and clasped my hands loosely at my waste. It was déjà vu.

The seriousness of the situation impacted my mood. Was Rome really threatened by some type of a weapon of mass destruction? Was POTUS in danger? Were there other threats? Unfortunately, I didn't know what to look for. My eyes kept darting the length of the Veneto. I tried to scan everything and not hover on any one person or street scene. In the old days, I looked for suspicious behavior or anything out of the ordinary. It was more instinct than training. But it seemed like more and more, there was no norm. A threat could appear from anywhere and be masked by the commonplace.

The presidential entourage had arrived at the American Embassy about thirty minutes before. After the first day of the G-20 Summit, POTUS's schedule called for an informal "meet and greet" to thank embassy staff for their assistance. Even family members of embassy staff were invited. Ana and the kids had come downtown for the appearance. The president graciously made a few remarks in the Bomcampani parking lot of the embassy to the assembled embassy staff and family members. President Rindler then walked the length of the rope line shaking hands. Ana texted me that Marie had received a presidential pat on her head. Afterwards, POTUS went into the chancery for discussions with the ambassador and a meeting with the embassy "country team."

My post was just inside the main gate of the chancery. My back was turned to the embassy and the "protectee." A threat would more than likely come from the front. The PPD detail covered the president within their working perimeter.

In the nineteenth century, the building now occupied by the American Embassy had originally been owned by the noble Ludovisi family of Rome. Serious financial problems forced them to sell it to the Italian royal family. Until 1924, Queen Margherita lived at the residence. After the Second World War, the United States bought the property and converted it into the American Embassy.

From my vantage point, I could easily see up and down the broad and stately Via Veneto. Looking to my left, the Via Veneto curved downhill toward Piazza Barberini. The section of Via Veneto going up from the embassy toward Porta Pinciana was part of the city's legendary *dolce vita.* Porta Pinciana was encased in the remnants of a crumbling brick wall that once surrounded ancient Rome. Modern Porta Pinciana marked the entrance to the Veneto and the *centro storico.* On the far side of the wall was Villa Borghese, the second largest public park in Rome. The Borghese gardens contained the Pincio or the Pincian Hill of ancient Rome. It overlooked the Piazza del Popolo. It was a favorite visiting place for Roman families. Children played in the park or fed the ducks swimming in the ponds and fountains. Couples often took a *passegiata* down the paths near the

Pincio in the Roman sunshine. They enjoyed magnificent views of the eternal city's skyline.

Despite the personal memories, historical location, and the surrounding views, I tried to remain alert and cognizant of the seriousness of my assignment and the very real threats. In fact, security services all over the city were on edge. Earlier that morning, Rome had witnessed the first of three successive days of scheduled massive peaceful demonstrations. Tens of thousands of people had marched down the very same Via Veneto. They joined an enormous rally in Piazza Venezia that had flooded outward, completely clogging adjoining streets and transportation arteries. The press had already conservatively estimated the rally to have included well over 200,000 people. The rally was designed to coincide with the first day of the G-20 Summit. Although many organized groups were present to promote various causes, both intelligence reports and the world media were reporting that the overwhelming majority of people were demonstrating their solidarity with the Palestinian people and their protest of Israel's West Bank settlements and confiscatory water policies. In contrast to many similar international summits, this time the organizers championed nonviolence and civilized behavior. However, Italian law enforcement and security services, joined by their counterparts in the G-20 delegations, were still very much concerned. The very size of the crowds could mask real threats.

In the late afternoon, the Veneto was still filled with demonstrators returning from the rally. They were not organized but walked singly or in small groups. Some held signs. A few still held banners aloft. Most looked tired and worn. Tens of thousands of demonstrators had announced they were fasting during daylight hours for the three days of the G-20 Summit to show their solidarity with the Palestinians. Continuing to draw on the lessons of Gandhi's nonviolence movement, they wanted to draw the world's attention to Israel's control of Palestine's water supply. Their tactics appeared to be working. Even from my limited vantage point, from time to time I spotted camera crews from the international media attempting to interview a particularly colorful or parched and disheveled-looking demonstrator. Undoubtedly the marches, demonstrations, and interviews were being broadcast around the world. I could only imagine the pressure building on the government of Israel.

Outside the embassy gate stood two armed Carabinieri. They were joined by additional Carabinieri, both at periodic fixed posts and others patrolling the sidewalks. Although the mid-morning demonstration had been over for hours, the Via Veneto was still blocked to all but official vehicular traffic. However, pedestrian traffic, both on the sidewalks and street, remained very heavy. The chancery gate was controlled by an Italian guard force under the direction of the embassy's regional security officer. As I was assigned my post, the Secret Service site agent directed me to be PPD's eyes and ears at the embassy gate. My encrypted radio was on the assigned frequency, and I could communicate directly with both the detail and the Secret Service command post. In close working proximity to my Italian colleagues, I could easily pass along needed communications.

Expressionless, I kept my eyes fixed toward the Veneto. The sun was low in the sky and long shadows covered what had become a very long and broad pedestrian walkway. I noted the variety of people passing by; young and old, well-dressed and unkempt. All seemed to be in good spirits. Most were obviously Italian, but there were many from other countries. In order to help stay alert, I played my old game of trying to distinguish nationalities. I noted everything from the style of dress, shoes, hair, and eye color of the passersby to the color of their skin. It was an international assembly in the best sense of the term. People had come to the G-20 Summit from around the world to express their views.

The radio crackled in my earpiece. "Country team meeting is breaking up. Turquoise will now be given a brief tour of the chancery."

President Rindler's call sign was Turquoise. Rindler was the first female US president. A former senator and popular governor of New Mexico, Ellen Rindler favored turquoise jewelry mined and fashioned in her native state. She ran a tough election campaign and early on had picked up the moniker *turquoise lady*. It had stuck.

I glanced down at my watch. POTUS was scheduled to depart the embassy in exactly twelve minutes. Barring the unforeseen, presidential events - even an "informal" meet-and-greet - are choreographed to the minute. I knew POTUS and her entourage would be leaving from the main door of the American Embassy directly behind me. The president would then walk the length of the driveway to the broad and shallow steps that climbed to the Bomcompagni gate parking lot and her waiting motorcade. In yesteryear, the steps were used by horses going to and from their stables. When my daughter Marie visited the embassy, she delighted in walking the big steps. She called them "elephant steps."

Although the detail leader was not happy about the arrangements, during the advance it was determined that the embassy driveway was not large enough to accommodate all of the vehicles in the motorcade. The Italians also vetoed the possibility of "stacking" the motorcade on the Via Veneto. As a result, when the presidential party emerged from the chancery they would momentarily be exposed to public view by pedestrian onlookers or from a number of buildings along the Veneto. To mitigate the president's being out in the open for more than a few seconds, one vehicle was parked in the embassy driveway. It would drive slowly and parallel the short presidential walk to the "elephant steps." The vehicle would provide cover and block direct line of sight.

Standing post, it was a struggle to keep worry and conjecture away. There were so many contingencies and "what-ifs." Farid's allegations remained in the back of my mind. Over the last few days when not with the Secret Service, I had spent whatever free time I had in my office trying desperately to develop additional information. My attempts to re-contact the source were not successful. It didn't surprise me. The fact that every combination of queries in ICE and other databases proved negative was also not a revelation. There was nothing to be found. I knew our best hope continued to be that the Guardia di Finanza might develop something by trying to follow the "value trail" to Italy, possibly from Pakistan. However, there just didn't seem to be enough time. I was on edge—which I knew was the wrong frame of mind.

A young man wearing jeans and a black leather jacket caught my eye. He had walked past the embassy gate at least three times in the last ten minutes. Approximately twenty feet away from me, his fists were clasped tightly onto the wrought iron embassy fence. He peered into the embassy compound. Over the previous few hours, I had seen others do the same thing out of obvious curiosity. They always moved on. This individual reappeared. He seemed to be South Asian. His demeanor was anxious. It was hard to articulate my concerns, but law enforcement officers learn to trust their gut feelings. Particularly given the totality of recent events, the individual's behavior seemed suspicious.

The embassy was American territory, but everything else was under the jurisdiction of the Italians. Opening the gate, I took a few steps and motioned to one of the Carabinieri standing guard quietly nearby. During the last three hours, we had occasionally exchanged pleasantries. Pointing out the individual standing at the embassy fence, I voiced my observations and concerns. Simultaneously shrugging his shoulders and offering the proverbial Roman expression "*va beh*" he motioned for me to follow. I explained that I could not leave my position near the gate. The Carabinieri then summoned his partner and the two of them walked over to the man who continued to stand transfixed, staring through the embassy fence. The Carabinieri started to question the individual, but I couldn't hear what was being said, and the subject didn't appear to respond to the Carabinieris' inquiries. One of the Carabinieri quickly ran his hands over the man's clothing, simultaneously probing and squeezing, undoubtedly searching for a possible weapon. When they were finished, the same Carabinieri who did the search loosely held the subject's elbow and escorted him back down the sidewalk to where I was standing.

As they were heading toward me, I heard the crackling again in my headpiece. "Turquoise is being escorted by the ambassador. They are stopping to see the Venus statue." I knew immediately that they were located at the main staircase, where a beautiful sixteenth century statue by Giambologna was displayed. The statue had been identified years ago in the embassy art collection by the embassy curator. Worth millions, it had been displayed in Rome's Capitoline Museums and the National Gallery of Art in Washington, DC. Now safely ensconced back in the embassy, it was a much-admired art treasure.

The subject stood in front of me. I estimated he was in his late teens or early twenties. He had longish coal-black hair, brown eyes, and the complexion and features of a South Asian. He was dressed in jeans. The subject's black leather jacket was unbuttoned over a bright green V-neck sweater. He wore running shoes. A Carabinieri stood on each side of him. I nodded to both saying, "*Grazie*."

Turning to the subject, I said, "*Buon giorno*, good day. I see you are interested in the American Embassy. Can I help you?"

He didn't reply. The subject had a blank look in his eyes. He was expressionless.

"*Come se chiama?*" What's your name? There was no response.

"He hasn't said a word since we approached him," said the Carabinieri in Italian.

"Does he have any identification?" I asked.

"We went through his pockets. He isn't carrying a wallet. He's not armed. We only found a money clip with a few euro notes. That's all."

I knew the president was due to depart shortly. In the back of my mind, I kept thinking of Farid's report and his allegations that a Pakistani of about the same age named Rafi Durrani might be in Italy with a weapon of mass destruction. The possible correlation to the subject in front of me was extremely weak. Nevertheless, I felt uneasy. The young man had a faraway look.

"Has this individual broken any laws?" I asked the Carabinieri closest to me.

"No. He should have identification, but we don't bother with that. Just standing by the embassy is not a crime. He is probably attracted to all the activity going on. Maybe he speaks a different language and he can't understand us."

"I think he's a bit *pazzo*—crazy in the head," said the other Carabinieri. "But he has done nothing wrong. He is just a bit odd."

Thinking it over for a few moments, I finally said, "Well, it's your call, but I suppose we should let him go."

Shrugging his shoulders, the officer I had first approached again muttered "*va beh*." He released the subject and with his hands motioned him to leave as if he was shooing away a pesky fly.

Still expressionless, the subject turned away and started walking back up the Veneto.

"*Grazie infinite*," I told my Carabinieri counterparts. "Thank you so much for your help."

I stepped back inside the embassy gate and the two Carabinieri resumed their nearby posts.

The radio again crackled in my ear, "We've got movement. POTUS is departing the chancery en route to the motorcade."

It was immediately followed by another transmission, "Jenson with the motorcade copies. We're standing by."

I sensed the movement behind me and stole a glance over my shoulder. The first of the staffers and aides in the presidential party headed out of the embassy toward the driveway. At the same time, I heard a shout up the Veneto. Turning my gaze, I saw some pedestrians directly in front of me motioning excitedly. I followed their pointed hands and my heart skipped a beat. The subject we had released just minutes ago was scaling the embassy fence. Perched precariously on top, he was pulling himself over. If he succeeded, he could easily jump into the embassy compound. Weapons drawn, Carabinieri on the Veneto were shouting and running toward him. He hesitated at the top of the fence. Simultaneously, POTUS, escorted by the ambassador and surrounded by staff and Secret Service agents, had already exited the embassy. They were headed toward the "elephant steps" and the waiting motorcade.

Training from years ago kicked in. Hitting the transmit button on my radio, I said, "This is Costa at the embassy front gate. We have a fence jumper. I'm responding."

From his perch on top of the fence, the subject looked back. The charging Carabinieri were shouting commands at him to get down from the fence. He turned his head toward the embassy. For a few long seconds, he hesitated. Then, leaping into the air, the fence jumper hit the ground inside the fence and sprawled on all fours. As he picked himself up, I started to run.

I was the closest agent to him. Shouts of "cover, cover, cover" filled the air. As the intruder got to his feet and took his first steps toward the presidential party, I lengthened my running strides and then lunged. I tackled the fence jumper on the lawn of the embassy, and the force of the impact caused us both to roll over. I righted myself and started to pinion his arms to the ground.

Simultaneously, seemingly dozens of hands went past me to the subject, holding him down. I was somewhat aware of more shouts and screams. Still on the ground, I looked through the pantlegs of an Italian embassy security officer. Closer to the "elephant steps" and the waiting secure motorcade than the chancery from which they had just exited, I saw the Secret Service use the security vehicle in the driveway as a shield. Some agents had guns drawn. Others formed a human cordon around the president. Turquoise was literally carried up the elephant steps to the waiting motorcade. The sirens were already wailing. Although things seemed to move in slow motion, the incident itself was over in seconds.

The front entrance to the embassy was bedlam. The intruder was handcuffed and seated on the ground. He was surrounded by security personnel. I saw some agents and embassy security officers running. They were no doubt frightened that the fence jumper might have been a diversion. Not knowing what to do, I picked myself up and slowly headed back to the front gate. Pedestrians had gathered on the outside of the fence. A television news crew was broadcasting. The embassy security force and the Carabinieri were moving people away from the vicinity of the embassy. My earpiece was barking. The command post was coordinating conflicting reports. I noted the Secret Service personnel using excellent radio discipline. In any incident, security is trained not to transmit unnecessarily so as not to "step on" vital communications. From the command post transmissions, it was apparent the motorcade had exited the embassy Bomcompagni gate and was headed to the nearby ambassador's residence. I could hear the noise of the sirens slowly disappearing. POTUS was unharmed.

I spotted Roy Williams from the Intelligence Division walking briskly down the elephant steps into the embassy drive. He scanned the scene in front of him. Checking briefly on the intruder, he walked over to the front gate.

"Welcome back to the Secret Service," he said with some bemusement. "What the hell happened?"

"Roy, it all happened very quickly."

"It always does. Take it one step at a time. Give me the details."

As I recounted the events, Special Agent Williams took a small pad out of his suit breast pocket and began taking notes. When I finished telling the story, he abruptly closed his notebook. "Without rushing to conclusions, it sounds like we might have a mentally disturbed fence jumper." He paused reflectively. "When I was in the Protective Intelligence Squad in the Washington, DC Field Office, we had a few of those. One incident was very similar to what just happened here. Two Uniform Division Officers at the White House approached an individual near the fence by the south lawn. As soon as they finished their conversation, they turned their backs and walked away. The guy jumped the fence."

"Very similar," I said. "But in this case, the guy didn't say a word. He was acting a bit strange, but I couldn't read his intentions. He hadn't broken any law and the Carabinieri and I basically concurred we should just let him go."

Roy nodded. "I understand." He paused and looked steadily into my eyes. "Joe, the two UD officers involved were subject to a lot of second-guessing. Don't be surprised if that happens here as well."

I nodded knowingly. "It's the nature of the bureaucracy."

"We're going to find out exactly who this guy is. I've got a lot of interviewing to do. I'll get Marco, the Secret Service attaché's FSN—foreign service national—to help me interview the Carabinieri. We'll talk again."

When Williams left, I turned away from the fence and headed toward the front entrance of the embassy. A crowd of staffers was gathering. They were standing together in twos and threes recounting events. The buzz quieted when the intruder was escorted to the Via Veneto gate to a waiting Carabinieri vehicle. He was accompanied by two Secret Service agents. Undoubtedly, he was being taken to a station for questioning.

I was certain that Ana had heard about the incident by now, and I wanted to give her a call and tell her I was fine. Reaching for my cell phone, I was startled when Susan Martinelli grabbed my arm.

"Joe, are you O.K.?"

"I'm fine."

Still holding my arm, she led me a few steps away. "I believe I know what happened," she said in an accusatory tone of voice.

"What do you mean?"

"Well, inside the chancery, the television news stations are already broadcasting the incident. They are saying witnesses told them that you interviewed him just prior to his jumping the fence."

"That's right."

"I saw the intruder on television and just now as they led him away." I saw anger in her eyes. "Joe, you singled him out because he is South Asian."

"What?" I asked incredulously. "No, Susan. He was acting rather strangely, so the Carabinieri and I had a talk with him."

"Are you telling me that your obsession with your so-called 'intelligence reporting' had no bearing on your decision to single him out?"

"No, it didn't," I said firmly.

"It could very well be that your interview was the catalyst that caused him to jump the fence."

I knew I had to measure my words carefully. "The individual was acting strangely. His race, ethnicity, and country of origin had nothing to do with it. It was the totality of the circumstances." I could tell my words were not registering. "Susan, I used my best judgment. I could not somehow divine his intent. I just spoke with Roy Williams from the Secret Service Intelligence Division. We still don't even know who he is."

"Exactly." Susan slowly wagged her head back and forth. "To me it appears that you were profiling. This is something that I personally abhor, and so does our department."

"It wasn't profiling," I said.

"Dennis and I both warned you not to get carried away. You seem to have forgotten your role as a HSI agent. I was afraid something like this would happen."

"That's ridiculous."

"Is it? Right now inside the chancery, Angie Coleman, the White House staffer in charge of this visit, is on the warpath. She is literally screaming that this visit has been ruined. The ambassador is trying to calm her down. You will definitely be hearing more."

chapter 27

I SAT QUIETLY in my G-ride, parked on the wide gravel drive of the American ambassador's residence. The car was underneath a row of cypress trees that darkened the night sky even further and also helped to deaden some of the nearby street noise. The car radio was turned off. The ambiance matched my gloomy mood. I was in no hurry to leave the sanctuary and solitude of my car and walk toward the bright lights and activity surrounding Villa Taverna. Glancing, resigned, at the luminescent hands of my watch, I let out an audible sigh. It was almost 2100 hours.

About an hour before, I had received a telephone call from the Guardia di Finanza's Colonnello Dario Rossi. He was adamant that he needed to see me. Rossi said that he had some information he wanted to share but would only discuss it face to face. I explained that I began my midnight shift with the Secret Service at 2200 hours. With the tone and the reasoning of an impatient man, Colonnello Rossi said he was working late and that he would be delighted to meet me at Villa Taverna.

The minutes ticked by as I awaited Rossi's arrival, and I became increasingly despondent. I didn't have any concrete facts, but I was convinced something catastrophic might soon happen in Rome. My gut still told me that Farid's reporting had to be taken seriously. In addition to the far reaching military/political/economic significance of a possible terrorist attack on Rome, my family's safety could be directly impacted. But I felt powerless. My inconsequential position in the bureaucratic hierarchy and limited power of persuasion butted up against the culture of the bureaucracies. The lack of specific "actionable intelligence" negated Farid's warnings. I knew I was being accused by some of "crying wolf," and by my own boss of getting involved in things that were not part of my job description.

I continued to replay in my mind the scene in front of the American Embassy. I had already given countless explanations of the fence jumping incident to Secret Service, embassy, Carabinieri, and DHS personnel. I also had to explain what happened to my wife and friends. Ana was fully supportive. Unfortunately, some of the others were not. As much as I told myself to ignore the criticisms, armchair critiques of my actions were eating at me. The attaché's accusations that I was profiling stung particularly badly. But even if I was unconsciously profiling, wasn't that understandable? Wasn't the threat level high enough to justify bending the bureaucratic niceties of political correctness? With limited information, how do we narrow down targeting?

The irony of the accusations by the attaché was not lost on me. I had done a lot of work with the Italian law enforcement agencies to target Italian-American organized crime—the Mafia—by proactively examining various databases. The financial databases, both American and Italian, proved particularly useful. By looking for anomalies, trends, and patterns, and then cross-referencing our findings in the law enforcement databases, it was possible to identify likely targets for further examination and possibly investigation. In short, we were using analytics to profile. Both the Italian and American governments endorsed the work. The financial targeting program was under the auspices of the attaché. This kind of targeting was acceptable. So what was the difference between proactively "profiling" possible Italian-American Mafia members and using many of the same methods and databases to try and identify suspect terrorists allegedly from South Asia or the Middle East?

My midnight shift aggravated my lousy mood. When I was in the Secret Service and regularly worked midnights, a former colleague used to say, "For every midnight you work, take a day off your life." The midnight shift was physically draining. In fact, Steve Rucker—the PPD lead agent—understood the physical and psychological reactions involved with the embassy fence-jumping incident and had passed word to me that, if I wished, I could be excused from further post-standing. Although I appreciated his offer, there was an unwritten code among agents in the Secret Service that they didn't back out of assignments unless absolutely necessary. The simple reason was that if somebody dropped out, somebody else had to take his or her place. The camaraderie in the Secret Service did not allow that to happen.

I knew POTUS was not yet at Villa Taverna. President Rindler was attending a G-20 dinner hosted by the Italian prime minister. She was not due back to the ambassador's magnificent residence until 2300 hours. As a comparatively low-ranking embassy employee, I had visited the historic sixteenth century villa only for the annual law enforcement Christmas party. The gathering was hosted by the ambassador, and the splendor of his residence always impressed the Americans and their Italian guests.

Although it was impossible to appreciate it during the nighttime hours, Villa Taverna also boasted one of Rome's largest and most spectacular gardens. The grounds were situated in a former vineyard called La Pariola. The land had been given to the German Hungarian Jesuit College by Pope Gregory XIII as a place of rest for pupils exhausted by their studies. Villa Taverna—then and now—was adjacent to Villa Borghese and at the entrance to the ancient catacombs of Sant'Ermete. In modern times, the surrounding area was called *Parioli* and was one of the most exclusive neighborhoods in Rome. I knew the area well, as I often drove through its backstreets on my daily commute to and from the embassy.

My thoughts were interrupted when I looked out the side window of my parked car. I saw some headlights approach the security checkpoint at the ambassador's residence. After a few moments, a car was waved through the gates. I immediately recognized it as a Guardia di Finanza vehicle. Opening my car door, I stepped out onto the gravel drive. I was momentarily illuminated by the headlights of the approaching car. Colonnello Rossi pulled up beside me.

"Buona sera," the Colonnello said as he stepped out of his vehicle. He shook my hand with a big smile on his face.

"*Salve,*" I replied. It was an ancient Roman greeting that, loosely translated, means *hail.* The acknowledgement was popular within Italian law enforcement circles.

"Joe, you're famous," he said. "The video of you in front of the embassy is playing over and over again on Italian television."

"Colonnello," I said with a grimace, "I'm not interested in that kind of fame. In fact, I'm trying to forget about the incident."

"*Ma, perché?*"—But why?

"We have an expression we use in the US, 'the culture of the bureaucracies.' Sometimes bureaucracies and managers don't want controversy. As a result, they stifle aggression. What's happening is that I'm getting some criticism for my actions."

Colonnello Rossi frowned. "*Lo capisco,*"—I understand. "But, Joe, we must continue to be aggressive. That's why I'm here."

"Colonnello, I only have about thirty minutes before I've got to report for my midnight shift."

"That's plenty of time. *Senti*—listen. There is something I must tell you."

"Please, continue."

Colonnello Rossi edged closer. Although nobody was in the vicinity who could possibly overhear our conversation, he still lowered his voice. "We have had some success in following the value trail."

Although it was dark in the parking lot, the lights from the villa caused some illumination. It was enough to let me see the sly grin on Colonnello Rossi's face.

I swallowed hard. "I'm delighted to hear that. Particularly after the last twenty-four hours, it is nice to hear some positive news."

"Joe, what I am going to tell you is just preliminary, but I want to let you know what we have discovered. Most of this has only come together over the last few hours."

"Colonnello, I appreciate anything you can tell me."

"Well, just as you suggested, we used our trade databases and we discovered some suspect imports of scrap gold and scrap metal coming into Italy from Pakistan."

I nodded. "That's what my informant suggested."

"That's right. It really wasn't very difficult to narrow it down. Italy does not import that much scrap metal or scrap gold from Pakistan. There was only one firm that imported both."

"So what did you find?"

"The name of the suspect company is *Riciclaggio di Oro* or RDO."

I laughed. "Riciclaggio means laundering or recycling."

"The owner may well have a dry sense of humor," Colonnello Rossi said. "We hope to find out."

"So why were the imports so suspicious?"

"Over the last two years, RDO consistently imported gold scrap at high prices. Sometimes gold scrap was actually imported at prices higher than four-nine gold or 99.99 percent pure gold."

"Were they legitimate imports or just a paper exercise to send payment abroad?"

"There is no way to tell right now," replied Rossi. "But the bottom line is that there is no rationale or legitimate market reason for importing gold scrap at prices higher than gold bullion."

"Exactly. However, if somebody wanted to use false invoicing as a way to justify payment, scrap gold would be an ideal medium. By the way, fictitious invoicing is what hawaladars sometimes do with counter-valuation."

"Joe, it is funny you should mention that. We think that is exactly what RDO was doing. It is value transfer via the scrap gold trade."

"Go on."

"The owner of RDO is an individual by the name of Hakim Faghoul. He lives and works in Brescia and is very active in the *clandestini* community. He is involved in what we believe is a hawala operation that serves Brescia's large immigrant community."

"Faghoul . . . isn't that a North African surname?"

"Yes, his residency permit shows he is Algerian. We are trying to gather additional information."

"Is there anything in the Italian law enforcement databases on him?"

Colonnello Rossi took a few steps away. The outdoor lights from Villa Taverna glimmered off the brass buttons of his uniform.

"There is only one record, and it is recent." He reached into his inside coat pocket and pulled out a plain white envelope. Wearing his black leather gloves in the chilly November night, it took him a few fumbling moments to open the flap and take out a half-dozen pictures. I moved closer. "These first pictures come from our internal security service. They are surveillance photos taken about two months ago at an immigrant rally in Milan."

"I see."

"The man circled here we've identified as Hakim Faghoul. The others are close-up photos from the rally. The last photo is from his residency permit."

I examined the photos closely. They showed a slight, sinewy, clean-shaven man who looked like he was in his late twenties or early thirties. There was nothing distinguishing about him. Yet I was transfixed by the stare in the identity photo.

"Look at his eyes. There is something disturbing about this photo. I can't place it, but his eyes look possessed."

Colonnello Rossi nodded. "There are a few other things that are disturbing."

"Tell me."

"For one thing, Hakim Faghoul is not in Brescia. He has been away from his home and business for about two weeks. His car is gone."

"Anything else?"

"A shipment of scrap metal arrived in the port of Napoli about ten days ago. The consignee is Hakim Faghoul and RDO. The shipment originated in Karachi."

There were a few moments of silence before I caught myself stammering, "My God. Are you sure?"

"Yes."

I shook my head. My mind was racing. "Scrap gold and scrap metal from Pakistan. That is exactly what my source said. What are the next steps?"

"This case is now getting a lot of personal attention by the Guardia's Commander, Generale Guglielmino. We will interview the freight forwarder and the driver who delivered the shipment of scrap metal. We are also getting a search warrant for Faghoul's home and business. Hopefully, we will learn more."

"Tomorrow I can play with Faghoul's name in our databases." I paused for a moment. "What about the Pakistani national who my source named, Rafi Durrani?"

"Joe, our services are coordinating closely. They are also working together on international inquiries. Record checks came back negative from Pakistan."

"That's disappointing."

Colonnello Rossi's voice tailed off. "Joe, maybe it is to be expected." Slyly smiling again, he added, "We also requested assistance from the United Arab Emirates. According to your source, Durrani has traveled there on multiple occasions."

"UAE authorities forwarded a copy of Durrani's passport photo. He has multiple entries into and out of Dubai. Our external security service is examining the information now."

"I'm sure you checked, but are there any records showing that Rafi Durrani entered Italy?

"*Purtroppo*—unfortunately—we have no records on Durrani. At least not under that name. But we're looking. I'm sorry to say that Italy does not have adequate biometric technology and eye retina scanning at immigration."

I nodded. "But even if you had the technology, we need data to mach it with."

Rossi was doing all that could realistically be done. In my work and travels I had found most of the time that good policing was universal. Law enforcement was about maintaining order in society. Laws and rules had to be enforced. Some police services had better tools, resources, and training than others, but officers who enforced the laws were generally organized individuals who approached their jobs and investigations in a methodical manner.

"We need more time," Rossi said wistfully.

"*In bocca al lupo*," I replied, using a traditional Roman euphemism meaning "good luck." The literal translation is "In the mouth of the wolf," which is often said to someone about to undertake a task. The expression seemed very appropriate.

Rossi nodded. Silently, he put his gloved hand on my shoulder. His smile offered unspoken support and encouragement.

"Colonnello, I think we both will be working midnight shifts."

chapter 28

Rafi left his room and walked down the narrow flights of hotel stairs. He exited into the lobby. Striding toward the front door and access to the street, he passed directly by the hotel's small front desk.

"*Buon giorno, signor* Kaker," said the receptionist. "I trust you and *signor* Faghoul are enjoying your stay with us."

Rafi was momentarily startled by the greeting. He still wasn't used to hearing his alias. Gathering himself, he turned toward the receptionist. "*Buon giorno, signor. Tutto bene. Grazie.*"

"It would be my pleasure if I could possibly be of assistance." continued the receptionist. He walked around the desk and directly approached Rafi. "Are you going sightseeing? Do you need any suggestions? Perhaps I could call you a taxi?"

Rafi smiled knowingly. The previous evening he had slipped the same receptionist an exorbitant sum of money to help him find two rooms in his "completely filled" hotel. It was quite obvious the receptionist was angling for more. "Actually, I am going for a long walk. I have some guidebooks of Rome with me and a good map. I think I have everything I need, but I thank you for your offer."

The receptionist rubbed his palms together. He looked over the rims of his spectacles and peered up directly into Rafi's eyes. "If you need recommendations for a good restaurant nearby, some female companionship, or anything at all, please do not hesitate to ask."

"Grazie. Signor Faghoul should be down shortly. Perhaps you should speak with him." Rafi slightly nodded his head in the universal sign of dismissal. The receptionist hurried to the front door. With a slight bend at the waist, he held it open as Rafi exited onto the busy sidewalk. Momentarily getting his bearings, Rafi turned to his right and began the short two-block walk back to Piazza del Popolo.

The hotel was perfectly situated. It was only a few short kilometers from the Circus Maximus and Via dei Cerchi where they planned to park and detonate the explosives-laden Scudo van. Afterwards, they planned to make a quick exit out of the *centro storico*, cross one of a number of nearby bridges over the Tiber, proceed up Via Flaminia, and make their escape from Rome. During the morning, Rafi and Hakim had practiced the route. Even though it was impossible to predict the vagaries of Italian traffic, they believed the routes they had selected—a primary and an alternate—would get them speedily out of Rome. They also wanted to check on the Alfa and the van. They were both parked in a secure parking garage. Just about everything was ready.

Rafi needed some exercise and some fresh air. He was still getting over his morning confrontation with Hakim. The Algerian seemed to enjoy toying with him by making cutting remarks. Rafi was trying desperately to maintain his self-control. He also thought the walk would help him go over his mental checklist one more time to make sure everything was covered. The enormity of what was going to happen was overwhelming.

Entering the massive oval-shaped piazza, Rafi passed the twin churches that stood on either side of the Porta del Popolo—Santa Maria di Montesanto and Santa Maria dei Miracoli. Instead of opting to walk back down the Corso toward Piazza Venezia where he knew he would encounter nothing but traffic and G-20 checkpoints, he turned and headed in the opposite direction. Rafi wanted tranquility. In the distance, he saw an expanse of green on a knoll overlooking the piazza. Without a glance at a map, he stretched his strong legs and headed toward it. From his thorough study of the guidebooks, he knew he was headed for the Pincio gardens and the nearby Villa Borghese.

He walked quickly. The exercise and the brisk, clear fall day were a perfect tonic. Rafi delighted in the weather, so different from his native Karachi. Leaving the bustle of Piazza del Popolo behind, he spotted a street that jutted up the side of the hill and seemed to lead directly to the Pincio. Step after step, his measured pace focused his thoughts.

He felt everything was in place for the operation. The only thing left to do was to notify his handler in Pakistan that the operation was a go. Adhering to the instructions they had received from their handlers in Karachi, both he and Hakim had maintained strict communications security. Outside of an innocuous email message after the shipment was delivered to the warehouse workshop in Campagnia, there had been no other contact. Tonight he would again send a coded message to a one time email address. It would read simply, *Allahu Akbar.* The pre-arranged signal was a common Islamic exclamation called the *takbir* in Arabic. It meant "Allah is the greatest" and was to be his battle cry.

Continuing his climb, Rafi worried again about Hakim. If he lived to report on this operation, he would tell his handlers that they had made a tremendous mistake in selecting the moody Algerian. Rafi had no doubt about Hakim's motivation or his technical skills. But Rafi was increasingly convinced that the man was not mentally stable. Over the course of the past week, he had observed Hakim's marked deterioration. There was not one thing he could pinpoint with certitude. Rather it was a combination of Hakim's actions, attitudes, verbal sparring, and uncontrolled hatred. Most of all, it was the haunted look in his eyes combined with his twisted smile. At times Hakim seemed almost as if he were controlled by an outside force. Something inside him seemed to be manipulating his thoughts and behavior. It gave Rafi a chill just thinking about it.

Making matters worse, Hakim had made it perfectly clear that after *maghrib*—evening prayers—he was going out to enjoy the Roman nightlife. He wanted Rafi to accompany him. Rafi also felt the need to relax. But he knew this evening—whether he survived the attack or not—could very well represent his final hours of freedom on this earth. He wanted to pray. He wanted to reflect. He knew he would need all of his senses and judgment. Although he realized he should probably accompany Hakim to try to keep him out of trouble, he politely turned down the invitation. He was afraid that if they spent much more time together, the increasing tension might threaten the success of the operation.

Replaying their most recent conversation in his mind, Rafi recalled how he reminded his partner that the following day would be jihad. They were Islamic warriors. They needed to prepare their minds, souls, and bodies. If sleep would come, it would be Allah's blessing. The words he had spoken to Hakim were identical to what he had heard over and over again in the madrassas and mosques. Rafi had not previously realized how much the preparation for jihad was embedded within him. He understood now that he had been unconsciously preparing for tomorrow's attack his entire life. Yet despite his appeals and the dutiful words, Hakim was not receptive. His mind was set on a night of merrymaking. Rafi's plea for Islamic piety had enraged his partner. So he said no more. However, before he left for his walk, he gave Hakim a final admonition to be ready before dawn.

Rafi continued his climb. The street he was traversing finally approached the top of the ridge. Cresting a shallow rise, Rafi entered a stunning park. In front of him was a small, beautifully manicured pedestrian piazza lined with trees, benches, statues, a fountain, and flower gardens. A small merry-go-round carousel came into view, flanked on both sides by venders selling *gelato*, pastries, popcorn, and drinks. While their parents sat on the nearby benches, small toddlers who were heavily bundled against the cool fall air awkwardly chased pigeons that likewise waddled over the piazza seeking discarded popcorn and other treats. Couples in their wool Italian coats held gloved hands as they took a *passeggiata*—a gentle stroll—around the Pincio. Some were lost in silence and others engaged in the kind of animated conversation that was uniquely Italian.

Turning to face the direction from which he had come, Rafi was overwhelmed by the magnificent view of Rome, particularly *Trastevere*, the western side of the city across the Tiber River. The sun was beginning to dip in the sky and the shadows highlighted the muted colors and tones of Rome. To his far left, Rafi could easily see Piazza Venezia and its imposing Monument to Vittorio Emanuele II. Behind the monument stood the ruins of the ancient Roman forum.

Two millennia ago, Roman armies left from this area to conquer the known world. As his gaze turned to his right over the broad panorama, he became fixed on the Vatican and the dome of St. Peter's basilica. Even from this distance it was the most impressive building he had ever seen.

Taking a few steps to the edge of the Pincio lookout, Rafi propped his hands on the railing. His gaze remained fixed on St. Peter's. The little he knew about Christianity and Catholicism he had learned from the popular Pakistani media, and the headmaster, teachers, and clerics in the Karachi madrassa.

The driving principle behind Islam, recited in the call to prayer, was *La ilaha illa Allah*—"There is no god but God." Muslims acknowledged the old prophets of Judaism and Christianity to be true messengers of God, but Muhammad was the last and the greatest of the prophets. The Quran was the final message from God. Islam's view of Christianity was that it started off as a religion based in Jewish tradition. Muslims acknowledged Jesus as both a prophet and a teacher. He followed Noah, Abraham, and Moses, but he was not the Alpha and Omega as Christians believed. Although the Quran taught that Jesus was born of the Virgin Mary, Muslims rejected the Christian belief that Jesus was both God's only begotten son and God incarnate. Islam condemned the Catholic doctrine of the Holy Trinity, stressing instead that God is unity. Muslims rejected both the crucifixion and resurrection of Jesus. According to the Quran, Jesus escaped the crucifixion and ascended directly to heaven.

Rafi's eyes remained fixed on the dome of St. Peter's Cathedral. He thought about how much he didn't know. Even with his broad practical education, international travel, facility with languages, and exposure to other cultures, he had never explored other religious beliefs. He had never felt the need or desire. He was very comfortable with his religion's absolutes. Rafi was taught that Islam was the only path. Freedom of relgion was not part of his background, belief, or thought process. In his short time in Italy, he had never stepped into any of the Catholic churches that seemed to be on every street corner. They somehow frightened him. Still gazing at the crown of the Vatican, he recalled the clerics' constant denunciation of the papacy and Christian beliefs. Although the crusades were initiated almost a millennia ago, the fiery speeches of the Karachi clerics made them seem like they were recent and, in fact, continued into the present times. The clerics fomented hatred, revenge, hostility, violent jihad, death, genocide of the non-believers, and the eventual eradication of the modern nation-state in favor of the *umma,* or caliphate, and international adherence to *Sharia.*

Tomorrow, Rafi was going to fight jihad. He was bringing the battle to the infidels in an effort to promote those goals. He would personally avenge the conquering Roman legions and the crusades, promulgated by a succession of popes who had dwelled and worshiped in the very Vatican that now held him transfixed. He would strike against the former colonial masters that subjugated foreign lands. Rafi was a slave of Allah. Submitting himself to His will, it would be by Rafi's hand that a "dirty bomb" would forever more stain the eternal city. Millions would be impacted.

Yet as he looked anew at a golden panorama of Rome, he realized that he didn't hate. He only felt confusion. For the first time in his life, he was beginning to question. He had doubts.

Finally turning away from the vista, he began to walk slowly toward the far end of the piazza. He walked among people, fellow human beings. They were men, women, and children, old and young, rich and poor, from various countries—innocent. The sight of them all made Rafi think; each individual had a different life, a different story. Every one of them was a gift from God. Like him, they had memories, joys, and secret sorrows; they were living day-to-day, complex lives and dramas; they had family, friends, and enemies. All had ambitions and dreams. Most believed in and worshipped God—the God of Islam, Judaism, and Christianity. And just like Rafi himself, he knew that their future would be indelibly shaped by his actions tomorrow.

Rafi suddenly found himself in the piazza in front a cart selling *gelato.* Deciding he needed refreshment in order to clear his mind of tormenting thoughts, he joined a few others in the short line for ice cream. Standing silently lost in his reflections, he was startled to feel something knock into his legs.

"Madonna mia! Alessandra, guarda che hai fatto!" —Oh, my Lady! Alessandra, look what you've done! *"Mi scusi tanto"* —I'm so sorry.

Looking down, Rafi saw that a very young girl had bumped into him. She was now seated on the ground holding an empty ice cream cone. A scoop of *gelato* had hit his pant leg and was now resting on his Italian leather shoe. The girl's small shoulders were beginning to quiver and she seemed to be on the verge of tears.

"It's O.K. It doesn't matter," Rafi immediately said with a laugh. He started to bend over to pick up the young girl but then knocked his head against another. The two simultaneously straightened. Rafi then looked into the loveliest eyes he had ever seen. The emerald green eyes simply sparkled. A beautiful young lady smiled. Her face radiated warmth and good will. Momentarily tousled, she took a red leather gloved hand and nonchalantly moved a long strand of chestnut brown hair that had fallen across her face. Rafi was instantly overwhelmed. With one appreciative glance, he was struck by how her bearing, features, and dress exhibited the Italian grace and stylishness he found so attractive. Smiling, together they both looked down again at the melting gelato on Rafi's shoe. They broke into laughter. The little girl broke into sobs.

"Il mio gelato!" —my ice cream!

Shushing the little one, the young lady turned to the counter and picked up a wad of paper napkins. Bending again, she tried to clean and quiet the toddler. While the young lady was occupied, Rafi bought three cones from the man across the counter. When she straightened, Rafi presented each of them with ice cream.

"Mille grazie. Ma sono io che dovrebbe comprare il gelato." —Thank you so much. But it is I that should buy the ice cream.

"É il mio . . . piacere." —It's my pleasure. Distracted by her beauty, Rafi stumbled to find the word. *"Mi dispiace. Italiano non é la mia lingua madre."* —I'm sorry, but Italian is not my native tongue.

"I speak English," she replied. Rafi was again mesmerized by her smile. "Thank you again for the ice cream . . . Are you here for the G-20?" she asked.

"No, not really. I'm traveling to Rome on business. My visit just happened to overlap with the G-20 meeting. I have some free time, so I decided to do some sightseeing."

"The Pincio gardens and Villa Borghese are beautiful," she said. Looking down, she saw the toddler start to pull on her pant leg. "I think Alessandra is going to need some help with her ice cream. Maybe we should sit on a bench . . . would you like to join us?"

Rafi's heart seemed to skip a beat. "I would like that very much." Rafi turned and scanned the area around him. "I see a free bench right over there next to the fountain."

"By the way, my name is Carla. The little one is Alessandra. She's my niece. Allesandra is two years old."

"I'm Shuja—Shuja Kaker."

Seated together, lost in conversation and her sparkling eyes, Rafi was only remotely aware of the passage of time. He vaguely realized after they finished the ice cream that Carla had sent Alessandra scurrying after the pigeons that flittered from one side of the piazza to another. He learned that Carla was a twenty-two-year-old student at the University of Rome. She was studying philosophy. She lived nearby with her parents in the Parioli district of Rome. When her schedule permitted, in the late afternoons she often took her beloved niece to the park to play. The two talked about Rome. Carla delighted in describing some of the city's insights and her favorite places. They laughed together as she described some of the eccentricities of the Roman people. When Alessandra returned to the bench after playing, the toddler climbed into Carla's lap. He watched with envy as Carla gently stroked Alessandra's hair until the girl's eyes grew heavy and she fell into a deep sleep.

As the sun began to set, they continued their conversation. Rafi—Shuja—told Carla a little bit about his life as an international businessman. She hung on his words as he described faraway places such as Karachi, Dubai, and other cities he had visited. Her eyes remained locked on his as he talked about his expanding business of importing and exporting. He also mentioned the more humorous characteristics of some of the people he dealt with and funny situations he had found himself in dealing with different cultures and languages. As he spoke, he caught himself trying to make her giggle and smile. Her beaming beauty was intoxicating.

Far too soon, the sun lowered. Rafi put the still-napping Alessandra in his arms. Looking down at the tiny girl's cherub-like face, her innocence momentarily intruded on his conscience. He forced those thoughts away. As he escorted Carla to her car, they continued their non-stop conversation. They were in no hurry to reach their destination. Finally there, Rafi helped Carla secure the slumbering Alessandra into the car seat. Then Carla turned to Rafi and put her gloved hand on his forearm.

Her eyes radiant, Carla said "I'll be back in the park again tomorrow afternoon at about the same time. I hope I will see you again."

Rafi could only nod. He desperately did not want to say farewell. He did not want this interlude of happiness to end. He was more confused than ever.

chapter 29

"BROTHER, YOU'RE STILL hungover," Rafi said disgustedly.

"I'm fine," Hakim replied. "Just leave me alone. We've got plenty of time."

It was just after sunrise and *fajr*, the morning supplication. Neither had slept. Rafi had spent the night alone. His worries and troubles were compounded as he had nervously waited for Hakim to arrive at his adjoining hotel room. Hakim finally stumbled back at three a.m. following a long night of drink and paying for women. After telling Hakim to take a shower and sober up, Rafi left the hotel and drove his motorbike up the Flaminia to where the Scudo van was securely parked. He put his bike in the back of the van and then, in the stillness and solitude of dawn, drove back down the Flaminia. Rafi was momentarily cheered when Hakim responded to his phone call and was waiting for the van to arrive in front of the hotel. In his backpack, the Algerian had timing devices and a few needed tools. Rafi's hopes soon evaporated, though, as he heard Hakim slur his speech.

Driving along deserted Roman streets, they arrived within minutes at Via dei Cerchi. They found it just as they had hoped. There was plenty of space for parking. With a short prayer asking for Allah's blessing, Rafi chose a spot midway down the portion of Via dei Cerchi that paralleled the Circus Maximus. Rafi was also heartened that he didn't see any Italian law enforcement officials. He wasn't sure if it was because of the early hour or because law enforcement and traffic police were stationed primarily on the other side of the Palentine Hill for the G-20 activities. What he did see in the early morning light were the ghostly shapes of large tour buses parked in the open field of the Circus Maximus. Parking was so scarce in Rome because of the G-20 that the authorities had built special ramps to facilitate entry and designated the area as a staging ground for the buses and their occupants.

"Brother, stay here and try to sleep. I'm going to take a long walk. I'll try to bring back some coffee."

"That's a good idea," Hakim mumbled as his chin slumped forward, hitting his chest.

Rafi exited the van. He saw lights in the far distance in the direction of Via di San Teodoro and the Bocca della Veritá. He hoped something would be open at this early hour where he could find some hot coffee.

On the other side of the Via dei Cerchi was the elongated oval field of the Circus Maximus—once one of the grandest and most impressive structures in ancient Rome. Approximately 250,000 Roman spectators could assemble on their tiered rows of marble seats while the emperor watched from his luxury box seat high on the overlooking Palatine Hill. For many centuries, the pomp and ceremony of chariot races—made famous in the movie *Ben Hur*—marked the basin. However, during the dark days of the fifth and sixth centuries, the barren Circus Maximus seemed to symbolize the imperial city's collapse. Later, medieval builders and scavengers in search of construction materials, marble, and fine statues reduced the grand circus to a great dusty field. By the twenty-first century, the Circus Maximus was a specter of its former self. The once blood-soaked racing track was covered with dirt and grass. The benches that lined the arena were gone. Only the slopes rising from the flattened basin remained, giving testimony to the frenzied spectators who once roared at the ancient races.

Rafi started to walk. He knew the crisp morning air and exercise would do him good. The long night weighed heavily on him. He had been absorbed in reflection and prayer, trying desperately to find guidance. He weighed his background, training, and his mandate to fight jihad against what he increasingly believed was a reality intertwined with differing perspectives and subtleties far more complex than he had previously understood. He was beset by what he was about to do—the repercussions of his actions. The previous afternoon's conversation in the Pincio with Carla and holding young Alessandra in his arms seemed to crystallize his concerns. Yet when he weighed his options, he could not escape his faith, ties to his homeland, the debt that he owed Majeed, and the trust given to him by a movement he still believed in. Feeling trapped and not knowing what to do, he proceeded forward.

While Rafi walked and wrestled with his beliefs and emotions, Hakim simultaneously stretched and twisted in the passenger seat of the van. The desperately needed sleep would not come. Although Hakim knew he had drunk far too much, he felt his mind was sharp. In the hazy consciousness of the sleep-deprived, the eves of previous battles flashed through his mind. In Iraq, many of his fellow al Qaeda fighters were tense and nervous before a fight. In contrast, he had always been calm. He had constantly told his comrades that it was just as important to fight with their heads as with their weapons. He felt the same way now. Although today would be the most important battle of his life, he was completely composed. He had no reservations. He relished the idea of being the bearer of death and destruction once again. After all these years, he was still inspired by his role model—the late Abu Musab al-Zarqawi. The martyr had never flinched from delivering righteous justice. Today, justice would be theirs again. Zarqawi's legacy would live on. The explosion and the dispersal of radioactive particles into the Roman air would sow panic. The infidels would be quaking in fear—not only in Rome but around the world. The vision of long-overdue Islamic ascendency roused him from his stupor. In fact, he sensed the familiar surge of adrenalin he used to feel before doing battle in Iraq. Adrenalin was a much more powerful drug than alcohol.

"No time like the present," thought Hakim. He wanted to work without Rafi hovering next to him. Moreover, at this early hour there would be no distractions from passing motorists and pedestrians. He was also confident Italian police would not be patrolling now. Grabbing his backpack, he got out of the van and walked to

the back. Opening the door, he immediately saw Rafi's motorbike. He took it out and put it near the curb beside the van. He made sure it was secured with a tamper-proof lock. Hakim caught himself smiling. Even though he had been an excellent thief years ago in Algiers, he was no match for the quickness and daring of the many thieves in Italy.

With the motorbike removed, there was enough space for him to jump up and enter the bed of the van. He fished his flashlight out of his backpack. Closing the door, he turned on the light. He slowly scanned the back of the van to get oriented. Carefully checking the van's contents, he saw that nothing had shifted. On both sides, stacked from floor to ceiling, were cardboard boxes filled with the scrap metal pieces that he had carefully selected in the Caivano warehouse. The washing machine containing the radioactive material was cinched down and stood solidly in the back of the van. Following instructions from their handlers, neither Rafi nor Hakim had tampered with it. They had even left on the red duct tape. Next to the washer, directly in front of him, was the freezer.

Hakim shimmied his way forward via a makeshift aisle that ran through the stacked cardboard boxes. Reaching the freezer, he slowly opened the door. He saw two bundles of dynamite sticks bound with black tape. Next to the explosives was another black-taped bundle containing two US military safety fuse igniters. Hakim knew they had been recovered from a battlefield in Afghanistan. He felt it fitting that the infidels' own weapons would be used against them. The van contained easily enough explosive power both to wreck havoc in the immediate vicinity and to blast the high-level radioactive material into the Roman sky. The message would be unmistakable.

Backing away, Hakim next opened a nearby plastic container. It held his tools. He reached for a battery-powered mechanic's light and flipped the switch. There was now plenty of light available. Once again, he reassured himself that the back of the van was windowless. He didn't want any light emanating that could possibly attract curious eyes.

Taking up his backpack, he gingerly lifted out his primary triggering device. He had checked and re-checked it over the last few days. Everything was in place. With some slight modifications, the device was nearly identical to the kind he had frequently used on the battlefields of Iraq. His improvised explosive devices or IEDs had proved deadly to the American invaders.

The primary trigger for the bomb was dependent on a cheap disposable phone that he bought at the Brescia flea market. Hakim chuckled in the silence of the van. Since the phone only needed to ring when called, he didn't even have to buy any minutes for it. The phone was simply not traceable. When the time was deemed right for the detonation, Hakim would place the call. The phone with which he was working rang by sending a pulse to two speakers. One speaker was in the phone head. The speakerphone on the back received a higher voltage, so it was more suitable for his purposes. To construct the trigger, he had simply popped out the speakerphone speaker. In its place, he had soldered the two lead wires to the trigger pin of a thyristor. Once the thyristor received the trigger voltage, it would allow the electric current to flow freely between the anode and cathode and the complete circuit—including the lead wires connected to the detonation fuse.

Leaning against a stack of cardboard boxes filled with shrapnel, Hakim took an LED monitor out of his tool kit and connected it to the triggering device. He turned on the disposable phone and checked to make sure it was fully charged. Next he made a test call. The LED monitor showed that sufficient current passed to trigger the device. Hakim opened a small nylon bag and removed a one-meter-long piece of detonation, or "det," cord, a thin, flexible tube with an explosive core. It would serve as his high-speed fuse. Since det cord was designed to explode rather than burn, Hakim knew that the sudden explosion, using the catalyst of the safety fuse igniter, would detonate the TNT, which in turn would blow up the contents of the van, causing the radioactive material to disperse.

He inserted one end of the det cord through the two bundles of TNT. Using black electrician's tape, he securely wrapped the homemade bomb into a tight package. Next, using an alligator clip, he connected the other end of the det cord to the safety fuse igniter. The det cord would act as a booster to the high explosives. The firing train was complete. Backing slowly away, he examined his work. The dirty bomb was now primed and ready. He was proud of its simplicity. He knew it would work.

As he double checked the connections to the device, Hakim thought of his partner. Although Rafi was obviously bright, he felt he was too young for this assignment. He was untested. He was soft. Hakim didn't want to use the word *coward* to describe him, but it was obvious that Rafi did not want to become a martyr. Hakim thought with remorse about his fallen comrades in Iraq. Many were younger than Rafi. They had willingly, gladly sacrificed themselves for the honor of fighting the infidels—fighting jihad. In contrast, Rafi knew nothing of the battlefield. He had never killed a man. However, what increasingly bothered Hakim was that Rafi was showing subtle signs of doubt. This they could not afford. He needed a partner he could rely on. *Well, it's over now.* He thought. *It doesn't matter. The bomb is here and it's rigged. I can do it all now myself if I have to . . .*

Hakim was certain that the primary device would work. But they could not afford to have anything go wrong. As a result, he had constructed another trigger—the failsafe. Opening another nearby plastic box, Hakim gingerly removed the back-up device. It was constructed of a washer/dryer machine timer secured to a small piece of particle board. The wires from the timer that he would use to complete the circuit lay exposed. Hakim took the folding knife he always carried in his front pocket and used it to strip the ends of the wires. He next removed a fully charged car battery from a nearby box. The battery would provide the electric current. Repeating his previous steps, he again used black electrician's tape to secure another piece of one-meter-long det cord to the bundle of TNT. As in the cell phone firing chain, a fuse igniter was connected to the end of the det cord. Alligator clips fixed the timer to the det cord booster and the car battery. All that was left to do was to set the timer. With a ninety-minute maximum setting, it would be the last thing he would do before he and Rafi left the van. Hakim did some quick calculations; depending on what transpired as they watched the events unfold on television, the call would be made to detonate the bomb sometime in the late morning. The exact timing would depend on gaining the most dramatic impact. *We don't want the bomb to go off too early or too late,* he thought. *If I set the failsafe just before we leave the van at 10:30, then if the backup is needed it will go off exactly at 12:00 noon.* The demonic grin reappeared on his face.

chapter 30

"JOE, the Coliseum is unbelievable."

I nodded my head in agreement. "I've been in Rome a few years now, and I'm still overwhelmed every time I come here."

"I'm sure that's why the G-20 organizers wanted the Coliseum as the backdrop for the last day's photo-op," continued Roy Williams.

Roy and I were standing together near a raised platform that would be used by the leaders of the assembled G-20 nations. Their motorcades were due to start arriving in thirty minutes. Each was given a precise time slot. It was my final post-standing assignment of the presidential visit. I was going to be working with the Italian police again, helping to coordinate the arrival and departure of POTUS. I was happy to be selected to work the last event of the G-20 Summit.

"Ana and I bring the kids down to the Coliseum quit a bit," I said. "On Sundays, they suspend automobile traffic on the Via dei Fori Imperiali, the street that runs in a straight line from the Piazza di Venezia past the Roman Forum to the Coliseum. We all come down and take a family stroll or *passeggiata*—just like the *Romani*."

Roy's gaze returned to the monumental structure. The Coliseum was an engineering marvel in the ancient world. It could hold fifty thousand spectators for games and spectacles. Although some of the walls had crumbled over the centuries because of earthquakes, and looters and scavengers had removed marble and building materials, the Coliseum remained imposing and structurally sound. "How old is this place?"

"Well, as any Roman could tell you, much of the surrounding land was made available as a result of the great fire of Rome, which happened in 64 AD. A lot of people blamed Nero for causing the fire so that he could add more grandiose buildings and gardens for his personal use. However, construction of the Coliseum actually started after Nero. I believe it was completed around 80 AD under the emperor Titus."

"It's amazing it has lasted all of these years," Roy said.

I shook my head. "Unfortunately, some observers believe more damage has been done to the Coliseum and other ancient treasures in Rome during the last fifty years than the previous two thousand."

"What do you mean?

"Most of the discoloration and pitting in the ancient facing and marble are due to modern-day airborne pollutants."

"Fascinating . . ."

Our conversation was interrupted. A bus arrived near where we were talking. We watched as it disgorged members of the international press. Talking noisily, they were escorted by Italian officials to a cordoned-off area. The "press-pen" was strategically placed to give visuals of the world leaders against the stunning backdrop of the Coliseum.

Roy's gaze came back to me. "Joe, that press bus reminds me. I came by to let you know about a couple of developments."

"Sure—go ahead."

"Well, the first is that I just spoke to Angie Coleman of the White House staff."

"She still has issues about what happened the other day at the chancery?"

"That's one of the things I wanted to talk to you about. I know you've been troubled."

I nodded. "I feel really bad about what happened. But given the same circumstances, I would do the same thing all over again."

"Don't worry about it. We finally identified the fence jumper."

"Well, who is he?"

"He's homeless. He sometimes stays in a shelter by Rome's Termini train station. One of the counselors at the shelter called the

Italian authorities after he saw him on television. Apparently, he's mentally ill and stopped taking his medications."

"That's a shame."

"Yeah. As I was telling you, the same type of thing happens fairly frequently around the White House. The president is just a magnet for people who have . . . issues."

"Do we know where he is from?"

"His name is Raj Malik. Apparently he is from India. The Italians are working with the Indian embassy to determine his status."

"Hopefully he will be O.K."

"I hope so too. Listen, let it go. You did exactly what you were supposed to do—both with the fence jumper and reporting the information from your informant. Don't second-guess yourself."

I nodded.

"People who criticize—well, they don't understand what it is actually like out on the streets."

"Thanks, Roy. I appreciate it. What's the other development?"

"Angie told me that there is going to be a major announcement here this morning. I don't know what it is all about. It's closely guarded. Anyway, after the photo op, POTUS will be joining some other G-20 officials on that platform over there to deliver some remarks. We just found out about it, so it wasn't included on the schedule or brief."

"O.K. Thanks for letting me know."

Roy grinned. "And then, it's all over. Wheels-up for POTUS is scheduled for 1600 hours back at Ciampino."

I smiled. "You must be anxious to go home."

"I'll miss you guys and Rome is great, but quite frankly I miss my family. There is far too much traveling in this work."

"Believe me, I understand." I momentarily thought of my travels away from home and the sacrifices made by my family. "Anyway, outside of that little incident with the fence jumper, everything has gone well. I'll feel a lot better after this final event. Maybe we'll make it."

"There has been a lot of behind-the-scenes work going on," Roy said. "With the corroborating information the Guardia developed about the Algerian and his metal recycling business, your report has gotten increased attention. The community is working hard with the new information. In fact, we had a meeting at the embassy early this morning."

While Roy talked, I heard another siren in the background. I glanced once again around the perimeter of the photo-op site at the Coliseum. I was staggered by the amount of security in view. Part of the purpose of the strong presence was to intimidate anyone who might consider causing trouble. Italian uniformed law enforcement officers were stationed everywhere. Even though the event was closed to the public and the Via dei Fori Imperiali was blocked to traffic, Carabinieri were lined along the wide street. Plain-clothes agents were visible along the outer security perimeter. I had been standing post at the Coliseum for the last few hours, and I had observed bomb-sniffing dogs and their handlers checking the entire location. I knew the tunnels below had also been secured. The Coliseum metro stop was closed. Looking up, I saw counter-sniper teams placed on the very top of the Coliseum. From that vantage point, they had almost 360 degrees of coverage. In addition, I could hear the occasional helicopter circling overhead, undoubtedly keeping a sharp watch below. The helicopters were the only aircraft allowed into Rome's no-flight zones. Without a doubt, the Italian authorities were very professional. They had done everything possible to secure the city.

The sound of the wailing siren was getting closer. "I'm sure the Italians are really working hard trying to locate him."

"We've offered them assistance, but there isn't much we can do. He's in their backyard—not ours."

"Has there been any thought of making a public announcement or canceling the last events?"

"No. It was vetoed again for political reasons. Nobody wants to cause panic or change the atmospherics of the summit."

Although I was used to security, I was a bit disconcerted by the show of force. "Roy, between us, I'm concerned about panic too. If something does happen, there will be chaos in this city. I've never done this before, and maybe I'm overreacting to the Guardia's news, but I told Ana to take the kids out of school and get out of Rome today." Before I could finish my thoughts, the noise of the siren suddenly stopped. A black car with yellow Guardia di Finanza lettering screeched to a halt. I saw Colonnello Rossi exit the car. He purposefully scanned the security activity around the Coliseum. Our eyes locked. He took long strides to where I was standing.

"Colonnello, I trust you had a busy night," I said with an outstretched hand. "I believe you have met Special Agent Roy Williams of the Secret Service's Intelligence Division."

"Joe, I was hoping to find you here. Yes, I have met Agent Williams."

Roy smiled. "Colonnello Rossi and I have been in a few meetings together over the last two days."

"*Senti*—listen—I am very sorry to disturb your preparations, but things are moving very fast."

Nodding at Roy, I said, "We are very appreciative that you have kept us updated."

"Of course," Rossi said. He paused. "You know, of course, that we obtain the nightly hotel registrations of those staying in Italy."

"Yes . . ."

"Over the hour we have learned that Hakim Faghoul is registered in a small hotel here in Rome very near Piazza del Popolo. What is more, another individual registered with him. His name is Shuja Kaker. He presented a Pakistani passport. Although we are not one hundred percent certain, his age and photograph fit those of Rafi Durrani."

For a few moments, nobody said anything. Rossi let Roy and I digest the news. I finally said, "So we at least know Faghoul is here in Rome. Coupled with the other information regarding the import of scrap metal, it appears the information by my informant is being corroborated."

"It looks that way," Rossi said.

"What are your plans?" Roy asked the colonel.

"The right people are being briefed. An assault team is standing by. We expect to go into the hotel and their rooms shortly."

"Do you have any idea of the whereabouts of Faghoul and the Pakistani?" I asked.

"No. We are getting our people in place now, but the suspects could be anywhere."

"Well, they will not get close to this event," Roy said conclusively. "Your services have this place locked down."

"We don't know for certain if they have hostile intent. But we can't take any chances," Colonello Rossi said. "We have to locate them."

Roy nodded. "Let us know if we can help."

Rossi smiled. "Actually, I am here on the orders of Generale Guglielmino. We thought Joe would like to accompany us. He can't go in with the assault team, but we thought it might be helpful to have him with us."

Of course I wanted to go. I looked at Roy.

"Roy, it's your call."

"I'll clear this with the detail leader, but I know what they are going to say—go!"

I could feel my face break into an impromptu broad grin. "Thanks."

"We want you to communicate back to us what is happening."

"Of course."

"What about my post-standing?"

"Don't worry about it. I'll talk to the site agent."

"Gentlemen, I must go back to my car and driver. I have some calls to make. Joe, please, join me within a few minutes. We will go to the staging area from here."

We all shook hands. I watched Colonnello Rossi walk briskly back to his waiting car.

I looked once more at the Coliseum and then turned back to Roy Williams. "Roy, remember I told you Nero torched Rome so that he could fulfill his ambitions and build according to his desires?"

"Yes?"

"Well, the fire got out of hand. He had to deflect criticism, so he blamed the new Christian sect for starting the fire. That started one of the first Christian persecutions. They continued over the years. Thousands were martyred right here. Right where the photo op is going to be."

"It's sad," Roy said.

"You're right. Modern lessons creep into the stories of history. The Romans were adept at using terror. Their enemies were butchered by gladiators. People were turned into human torches. In the Coliseum, many were pulled apart by wild animals. Even crucifixion was developed as a form of terror."

"Sadly, madmen still use religion to justify killing and greed."

chapter 31

RAFI AND HAKIM slowly got off their motorbike. They parked and locked the bike in a narrow parking space about ten meters from their hotel. Keeping their caps pulled down and their sunglasses on, they took a few moments to remove their gloves, straighten their leather jackets, and compose themselves. They were still flushed from the ride and the reality of what was happening.

The countdown had begun. The dirty bomb was armed, and the triggering devices in place. In a conscious effort not to attract attention, Rafi had driven the bike carefully and under the speed limit along Via dei Cerchi. As they had anticipated, the area was filled with vehicles and people. The *vigili*—traffic police—were trying to control order and transit through the area. Skirting the periphery of the Circus Maximus, Rafi headed toward his left and picked an alternate route that kept them away from the roadblocks leading to the Piazza di Venezia, the Via del Corso, and the activities of the G-20 Summit. Taking side streets, they exited near the Tevere and followed the river until they reached the Piazza del Popolo and their hotel. Although there was somewhat more congestion than they had counted on, so far everything was going according to plan. They were adhering to their schedule.

Scanning the area in front of the hotel and seeing nothing out of place, they walked the short distance to the front entrance. As they entered the lobby, the receptionist looked up from his desk.

"*Ah signori, buon giono. Tutto bene?* - Good day, sirs. How is everything?

"Benissimo, grazie. Abbiamo fatto un giro turistico. Roma è una città incredibilmente bella," — Everything is wonderful. Thank you. We did some sightseeing. Rome is an incredibly beautiful city, Rafi replied.

"Splendido. Fatemi sapere se avete bisogno di qualcosa." — Splendid. Let me know if you need anything.

Hakim smiled broadly. "*Grazie.*"

The two terrorists proceeded through the lobby and took the narrow stairs to the third floor. Rafi fished his card key from his wallet and opened the door to his room. Looking over his shoulder, he said to Hakim, "Get whatever it is you want to take with you out of your room. It must fit into your backpack. Then come join me here."

Rafi entered. He took his cell phone out of his inside jacket pocket and placed it on top of the television. He next removed his jacket and threw it on the bed. Taking the TV remote control, he switched it on and channel-surfed until he found what he was looking for—live local news coverage of the G-20 Summit. With their faces transposed in front of the backdrop of the Coliseum, the news commentators announced that the leaders of the G-20 and their finance ministers would soon appear for a photo session and a final communiqué. Rafi smiled with satisfaction. Everything was on schedule.

Still following the running commentary, Rafi opened his closet door and removed his backpack. He had organized it the night before. It contained the few essential personal items he would need as he fled Italy with Hakim. Getting ready for a quick exit, he threw it on the bed next to his jacket. Going through his mental checklist, he patted his hidden money belt. Even if the situation deteriorated, and they judged it was no longer safe to use credit cards, between the two of them they still had plenty of cash. Besides, before he left Pakistan, Rafi had been briefed by his handlers on how—if needed—additional funds would be available via ATM or forwarded to him by money remitters.

Waiting for Hakim to arrive, Rafi walked over to the balcony. He pulled open the drapes, unlocked the door and stepped outside. His third-story room overlooked a small narrow street. Although his view was partially blocked by buildings across the street, he could still make out a limited panorama of the Roman skyline through the gaps.

The view of the cloudless brilliant blue sky triggered within Rafi the return of remorse and confusion. Over the last twenty-four hours, he had desperately tried to suppress his doubts and misgivings. With concentrated mental effort and prayer, he thought he had succeeded. He had resigned himself to follow his training, allegiance to jihad, and his affection for Majeed. They were guiding his actions. *It is as Allah wills*. Yet, as he gazed upward, he found it hard to accept that within thirty minutes that same sky would be polluted with radioactive fallout.

He heard a tap on the hotel room door. Leaving the door and the drapes open, he came back into the room. Looking through the peephole in the door, he saw Hakim with his backpack on. Rafi quickly unlocked the door and motioned for him to come in.

"Put your backpack over there on the bed next to mine. We'll be ready for a quick exit."

In quick motions, Hakim slid the strap of the backpack off of his shoulder and tossed his backpack next to Rafi's. He then took two steps toward the television.

"They just announced the G-20 leaders and their foreign ministers will be appearing shortly for a photo shoot and a final communiqué," Rafi said.

Hakim's twisted smile appeared. "Perfect." He took his phone out of his shirt pocket. Turning it over and over, he examined it yet one more time. "We're ready," he announced. "I just have to input the number of the trigger phone."

"I wonder if we will hear the explosion from here."

"We should," Hakim replied. "Hear it and feel it. But this is a densely packed city, so both the sound and shock waves will be partially blocked."

"I just opened the balcony door. Maybe that will help."

As they were talking, they overheard the commentators announce that the G-20 leadership had assembled. The television showed the chiefs of the countries' respective delegations start to assemble on a podium in front of the Coliseum. Hakim noted the smiling faces, handshakes, and pats on the back. "They will not be smiling much longer," he said.

The Italian prime minister, hosting the final event, encouraged his colleagues to form rows behind him. He then stepped to the podium.

Hakim held up the phone again. His twisted grin reappeared. "Now?"

"No!" Rafi replied forcefully. "We have time. Let's see what they have to say."

His thoughts racing and his heart pounding, Rafi barely comprehended the Italian prime minister's remarks. All he could think about was that within minutes the man standing next to him would enter numbers into a mobile phone, and the world would irrevocably change. And he, Rafi, was in large part responsible. He felt he was outside his body, watching the scene unfold. The television screen jumped from the prime minister. The camera slowly panned the assembled world leaders. He watched intently. Varied in age, sex, skin color, and dress, they were a microcosm of humanity. They were from both developed and developing nations. The leaders and the countries they represented all had faults but all worked to improve life for their people. Rafi realized that the people he saw in front of him on the television screen were members of the world's primary religions. He knew that the leaders of Saudi Arabia, Indonesia, and Turkey were Muslim. Others could be as well. His palms began to sweat. Within his mind, the words of the television commentators became pulsating echoes. Shaking his head and making himself focus, he became aware that the Italian prime minister was leaving the podium. President Ellen Rindler of the United States stepped forward.

"Scum—murderer of innocents," growled Hakim. "Let's do it now!"

"Not yet." Rafi said firmly. "A few more minutes will not make a difference. She might say something of interest."

President Rindler stepped to the podium and adjusted the microphone. "Mr. Prime Minister, I wish to thank you personally, the Italian Finance and Foreign Ministries, and the Italian people for hosting the G-20 Summit. As you noted in your remarks, the meetings were extremely productive, and we have made good progress establishing a collective framework to reach some of our joint economic goals. I would like to add, on a personal level, that many of us gathered together here have also furthered our individual relationships. Important dialogs on a wide range of subjects have been initiated—including the situation in Palestine."

"What is she talking about?' Rafi asked.

As if to answer his question, President Rindler continued. "The G-20 is not tone-deaf to the deteriorating situation in the Middle East. We hear the anguished cries of the Palestinian people who have been denied drinking water. We have noted the massive worldwide nonviolent demonstrations and marches. It is in our collective interest to see a speedy resolution to this crisis. In fact, many of our private discussions here in Rome over the last few days have been about how we can ease the burden economically on those who are calling out for recognition and assistance. We all agree that fundamental human rights need to be addressed, including the right to work, the right of individuals to be secure in their own homes, and the right of access to basic necessities such as clean drinking water." Rafi noted that it appeared she was speaking without the use of notes or a teleprompter.

"To this end, I have had a number of very productive conversations with many of my colleagues here today." President Rindler turned and looked around at the assembled leaders behind her. She nodded her head. Smiling broadly, she added, "I have also had substantive talks with others involved in the water disputes." As a seasoned politician, Rindler paused for long moments. Gaining dramatic effect and looking directly into the cameras, she said, "The outline for a resolution to this matter has been formed." Although the public was not in the vicinity, a few audible gasps and an impromptu ripple of applause could be heard in the background.

"Since the United States will be hosting the next G-20 Summit and has played an integral role in coordinating these recent developments, I have been asked by my colleagues to make the following announcement."

President Rindler slowly opened a folder that had been placed on the podium. She started to read. "Under the sponsorship of the G-20, a special meeting will be held this coming January in Amman. The exact dates are yet to be determined. At that time, his Excellency the King of the Hashemite Kingdom of Jordan will host representatives from Saudi Arabia, Lebanon, Egypt, Turkey, the transitional government of Syria, the Palestinian peoples, the government of Israel, and a working group of the G-20." Rindler looked up from her notes and smiled. "Their mandate will be to put an end to this crisis by finding a way to provide and guarantee access to water for all. It is a regional problem and there must be a regional solution. As a collective group, the leaders here assembled have agreed to assist." Rindler paused again. "This will be the first time that Israel will participate in such a conference." She looked up and appeared to ad-lib, "As most of you know, this will also be the first time that Saudi Arabia and other Arab nations will officially meet with Israel."

"It's a trick. She's lying," Hakim hissed.

"As a sign of good faith, the prime minister of Israel has promised the lifting of all previously imposed water restrictions. There will be a detailed announcement this afternoon in Tel Aviv." President Rindler slowly stepped back and turned to look at the G-20 leaders. Dramatically, she moved her gaze from left to right. She then directed her attention back to the cameras. "Speaking for the entire G-20, we expect that the extension of this olive branch by Israel will be met in kind. We are asking that the Palestinian people and their supporters, protestors, and activists immediately end their strikes, work-stoppages, and demonstrations. The world has heard you. We applaud the nonviolence. The time has come for the next step. This situation must be resolved via direct negotiations." President Rindler smiled broadly before continuing. "Collectively, the G-20 is hopeful that these discussions could be the catalyst for future discussions about securing a lasting peace in the Middle East."

Still clutching his phone, Hakim shook his head. "No. It is a plot by the Zionists and the Crusaders. They will continue to oppress Muslims."

"Are you blind?" Rafi asked incredulously. "Don't you see the Muslims on the stage behind Rindler? Other Muslim countries will be attending the conference in Amman."

"They are corrupt puppets," Hakim spat. "Their only interest is to cling to power. That is why they want 'peace.' They want to maintain the status quo because it suits their interests. If they really want to solve the problem, they will join us in fighting jihad. We can start it right here. Right now!"

Something snapped inside of Rafi. In an instant, his thoughts crystallized.

"Brother, wait. Listen to what I have to say. This is not right. You and I—all Muslims—are supposed to be the messengers of peace for humanity. Islam and its Prophet, peace be upon him, were sent as God's gift and mercy to all of mankind. The message of belief, mercy, and peace is not just for Muslims."

"The infidels have rejected our message," said Hakim coldly.

"That is because the message has been hijacked. You speak in glowing terms of al Zarqawi, but what did he do? He killed Muslims. You were there. You saw it. The September 11 hijackers? The countless misguided brothers who butchered innocents in Amman, Mumbai, Istanbul, Madrid, London, Bali, Nairobi, Dar-es-Salaam, Saana, Algeria, Libya, Somalia and countless other places? What has their carnage brought us? Our jihad has just distorted and degraded our noble religion. It has turned the whole world against us. How long are we going to continue this? How long are we going to kill and be killed to avenge Western excesses and injustices?"

Hakim's face reddened. His eyes glared. Rafi didn't care. President Rindler's announcement had been his own catalyst. The myriad doubts and misgivings swirling in his mind were now falling into place. He knew there was no going back. He had to finish.

"I have seen peaceful demonstrations in Rome, Karachi, and Dubai. They have been held around the world. These events follow the 2011 Arab Spring. We have seen that it is nonviolence that affects change. Not terror." Rafi continued. "If our jihad is a war against the United States and its allies for their blind support of Israel, our actions have yet to make the West change its policies. In fact, every attack, successful or not, makes Americans and the rest of the world even more hostile toward Muslims everywhere and strengthens their enemies. After Rindler's announcement today, this dirty bomb will have disastrous consequences for the Islamic world. Muslims have enough problems already. Our actions will just make ordinary peace-loving Muslims suffer more!"

Hakim trembled with rage. "No!" he shouted. "You are a coward. It is time to kill the *kafirs,* the crusaders." With his left hand, he grasped his phone. Quickly he started punching numbers. Without thinking, Rafi grabbed the phone from Hakim's hand. The suddenness of the move surprised them both. The growing tension between them and the fracture they both had long wished to avoid was now out in the open. For a moment they both stood and stared at each other. Rafi saw pure contempt in Hakim. His lips began to curl. Still standing in front of the television, Rafi spotted his cell phone lying nearby. He grabbed it with his free hand. Still, Hakim did not move. Rafi took a step away.

"What do you intend to do?" Hakim taunted. "You're a fool, a coward, a disgrace, an imposter. You never did want to fight jihad."

In an instant, Rafi bolted through the open curtain to the balcony. "I'll fight jihad!" he shouted. "The jihad of peace!" Taking the two phones, he threw them with all his might toward the brilliant blue Roman sky. "*Allah Akbar!*" God is Great! he cried.

Hakim was right behind him. Reaching into his pants pocket he pulled out the knife he had used a few hours earlier to strip the wires for the timing device. Quickly unfolding it, he clenched it tight and aimed for Rafi's back. Rafi sensed the coming knife thrust. With catlike quickness, he turned and stepped aside, partially parrying the driving force of the knife. The passing blade deeply gashed Rafi's upper left arm. Blood splattered. Hakim laughed the laugh of one possessed.

"You're a madman!"

With adrenalin flowing, Rafi used his right hand to grab Hakim's still-outstretched arm. With the advantage of youth, strength, and weight, he pulled with all his might. Hakim flew past him. He landed, stunned and sprawled on the balcony at the base of the railing. Not giving him a chance to recover, Rafi kicked Hakim hard in the kidney area. Groaning in agony, Hakim tried to turn. Still holding the knife, Hakim raised his arm again. Rafi reloaded and kicked a second time. This time he aimed for Hakim's groin. There was a soft thud of boot hitting flesh. Hakim gasped. His face twitched. His hands started to spasm and he dropped the knife. Rafi bent low. He stared hard at his partner in terror. Then he put a knee on Hakim's chest. He picked up the nearby knife. He noticed blood on the blade and understood it was his. Hakim lowered his eyes and began to focus. Pressing the blade to Hakim's belly, Rafi hesitated just a moment. Then he increased pressure on the knife. Slowly puncturing the skin he gently eased it into Hakim's flesh. As if the reality of what was happening hit him, he stopped. Hakim's haunted eyes smiled with the pain.

Hakim began to slowly compose words. "You are a coward." Gasping, he added, "And you forget, I have a failsafe device. It goes off at noon."

As the words escaped his contorted face, the twisted grin reappeared.

Exorcising evil, in an upward motion, Rafi thrust hard.

With his knee still holding him down, Rafi watched Hakim coil in agony. A look of panic came across his face. Then terror. Hakim twitched violently and then went still.

His heart pounding, Rafi slowly got to his feet. Dripping blood, he staggered back into the room. Alarmed about the deep cut on his arm, Rafi took two T-shirts from his suitcase. He used one to soak up the blood from the seeping wound. He tied the other tightly over the wound using his mouth and free arm. He hoped the steady pressure would staunch the bleeding. Rafi next looked at his watch. It was 11:44. The second hand on his watch was ticking precious seconds away. He asked for Allah's blessing. Rafi picked up his leather jacket and sunglasses from the bed and gingerly put them on. As he draped the backpack over his good shoulder, the sound of the television commentators came back to his consciousness. He heard them say that the G-20 Roman Summit was officially over.

The assembled leaders were leaving the Coliseum. Simultaneously, Rafi left the room.

Bounding down the hotel stairs into the lobby, Rafi knew he had a decision to make.

"Buona giornalta. Tutto bene?" asked the startled receptionist.

Ignoring the man and his greeting, Rafi ran out the front door into the street. Spotting his motorbike, he quickly unlocked it. Positioning himself on the bike, he gunned the engine and burst onto the street. The seconds ticking, Rafi looked again at his watch. Was there enough time? His mind was racing at fast as his bike. He was simultaneously calculating, cursing, and praying. Within moments, he rode directly into the Piazza del Popolo. He looked to his right. Via Flaminia beckoned him. It was the escape route out of Rome that he and Hakim had planned to use. It would be so easy. Rafi took a deep breath. In the Piazza, he steered his bike in a wide semicircle. The jihadist recited the prayer of martyrdom, "Allah is most great, Allah is most great, there is no God but Allah." His decision made, Rafi was at peace. He smiled as an internal calm momentarily enveloped him. He made a sharp left turn and entered onto the Via del Corso. Throttling the gas on his bike, he began his race back toward the dirty bomb.

Rafi knew that the Via del Corso ran in a straight line from the Piazza del Popolo to the Piazza di Venezia. It was an anomaly in a city famous for its labyrinth of twisting streets, piazzas, and meandering alleyways. If he had any chance of reaching the Scudo van he had to take it. With his watch ticking down minutes, he could not afford to follow the indirect route along the Tevere.

The "*corso*" or race track was aptly named. For centuries, Rome's central thoroughfare was the scene of jockeyless horse races. The horses pounded down the street, cheered on by people on the walkways and waving from the balconies. Today, the Via del Corso barely had enough space for two lanes of traffic and two narrow sidewalks. It was lined on both sides with high-end shops and boutiques. During the G-20 Summit, the authorities had sometimes closed the Corso for security concerns and to facilitate motorcade traffic. Rafi gambled that it was now open.

Rafi's bike was not powerful. He opened it up to full throttle. He felt fortunate. The traffic on the Corso was relatively light. He darted, weaved, and raced around the automobiles and bikes in his path. Halfway down the Corso, he saw a column of police vehicles charging toward him from the opposite direction. There were no sirens, but lights were flashing. Some of the police cars were staggered. They were almost abreast. In the lead car that was coming directly at him, a police officer on the passenger side leaned out the window. He was frantically waving a hand-held traffic indicator, motioning oncoming traffic to get out of the way. Momentarily forced to slow down, Rafi jumped the curb from the street onto the sidewalk. He scattered pedestrians in front of him like children scatter pigeons in a piazza. Finally free of the motorcade, he gunned his bike back over the curb and roared anew down the Corso. The buildings that lined both sides of the Corso functioned as a sort of wind tunnel. Rafi's jet-black hair streamed behind him.

Approaching the end of the Corso, Rafi blew through the red light and the frantic motions of the *vigili* directing traffic in the Piazza di Venezia. Streaking past the Capitoline Hill and its Piazza del Campidoglio, he entered the Via del Teatro di Marcello. The roar of his bike pulsated in his ears. Shifting gears with a flick of his wrist he winced in pain. The deep cut caused his arm to throb. The loss of blood was causing him to feel lightheaded. He shook his head and then hazarded another glance at his watch. The minutes were disappearing.

He heard a siren behind him. Rafi didn't look back. Twisting through traffic and pedestrians who were unfortunate enough to find themselves in his path, Rafi kept praying.

"Allah is most great, Allah is most great, and there is no God but Allah."

He knew he was getting close. He was also aware that he was running out of time. Rafi was hopeful that Hakim might have miscalculated the time or that there might be a slight maladjustment of the timer. Perhaps there would be extra seconds that would work in his favor.

Turning left, Rafi saw the Via dei Cerchi. As if he was riding a horse, he slapped the metal handlebar and urged his bike to go faster.

Rafi raced along the embankment of the Circus Maximus where crowds of spectators had assembled in yesteryear. He was just above the course of the chariot racers of old. On his left, the Palentine Hill loomed. From their palatial seats high above, emperors of long ago had looked down on the races below.

Rafi was getting closer and closer to where the van was parked. But he couldn't see it. His vision was blocked by a line of huge tour buses directly in front of him. He squeezed back on the brakes. One bus on Via dei Cerchi was stopped diagonally in the road. The roadblock attracted a cluster of Italians yelling and gesturing. Breaking fast, Rafi instantly surmised that the bus driver had not been able to complete a Y-turn or negotiate traffic. All he had managed to do was wedge the bus between others. Rafi momentarily stopped. Straddling the bike, he looked left and then right. There appeared no way around the giant vehicle. Muttering another prayer, he yanked the bike to the right and once again gunned the engine. Bobbing up and down on the saddle seat, he headed straight down the washboard-like embankment onto the field of the ancient racetrack.

Spraying gravel, dirt and grass when he reached the flat, resembling a charioteer of antiquity, he weaved and careened around the obstacles in his path. The field was filled with all kinds of vehicles, vending carts, and demonstrators. The people who saw the madman on the motorbike shouted at others to get out of the way.

Calculating that he had cleared the bus above him on Via dei Cherchi, he cut to his left. Back up the embankment he flew, tires whirling. When he was about to clear the ridge of the embankment that hinged the road, he momentarily lost his field of vision. Riding blind, Rafi atop his bike jumped back onto the road. A group of demonstrators appeared suddenly in front of him. Rafi turned sharply to avoid them. He felt his bike lose traction and begin to slide. He lost control. Momentum carried him forward. Its wheels whirled in the air. Still straddling the bike, Rafi's left leg raked against the ground. Both the bike and its rider finally came to a stop.

Pain searing through his leg and injured arm, he somehow managed to push the bike off himself. He hobbled to his feet. Rafi shook his head to try to focus. The terrorist looked at his watch. He saw both watch hands laid flat against the other pointing at 12.

With all the physical and mental strength he could muster, Rafi willed himself forward. Step after crippled step. His jeans were blood-soaked. People shouted. Some ran forward to try to assist him. With his good arm, he forcefully waved them away. Dragging himself forward, he finally spotted the van on the opposite side of the street. Murmuring a prayer of thanks, he moved forward.

There was stillness. Complete quiet. A motionless wave of calm. Then a blinding flash. A brilliant radiance. In the instant before Rafi was vaporized, he asked for forgiveness.

"Allah is most great, Allah is most great and there is no God but Allah."

chapter 32

THE SOUND OF the explosion reverberated down the Corso and funneled into the Piazza del Popolo. Some of the surrounding buildings seemed to shake on their foundations. For long seconds, nobody moved. Colonel Rossi and I looked at each other. Neither one of us said a word. Around us there was silence. A few moments later there were a few audible gasps. Then screams. I looked at my watch. It was exactly twelve noon. It was hard to tell where the blast had come from, but it appeared to be back in the direction from which we had come.

"I'm afraid we are too late," I finally said.

"*Madonna mia*," Rossi replied. "Pray for us."

Just minutes before, we had raced up the Via del Corso and arrived outside what we believed was the terrorists' hotel. The special assault team had already burst through the front entrance. A line of other Carabinieri stood almost shoulder to shoulder along the perimeter of the building. Uniformed officers were already establishing a perimeter, marking off an area outside of the building in order to safeguard the scene. I was impressed with their discipline. However, I couldn't help but notice their expressions. When the sound of the explosion hit, all had various looks of surprise, anger, fear, and frustration. Some looked to the sky. Many reached for their cell phones. Others crossed themselves. Their lips formed silent prayers. I thought that their actions were a probable reflection of the human reactions occurring simultaneously throughout Rome. When and if it was determined that this was a radioactive dirty bomb, I was confident fear and then panic would be added to the mix.

Colonel Rossi's radio started to crackle to life. Through my earpiece, I heard the Secret Service's command post simultaneously request information and issue instructions. Once again, Turquoise was being evacuated to the ambassador's residence.

"*I bastardi*," Rossi said. "*I bastardi*," he repeated. Taking a few steps forward and then back, he said, "Joe, the team has been inside for five minutes now. I haven't heard any gunfire. We need some answers. Let's go in."

Colonel Rossi gave a nod to the Carabinieri standing guard at the door to the hotel. Walking into the lobby, I immediately spotted the hotel receptionist. There were two heavily armed assault troops on either side of him. They were dressed in black and wore body armor. The receptionist was trembling. He started to babble.

"Signore Sakir é un uomo cosí gentile, cosí generoso. Ha lasciato l'albergo venti minuti fa."—Mr. Sakir is such a nice man—so generous. He left the hotel twenty minutes ago."

Rossi checked with others in the lobby to determine if it was all clear. Directed to the third floor, we quickly climbed the stairs. Reaching the third-floor landing, we stopped. There was a crowd of people in front of us. Most were members of the assault team. Others apparently were hotel guests drawn to the excitement. In typical Italian fashion, everybody was talking at once. An officer finally raised his voice and directed the guests back to their rooms. Barking further orders, he told members of the entry team to verify that the other floors were clear. He told the officers that they should order any other guests they encountered to stay inside their rooms. He also posted team members to secure entry into the subjects' two rooms. They had to preserve the crime scene.

Colonnello Rossi and I stayed in the background until order was maintained. Motioning for me to stay behind, Rossi approached the ranking officer. He was a colonel in the Carabinieri in charge of the assault team. Speaking in hushed tones, at one point the two colonels looked over at me. I nodded my head in acknowledgement. Finally, Rossi came back to where I was standing.

"Apparently, the assault team arrived about ten or fifteen minutes too late. We're not sure what happened. However, an individual they believe is Hakim Faghoul is inside the room to our right. They found him on the balcony with a knife still in his stomach. By the looks of the balcony and room, it appears there was a struggle."

"What about the other one—his partner?"

"They don't know. He's not here. But you heard the receptionist. Apparently Sakir left the hotel just a short time ago."

"Have they found any bomb making materials?"

"Nothing so far."

"The room with the murdered Faghoul is registered to Sakir." Colonnello Rossi pointed to his right. "The adjoining room is registered to Faghoul."

I nodded. "Can we go in?"

"The colonel graciously gave us permission. Don't touch anything."

"Of course."

I followed Colonnello Rossi inside the room. I heard the television before I noted anything else. The news commentators were talking about a massive bomb that had been detonated near the Circus Maximus. Few details were available, but there seemed to be hundreds of casualties. The commentators promised live video coverage shortly. Walking to the other side of Rossi, I could clearly see that there had been a struggle in the room. A chair was overturned. A dresser drawer stood open. I saw socks and underwear scattered on the floor. Large drops of blood were splattered on the carpet, not yet dry. The red trail led into the bathroom. A jacket and a backpack rested on the bed.

A member of the Carabinieri assault team stood by the open balcony door. He stepped aside. Colonnello Rossi and I immediately saw the body of a man on the floor in front of us. He faced up, but his body was turned on its side and curled in the fetal position. He lay in a pool of deep crimson blood, a knife protruding from his stomach, and his eyes had rolled back in his head as if he were staring up at the Roman sky. Rossi reached for an envelope in his breast pocket and took out some photographs. The colonnello glanced back and forth from the photographs to the dead man.

"That's him. That's Hakim Faghoul, or whatever his real name is. We'll find out."

I nodded. "We have to find the other one—Sakir."

"We will," replied Rossi. "All the services in all of Italy will be mobilized." We walked back into the room. Looking around once more, Rossi said, "I've got to get back downstairs to make sure that alerts are immediately sent out."

"I understand. I also want to report what has happened to the Secret Service and embassy."

Exiting the stairwell on the ground floor, I had a good view of the busy scene in the lobby. Ranking officials and their aides—some uniformed and some in plain clothes—who represented various intelligence and law enforcement services were huddled in small groups. A television in the lobby attracted a group of functionaries. The first pictures of the bomb scene were being broadcast, apparently taken by bystanders with camera phones in the vicinity of Circus Maximus. The carnage shown on the screen was horrific. One picture of torn and bloodied people cowering in front of blasted and overturned buses was particularly unsettling. The hotel receptionist remained behind his desk as the officers continued to pepper him with questions. I overheard him say that the lobby surveillance footage would certainly have captured the comings and goings of Faghoul and Sakir, and would immediately be made available to the authorities. Outside the door, I could see people pleading with the guards for access to the hotel. Somebody was taking photographs through the windows.

Colonnello Rossi was observing the same scene. He shook his head in obvious frustration.

I nudged him gently on the arm. "I'm very much the outsider here, but if you would permit me, I have a suggestion."

"*Per favore . . .*"

"The services should set up a command post away from the hotel. This investigation has to be coordinated in an orderly fashion. The evidence here must be preserved."

"Yes, of course. This is our policy as well. The security command post for the G-20 has contingency plans for just this type of thing. I think what we are witnessing here is still the initial confusion. But I'll make the inquiries."

As he walked away, I pulled out my mobile phone and dialed Roy Williams. The phone rang and rang. I finally heard a voice.

"Joe? Is that you?" he said. "It's crazy here! We've got to keep this short. What's the situation where you are?"

I relayed what Rossi and I had seen in the hotel.

"O.K. I'm glad you're there. Keep us updated."

"Roy, I'm assuming POTUS and the other G-20 leaders and delegations are safe."

"Yeah. Some people in our delegation are a bit spooked, but physically everybody is fine. The explosion was on the other side of the Palentine near the Circus Maximus. The Palentine blocked the blast."

"That's good."

"Joe, one more thing."

"What's that?"

"We are getting preliminary reports in right now. There are high levels of radioactivity in the air."

I paused. The news didn't really surprise me. Everything Farid reported had proven correct. "That's what I was afraid of," I finally said. "Right now, most people just think this is a regular car or truck bomb. Rome has had those before. The Mafia unleashed a number of bomb attacks in this city and elsewhere in Italy in the mid 1990s. But when the people find out this is a dirty bomb, I'm afraid panic will start."

"Try to stay indoors."

"O.K. When I finish up here, I'll head back to the embassy. I'll check back later."

"Please do. We will be making some contingency plans. There are also some people who want to talk to you."

"O.K. Ciao."

Putting the phone away, I started looking for Colonnello Rossi. The scene in the lobby was getting more and more chaotic. Tempers were starting to flare. Arguments between representatives of the various Italian law enforcement services were breaking out. I was well aware of many of the protocols and memorandums of understanding between the enforcement and intelligence agencies. Some of them impacted HSI and other US agencies' work and parameters in Italy. Nevertheless, issues of jurisdiction, competence, and venue were being heatedly debated. The Italian bureaucracies, similar to those in America and every other country I had ever worked with, were fixated on turf and rivalry.

Everything was cut short by the wailing of what sounded like an old-fashioned air-raid siren. An alternating pattern of long and short wails sounded in the lobby. Outside, the blasts of noise must have been even more forceful. People in the lobby stopped what they were doing. They looked at each other with quizzical looks. Unfortunately, I knew what the alarm signaled.

"Sembra essere una bomba radioacttiva," I said loudly to no one in particular. *"Ci sono reporti di radioactivita nell' aria."*—There are reports of radioactivity in the air.

Gasps in the room punctuated a new round of siren blasts. Some around the television shouted that the mayor of Rome was going to be addressing the city residents. In unison, everybody reached for their phones. They were calling home. Within minutes they all gave up. The cell phones and mobile devices were not functioning. Everybody surmised that the communication networks were overloaded. I was just thankful that Ana and the children were not in Rome. I would try to contact them when I got to the embassy.

I spotted Rossi nearby. Maneuvering over to him, I waited until he finished speaking with a counterpart in the Polizia di Stato. As he turned toward me, there was a hardened look of purpose and resolve on his face.

"Joe, I know this appears like bedlam, but we're making progress. This is just the Italian way. We have a plan in place, and we are sorting things out."

"Colonnello, I have no doubt that all of the Italian law enforcement, intelligence, and military services will cooperate fully—as well as the Italian people."

"I'm only sorry that we didn't have more time. We worked so hard to develop the information from your source. If we'd had another hour, I think we could have intercepted the attack."

I nodded. I believed he was right. "I relayed our observations here at the hotel to Agent Williams. Is there anything I can do?"

"No. In fact, all unessential people will be ordered to leave here shortly."

"That's for the best. I should probably head back to our embassy."

"I'll have my driver give you a ride. Come, I'll escort you outside."

As we twisted our way through the crowded lobby, I noted that the Mayor of Rome was on television. He was announcing that the bomb blast apparently had released radioactivity. He appealed for calm and advised people to remain indoors. When we reached the front door of the hotel, it was a mob scene. The posted guards were muscling people away. I was shocked at the activity in the street. Television camera crews were arriving and jostling for position outside the area the police had already cordoned off. *How did they find out so quickly what happened here?* Since we had just come from the hotel crime scene, reporters began shouting questions at us. I couldn't help but smile. Despite the severity of the situation, the scene was almost comical. In attempts to somehow minimize their exposure to radioactive fallout, some of the journalists were already arrayed in various combinations of masks, goggles, and air-filtering devices. A few looked like they had stepped from a 1950s sci-fi movie. A team of technicians dressed in bright yellow radioactive-proof suits was drawing lots of attention. They were retrieving materials from their nearby van. Dressed in full protective gear that included rubber boots, gloves, and full head covering and masks, they made a good visual for the photojournalists. I overheard some in the crowd shouting offers of thousands of euros for the technicians' suits. Behind the police line holding back the press, I spotted a few broadcasting vans with satellite dishes. Double-parked on a nearby cross street, their presence had apparently blocked traffic. The cacophony of horns from every sort of vehicle, the howling sirens of emergency vehicles, and the shouts from the aggressive press combined to create an overwhelmingly deafening din.

I followed Colonnello Rossi to his waiting car. I saw him talk animatedly for a few moments with his driver. Turning back to me, he said, "Gino knows to take you to the American Embassy. Afterward he will come back here."

I nodded. "*Grazie*. You have my number. Over the next few hours, I'm sure the telephone situation will improve. Our command posts can also communicate. If you can, please provide updates."

"Joe, we are going to continue to need your help."

"Of course," I replied. "Let me know what I can do."

I looked directly in Rossi's eyes. I saw fatigue, anger, despair, and determination. Grasping his hand firmly, I said, "*In bocca al lupo.*" —Good luck! I got into the car and the colonnello closed the door behind me. The driver inched forward.

"*Ho sentito alla radio che il traffico é completamente bloccato*," he said.—I heard on the radio that the traffic is completely blocked. "*Non credo che possiamo arrivare a l'ambasciata.*"—I don't believe we can make it to the embassy.

"*Capisco.*" —I understand.

"*Tutti cercano di scapare dalla citta.*" —Everybody is going to try to flee the city. "*La gente e´ disperata.* — People are desperate

chapter 33

Carla slammed the dashboard of her Fiat Uno. She had been sitting in her car for the past two hours and hadn't moved one meter. Via XX di Settembre was completely blocked. Nothing moved. Frustration, fear, rage, incomprehension, denial, and panic were just a few of the emotions that were alternately pulsating within her. Carla desperately wanted to talk to her family. She needed to know if they were O.K. and at the same time assure them of her safety. However, millions of others in and around Rome had the same thoughts at the same time. The communications networks had crashed. Carla had long since given up trying to use her phone. Both calling and texting were impossible. So Carla resorted to playing the buttons of the car radio, frantically trying to find news updates that would clarify what was happening in her beloved *citta eterna.* The news reports were not good.

The latest announcement from the mayor of Rome confirmed that the bomb had apparently released radioactive particles into the air. The mayor encouraged people to avoid the roads and stay indoors. He appealed for calm and reassured listeners that the authorities had control of the situation.

"But what about those that are already trapped in traffic? We can't move! What about us?" Carla thought in frustration. Feeling more and more helpless, she couldn't hold back any longer. She began to weep.

Only hours before she had been enjoying a routine day. It was a beautiful late November day. Despite the brilliant Roman sunshine, the air was crisp. The chill was the excuse she needed to wear her new white wool jacket with leather trim cut in the latest Milanese fashion. She knew the lines of the jacket accentuated her figure. Carla was hoping to see Shuja again later that afternoon.

Leaving home at the normal time, Carla drove directly to Rome's Sapienza University. Her class began at 11:00. Her professor was lecturing on the philosophy of religion while Carla was daydreaming of the young man she had met in the park the day before. *Shuja was so kind*, she thought. And he made her laugh. Carla felt she could also detect his sensitive side. She was taken by how Shuja had not hesitated to play with little Alessandra. It wasn't that the Italian men she knew weren't nice; it was just that Shuja was so worldly. As she half-listened to her droning professor, she thought about a possible relationship with the handsome young Pakistani businessman. Although dismissing it as impossible, she nevertheless knew she would go to the park after class. Maybe he would be there. Her thoughts were interrupted when the windows in her classroom rattled with the muffled sound of an explosion.

Thirty minutes later, after news of the dirty bomb swept through the campus, Carla was caught up in a stampede of people racing for their cars or public transportation. Headed home, she found herself on Via XX di Settembre when the traffic simply stopped.

Carla looked again out the car windows and saw nothing but blocked traffic. "*Perche´?*" "*Perche´?*" And then she silently recited one more prayer.

Nearby, two men suddenly exited their cars. Their long verbal sparring, gestures and horn honking had escalated. Although her windows were rolled up tight in an attempt to protect herself from the unseen radioactivity, Carla could still hear shouts of rage. One driver had apparently tried to maneuver his car around the other - as if one or two meters of progress meant anything. The shouts soon turned into shoving. Carla screamed when one of the two landed a solid punch. She could hear the soft thud of fist hitting flesh from inside the car. The victim lurched backward and sprawled on the car hood. As he slid to the ground, the aggressor glared at the victim. His eyes then turned to Carla. With a shrug of his shoulders, he stormed away abandoning his car and leaving his prey in the street.

Carla shook herself and tried to regain her composure. She couldn't believe all of this was happening. Up to this point she had lived a normal life. She was blessed with a wonderful family and had a close circle of friends. Carla was privileged to live in a beautiful home in one of the nicest areas of Rome. Although she enjoyed her studies, Carla knew that one day soon she would have to leave the nest and face the challenge of trying to find a job in an Italian economy hit hard by economic downturn. But her family was supportive and well connected. They would help. Before today, Carla felt her future was bright and promising. Now everything was turned upside down.

Her introspection was interrupted by a news report that the underground metro system and the trains at Rome's Termini station had stopped running. The crowds of people thronging the rail stations had become unruly. The authorities felt that the only way to control the situation was to announce the temporary curtailment of service. With another transportation option shut down, she felt more trapped than ever.

Carla began to calculate. Should she abandon her car and try to walk home? It appeared that many around her were now making that decision. Undoubtedly, abandoned cars were contributing to the blocked traffic. The Fiat Uno's gas gauge was already perilously close to empty. She was also thirsty. She told herself her discomfort was nothing compared to those who were injured by the bomb. Carla said another prayer.

In the next instant, her racing mind remembered Shuja. Carla wondered how he was dealing with the situation. Was he also trapped somewhere in Roman traffic? What would he think of Rome now? Missing the meeting in the park, she knew she would never see him again.

"*Perche´´?*" "*Perche´?*" Carla kept asking herself. "*Who would do such a thing? Why do innocents have to suffer? Why on this beautiful late November day would God allow such a thing to happen?*"

chapter 34

I SAT ALONE in a conference room at Aviano Air Base in northern Italy. The previous seventy-two hours had rushed by in a blur of activity and emotion. Since the detonation of the dirty bomb in Rome, it felt like everything had been turned upside down and shaken. Over the centuries, Rome had suffered countless attacks. Yet the eternal city had never experienced anything like what happened in the second decade of the twenty-first century. The old realities were no more. The world had changed.

Although the explosive impact of the bomb was horrible, direct casualties from the blast totaled less than one hundred dead and wounded. There was still an undetermined number of missing. Those closest to the bomb were blown to pieces. At the furthest end of the kill zone, the victims were killed primarily by the shock wave.

It was the real and perceived threat of radioactive fallout that caused the subsequent panic. After the attack, the city spiraled into confusion and then disorder. The population of Rome and environs before the attack totaled approximately three million people. Despite pleas from the authorities for calm, hundreds of thousands of Romans simultaneously decided to flee. The situation was exacerbated by the additional hundreds of thousands of people who were in Rome for the G-20. For Romans and non-Romans alike, total traffic gridlock developed. It was simply not possible to travel within the city via motor vehicle. Moreover, the *grande riccordo annualare*—the beltway surrounding the city—and major highways leading out of Rome were also blocked by the sheer numbers of vehicles. Although there were examples of virtuous behavior, fear and panic caused many people to resort to selfish aggression and sometimes violence. It was as if the worst aspects of human nature also had been loosed in the radioactive air. In the rush to save themselves and their families, some people turned on their neighbors. Television broadcast ugly scenes of fights breaking out between frustrated motorists. Gasoline was impossible to buy. Businesses and schools simply closed. Mobs broke into food stores. Vital government offices and services didn't function because civil servants couldn't report to work. After forty-eight hours of increasing chaos, martial law was imposed.

Seated in a comfortable chair at the large conference table, my head bobbed toward my chest. Like many at the air base, the lack of sleep was beginning to take its toll. In my exhaustion-induced daze, I recalled the hours immediately after the blast. After leaving the hotel that had hosted the two terrorists, I was forced to abandon Colonnello Rossi's car and driver. The roads in the *centro storico* were simply paralyzed. Like many others, I soon realized that walking was the only viable form of transport. Despite the threat of exposure to radioactive fallout, there was no other choice. Walking through the jammed Piazza del Popolo, I witnessed the first ugly scenes that were increasingly repeated throughout Rome—panicked drivers releasing their frustration by turning on each other. The *vigili*—traffic police—gave up and abandoned their posts. Chaos reigned. However, I was fortunate. Once I reached the Pincio and Villa Borghese gardens, it was a short distance to the embassy compound.

The entire embassy immediately became a beehive of activity. The G-20 command post was quickly reconstituted to deal with the immediate crisis. President Rindler insisted on a coordinated US political, military, diplomatic, and humanitarian response. Italy, a member of NATO, appealed for assistance. For only the second time in its history, Article 5 of the North Atlantic Treaty was invoked, whereby "an armed attack against one or more of them in Europe or North America shall be considered an attack against them all." For years, NATO planners had envisioned just such a "dirty bomb" scenario. The attack on Rome triggered NATO's implementation of a massive logistical, security, and humanitarian response.

President Rindler and other world leaders were determined not to succumb to the new terror threat. There is a truism in counter-terrorism operations. Although terrorist groups have the advantage of surprise, once the trigger is pulled the network exposes itself. Thus far there was no conclusive proof of a specific extremist group's involvement with the Rome bombing. However, preliminary signs including social media analysis and intelligence "chatter" pointed directly toward a consortium of individuals and factions aligned with the Pakistani Taliban. Rindler strongly believed that the tragedy presented an opportunity. She felt that the immediate worldwide condemnation of the barbarous attack, coupled with the previously announced progress to settle the water crisis in Palestine, could be used to finally cripple Islamic extremists. To this end, the president opted to stay in Italy for a few days and continue to work with many of the G-20 partners.

Although her safety was not directly threatened, it was impossible to work in Rome. The president had to relocate. Helicopter transport ferried POTUS and essential staff to Ciampino Airport and the waiting Air Force One. Aviano was the destination.

Located in the northeastern part of Italy at the base of the Italian Alps, Aviano Air Base was a major command of the Air Force and also the air component of the United States European Command. The base offered a secure environment and state of the art communication facilities. The airfield, under the protection of the 31st Fighter Wing, was also available to support the aircraft of many foreign counterparts that were gathering to design a worldwide response. For the previous forty-eight hours, Aviano had turned into the logistical center for a new type of "shuttle diplomacy." A steady flow of aircraft in and out of the base had ferried US, NATO, Italian, and international officials. A series of seemingly endless meetings had been held to coordinate the immediate response to the Rome terror attack.

I found myself at Aviano due to some of the security issues that had to be confronted. Since it was not known whether the terror attack on Rome was isolated or part of a broader offensive, police forces around the world went on alert. Customs services were given urgent orders to closely track, monitor, and inspect containers that fit the profile of the suspect shipment from Pakistan. Intelligence agencies began the arduous task of trolling—searching for human sources of information who might provide insight. Telephone, airwaves, Internet communications, blogs, message boards, chat rooms and other forms of social media were examined using sophisticated analytics.

For example, nouns were analyzed to determine relevance to specific topics of concern and the use of adjectives helped determine positive, negative and neutral sentiments. All of this was done in multiple languages. Officials were searching for suspicious communications. The overriding priority was to try to detect whether or not another attack was in the offing.

Since I had reported the initial intelligence, I was invited to Aviano. A joint intelligence and law enforcement task force was formed to help focus the preliminary steps of the investigation. As yet, we didn't know with certainty who or what had orchestrated the Rome attack. Although it would take time, we were confident the subsequent international investigation would be successful. With a massive outpouring of international cooperation, we were already receiving very useful data and intelligence that helped us follow the suspicious money, value, logistical, and people trails. We were determined to follow those trails to their starting point.

Looking out the window of the conference room, I saw Air Force One parked on the tarmac. With its unmistakable powder blue and white color scheme, the plane was an immediately recognizable symbol of American power and presidential authority. For a few minutes, I watched transfixed as the final preparations were made for the president's departure. Air Force and Secret Service security maintained a tight perimeter around the plane. The ground crew was busy with final preparations. Although much progress had been made in just a short time at Aviano, President Rindler felt she had to get back to Washington, DC. A presidential address to the nation was scheduled for the following evening. Rindler and many other world leaders were also expected to address an emergency special session of the United Nations.

Lost in reflection and exhaustion, I was startled with a perfunctory knock on the conference room door. Without waiting for a response, the door opened and Frank Fortuna, the Secret Service attaché from Rome, walked briskly into the room.

"Joe, thanks for waiting. The chief of staff will be here momentarily."

"Thanks, Frank. I appreciate the heads-up. I was about ready to fall asleep sitting at the table," I added sheepishly.

"Turquoise is attending a final brief. We have a wheels-up scheduled in a little over one hour," Fortuna said.

"By the way," I said, "How is your family? Did they make it out of Rome yet?"

"Yes, they were evacuated last night. They've got housing at our base in Livorno."

"Ana and the kids are there as well. The doctors said that those with minimal exposure will all be fine."

"I sure hope so," Frank said. "I just feel so badly for the others still there. The reports this morning are that the radioactivity levels remain far too high."

I nodded. We all thought of our friends, co-workers, and the Romans themselves still in the contaminated city.

"We're learning a great deal about the after-effects of dirty bombs," added Frank. "Apparently, what is happening is that some of the radioactive material was deposited onto surfaces. Over the last few days, the deposited materials became airborne again due to wind and vehicle movement. The experts call the phenomena 'resuspension.' Because of the new circulation, people are being exposed to additional doses of radioactivity."

Before I had a chance to comment, a distinguished-looking man in his early forties with a mop of prematurely white hair entered the room. I recognized him immediately.

"Joe, I would like to present President Rindler's chief of staff, Carlos Santos," Frank said.

I got up from behind the table and walked over to Santos, extending my hand.

"It's a pleasure to meet you, sir."

"Joe, the pleasure is mine. I've heard quite a bit about you over the past few days."

I shook his extended hand. I wasn't sure what he meant by those words. "I'm sure it has been a very memorable trip to Italy," I finally said.

"Very much so," Santos replied. "This is such a beautiful country. I just wish the circumstances were different."

"Joe and I were just talking about the investigation," said Fortuna.

"From your perspective, have we been making progress?" asked Santos.

"I'm working here in the task force," I said. "Considering that it has only been a few days since the attack and the difficulties working away from Rome, I feel there has been substantial progress."

"That's good to hear," said Santos.

"For example, the Italians have now positively identified the individual found in the hotel room with a knife in his stomach as Hakim Faghoul."

"Yes, I understand the Algerian government has pledged complete cooperation," replied Santos.

"Has there been any progress on identifying the other individual involved?" asked Fortuna.

"The hotel videotapes were helpful in identifying Sakir," I said. "The Italians are also analyzing surveillance videotapes from fixed posts around Rome and from overhead helicopters."

Fortuna nodded. "Those could be very helpful."

"Yes. For example, the security CCTV cameras along the Corso show somebody riding a motorbike like a madman. It appears that individual is Sakir. Interviews of the survivors around the blast scene seem to suggest that the same individual was racing toward the van when it exploded. Unfortunately, they haven't yet found any remains that can be positively identified as Sakir."

"Our FBI has offered to assist," added Santos.

"The Italians are very capable," I said. "But there is an excellent working relationship between our law enforcement services. It will definitely be a multilateral effort to conclusively make the link between Sakir and Rafi Durrani."

"I also understand that the truck driver who delivered the shipping container confirmed from photographs that Sakir and Faghoul received the consignment in Campania," added Santos.

"That's correct," I said. "The Italians are still investigating what happened in Naples—specifically how and why the container was cleared."

"Excellent. There may be lessons to be learned. We might have to adjust our own clearance procedures," said Santos.

"The whole thing is strange," said Fortuna. "The stabbing of Faghoul. Sakir apparently riding back to the van. Perhaps others were involved. Our experts tell us that the bomb could easily have been detonated a number of ways. I wonder if we will ever find out what happened?"

"One of the things we hope to do shortly is to try again to approach the original source," I said. "Perhaps he will now agree to provide additional information."

The chief of staff nodded his head. As he did so, President Ellen Rindler entered the conference room. She smiled broadly and walked directly to me.

She extended her hand, which I grasped. "Joe, I wanted to stop by and meet you before I fly back to Washington."

"I'm honored, Madam President."

"Unfortunately, I have just a few minutes. But before we discuss the terror attack on Rome, on a personal level, I want to thank you for your action with the fence jumper at the embassy gate."

I could feel my face start to redden. "I just did what I thought was required."

"Joe, we all know the amount of pressure you have been under. We also are somewhat aware of the amount of manufactured flack you took from certain quarters regarding your actions," said Frank.

"Frank told me a little about the type of work environment you have had under the new HSI attaché," said Santos with a twinkle in his eye. "She will soon be recalled to Washington, DC, for consultations." I could feel my face redden some more. The president smiled.

"We were just discussing the latest developments in the investigation," Santos continued. "Joe thinks we are making progress."

"Excellent," said President Rindler.

"The task force is quite confident that, using our intelligence, analytic, and investigative tools, we will be able to identify many of those involved with the conspiracy. However, there will be challenges."

"For example?" asked the president.

"Well, for one thing, we haven't even yet begun to identify the source of the radiation. The task force wants to examine clues from the fallout and radioactive debris. Speaking as a criminal investigator, we are going to be dependent on science to help us."

"Actually, we have already had some discussions about this," said President Rindler. "Unfortunately, our capabilities in this area have eroded. In studying our options for retaliation, we have to let terrorists and those who sponsor terrorism know that even crude nuclear devices have fingerprints that specialists can find and trace. As a result of this attack, I believe Congress will find money to enhance our detection capabilities."

"It is good to hear that positives will result from this tragedy."

"Joe that is exactly the message that I am going to deliver to the American people and to the United Nations. Over the last few days, countries have joined together in an unprecedented diplomatic initiative. An international consensus is developing that enough is enough."

"It is amazing how the imminent threat of death and disaster focuses the mind," said Chief of Staff Santos with a very slight suggestion of a smile. "Some of our international colleagues have had a change of heart."

"We've also learned a lot since the September 11 attacks," said President Rindler. "We are not going to repeat the same mistakes. I firmly believe only Muslims can defeat radical Islamic groups and the pernicious ideology they represent. The West can't do it—at most we can contain them."

The three of us nodded our heads in agreement. Rindler was warming to the topic. "The Muslim extremists hate the West. They will continue to attack us, in part out of hatred but more so as propaganda tools. They have to keep trying to convince Muslims that they represent the avenging hand in a struggle to defend Islam from

Western control and contamination. That's what they will undoubtedly say happened in Rome. They justify the so-called 'clash of civilizations' because that becomes the justification for their existence. But the tide is turning. Even before bin Laden's death, Muslims around the world began to realize that al Qaeda and its allies have murdered their way across Muslim lands in a brutal attempt to overthrow order and impose their view of *Sharia* law. I don't understand how those extremist groups claim to speak for Islam when they betray their very religion with their worship of death and punishment of the innocent."

Rindler stopped to gain control over the quiver in her voice. "And their lie is exposed in the contempt they have for Muslims themselves. From Algeria to Afghanistan the radicals have killed Muslims by the thousands. It is in the Muslim world where the battles are primarily being fought. Our Arab friends and others in the Islamic community have assured me that they are making some progress with a combination of police action, intelligence, and re-education campaigns. Extremist ideology must be condemned. The ruling elites realize that they have to listen and give the alienated a stake in society."

I noted the passion in President Rindler's voice. This was a side of her that the average person did not get to see. She was not reading the impromptu speech off of a teleprompter. It was obvious she was deeply affected by the events in Rome.

"During my conversations over the last few days with our Muslim friends," she said, "I was told over and over that they increasingly understand that the real battle is between a twisted, backward, and bankrupt philosophy and a global Muslim community of over 1.8 billion who see no conflict between their faith and being fully part of the wider world. The Pakistani Taliban want to take over Pakistan and impose their version of Islam. But I have been assured that this is exactly where it will be defeated. And I am confident that it will be ordinary and faithful Muslims who defeat it."

"Let's hope so," I said. "Pardon my directness, but I have traveled in the Middle East and South Asia for years. There is a lot of talk and cosmetic attempts at reform, but most of the time very little action."

"Joe, I share your concerns," the president said. "But I believe this time it will be different. Regarding Pakistan, our Muslim interlocutors say themselves that Pakistan should be forced to find a different future. 'Forced' is their word, not mine. Pakistan cannot achieve its national ambitions until it honestly gets its head straight about terrorism. The pro-madrassa, intolerant, and myopic view of the world resulted in the dirty bomb attack on Rome. Everybody knows it can happen again—anywhere. Assurances have been given here at Aviano that enormous pressure will be applied by the Muslim world itself. I am confident that Pakistan and other countries will make needed reforms."

"Specific promises were made," added Santos. "Further steps will be discussed at the United Nations."

"It all comes down to implementation," I said.

"I have made it crystal clear, and so have our NATO allies, that our patience will not last long."

"What about the water crisis?" I asked. "That seemed to be the catalyst for the attack."

"The framework for a settlement negotiated at Rome during the G-20 meetings has taken on even more urgency," said President Rindler. "In the short term, Israel will make painful concessions. Long term, the United States, many European allies, and some of the wealthy Gulf states have agreed to finance the construction of desalinization plants. We have to identify the best locations along the Mediterranean coast and perhaps along the Red Sea. There is agreement that the entire region must benefit from new freshwater sources. Safeguards will be put in place to assure that water will never again be used as a tool to exert pressure or control."

"Maybe good will come from this after all," I said.

"The struggle between good and evil has been going on since the beginning of time," Rindler said. "I choose to be optimistic. I believe good will triumph."

I nodded my head in agreement. Perhaps it was the exhaustion I felt or the raw emotions unleashed by the events in Rome, but something pushed me to say more. "I just feel horrible that we did not succeed in stopping the attack. We came so close."

There was silence for a few moments before the president said, "Joe, don't beat yourself up over it. I understand you did all you could."

"Yes, but the system should work better," I replied. "Just like the events surrounding September 11, there are lessons to be learned."

"What do you have in mind?" asked the president.

"There are many things. One issue in particular I feel strongly about is the importance of promoting transparency in international trade. We have to do a better job of identifying and investigating illicit value transfer. Besides the massive amount of trade fraud, tax cheating, and money-laundering going on around the world via the misuse of trade, we have also found trade can be a back door to help monitor underground finance."

Both Santos and the president nodded.

"With more and more data and advances in technology, we can also do a much better job of using advanced analytics to detect dangerous shipments of cargo."

The President and her chief of staff didn't stop me so I continued. "We do not have enough law enforcement personnel to keep up with all the dangers out there. At the same time the intelligence and law enforcement communities are drowning in data. The only way we are going to stay ahead of the threats we face is to better exploit data. That's our strongpoint and our adversaries' weakness. We are going to have to increasingly rely on predictive analytics."

"I'm very interested in your ideas," the president said. "I'm also interested in the details of how your investigation was initiated."

"Undoubtedly there will be various investigative commissions into the Rome attack," added Santos. "They will be interested as well."

The president smiled. "Joe, we need to learn the hard lessons. Please write the story from the beginning."

Epilogue

The Wazir tribal compound was located in a small valley carpeted by black pebbles. The land was almost devoid of vegetation. Rugged russet-colored terrain made the compound almost invisible from the dirt highway. There were no signs. One knew to take the 300-meter long, narrow dirt and gravel road that led to the compound gate. Permission was necessary to proceed. Twin gun towers with armed sentries hovered over the entryway. The gunmen, with their AK-47s resting nearby, held sniper rifles. They faced outward toward the highway. Guarding against threats from above, the gunmen also boasted Iranian-made shoulder-fired surface-to-air missiles. Additional sentries could occasionally be seen standing like so many scarecrows propped against lookout perches on the surrounding steep cliffs.

The cluster of buildings inside the compound was surrounded by high sand-colored mud-packed brick walls. The decrepit mud buildings were uniform in their dreariness. Only the mosque and its attached *madrassa* offered newness and a hint of color. They were financed by a wealthy Saudi donor. On the roof of the *madrassa*, the antenna of a powerful radio transmitter reached skyward like a flagless pole. Nearby, a satellite dish also pointed toward the heavens. Black wires that hung like drooping clotheslines stretched from the roof of the *madrassa* to a nearby building.

Loyal to neither Pakistan nor Afghanistan, the Waziri were loyal to their tribe. Like all Pashtuns, they live by the code of *Pashtunwali.* Blood feuds and the defense of family and land were some of the primary tenets of their honor code. So was *melmastia* or hospitality and *nanawatai* or asylum for guests seeking help.

Inside the largest of the mud-bricked buildings, the dirt floor was strewn with carpets and embroidered pillows. Majeed and his son Tariq were seated together cross-legged. They had come as refugees seeking a safe haven. The nearby television broadcast Pakistani and international news. Most of the news focused on the harsh and widespread government crackdown on extremist groups. Listening intently, Majeed sometimes swayed back and forth. The reports were not good. Unconsciously, he sometimes pulled on his ragged beard or fingered his prayer beads. The occasional moan of despair could be heard.

Majeed suddenly uncrossed his legs and kneeled on the floor. As if in supplication and prayer, he held his head in his hands. Pressing his face low, the two large gold rings on each of his pinky fingers seemed to dig through the carpet into the hard-packed dirt floor. Slowly rocking forward and backward, the bookkeeper started to moan. "What have I done?" he repeated. "What have I done?"

Tariq watched his adoptive father's anguish. During the last few weeks, as things unraveled around them, he had wanted to help. But there was little he could do. Majeed received advance notice of the coming massive and brutal Karachi crackdown. Tariq joined his father, and together they fled the city and finally settled into this forsaken Waziri compound. He too felt the betrayal of many. Their banishment hurt deeply. But it was the realization of Rafi's loss that was most difficult to bear.

Yet Tariq had the outlook of a young man of the streets; by nature he was a fighter. He believed that what they were facing was nothing more than a temporary tactical setback. In deference to his father, he had said little. But now he knew he had to speak up. It was time to take the offensive.

Gathering himself, he rose to his feet. Putting his hand on Majeed's shoulder, he uttered a prayer. Then he helped his father to rise. Looking directly into Majeed's reddened eyes, he gripped both of his hands in his.

"Rafi would not want this," Tariq said slowly and firmly. With emotion and resolve in his voice he continued. "We should be proud. Rafi died a martyr and is in paradise. We shocked the infidels with our operation. We should celebrate. And the best way to honor Rafi's memory is to fight back."

Majeed's eyes focused. The wisdom in the few words of his remaining son was exactly what the older man needed to hear. Majeed collected himself. His grief was over. He knew Tariq was right. The operation had gone perfectly. They had made the West quiver in fright. They should be proud. Who knew that most of the Muslim world would turn on them and ally themselves with the infidels? It was blasphemy. Who knew that the Rome attack would dramatically expose the deep divide in Pakistani society between religious and secular forces? Who could have foreseen that the end result would be that the weak Pakistani government, bowing to massive international pressure, would finally be forced to show resolve? It was sacrilege. Didn't they understand? Tariq was right. Instead of cowering, it was time for revenge. Majeed straightened. His bookkeeper's mind was already calculating. Almost hidden under his beard, a smile came to his lips. He had a new reason to go forward.

He increased his grip on Tariq's hands. With a strong voice and a look of renewal, he slowly quoted an ancient proverb. "My son, a Pashtu's enmity is like dung fire. That is, it smolders and burns for a long time. The fire is not easily quenched."

The father and son smiled warmly. A look of renewed purpose glowed in their eyes. They embraced.

Made in the USA
Charleston, SC
17 September 2013